BI

Michael McDowell was born in 1950 in Enterprise, Alabama and attended public schools in southern Alabama until 1968. He graduated with a bachelor's degree and a master's degree in English from Harvard, and in 1978 he was awarded his Ph.D. in English and American Literature from Brandeis.

His seventh novel written and first to be sold, *The Amulet*, was published in 1979 and would be followed by over thirty additional volumes of fiction written under his own name or the pseudonyms Nathan Aldyne, Axel Young, Mike McCray, and Preston MacAdam. His notable works include the Southern Gothic horror novels *Cold Moon Over Babylon* (1980) and *The Elementals* (1981), the serial novel *Blackwater* (1983), which was first published in a series of six paperback volumes, and the trilogy of "Jack & Susan" books.

By 1985 McDowell was writing screenplays for television, including episodes for a number of anthology series such as *Tales from the Darkside*, *Amazing Stories*, *Tales from the Crypt*, and *Alfred Hitchcock Presents*. He went on to write the screenplays for Tim Burton's *Beetlejuice* (1988) and *The Nightmare Before Christmas* (1993), as well as the script for *Thinner* (1996). McDowell died in 1999 from AIDS-related illness. Tabitha King, wife of author Stephen King, completed an unfinished McDowell novel, *Candles Burning*, which was published in 2006.

Dennis Schuetz was born in 1946 in Parkersburg, West Virginia. He graduated from West Virginia University and later moved to Boston, where he attended the Orson Welles Film School and began to write fiction. He collaborated with Michael McDowell on six novels (the two "Axel Young" books and a series of gay-themed mysteries published under the name "Nathan Aldyne.") For the last ten years of his life, Schuetz worked for the Massachusetts Department of Public Works. He died of a brain tumor in 1989.

BLOOD RUBIES

MICHAEL McDOWELL
& DENNIS SCHUETZ

(*writing as* Axel Young)

VALANCOURT BOOKS

Now that you are sweetly dead to the world,
and the world dead in you,
that is only a part of the holocaust.

SAINT FRANCIS DeSALES

Prologue

Leaden clouds driven in from the west hastened the end of a frigid winter day. All of Boston was bathed in chill blue twilight. The vast reflective surfaces of the harbor and the Charles River subsided from dull silver into blackness. By nine o'clock the low clouds domed the city, and the predicted snowstorm seemed inevitable. Still, in the final hour of the day, the year, and the decade, anticipation of midnight, 1 January 1960, far outweighed Boston's concern over the possibility of a snowstorm. On Beacon Hill, braceleted hostesses discreetly shuttered their windows against the harsh glare of the lightning; in the barrooms of the West End and along the waterfront, the jukeboxes and the television sets were turned up to cover the noise of the thunder.

The temperature dropped steadily as a chill wind streamed in from the Atlantic.

On the corner of Salem and Parmenter Streets in Boston's North End, the dusty windows of a four-story tenement rattled with each explosion of thunder. The building, constructed in the eighteen fifties for a prominent judge and his two motherless children, was now home to some forty people, most of them of Italian extraction.

In several of the windows hung poignant attempts at holiday cheer. Suspended lopsidedly by the neck in one cloudy window was a small fat Santa Claus, illuminated by a red light shining garishly through his broken plastic face. Two floors below, the Virgin Mary perched precariously on a narrow sill, one raised hand poking through a jagged hole in a windowpane, as though signalling for assistance from someone passing below, along Salem Street.

Within, the glum hallways and staircase were laid over with the texture of noise from every apartment, every room. Even those flats whose occupants were out contributed the sounds of shuddering, malfunctioning refrigerators, hissing radiators, mewling and yapping pets, even radios, left on to discourage any burglar stupid enough to come to such a place as this.

Heated voices of two men and a woman on the fourth floor, all shouting in coarse Italian, rose over the noise of a dozen television sets, all tuned to Guy Lombardo's orchestra playing "White Christmas." The caterwauling of small children sputtered here and there on the lower floors.

Outside, hail fell suddenly from the night sky, smashing against the streets and buildings like machine-gun fire. Lightning, in blinding, flashing waves, lighted up the pellets of ice as they fell. A flock of bedraggled pigeons that made their home on the roof of the tenement suddenly flew down and took refuge in the leafless forsythia that lined the building on Parmenter Street.

The scantily furnished bedroom of the third-floor corner apartment was illumined only by a chipped Kewpie-doll lamp on a table next to the door. Its pale light fell softly over the face of the woman who writhed beneath the stiff, soiled sheets of the narrow bed. She was young, no more than nineteen.

Mary Lodesco's head was thrown so far back on the pillow that her shoulders were arched entirely off the bed. Her teeth were clenched and bared, and her body twisted as another spasm of pain shot through her. Her knuckles whitened as she grasped the rungs of the iron bedstead, and the black paint dropped in flecks over her forehead and the top of the sheet.

Thick with salt and mucus, tears flowed from her tight-shut eyes. Discolored saliva glistened at the corners of her mouth. The spasm passed and the woman dropped heavily onto the mattress, breathing laboriously. Behind her head, Mary Lodesco's hands slid to the bottom of the rungs. Her head lolled to one side, and her blond hair fell in damp tangles across the pillow.

Flashes of chain lightning seared the room to a brilliant white, and the thunder that followed immediately shook the walls and rattled all the windows. The woman in the bed cried out. Her green eyes were filled with terror, and her fingers pressed hard against her enormously bulging belly.

In the next half hour the shower of hail slackened, then

regained its strength. The tiny pellets of ice that smashed on stone and concrete melted, only to be frozen together again. Sheets of perilously slick ice formed over streets and sidewalks.

Theresa Lodesco stood with her knees pressed against the cold frame of the iron bed as she gazed at her daughter Mary. A floor lamp, with its shade removed, had been brought in from the adjoining bed-sitting room occupied by the old woman.

Nestled in Mary's arms were two baby girls, thin and pink and unmoving beneath their linen wrappings. The mother, holding them protectively in her quaking arms, looked wearily from one child to the other. Ice pelted the two windows of the room. The radiator hissed weakly and sent up steam that obscured the view of Parmenter Street.

Mary Lodesco inclined her head to stare up at her mother.

"This one," Theresa was saying, pointing to the infant in its mother's right arm, "was born in nineteen fifty-nine. Then the bells chimed, and the other one came. She was born in nineteen sixty. And those two can thank God for the rest of their lives that the midwife came on a night like this."

With apparent effort, Mary Lodesco whispered, "The rings . . ."

Confusion creased Theresa's face. Mary Lodesco flopped one hand weakly beside her head and touched a minute gold earring set with a sliver of ruby. An identical jeweled setting pierced her other ear. "The babies," she whispered. "Pierce them . . ." she gasped finally, as if with the last of her strength.

"They're too young!" exclaimed her mother.

"Pierce them! One for each."

Theresa turned her face away. "They're too young. They . . ." She sighed and settled her bulk onto the edge of the bed. She touched one of the little girls with the back of her hand. "My mother gave them to me, and her mother gave them to her, and so on back before anyone could remember. The oldest daughter gets them, but . . ." She waved her hand over the babies: ". . . you have two!"

"It's all I have to give them!" rasped Mary Lodesco. "Do it!"

Theresa sighed. In a few minutes she returned from the other room with a cup of ice, alcohol, cotton, and a large sewing needle.

Each child lay for a few seconds across her grandmother's wide lap. A ruby earring—all that their mother had to give them in this life—was secured in the left earlobe of one of the infants, and in the right earlobe of the other. "Not good," Theresa muttered darkly. "Not good to separate the rubies. Bad luck—bad luck will follow until the rubies are together again . . ."

When she had returned the second infant to the cradle of its mother's arm, Theresa Florenza went to the window over Salem Street and sighed. "The storm is nearly gone." She glanced once more at the new mother: "You're so thin—no flesh on you. Hardly enough to give to one baby—and now you have two. How will we take care of them?" Theresa Lodesco muttered a short prayer, twice over, for the souls of the two infants whose lives she did not believe would be of more than a week's duration. Without another word, she snapped out the light and returned to her own room, closing the door behind her.

In the hour after midnight, many of the inhabitants of the tenement at the corner of Salem and Parmenter had taken themselves to bed. Mary Lodesco and her twin infant girls slept; in other apartments the children who had, only with difficulty, remained up until the chiming of the New Year's bells now slumbered soundly. And in the room at the very back of the first floor, an old man fell into the dead sleep of the confirmed alcoholic. The cigarette he had lighted only a moment before, the last in the pack, slowly dropped from his fingers. The hot orange tip of the cigarette rapidly burned down and ignited the mattress ticking. Tiny serrated flames crept across the edge of the mattress toward the cuffs of his grease-stained trousers.

Mary Lodesco snapped her head up, eyes wide, her mind alert but without memory. She stared about the darkened room, and then gasped as a tiny claw brushed against her breast. Then she felt the two infants nestle against her at the same time, in just the same manner, and the remembrance of the terrible labor and delivery flooded back. She cut it off with a smile directed at her two little girls. Both infants began to cry at once. With heavy-lidded eyes, their mother regarded their tiny, insistent hands.

Slowly the sounds of running feet and garbled shouts in the hallways brought her to full, if perplexed consciousness. She struggled to sit up. The room was as uncomfortably hot now as before it had been cold. Then, at the same time she felt the discomfort in her eyes and her throat, she saw the thin veil of smoke wafting across the blue light from the two windows.

The infants shrieked, and their cries blended with the approaching sirens outside. From the street there was a babble of moanings and shouts of distress. Audible beneath it all were pinpoint sounds of shattering, tinkling glass, and a dull, low-volumed roar that Mary Lodesco could not identify.

She eased out of the bed, sliding the babies close together into the center of the sagging mattress. When she tried to stand on her feet, she doubled over with the pain that shot up from her groin. She grasped the foot of the bed for support, crying out until the pain had subsided. She stood erect, breathing hard, and stumbled to the front window. Salem Street was amass with people, dark and colorless, all standing with black mouths agape.

A bright arrow of flame, fiercely colorful amid the black-and-gray scene, shot out of the window just below her, and Mary Lodesco gasped in terror. She unlatched her window and tried to slide the frame up, but ice had frozen into the wooden seams and held it fast.

In the street, firemen from two trucks dragged out the hoses and rapidly fixed them to hydrants down the way. An ambulance appeared, coming the wrong way up Parmenter Street, the drivers bringing the vehicle right up against the fire engine that blocked the intersection. Two attendants jumped out with stretchers.

All the inhabitants of Salem Street leaned out their windows. Those who had no view came out into the cold, watching, horrified, as an old woman trapped on the third floor of the building flitted past orange windows, her hair turned to matchsticks of flame.

On Parmenter Street, the views of the burning building were

obscured by smoke. The only spectator here was a young woman returning home to her ill husband after a long formal dinner at Polcari's restaurant. She wore a black wool coat over a full-length white evening gown. A white woolen shawl was draped over the woman's shoulders, and she held one corner of it to her mouth against the cold. Her eyes darted up the building and stopped at the third-floor corner window. She drew in her breath sharply as she watched a woman trying to break open the window with one hand, holding in the other a small white bundle.

Mary Lodesco drew back from the window over Parmenter Street. She hit at the frozen wooden frame as she held one of her daughters tight against her breast. Tears of fear and frustration streamed down her soiled face. The room was filled with smoke, and flames ate steadily at the bottom of the door.

Mary lunged, her arm straight out, the hand splayed open. The glass smashed, shearing open her hand in half a dozen deep cuts. She grabbed at the sticks in the frame and, not minding the shards of glass still stuck there, ripped out the wood. She ran back to the bed and slung the single pillow out of its sweat-stained case. She dropped the baby into the cotton sack, swung it round a couple of times to close the infant in, and then carefully pushed the case through the large hole that she had made in the window over dark Parmenter Street.

"Wait for the net!" cried the woman in the black coat and the white evening gown. For a brief, intense, unthinking moment, Mary Lodesco locked eyes with the woman below, who, as if mesmerized, had moved directly below the window.

Mary Lodesco opened her bloody hand, and the pillowcase dropped three stories.

At the last instant the woman below threw out her arms and caught it. She looked up again in surprise, but Mary Lodesco had already retreated from the window. She slipped on a patch of ice and fell to her knees, ripping open her white gown, but the bundle was still in her arms.

The bloody top of the pillowcase slowly unwound itself and a little bloody hand shot out into the cold night.

*

Mary Lodesco, afraid to know whether the woman had caught the baby or not, grabbed up her second child. She was possessed by a single thought—that at least one of her daughters should survive. She yanked the blanket off the bed and wrapped it carefully about the silent form. She could not see for the thickness of the smoke, and could not catch a breath to fill her lungs. She began to cough uncontrollably. Blood poured out of her right hand.

Mary Lodesco collapsed and sprawled heavily on the floor. Flames shot under the door and surged towards her in thin parallel lines along the floorboards. She crawled toward the window over Salem Street, pulling after her the baby, almost smothered in its blanket. Her hope for the child provided her strength. Pressing the infant to her breast, she struggled to her feet. But with that motion she lost all and fell with full force against the window frame. The frame splintered and Mary Lodesco died, her abdomen pierced by a sharp peak of shattered glass.

The crowd on Salem Street uttered a great cry as the woman's body thrust through the third-floor window. The falling shards, caught in the great spray of one of the hoses, were smashed against the side of the building. The blanket in the dead woman's arm was tossed free, and the firemen below instinctively jerked the net to catch the falling object. The blanketed bundle hit the rim of the net and bounced into a large puddle of icy water in the street.

In a black recessed doorway on Parmenter Street, Vittoria LoPonti gazed at the naked infant whose face bore the imprint of a bloody hand. The sliver of ruby in its ear dully reflected the orange fire in the tenement house. She carefully wrapped the child in her white shawl, and kicked the empty pillowcase aside. Holding the child tight to her breast, she hurried along Parmenter Street, dodging precariously through the crowd on her high heels, glancing neither at the firemen, nor at the rapt crowds, nor at the moaning victims who were being lifted into the backs of the ambulances.

PART I

Katherine

I

Fourteen persons were thought to have perished in the terrible North End tenement fire of New Year's Eve, 1959. This number included Mary Lodesco, her mother, Theresa, and one of the pair of infants who had been not an hour old when the blaze broke out. The existence of this child was known at all only through the testimony of the midwife who had attended the double birth.

The baby girl that had bounced out of the firemen's net into an icy puddle on Salem Street was taken to Massachusetts General Hospital, kept there for seventeen days, and then released to a state adoption agency. Seven months later the baby was adopted by James and Anne Dolan and named Katherine, after Mrs. Dolan's grandmother.

The puny child was brought home that hot July afternoon in 1960 to the second-floor apartment of a triple-decker house on Medford Street in Somerville, where the Dolans had lived since their marriage seven years before. Below the couple's two-bedroom flat was another just like it, and a third one stood just above. On their block were five identical buildings to the left and four more identical buildings to the right. Across the street was another block with ten triple-deckers, and eleven had been squeezed onto the block behind. And in the winter, when the dying maples and the vigorous oaks had lost their foliage, Anne Dolan had a view of two dozen more blocks of triple-deckers; they extended in every direction from the house on Medford Street.

Somerville, Massachusetts, a suburb only a mile or so north of Boston, has an area of only six square miles, but a population of over one hundred thousand, making it one of the most crowded municipalities on earth. It has no industry whatever, and its shopping areas are of only the most desultory nature. Its parks are small and woebegone, and its single distinctive feature is the thousands and thousands of triple-deckers, built in the decades around the turn of the century, that are terraced round its gentle hills.

Religion plays a large role in the lives of Somervillians. It is still the rule, even in the poorer families, that the wife remains at home and the husband's meager paycheck is stretched unaided across the family's entire expenses. In consolation for their straitened lives, women often remain in the fervid embrace of their religion. Certainly there are Unitarian and Methodist and Congregational and Baptist churches to be found within the city's limits, but they are scarcely to be compared in number, size, grandeur, or social importance to the Catholic churches, which seem to rise at the end of every third block. These churches are well-off, for women skimp and pare in order to present a larger contribution to Sunday's collection plates than their near neighbors. The lawns of the churches are manicured, and the statues of the Virgin Mary are never defaced. Some scheme of building or remodeling or adding on seems always to be contemplated or in the works or just completed.

In Somerville, enrollment in Catholic schools exceeds that of the public schools. Of the three principal parochial schools, the strictest, best endowed, and most highly regarded is run by a chapter of the Slaves of the Immaculate Conception, a sorority of missionary nuns. In the great sprawling buildings of the School of the Immaculate Conception, girls could be educated from the nursery through the senior year of high school. The convent and school are located on Lowell Street, within half a dozen blocks of the Dolan home. The church attached to this complex is dedicated to St. Agnes.

It was there that Katherine Dolan had been enrolled since kindergarten, and the walk from her home to the convent-school was more familiar to her than the lineaments of her own face in the mirror.

In the autumn of 1968 Katherine Dolan was eight years old

and in her third year of the elementary level of ImCon, the students' irreverent designation for the school. On the day before Thanksgiving, as she hurried down Medford Street toward her home, she held her reader close to her breast and burrowed her face into the turned-up fake-fur collar of her brown wool coat. The wind blew hard down the grimy street, stinging her bare, chafed knees above the green plaid socks and freezing her toes inside her scuffed oxfords. Tufts of her straight, light-blond hair whipped at her thin face from beneath her green knit hat, and her intense green eyes began to water. She stopped at the end of the sidewalk and glanced up at the windows of the second-floor apartment. Behind the lace curtains she could barely discern the gray flickering of the television. She saw her mother stand, lean forward to adjust the set, and then drop back out of sight.

A sharp tapping at glass drew her eyes a story upward, where Mrs. Shea was waving down at Katherine; Mrs. Shea had recently married a Marine Corps sergeant who had been sent to Vietnam on the day after their honeymoon. Although Mrs. Shea was not Catholic, Katherine thought her very nice and sometimes visited her upstairs.

The warmth of the narrow stairwell that led up to the second and third floors made Katherine's face ache. She rubbed the back of her hand against her cheeks as she slowly mounted the stairs. She opened the door of the apartment slowly, as if trying to slip inside without attracting her mother's attention, and placed her book on a little rickety table next to the clothes tree.

"Katherine!" called her mother. "Don't sneak around like that!"

Anne Dolan sat in a formidable armchair placed no more than four feet from the screen of the portable television. Her back was to Katherine, and she didn't look round to see her daughter. A large lace tablecloth was spread across Anne Dolan's lap, and she was mending a tear in a big rose design as she watched *Candlepins for Cash*.

"You were so late," said Anne Dolan, "I almost thought it was your father. Now he's late too."

Katherine seated herself on the frayed arm of the chair next to her mother's, folded her hands over one another in her lap, and said softly, "Ma, I told you I was going to help the sisters."

Katherine glanced into the dining room. The Dolans' good china was set out on one end of the table and covered with a large sheet of plastic that after Thanksgiving would be nailed over the kitchen window as stormproofing. Now that she began to adjust to the warmth of the room, Katherine could detect the too familiar odor of stringy beef that had been stewing for hours on top of the stove.

"They ought to pay you," said Anne Dolan. "The nuns are good, nuns are at the heart of the church, but they're running you into the ground over there, because you let 'em. It's a sin to take advantage of a child the way they take advantage of you. And it's a sin in you to let 'em do it."

"I love to help, Ma. I like to do everything I can."

"I know you do," snapped Anne. "I just wish you spent half the time helping me that you do over at the convent."

Katherine slid off the arm of the chair into the seat. She fisted both hands and dropped her chin upon them, as she stared at the television.

It was only in the convent of the Immaculate Conception that Katherine Dolan was happy. For any number of reasons, she didn't particularly like school, but it was a distinct pleasure to her to think that so close to the noisy classroom, with the jarring bells and the constant giggling and whispering, there lay the quiet, empty halls, the spare chambers, and the peace and serenity of the Convent of the Slaves of the Immaculate Conception. There, at all hours of the day and night, there walked, in smiling content-ment, the three dozen nuns who were daughters of the church.

In the school Katherine felt herself to have no part of the lives of her peers. She considered it her duty to report which of the boys or girls passed notes during religion class or secretly devoured candy during the mass they were compelled to attend on First Fridays. But she made her reports quietly, when none of the students were around, and was always disappointed that the offending child wasn't sent home, deprived of recess, or other-wise punished by the nuns. Katherine was a diligent student, but no matter how she agonized over the reading assignments or the simple math problems, her attention was continually drawn away from what was taught, to the teacher herself—to the nun who stood at the front of every classroom.

Katherine had heard the jokes of her classmates, in which nuns figured as penguins, but she found these crude witticisms blasphemous. To her the Slaves of the Immaculate Conception were beautiful and mysterious creatures. She knew the phrase *enter the convent*, of course, but the idea was still with her that these women were born to the robes, that they had been set apart and blessed to the order since birth. When, for whatever reason, she found herself standing near one of the nuns, Katherine would run her fingers lightly along the material of the voluminous black robes until she knew the feel of that coarse cotton as well as she knew her own skin.

Each year the third grade put on a Thanksgiving pageant, solely for the entertainment of the nursery, kindergarten, and lowest elementary level, and this year's show depicted highlights of the life of Mother Cabrini. Katherine pled with Sister Mary Claire, who had a flair for drama and directed all such affairs, that she be allowed to play the saint. So fervent was Katherine in this wish that she was given the part. Anne Dolan had refused to make the costume, but Mrs. Shea, upstairs, was an expert needlewoman and, going only by photographs, had produced a beautiful copy, in exquisite miniature, of a nun's habit. Katherine kept it at home a full week—telling Sister Mary Claire that it wasn't quite ready yet—and whenever her mother was out of the house, Katherine put the robes on. She locked the door, knelt by the side of her bed, and prayed, pretending that she was in a chapel, surrounded by her sisters.

Katherine felt pressure on her foot and looked over at her mother. Anne Dolan, breaking the white thread with her teeth, had pushed the toe of one worn slipper against Katherine's oxford.

Katherine blinked. "What were you saying, Ma?"

"Never mind now. What's wrong with you? Always going into a trance: I'm surprised you haven't been run down by a truck before this. It's a wonder to me that you can get to and from the school every day."

Anne Dolan had rethreaded her needle and began working on a delicate stitch. She leaned close over the material.

"What did you say, Ma?" said Katherine with resigned patience.

"It's not important. You don't care what I say or you'd listen the first time." Anne Dolan pushed back a black wave of dyed hair from her forehead and pursed her bright-red lips.

Katherine sighed. "That's not true."

"I asked you what you were doing at the convent so late."

"Sister Mary Claire asked me if I wanted to help them get the food for Thanksgiving, and—"

"And of course you said you'd let them put you in chains if they wanted to. There's probably sixty of 'em, don't have a thing to do with themselves all day long but say half a dozen prayers, and they need your help, when I'm here all by myself, with five thousand things to do before tomorrow morning. I haven't even started the dressing yet and—"

"Grandma always says I get in the way when I try to help."

"Well Grandma's not here now. I need that bread broken up in crumbs, and make sure they're small. You never break it up small enough. And when you're through with that, you can scrape out the pumpkin, and make sure you don't get the seeds all over the floor. And this room needs to be dusted, and be sure you move all the furniture when you sweep."

Katherine went into the kitchen to begin the work that had been set out for her. Her obedience was not to Anne Dolan, but rather to the nuns, who had always stressed the importance of obeying one's parents. Katherine was ashamed of her mother: ashamed that Anne Dolan dyed her hair black, that she used rouge on her pale cheeks, that she disguised the wrinkles at the corners of her eyes with pearl powder, that she wore pants that were too tight and dresses that were too short.

For her part, Anne Dolan resented her daughter; had resented her from the first month after the adoption, when she had realized how much of a responsibility the child was. It had been her husband and her mother who had insisted upon the necessity of adopting a child, for seven years of marriage had proved that Anne was barren. The plan had been to adopt a number of

children as Jim Dolan rose in importance and salary in the Necco
Wafer factory in Cambridge; but James Dolan was not advanc-
ing, and Anne had used his failure to get any but cost-of-living
raises year after year as an excuse never to trouble the adoption
agency again. At least once a week, Anne Dolan told Katherine,
"You've made me old before my time." She had used the fact of
Katherine's adoption as a taunt and weapon against the child,
since long before Katherine even knew what the word meant.
"You're adopted!" her mother screamed at her once, when she
was two and had upset a plate of food: "Your real mother burned
up in a low-down sleazy apartment house, and she threw you
out the window! Your real mother burned to ashes, and then got
washed away by the fire hoses!" Anne Dolan had got the confi-
dential information on Katherine's parentage from a worker at
the adoption agency who was also a member of the Daughters of
the Sacred Heart.

This "real mother," to whom Anne Dolan still sometimes
referred, had taken on mythic stature in Katherine's mind: she
saw her as a saint who had undergone the martyrdom of flame,
like Catherine of Siena. But when the child asked questions
concerning this woman, Anne Dolan would say that she knew
nothing at all about her, that Katherine was got from an adoption agency, and that's all there was to it. Anne Dolan knew that
Katherine had been born out of wedlock and was reserving this
information as ammunition for a time when Katherine understood fully the shame of bastardy.

Katherine sat at the kitchen table scooping the seeds out of
the pumpkin. As usual, she was thinking about the convent,
where at this very moment the nuns were filing into the chilly
gold-and-purple sanctuary of the Church of St. Agnes for ves-
pers. She wished that she could be there with them. Sister Mary
Claire, Katherine was virtually certain, had never even heard of
Candlepins for Cash.

So intent was she upon her homely task and the bright vision
in her brain that she was startled when she looked up and saw her
father in the doorway. James Dolan was thirty-three, just a year
younger than his wife, but a man to whom the years had not been
kind. He was noticeably overweight, he had lost much of his fine

dark hair, and his face was blotched red; he had drunk too much liquor on too many days after work.

James Dolan was not the man to miss so good an excuse as its being the first really frigid day of the year, or the eve of a paid holiday, to go out drinking after his eight-to-four shift.

"Hi, Kathy." He grinned. "I brought you something." He waved a paper bag in front of him. Much wrinkled and torn about the top, it bore the logo of a women's clothing store in Central Square, Cambridge.

"Hi, Daddy," said Katherine softly, and continued to spoon out her pumpkin seeds.

"Aren't you going to give Daddy a big hello hug?"

Katherine put the spoon carefully down on the table and wiped her hands on a dish towel. She slid down from the chair and stood before her father. James Dolan lifted her in his arms and nearly squeezed the shallow breath out of her. "Daddy!" she protested. "Please put me down!"

James Dolan's large fleshy hand rested at the base of her spine. "You been a good girl, honey?" he whispered hotly in her ear, then pressed his own ear against her mouth, for her to whisper back.

"Yes," she answered, trembling. "I always try to be good."

Anne Dolan's heels could be heard on the bare dining room floor. James Dolan lowered Katherine to the floor.

"Jim," said Anne Dolan, "go watch the news or something, 'cause I have to get dinner on the table and you're in the way."

Katherine ran back to the spoon and pumpkin. James Dolan did not look at his wife as he passed her in the doorway. He switched channels on the television set and fell heavily into the large chair before it.

As Katherine placed aside the last of the dinner dishes to dry, she reached through the hot, greasy water and pulled the rubber plug to drain the sink. From the living room she heard the taped laughter of a situation comedy on the television. Katherine hadn't watched much television since she learned that there were no sets in the convent. When she went into the dining room to refill the salt shakers—this had been the last of her mother's directions before she left for Wednesday night bingo at the Knights of Columbus—she glanced into the living room and started to find her father slumped in his chair and staring not at the television, but at her. The cold gray light, the only illumination in the room, played off his pale, fleshy face.

She turned out the lights in the kitchen and dining room and crept softly through the living room. What she feared, happened: her father called her over to him.

"Come and sit with Daddy, sweetheart. Come over here and watch television with me."

"I got to do reading tonight. In the third grade they give us homework."

"You can do that later, Kathy."

She nodded obediently, and was about to settle into her mother's chair when James Dolan sprung at her and lifted her onto his lap. "There," he said, "isn't that more comfortable now?"

"Yes . . ."

James Dolan shifted, and Katherine suddenly felt a growing hardness against the inside of her thigh. She pressed the palms of her hands against the chair arms and tried to move away, but her father clasped her more firmly against his lap. He held her secure against him and pushed his chin against the top of her head so that she could scarcely move. Her head bobbed up and down whenever he laughed at something that happened on the television.

"I like holding my little girl like this," he said slowly. "And I bet you like it too, don't you? I tell you something, Kathy, in about eight years you're going to be the prettiest girl on Medford Street, and I know what I'm talking about, too! I'm going to look out the window and I'm going to see a line of boys a mile long following you around like you were the queen of this town—Kathy Dolan, the Queen of Somerville!"

Katherine drew away from her father. "I *have* to do my homework now, Daddy. It's getting late."

"Let me help you, why don't you?"

"I don't need any help. We're supposed to do this by ourselves."

"I won't help you then, I promise," he said, pressing hard with the flat of his hand against the bulge in his trousers. "But I'll let you read to me, and you'll show me how good you can do it. I don't think I've ever heard you read, Kathy. You're growing up faster than I can keep track of."

"All right," said Katherine reluctantly.

He stood. "You go get that book and then come in the bedroom and you can read to me there. I got to lay down for a while."

James Dolan lumbered down the hall and through the open door of the large, darkened bedroom at the end. A sharp gale of tinny laughter erupting from the television behind her made Katherine jump. She turned round and flicked off the set.

"Kathy," her father called, "you come in now and read to me."

Katherine lingered a moment longer, staring at the small tapestry of the Last Supper that was hung above the couch. She nervously fingered the hard ruby that pierced the lobe of her left ear. At last, when her father called again, she took her book from the table and advanced toward the partially opened door of her parents' bedroom.

The shade on the bedside table lamp had been tilted, and the room was in heavy shadow. James Dolan lay on the bed with two pillows propping him against the scarred mahogany headboard. He was flicking the ashes of his cigarette into the ashtray that rested on the smooth flesh of his bare chest. His belt buckle had been loosened, and the bulge had returned beneath his gray cotton work pants. Katherine's hands tightened on her book.

James Dolan patted the mattress beside him. "Come sit over here, Kathy."

Katherine moved to the bed. James Dolan crushed his cigarette and set the ashtray aside. He took the book out of her hands, glanced at the title, and then dropped it on the floor. Katherine blinked in surprise.

"It's cold in here, Kathy. Give your daddy a hug to warm him up." He took her hand and held it flat against his belly. Then he drew her down close to him.

2

When Katherine was thirteen her menstrual cycle began. The unexpected blood so frightened her that she thought it was God's punishment for what her father had been doing to her—a vengeful stigmata. When she realized she could control neither the flow of blood nor the cramps that made her ill, she went in desperation to Anne Dolan. Her mother told her only that all women were cursed with such a bloody discharge, and commented that none deserved it more than Katherine. After that Katherine never again brought up the subject with her mother, but would find, each month thereafter near the time of her period, a box of sanitary napkins tucked into her top bureau drawer.

Katherine accepted the monthly bleeding as a deserved penance. She was certain that her mother exaggerated when she said that *all* women were thus afflicted; she could not imagine that the Slaves of the Immaculate Conception also experienced this biological event, and finally decided that the women of the Convent of Saint Agnes had been miraculously spared the humiliation as reward for placing their lives in the service of God.

At about this time Katherine's sleep became haunted by dreams—dreams that were no less disturbing for their being bright and joyous. In them she was always happy, her hair always fixed prettily, her clothes costly and flattering. She played with girls her age and was ever their favored companion, sought after, adored, and emulated. Even when her father appeared in these dreams—his shadow looming first upon an endless wall behind her—she would stare up at him without fear, almost without recognition. When he tried to touch her, she avoided him easily and still was not afraid. By the time she was fourteen Katherine began to think that perhaps the girl in her dreams was a vision of what she might someday become, and this prospect disturbed her the more. In the dreams were no nuns, no sense of the presence of God; sometimes she would see young men vying for her favor and herself accepting one or another, and although they were innocent, even gallant exchanges, she found these visions to be the most sinful of all.

When she entered the last year of the junior high school level, Katherine felt substantial alienation from her classmates as their conversation turned increasingly to the topics of hairstyles, clothes, rock music, and boyfriends. Katherine found their pre-occupations distasteful, and it dismayed her that so many of the girls drank liquor and smoked—with or without their parents' knowledge. She went into an agony of conscience whether she ought not tell the nuns which of the girls had admitted to trying marijuana. Talk of sex immediately put Katherine to flight.

By the time she graduated into the high school of ImCon, Katherine had only two interests in her life: her studies and the Convent of the Immaculate Conception. Unfortunately, no matter that Katherine read every assignment through twice, studied three or four hours for the simplest exam, and worked for weeks on every paper, she seemed never to struggle above C grades; however, on her report cards year after year, these were recorded as B-minuses by the nuns, who knew how hard Katherine tried.

She would have done better work in school had her thoughts not so unremittingly centered upon the convent. As she read about Charlemagne and Renaissance art, her mind would drift to the spotless halls and spare chambers of the convent. She thought she could hear the sisters' soft, squeaky tread on the quarry tiles, smell the odd combination of incense and starch that pervaded the convent's atmosphere, taste the particular kind of China tea that was brewed there in astonishing quantity. She cast herself in the role of confidante to the nuns and imagined that she heard the secular confessions of this nun and that as they walked those quiet halls together. They would seek her advice on the problem of a difficult student; they would request her assistance on some outing with the younger classes. Time and again Katherine lost herself in these reveries, which were likely to capture her at any hour of the day, but were particularly distracting when she was at ImCon, so near to the cloistered halls.

Katherine was certainly not disliked by her classmates, but she knew that they patronized her. At least once a week, a girl would offer to set up a double date with her brother or promise to accompany Katherine to Filene's Basement or the Lodge in Harvard Square, where she might find attractive "with-it" outfits. Katherine always thanked the girl profusely, but said she was busy on the day suggested for these mild adventures. Because ImCon required a uniform—green plaid skirt, white blouse, black stockings—Katherine did not stick out from the ranks of the other girls so much as would have been the case had they all been clothed out of their own closets. The fact was that the most stylish outfit that Katherine had was her school uniform. She was actually embarrassed for her classmates when she met them on the street on Saturday and Sunday; their pants and their short skirts, their halter tops and their tight sweaters seemed to her only gaudy and whorish. How could Christ love a woman who went without a brassiere?

The stark white wimples and flowing black robes of the Slaves of the Immaculate Conception set off their flawless pale complexions as though they were fine porcelain, and their beatific features seemed painted with the finest brushes and the purest inks. Katherine thought the heavy pewter crucifixes about their necks and the heavy-beaded rosaries dangling from their belts far more desirable than the jewels hung in the windows of Shreve Crump & Low. Katherine disapproved of the current practice of nuns wearing "street clothes" and taking up residence in apartment complexes or rooming houses. She could not understand how a nun could devote herself wholeheartedly to her calling and her God when she was at liberty to live and dress as the lay population of the community. Katherine could see little sacrifice in *that* kind of life.

In her senior year Katherine grew particularly attached to Sister Mary Claire. The small, stout nun was now sixty, with clear, bright-blue eyes behind the round silver frames of her glasses. Katherine had been delighted when the nun had earned a certificate that enabled her to transfer from teaching in the lower grades to the high school. They had come up exactly together. Sister Mary Claire had no end of energy, and her classes in ancient and European history were lively and popular. But no matter how attentively Katherine listened to Sister Mary Claire, how detailed her notes, or how many hours late into the night she reread her texts, she did no better here than in any of her other classes.

Of the few gifts that Katherine received that Christmas of 1977, her last year at ImCon, two were important to her. The first was a joint presentation by the nuns of the Convent of St. Agnes, in grateful recognition of all the cheerful work that Katherine had performed over the six years. It was a simple gold pendant that contained a tiny chip of bone from the thigh of Saint Adelaide, tenth-century empress of the Roman Empire, who had given up power, honor, and wealth to enter a convent. The relic had been blessed by the last pope but one, and thus was doubly sacred to Katherine.

The second gift was from Sister Mary Claire alone: a small gilt-edged volume bound in fine oxblood leather, with a gold latch and a gold key.

"It's a diary," said Sister Mary Claire, when Katherine appeared puzzled why a book should have a lock on it.

"A diary?"

"Yes, Katherine dear, for your personal observations and meditations. *I* keep a diary," smiled Sister Mary Claire, "and I can't tell you how often it's proved a comfort to me. A diary is a perfect sounding board for our brightest hopes and deepest fears. It should of course always be employed only in conjunction with regular and full confessional."

Never having kept an account of her activities or thoughts, Katherine was not sure what information about herself she should inscribe on the thin, almost transparent pages. She wished that Sister Mary Claire had given her a better idea of what sort of thing she wrote in her own diary, but Katherine had been so surprised to discover that Sister Mary Claire stood sometimes in need of comfort and consolation that she had not the presence of mind to question the nun. Katherine could think of nothing in her own life that was worth the trouble of recording.

"What do you think I should write about?" she asked Sister Mary Claire on the following day, as they stood in line next to one another in the school cafeteria.

"About what matters to you, of course. You could, oh say, describe your parents, talk about the house you live in and the people in your neighborhood and what seasons you like best. Once you've started, it will be difficult to stop. There are a million billion things in our lives that are worth taking notice of, Katherine, even in lives that are as quiet as ours . . ."

Katherine was thrilled that Sister Mary Claire would say such a thing as "lives as quiet as ours," because it suggested that they were almost spiritual equals. But Katherine was brought down a little when she realized that when she said "ours," Sister Mary Claire meant not the lives of herself and Katherine, but rather those of herself and the other Slaves of the Immaculate Conception.

That evening, Katherine shoved a chair against the doorknob —her father kept the only key to her room—sat down at her little writing table, and opened the diary. She decided to begin with a description of her parents, but stopped mid-page, flushed with embarrassment, when she realized that everything she had written was uncomplimentary and disapproving. She tore out the page and cut it up into tiny pieces, which she hid in her pocketbook so that her mother couldn't find them and piece them together again.

James and Anne Dolan would have no place in Katherine's diary.

Instead, she made a list of all the nuns whom she knew by name and noted after each her position and duties in the convent. Then she listed all the religious holy days and the special prayers that were accorded to each. She ruled off half a page and made a little diagram of the nuns' sleeping quarters; she showed where Sister Mary Claire's room was and marked which windows had the best view. Then she went back over the past week and told what work she had done at the convent each day and how the nuns had praised her pious industry. Though she had filled three and a half pages in her tiny, crabbed script, Katherine wanted to go on, but she forced herself to close the book and lock it, to preserve for herself the pleasure of writing more the next day.

Katherine kept her diary on the top shelf of her locker at school. She dared not leave it at home, for she knew that her mother, upon pretense of cleaning, searched through her room every day. Every Monday afternoon Katherine took the red leather book with her to study hall and wrote about the previous day's services in the church; on Wednesday she described that morning's confessional; and on Friday she told of the week's work in the convent, the school's day-care center, or the church's charity kitchen.

More than once Katherine told Sister Mary Claire how much she appreciated her gift and how much the diary had come to mean to her; but she was always disappointed that the sister did not ask permission to examine the book.

In the first week of March, on a Tuesday, Katherine took the diary home, shut herself in her room, and, in an unsteady hand, while dropping tears on the pages, wrote of the death of Sister Bibiana, a nun in her late forties who had taught Katherine American literature. She had died in the collision of a trailer-truck with the taxi in which she had been riding. At the end of this unhappy entry Katherine inscribed passages from the Mass for the Dead, which she knew by heart, pronouncing each word silently as she wrote it.

That night Katherine cried herself to sleep, unable to drive from her mind the picture of dark-robed Sister Bibiana struggling wildly to free herself from the fiery backseat of the taxi on the rain-soaked roadway beside the Charles River.

The teaching vacancy left by the death of Sister Bibiana created a problem for the School of the Immaculate Conception. The nuns who were certified to teach literature at the high school level had full teaching loads already, and the principal of the school reluctantly decided that a lay teacher must be hired to fill out the semester.

On the Monday morning after Sister Bibiana's Saturday funeral, when Katherine entered her American literature class, she was greatly surprised to see at the front of the classroom not a nun—not a woman at all—but a handsome young man whose name, Mark Robbins, was scrawled on the blackboard behind him.

Katherine slid into her seat near the back of the room and beside a window that looked out onto a side wall of the convent; but today, instead of hoping for glimpses of the nuns in the windows of their chambers, she fastened her eyes on Mark Robbins.

Once she had got over the oddity of a man's conducting the class, she realized that she felt a decided resentment against him. No matter how affable he tried to make himself, no matter how much he stressed his willingness to help the students in any way he could, Katherine knew that she would not be able to confide in him if she had difficulty in the interpretation of a Robert Frost poem or a short story by Saroyan.

Sister Bibiana had always been lenient in grading, and Katherine's marks in her classes were, she knew, better than she had deserved. Watching Mark Robbins, Katherine had uneasy visions of long and difficult reading assignments, unduly hard examinations, and low grades on her report card. Katherine did not hear the dismissal bell, and looked around her surprised when the other students suddenly rose from their chairs and began to file out.

Mark Robbins cast a brief, curious glance in her direction. Katherine blinked, and realized that she'd been staring at him through narrowed eyes for a full fifty minutes. She gathered her books and hurried out of the room, almost in tears; whether she was more angry than embarrassed, she didn't know.

That night Katherine's sleep was restless with uneasy dreams. Again she dreamt of herself, but an altered self: her blond hair was longer and fell in soft waves about her face. She had slight, subtle makeup about her eyes and cheeks. She wore expensive dresses that, although tasteful, emphasized—rather than hid—her full figure. She had numberless friends her own age, as fashionably got up as herself, with whom she laughed and talked as if nothing in the world were more natural than that she should be popular and admired.

The next morning, her mother commented on how "poorly" she looked. "Nuns are working you too hard, Kathy, that's what's wrong with you."

"No, Ma," returned Katherine, "it was only the dreams that I had. I think I had dreams all night long."

"Just like you used to," said her mother.

"What? I never dreamed like that before, did I?"

"Yes, you most certainly did. When you were twelve, you had dreams all night long, every night. I remember well enough: you used to wake me up every morning at four and say you didn't want to dream anymore. Those dreams started right at the time you got the curse."

Katherine blushed and asked, "What did I dream about?"

"About a little girl. You."

"Me?"

"Now I suppose you're dreaming about the nuns all night long."

"No," said Katherine uneasily, "I'm not . . ."

3

Katherine's resentment of her only male teacher was short lived; soon she found herself looking forward eagerly each day to Mark Robbins's class. She stayed up late at night in order to read through every assignment twice and then kept herself awake in bed, imagining what questions he might ask of her and formulating loquacious replies to them. She began, in fact, to create entire dialogues between him and her on the subject of Vachel Lindsay's poems or Thornton Wilder's plays, in which the rest of the class sat by silent and jealous of their camaraderie.

Mark Robbins was in his early twenties, with close-cropped auburn hair, large dark eyes, a square, strong-featured face, and a ruddy complexion that held a year-round tan. He was not much taller than she and had broad shoulders and a slender, athletic body. It did not escape Katherine's notice, although she felt some guilt about it, how Mark's shirts on warm days clung damply to his chest so that the faint outline of curly hair was visible through the white cotton.

The final weeks of Katherine's senior year went by rapidly. Prom committees were formed, yearbooks were distributed, concerts and exhibits were given by the various clubs and organizations within the school; throughout the senior class there prevailed an air of great expectancy. Katherine was unhappy, however, and refused to participate in either the senior dance or the senior picnic. She could not understand why all her classmates were so excited by the prospect of leaving ImCon behind;

ImCon was Katherine's greatest happiness—almost her only happiness—and the thought that a single ceremony, on June third, would sever her from that contentment was almost more than she could bear. When the nuns asked her why she seemed so dispirited, Katherine replied that it was only the thought of final examinations.

Her dreams during this difficult period only increased in frequency and intensity; and although they were pleasant or at least innocent dreams in themselves, Katherine was disturbed by them. She would dream of herself transformed, and with each succeeding night she seemed to become prettier—prettier still than even the most popular and admired of her classmates. Mark Robbins had found a space in those dreams as well. He would walk quickly up behind her, then run to catch up with her when she increased her pace, but he never reached her—and she could never hear what it was that he was saying to her.

When he came to Katherine at night, he appeared bare chested and damp with sweat. She'd wake with a start, her own face glistening with perspiration in the pale morning light. She'd turn on her side and fix her stare on the crucifix above her bed until her eyes grew heavy again.

Mark Robbins had given his senior students the option of writing a ten-page paper instead of taking the final examination, and Katherine, knowing that she would panic when confronted with that mimeographed page of questions, had asked her teacher if he could think of a topic that would suit her. He suggested that she read some of Emily Dickinson's poetry, perhaps with an eye toward writing about the poet's unorthodox views of heaven and hell.

The topic exactly suited Katherine, and, with a little help from Mark Robbins, she researched the paper, studied the poems until she knew many of them by heart, and finished the assignment two days before it was due. Yet, on the last day of class, she told Mark Robbins that she still needed to copy it out in her best hand —Katherine felt vaguely that there was something religiously offensive about typewriters—and asked if, possibly, she could deliver it to him that next day, Saturday.

He agreed and gave her his address. Katherine recognized the name of the street and knew it to be just over the Somerville line, in Cambridge.

That Saturday Katherine rose early, bathed slowly, and dressed in the clothes that she normally set aside for mass on Sundays—a white silk blouse with off-white stitching on the collar, a black skirt, and a black leather belt. She placed her oxfords in the closet and put on her loafers. She had purchased a pair of sheer hose at the discount center in Lechmere and wore these also; a girl at school had told her that hosiery lent flattering sophistication to any outfit. Viewing herself critically in the full-length mirror in the bathroom, she was satisfied, but then, as a final touch, fixed a length of blue ribbon in her hair. She took the manila envelope containing her term paper and left the house.

Although she could have walked the distance to the street on which Mark Robbins lived, Katherine waited for the bus. It was a warm morning, and she did not want to risk soiling her blouse with perspiration. As the bus rattled through the dusty streets of Somerville, she folded her hands gently over the manila envelope and stared out the window. She envisioned herself sitting in Mark Robbins's living room, conversing with him casually, as would never have been possible at school, with one happy subject lapsing gracefully into another. He would ask her to assist him in grading papers or recording scores in his book. They would work for a while, side by side on the couch, stopping to put questions to one another about the papers or the exams, and then they'd break for lunch. Something soft and without words would be playing on the stereo. After lunch they'd resume their work, but in a manner that was even more relaxed than before. Mark would tell her this and that thing about his personal life—things unimportant in themselves and not really secrets, but things, nevertheless, that he had revealed to no one else at ImCon.

On the bus, Katherine started nervously when she realized that the object of her little waking dreams was now her male teacher, and no longer the Slaves of the Immaculate Conception. But then she told herself that what she was really interested in was *teaching*; what she really wanted was to see how teachers—any teachers, really—felt about their classes and their students and academics in general. From Mark Robbins, she told herself comfortably, she would find out what it was all like.

Mark Robbins lived in a spacious Victorian duplex painted a shade of yellow that would have been much too cheerful for Somerville. Katherine walked slowly up the walk, taking care to appear graceful in case Mark was watching for her out the window. On the nameplate beside the door that led up to the second floor was a piece of ripped notepaper with "Robbins" written in neat block letters. Katherine pushed the buzzer, and only a moment later heard footsteps descending the stairs. She tried to peer in, but the lace curtains obscured her view.

The door was unlocked and pulled open by a young woman with long dark hair and large dark eyes. "Yes?" she asked pleasantly.

She was dressed in a red Chinese print robe, its black sash gathered to one side and tied in a loose knot. The toes of her shiny black slippers showed beneath the wide ornamental hem.

Katherine wanted to flee across the shaded veranda, but found that she could not move beneath the young woman's polite but curious stare. Sister Mary Claire had told Katherine that Mark Robbins was not a married man.

"May I help you?"

"Eden, who's there?" It was Mark's voice, issuing from the top of the stairs. Katherine saw his head come suddenly into view as he leaned over the railing. "Who in the hell—oh, Katherine . . . Bring her on up, Eden. A student of mine."

The woman smiled warmly and stepped aside to admit her, but Katherine didn't move. "Don't be shy . . . what was your name again?"

Katherine coughed and told her. This woman, Katherine was horrified to think, was not Mark Robbins's wife, and yet was so comfortable with her unlawful position in his household that she would answer the door even in her robe. Such an easy acceptance of a blatantly sinful situation astounded Katherine.

"I'm Eden," said the woman, "a friend of Mark's," and then waved toward the stairs. Katherine, a little dazed, passed inside. Eden relatched the door, gathered up the hem of her robe with one hand, and quickly followed Katherine up. As Eden showed her across the landing and into the living room, Katherine caught the faint scent of gardenia.

Mark, wearing a blue velour bathrobe, was sitting in an over-stuffed wingback chair, drying his hair with a thick red towel. Eden indicated a chair on the opposite side of the hearth from Mark, but Katherine sat on the sofa across the room. Beyond the wingback, through opened French doors, Katherine could see the bedroom. What she imagined to be a waterbed was brightly illuminated by shafts of green-filtered sunlight through the large bedroom windows. The rust-and-tan striped sheets had been thrown back, and one pillow had fallen off onto the floor. A pile of women's clothing was strewn over a straight-backed chair. Katherine was scandalized and hot with embarrassment.

"Coffee?" offered Eden.

"Please," said Mark. "Katherine?"

She nodded, and Eden disappeared through the dining room and into the kitchen.

"Instant all right, Katherine?" she called back.

Katherine nodded silently.

Mark laughed. "Instant's fine!" he shouted. He rumpled the towel once more through his hair and then dropped it on the floor beside the chair.

"I brought the paper," Katherine exclaimed suddenly, and looked down at the manila envelope in her hands. "It's all done, and . . . ah . . ."

"And I'm sure it's fine," said Mark Robbins.

She placed the envelope next to her on the sofa, and was embarrassed to see that the moisture from her sweating palms had glued down the flap. She flipped the envelope over, hoping that from across the room Mark Robbins couldn't tell how nerv-ous she was.

"I hope you didn't have far to come this morning?" he said.

"No," said Katherine.

Mark smiled. Then, after a few moments had passed, he asked, "You live near ImCon?"

"Yes," said Katherine, and folded her fingers into themselves.

Eden returned with a tray holding three mugs, a dish of sugar, and a small carton of half-and-half. She set this on the coffee table before Katherine, and then seated herself cross-legged on the floor between the table and Mark. She tossed her long hair back off one shoulder and then handed Mark a mug of steaming black coffee.

"Black or with cream and sugar?" she asked Katherine.

Katherine nodded.

Eden glanced at Mark, and he said, "I think Katherine's the cream-and-sugar type. Am I right?"

"Yes," Katherine said. "No, I don't drink coffee. Thanks anyway," she murmured.

Eden smiled and shrugged. She fixed her own coffee, took the mug in both hands, and sat back.

"So, *you're* Katherine Dolan," Eden said. "Mark mentioned you, but he didn't tell me you were such a pretty girl. He did say you were shy."

Even with her black hair falling uncombed about her shoulders, with no makeup, and wearing nothing but the Chinese robe and slippers, this woman was beautiful, Katherine thought. Involuntarily she looked down at her white blouse and black skirt and then saw with horror that there was a run in her new hose. She crossed her legs and held her ankles tight together.

"Why don't I look over your paper while you're here, Katherine?"

Before she could protest, Eden had snatched up the paper from the couch and handed it over to Mark. He pried open the gummed flap and began reading immediately.

Eden asked Katherine where she lived, how she filled her spare time, what she planned to do after graduation. Katherine answered tersely when she couldn't simply shrug her shoulders. As she watched Mark turn the pages of the paper, she began to fear that he would never get to the end and she would never be able to leave.

At last the paper was pronounced acceptable, and Mark said she had received a B-plus. Katherine thanked him, mumbled her good-bye, shook hands clumsily and damply with Eden, and nearly slipped on the stairs in her haste to get away.

She was shaken by her first brush with blatant concupiscence. Mark Robbins's and Eden's complete ease in their relationship disturbed her more than the relationship itself; they evidently had felt no embarrassment that she had come in upon them in their robes. They hadn't closed the door into the bedroom; Eden hadn't made some feeble excuse for her being at Mark's apartment so early in the morning; she hadn't tried to pretend that she didn't know where anything was in the kitchen. They had, in short, expected her to accept them just as they were.

If she had run forward only a few feet, she might have caught the bus that would take her to Medford Street again, but Katherine deliberately allowed it to go by. She walked home by the longest route she knew, clenching and unclenching her fists all the way.

4

When Katherine returned home that Saturday, she was limp and exhausted and wanted only to lie down in the cool darkness of her room and sleep. Her mother had just left for her regular Saturday afternoon bingo with the Daughters of the Sacred Heart. In the bathroom Katherine splashed water on her face and patted the cloth hastily over her cheeks and forehead. For a long moment she stared at her reflection in the mirror: she appeared haggard and stupid. Angrily, she yanked the blue ribbon from her hair and flung it into the toilet. She pulled the chain with such force she thought it would snap free.

Katherine went into the kitchen. Through the back door she saw her father lounging in the large green armchair in the corner of the screened porch. His thick fingers were wrapped firmly about a beer can and he stared stuporously at the television resting on a small table just before him. On fine weekends from May through September he invariably sat out on this porch, drinking beer and watching whatever sports happened to be on. He laughingly referred to this as his "out-of-doors exercising." He rose only for trips to the bathroom or the refrigerator.

As quietly as possible, Katherine filled a glass with water from the tap. She turned to go back to her room, but stopped short. Her father stood at the screen door watching her, a grin playing uncertainly about his mouth. The girl blurted a hasty greeting as he pulled open the door and came into the room. He stumbled as he stepped in front of her, blocking her exit to the dining room.

As she tried to step around him, he grabbed her chin, turning her face into the light. "Your eyes are red," he said. "You been crying?"

Katherine shook her head no.

James Dolan ran his thumb across her lips. He let her go and scratched his chest. "You been crying. Some boy did that to you, didn't he? Some boy." His mouth expanded to a full grin. He kept his eyes on her and did not allow her to look away. "Who was that boy, Kathy? Come on, tell me."

"Daddy, please," Katherine said, and again tried to step around him. "I don't feel good and I want to lie down."

"You tell me his name, and you tell me what he did to make . . ." James Dolan could not keep down a belch that rose in his throat. "Nobody can do that to my little girl. You just tell me his name and I'll go right over there and beat his ass."

Katherine's hand trembled and the water in the glass sloshed over the rim, moistening her hand. She bit her lower lip to keep the tears from rising again. For one brief moment she wanted to shout out Mark Robbins's name, to tell her father how the man had humiliated her, brought her in contact with his whore, but she only cried: "Daddy, nobody did anything to me! I just don't feel good!"

Katherine's sudden anger surprised James Dolan, and he swayed back. She took the moment to dodge past him, but as she did so, he grabbed her arm. The water she carried spilled down the front of her blouse. The thin material clung to her brassiere, now plainly visible beneath. The cold liquid was fire on her breast. James Dolan's hand tightened about her elbow.

"Let me go, Daddy!" Katherine hissed in shame and terror. Her father stared bleary-eyed at the curve of her breasts.

"Let me go!" Katherine shouted, her eyes wide with fright.

"Your mama won't be back before five, honey," he said huskily, his face close to hers. The fumes of his alcoholic breath came hot against her cheek. James Dolan jerked forward, the hardness in his groin pressing firmly against her hip. "She ain't really your ma, you know, just like I ain't really your daddy. I ain't—"

Katherine wrenched her arm free with such force that her father slipped backward. The glass fell from her hand and smashed on the linoleum about his feet. Katherine ran through the apartment and did not stop until she had entered her room, at the end of the hall. She slammed the door, fell heavily back against it, and covered her face in shame. Her breath came in labored gasps. She was suddenly thrust forward as the door flew violently open and her father came into the room. He shut the door and, with the key clutched in his hand, secured the latch. He turned to Katherine.

She backed against the closed window, rattling the lowered shade. The late afternoon sun against the shade filled the room with ochre light.

"Leave me alone, Daddy," Katherine said evenly. "Please, leave me alone."

James Dolan said nothing, but his moist eyes were bright with desire. Katherine clasped her arms across her breasts as he moved to within a few inches of her.

His stale breath seemed to fill the small room, and Katherine turned her face away from him and shivered despite the stifling closeness. "Get out. I'll scream," she whispered. "Mrs. Shea is upstairs. I saw her when I—"

"I saw her go out half an hour ago, Kathy. If you yell, you'll have to yell loud enough to bring the nuns. Go on, yell—bring in the nuns. You want the sisters coming in this house and seeing how you show yourself off to your father? You'd be ashamed of yourself, Kathy. D'you ever tell the nuns about how you turn your daddy on, just walking around the house?"

Katherine realized that she was trapped. An expression of stony resignation came over her face. She did not resist when James Dolan pushed her arms tight to her sides and drew her close against his chest.

"Don't, please . . ." she whispered, but her voice was expressionless.

"You want me to, Kathy," he whispered. "You know you want me to. Not like I was your real father."

His fingers fumbled at the buttons of her blouse, but he was impatient and clumsy and could not undo them. He caught the material in his fist and ripped it apart. Katherine gasped and tried to shove him away. James Dolan wrestled her the few steps to the bed and toppled her onto it. He came down upon her with such force that her breath escaped in one heaving blast, and she could not catch it again. A sharp ache pulsed in her chest, and Katherine writhed to free herself. Her father clamped his wet mouth over hers, and she gagged as his tongue probed within her. He tore off her brassiere and yanked at her panties until they were stretched about her thighs. Dolan frantically undid his pants, leaned back and roughly threw her legs up. He dropped forward against them and entered her body in one thrusting motion. Katherine groaned uncontrollably and shut her eyes tight.

"You been wanting it again, you know you have, big girl like you, it's been so long, Kathy, been so long . . ." He grunted his litany over and over as he drove her into the mattress. "No boy can fuck you like this, like my little girl wants to get fucked, right through the fucking floor, Kathy . . ."

Katherine had stopped fighting him. She yanked her face to the side, and for one long flashing moment she envisioned Mark Robbins atop her. It was his mouth that burrowed into her neck, his arms that pinned her to the blanket, his muscular legs that slapped against the flesh of her thighs. And when her father was nearing orgasm, she moaned with such pleasure that James Dolan pulled back, staring at her with an expression of revulsion. His hot seed spattered over her heaving belly.

Katherine opened her eyes and parted her lips in a grotesque smile. It was her father that leaned above her on outstretched arms, but it was Mark Robbins she saw. James Dolan weakly climbed off the bed and pulled his pants up, unable to take his eyes from her altered face. Finally he turned away, unlocked the door, and stepped unsteadily into the hall.

Katherine's smile turned into a scream that she blocked with her fist. She writhed on the bed until she had struggled out of all her clothes. Dazed, she staggered naked into the bathroom—ignoring her father standing perplexed and guilty in the doorway of his bedroom—and vomited on the tile floor.

★

One night the following week, at the dinner table, with her knife in one hand and her fork in the other, Katherine told her adoptive parents in a flat and emotionless voice that she intended to become a Slave of the Immaculate Conception. Nothing they could say or do would shake her out of that resolve or prevent her from assuming the beloved black robes of the missionary order.

5

"You were the lucky one! You had a sister, a twin sister, and she burned to ashes in that fire in the North End! Burned to death with half a dozen bums and half a dozen whores! One of the bums was your father, and one of the whores was your mother! You think a woman like that would have been a mother to you like I have? You were the lucky one! You didn't die, you didn't have a prostitute for a mother, you didn't grow up in a slum! You're our only child, we've treated you better than if you were our very own! And what do you do for appreciation, tell me, *what?*"

Katherine didn't reply.

"You decide to become a *nun!*"

Anne Dolan turned away in her bitterness. The more she thought about it, the more she was aggrieved that her daughter had determined to take the veil. Anne Dolan conceived that Katherine was taking this step merely to flee from the house on Medford Street.

"Well," argued Anne Dolan in her cooler moments, "I don't know why you have to become a nun, why don't you become a secretary instead? Who knows—your father could have an accident in the candy factory tomorrow, and then where would we be? People die in the candy factory all the time."

"I don't think anybody dies in the candy factory, Ma. I don't think they have that kind of machinery."

"They do!" snapped Anne Dolan. "If you were a secretary, you could live here at home and put all your money in the bank, and then we'd have something to live on besides Social Security. What good will you be to us locked up in a convent? You know the old saying: a daughter in the convent is a daughter in the grave."

"I never heard that," protested Katherine mildly.

"I hear it all the time! So does Jim!"

"Ma," said Katherine patiently, "it's not something I decided for myself. It's—"

"Of course not! The *nuns* decided. That's who decided. I'm surprised they didn't just throw a hood over your head and drag you away."

"God decided," said Katherine. "It was God's voice in my heart. I hear God's voice in my heart every minute of the day. I'd never be happy anywhere else. I'd never be happy leading any other kind of life. God wouldn't let me be happy."

"What about us! God is making us miserable by taking you away. Does God want us to be miserable? We're good Catholics. What's God got against us?"

"Nothing. He loves you just as much as he loves me. But the fingers of Christ have wrapped themselves around my heart, and they're squeezing it till I can hardly breathe. That's what it feels like, Ma."

Anne Dolan observed her daughter with disdain, a tight smile creeping across her carmine lips. "I'm sorry to hear that, Kathy, 'cause Jim and I are going to see to it that you don't get into that place."

The calm words came like a frigid slap across Katherine's face. "What're you going to do, Ma?"

"Your daddy's taking a day off from the factory next week and I'm calling the mother superior and set up an appointment. We're going up there together and tell her all the reasons why you can't go into the convent."

"Ma . . ." There was real fear in Katherine's voice.

"I won't let you do this, Kathy! If I have to use my last single dying breath to keep you out of there, I'll use it!" Anne Dolan's face was hard with determination; then, suddenly, her brow smoothed and she sauntered triumphantly from the room.

A few nights later, while Anne Dolan was taking a bath, James Dolan knocked softly at the door of his daughter's room. It was inched open, and Katherine's nervous eye appeared in the crack.

"Come on here in the living room," whispered James Dolan. "I want to talk to you about something real important . . ."

"I'll be there in a minute," said Katherine, and the door was pushed shut.

A few moments later she came into the living room and stood just at arm's length from her father.

"Yes, Daddy?"

James Dolan sat on the edge of the chair before the blank television screen, with his hands clasped tightly before him. Katherine realized with a sinking heart, when she smelled the stench of stale beer and the cigarette smoke on his shirt, that he had just come in from the Paradise Cafe.

"I haven't said nothing to you about . . . about what you want to do, Kathy, have I? I haven't said nothing about it."

"No, you haven't," said Katherine.

"But I got to. Honey, I got to know why you want to lock yourself up with all those nuns. I mean it's not . . ." His chest heaved in a belch, and, almost tearfully, he broke off.

"Not what?" said Katherine tonelessly.

He looked up pathetically. "Not natural, that's what. It's not natural. Young girl like you, pretty girl like you. You could have a boyfriend for the asking and get married, and you know how much your mother would like a big wedding, and I would too, and there'd be kids, kids'll make any woman happy, and that's what you are now, you're a woman, and that's what I don't understand, why a woman would want to lock herself up, you could be happy with a husband and kids, and we'd always have you. You wouldn't be lost, and that's just what you're going to be if you go in that place. They'll take you away, they'll transfer you somewhere where we won't ever see you again, they'll take you to Minnesota or some place like that, and then they'll never tell us where you are . . ."

"If I thought I wouldn't be staying right here in Somerville, I'd never even think of joining the convent."

"It don't matter," said James Dolan. "We still won't see you. They won't let us see you."

"It's still what I have to do."

"Don't you care what people think? You know what people think when somebody like you goes off to a convent? They think it's not natural, they think there's something wrong with you.

You know what I mean, they think there's something wrong—
down there. Maybe you're afraid of boys, maybe something happened to you—you know what I mean."

Katherine backed away. "I don't care what people think about
me. I'd be doing this for God. I wouldn't be doing it for anybody
else. I *know* this is what I have to do!"

"You're too young to know that!" He reached out and snatched
her arm. "I been good to you," he whispered hotly. "I work for
you, you don't think I go down to that goddamn candy factory
every day just because I like the work. You don't think it's because
of *her!*" He jerked his head toward the bathroom.

"Daddy," pleaded Katherine, trying to pry his tobacco-stained
fingers from her wrist.

"You're the only thing I care about, and it's going to kill me to
lose you to a pack of wrinkled old women, every damn one of
'em still got their goddamn cherries—"

"Daddy!"

"Every damn one of 'em," he hissed, "ought to get their cherries busted, and that's why your ma and I are going to stop all this.
We're not going to let you go in that place—they'll never get you
away from me—"

In a fever, Katherine pried herself loose and ran back into her
room. She slammed the door and shoved the chest of drawers
against it.

It was perhaps when she was most patient with her parents
that Katherine played her most deceptive part. If she over and
again described what it was to feel in her heart God's call, if for the
tenth or twentieth time she recited her irreproachable motives
for joining the convent, it was not because she wanted her parents to understand, to be brought over to her side, to support her
in this decision—it was only so that they might not interfere. But
now she was frightened that her parents would find some way,
working together, to prevent her from becoming a nun. Legally,
it was beyond their power. Her eighteenth birthday, which had
arbitrarily been celebrated on February fourteenth, Saint Valentine's day, was some months past, and it was now possible for her
to join the convent without her parents' permission. With it, she
might have gone in two years earlier, but Katherine did not like

to think of this; the notion that she had squandered two years in the outside world made her tremble, and she consoled herself to the lost time by saying to herself that her adoptive mother and father would never have agreed to sign the papers. Her only concern now was to get into the convent. Katherine knew that, even though she was legally in the right, a visit by her parents to Mother Felicitas might prove disastrous to her cause. She hoped that she would be able to play her parents off one another, to make their rage impotent; Anne and James Dolan were natural antagonists anyway. Katherine remembered certain times past when her parents had gone at it with some ferocity, but not the most frightful of those memories matched what she heard from them now every night.

James and Anne Dolan fought about their daughter's decision, but they also fought about James's drinking and James's friends; they fought about Anne's bingo and Anne's cooking and Anne's temper. Twenty years of constant friction, twenty years of smoldering anger, glowed nightly now like worms of red fire. Katherine, without realizing it, found herself waiting for the great explosion when both would be engulfed by the combustion of their implacable rage. And in that confusion of light and heat, she would make her way to the cool, dim safety of the convent.

6

On the day after her graduation from high school, Katherine Dolan sat in her room with the door closed and the curtains drawn against the early Saturday morning heat. In her diary she recorded her mingled feelings about the ceremony. Of course, for months before, she had at great length written of what her misery would be to leave the school, the convent, the church, and the nuns. But once she had made her decision to join the order of the Slaves of the Immaculate Conception, the school year became merely a barrier of time to be got across, and she regarded the end of it with nervous, yet happy anticipation.

Just as she was turning the key in the lock of the diary, Katherine was startled by a knock at her door: not her father's heavy hand, nor yet her mother's peremptory rap. She thrust the diary into the drawer of her little desk, rose, and opened the door.

Mrs. Shea stood there, and Katherine smiled and regarded her questioningly.

"Oh Katherine," cried Mrs. Shea, "I hate to bother you like this, but would it be possible for you to come up and keep the children? My sister—you've met her, she lives in Brockton—broke her arm this morning, I don't know how she did it, she was hysterical over the phone, I've got to get over to Brockton this minute, and I was wondering could you please stay with the baby? Bill's off with the Reserves this weekend. Oh, and congratulations, I wish I could have been there last night to see you graduate!"

"Of course," said Katherine. "You go on right now, and I'll be up there in about two minutes. I just want to gather some things together. You take as long as you want. I'll even spend the night, I just have to be out in time for mass in the morning, that's all."

"Katherine," cried Mrs. Shea vehemently, "you're too good for this earth!"

Katherine was glad of an excuse to be out of the apartment. Each Saturday afternoon Anne Dolan attended her second weekly bingo game with the Daughters of the Sacred Heart, and Katherine was left alone with her father. James Dolan had already taken his place on the screened porch and was dozing off in front of the Saturday morning cartoons. He refused to open a can of beer before noon, because he was convinced that only a man who drank before noon was alcoholic. And if he could not drink, then he must sleep. Katherine did not want to give her father the opportunity to repeat the scene of a few weeks past; and she knew he would never, no matter how much liquor he consumed in the course of an afternoon, mount the back stairs to the Shea apartment. She would be as safe there as within the confessional at the Church of St. Agnes.

Upstairs, Katherine played for a while, with little John Shea on the floor before the television set. She prepared his food, held him close to her as she watched a Doris Day film on television, and later tucked him into his bed for a nap.

Alone in the Sheas' living room, Katherine drew the curtains against the hot afternoon sun. She hooked the back screen door in the kitchen, through which she could hear the sound of the baseball game drifting up from the screened porch just below, and settled in to watch *Anthony Adverse*. Her attention held not on the film, however, but on the crowding events and changes of the past two weeks. Her thoughts reeled darkly as she tried to find some way to prevent her parents from making the appointment with Mother Felicitas. Her head began to ache with the effort. With a fervor that obscured the sound of the television, that distorted her sense of passing time, that blocked out even her knowledge of where she was, Katherine Dolan prayed that nothing might interfere with her induction as a postulant into the order.

She closed her eyes as she whispered one prayer after another. The blackness behind her lids was suddenly filled with a vision of dead Sister Bibiana, her robes streaked with lapping tongues of flame. The nun's face was turned heavenward, eyes rolled back, as her lips formed the same prayers that Katherine huskily chanted. Sister Bibiana's head began to loll in rhythm with their echoing chant, and then her voice suddenly intoned clearly in Katherine's head: "You will wear my robes, Katherine. God's eternal love will first sear and then consume your heart."

Katherine opened her eyes. Her hair clung damply to her forehead, and her back ached from the tortured posture she had held in the overstuffed armchair. She stood and walked, as if by a silent command, through the Shea apartment toward the entrance hall. She stole down the front stairs and through the unlocked door of her own apartment. She moved through the hot, shadowed rooms until she was standing in the kitchen. The baseball game blared loudly on the back porch, but when she peered through the screen, Katherine did not see her father. Her eyes drifted about the room, briefly examining things as if for the first time. As she turned back toward the dining room, she stopped. James Dolan stood grinning in the doorway.

"Didn't want me to hear you, did you?"

Katherine's tongue slid across her dry lips to moisten them; they had been seared by the vision of Sister Bibiana.

"Do you love your daddy, Kathy?"

He had evidently come back from the bathroom, and the fly of his baggy green pants was unzipped.

"I love God, Daddy," she murmured, but he did not hear her. She stepped to the counter beside the sink and rested her hands flat on the cool red Formica. Her eyes languidly skimmed over a small joint of cooked ham resting on a crumpled sheet of tinfoil, and the carving knife beside it.

"You shouldn't leave the ham out, Daddy, it'll go bad." Katherine wiped the blade of the knife with a sponge and then began methodically slicing the remaining meat.

"Do you love me, Kathy? I'll keep asking till you tell me, honey."

"Yes," said Katherine.

"Yes what?"

"Yes I love you."

James Dolan leaned heavily against the door frame. "You hurt me, Kathy. All the time. Every time I look at you, I hurt . . ."

"I'm joining the convent, Daddy," she said calmly as she continued to run the blade smoothly through the pink meat, cutting the slices thicker and thicker. "I'm joining the convent, and then you won't have to think of me anymore."

"Don't talk about that! Don't talk about that—because it's not going to happen. I'm not going to let it happen."

James Dolan stepped closer to his adopted daughter. He swayed badly, then grabbed at his crotch as if that would help to balance him. "But I worry about you all the time, honey," he whispered. "All the time, honey, I worry about you all the time."

Katherine put the knife aside and pressed both hands onto the counter. "Then leave me alone," she hissed, *"just leave me alone."*

"All I want's a hug," said James Dolan, coming up so close behind her that his alcoholic breath seemed to envelop her. "A hug to make me feel better. You don't think I could ever let you go, do you? Even if you got in that place, I'd break in and drag you right back out again. And nobody would stop me." His arms reached suddenly round her and his hands clapped over her breasts.

He let go only long enough to turn her toward him and pin her against the counter. He pressed his mouth to Katherine's, but she turned her head and he streaked her cheek with saliva. He brought one hand up and pressed it flat over her breasts. With his other, he grabbed Katherine's hand and held it against his erection.

"Oh, Kathy," he moaned, "I love you so much, I—"

Katherine stamped on his foot, but he seemed not to notice. He pushed her hand inside the open fly of his pants. As she struggled in vain to withdraw it, he rubbed his fleshy body against her and bit at her neck.

Katherine's free hand reached determinedly behind her and skittered across the counter until the fingers had closed round the handle of the carving knife. She dug her fingernails into her father's genitals until he drew back in sudden pain, groaning. She brought the knife before her in a careful arc, grasped the handle with both hands, and plunged it into her father's chest. She was surprised how difficult it was to press it in all the way to the hilt; but she stared into her father's terrified eyes and pushed. Blood spilled thickly down the inside of his shirt. Then she pulled the knife out and plunged it in again, an inch to the left. This time a thick stream of shining blood spurted out through the tear in his shirt and splashed heavily on the floor. Katherine released the knife and backed along the counter, away from her father.

Death rattled in James Dolan's throat. He swayed for a couple of seconds, then fell sprawled on his back; his arms withdrew stiffly to his sides, and his hands clenched. A scarlet bubble formed at his mouth and popped. A little geyser of blood drenched the knife that was still in him. His chest sank and he was still.

Katherine's fingers were sticky with blood, and her blouse was stained. She took off the blouse, and with it wiped clean the handle of the knife still stuck in James Dolan's body; the movement brought up more blood from his unbeating heart. She folded the blouse and let it rest on her father's belly. She went to the sink, washed her hands, and sponged her stomach clean. She quickly but carefully cleaned the sink, then took the sponge and her blood-stained blouse and secreted them in a shoe box at the back of her closet.

She put on a blouse that was the same color as the one she had worn that morning, went back into the kitchen, being careful not to step even near the blood that had spilled onto the floor, and returned to the Shea apartment by the back stairs. She changed

John Shea's diapers, then sat by the front window for half an hour, watching for her mother.

When Anne Dolan came up the sidewalk of the house, Katherine retreated from the window so that she could not be seen. She turned on the television and resumed her place in the armchair. She listened for the sound of the front door opening and for her mother's footsteps upon the stairs. She followed them upward, and then heard her mother open and close the apartment door behind her.

Five minutes later Katherine heard Anne Dolan's screams.

They beat up from the kitchen: piercing long screams with only the slightest catch of breath to separate them. Katherine clawed the arms of the chair.

John Shea cried out for Katherine. She rose, went to the child, soothed him with inarticulate words, and then shut him in the bedroom.

Katherine hurried through the Shea apartment, clattered down the back stairs, and stopped for a moment before the television on the back porch. A shaving cream commercial played to her father's empty chair. Katherine switched off the set.

She turned and stared through the screen door of the kitchen. With the air so bright without, the room was but dimly illuminated; all within seemed dull and gray. James Dolan lay upon his back, half beneath the kitchen table. H is eyes were wide and milky. Blood was flecked upon his face and dribbled from the corner of his mouth. The front of his tan knit shirt was ripped, and dark blood was just beginning to coagulate along the deep, livid gashes in his chest. The crotch of his green work pants was stained with urine.

Anne Dolan stood behind her husband's corpse, staring at Katherine with eyes slack and dull. Her mouth was opened wide, but sound was caught in her throat. With one hand she held a kitchen chair balanced crazily upon a single leg, so that it twirled and dipped in an oddly graceful, if jerking fashion; and with the other she grasped the long, bloody, carving knife.

7

Two squad cars arriving at the house on Medford Street, summoned by a woman who had heard Anne Dolan's screams through her kitchen window, brought the neighbors out onto their porches and raised windows all up and down the block. The ambulance came, and with it reporters from Channel 5, the *Herald*, and the *Globe*. Now, as neighbors came down from the porches and edged the property, pointing and whispering and guessing on which floor the crime, tragedy, or accident had occurred, the only noise that could be heard from within the house was the wailing of the Shea child, left alone on the third floor.

Inside, one of the paramedic ambulance drivers slipped Katherine a couple of sedatives for her mother, who was weeping hysterically. There was no need for him to hurry with the man on the kitchen floor. James Dolan would wait for the police photographers.

Anne Dolan sat on the edge of her bed; Katherine was beside her, holding her about the shoulders and whispering reassurance in her ear. Photographers stood in the doorway and photographed them there. An inept policeman asked irrelevant and distressing questions until Katherine begged him to leave off for her mother's sake.

When a detective had taken his place, Anne Dolan said that she had returned home from bingo shortly after six, gone to her bedroom to change shoes, and then walked into the kitchen, where she found her husband dead on the floor. In her panic, she told them, she had yanked the blade from his chest in hope that she might revive him.

While her mother wept anew with the terrible remembrance, Katherine stated that she had been baby-sitting in the apartment upstairs, that she had heard nothing and suspected nothing until she heard her mother's screams. Neither the front nor the back door of the Dolans' apartment had been locked, but then on the weekends, it never was.

The murder made the late-night television news and Sunday's papers. The police said that there were no definite suspects, but strong leads would doubtless result in a quick arrest.

When questioned by the police, neighbors reported the presence of strangers in the neighborhood that afternoon. It was found that James Dolan had had several heated arguments with two different men on the loading dock of the candy factory, and that he had once come to blows with a truck driver at the Paradise Cafe. Only Anne Dolan's fingerprints were found on the knife that had killed him, but the police laboratory report suggested that her erratic handling of the knife might well have obliterated any others on the handle. The working hypothesis of the police was that a thief had entered the unsecured dwelling. Surprised by James Dolan's presence and perhaps attacked by him, the thief had murdered him.

Over the next few days the publicity dwindled and the neighbors sometimes forgot to stare when they walked by the house. The police could no longer assure Anne Dolan and her daughter that a suspect would soon be found and arrested.

Fifteen years before, the union at the candy factory had supplied James Dolan with a burial policy, and his corpse was laid out in an ornate metallic coffin with purple satin lining. The brief, simple service was conducted at the Church of Saint Agnes. Because Anne Dolan had never come out of her sedated haze since the afternoon of the murder, the burden of the preparations fell upon Katherine, who was greatly assisted by Mrs. Shea and Reverend Mother Felicitas. At Katherine's request, the coffin was sealed during the service, and many who had attended merely out of curiosity went away disappointed. During the service Anne Dolan, with a great black veil covering her face, sat heavily against Mrs. Shea in the front pew and wept loudly and without ceasing. Katherine sat a little apart and stared blankly past the coffin to the altar. She betrayed no emotion at all, and Medford Street neighbors who attended whispered among themselves that this was something the girl never *would* get over, as long as she lived. Because the diocese grave diggers were on strike, there was no graveside service, and James Dolan's coffin went into the cold storage with some hundred others similarly detained.

And although her father's co-workers grumbled, Katherine refused to entertain them at a wake. Anne Dolan had pleaded for this melancholy celebration with as much energy as her drugged state would allow, for she wanted the opportunity to display her grief; but, arguing economy, Katherine held firm, and the Medford Street apartment was kept locked. After the funeral Anne Dolan returned home and sat in front of a flickering television set, keeping the sound turned off in an irrational gesture of reverence for her dead husband's memory.

The next morning Katherine took from her bedroom closet the shoe box containing the stained blouse and bloody sponge and put it into her book bag. On her way to ImCon she tossed it into a large dumpster that stood behind a row of small stores. She had vaguely expected a sense of relief, but none came. It was mild exhilaration that Katherine felt, as though she had taken one step more on the road that would lead her to the convent door.

A month before, it had been to Sister Mary Claire that Katherine first confided her desire to become a Slave of the Immaculate Conception. And although she began with trembling diffidence, Sister Mary Claire's smile had encouraged her. When, in an excess of emotion, Katherine broke off a few sentences into her little prepared speech, Sister Mary Claire said, "Of course, dear. We've seen this coming for a long time. This won't surprise anybody around here. We're all anxious to have you become one of us. Of course it can't be decided as easily as just saying 'Welcome,' you know. There's no end to rules and regulations, and things to be signed, and things to be memorized, and ceremonies, and letters that have to be written, and you'll have to be interviewed, and you'll have to talk to three different priests, and you'll have to undergo psychiatric examinations—in short, dear, this place is harder to get into than Radcliffe."

"You don't think—"

Sister Mary Claire took Katherine's hands affectionately between her own: "I think it's a matter of time. You'll be the newest and brightest flower in God's meadows this year, Katherine."

One week after her father's burial, Katherine returned to

Sister Mary Claire and repeated her fervent desire to join the sisters at the Convent of Saint Agnes. But Katherine noted with dismay the new tone of caution overlaying Sister Mary Claire's encouragement. The nun explained that the final decision must be made by Mother Superior Felicitas, and that her word was law in the convent.

"Have you told her about me?" asked Katherine uneasily.

"Of course!" said Sister Mary Claire, surprised. "Your desire to join us is no secret here, Katherine! I think we probably knew it before you did yourself!"

That very morning, Sister Mary Claire led Katherine to the office of Mother Superior Felicitas, the spiritual and administrative head of the Convent of Saint Agnes.

"You know, Katherine," said Mother Felicitas without preamble, "joining the church is a greater, more important step for a girl even than marriage. It is marriage with the ultimate Bridegroom. The Virgin is wedded to the Church itself. You *must* understand all that it entails." She sat with one hand laid gently over the other on the polished oak desk before her.

Katherine kept her eyes cast down and traced the floral pattern on the carpet. "I do understand, and I'm ready to accept."

There was a substantial silence. When Katherine raised her head, she found Mother Superior Felicitas staring out the window to the school playground and a soccer game there. The nun turned her head and held Katherine's gaze, lengthening the already uncomfortable silence. "I'm not entirely sure you *do* understand, Katherine." There was no reproach in her voice. She shifted in her chair, adjusting the fold of one black sleeve.

"I have no doubt of the sincerity of your desire to become one of us. But in light of your recent tragedy …" Her voice trailed off, and she sighed. Then, she continued: "I don't think it's a good idea to rush into such an undertaking in the wake of the emotional upheaval of your father's …" She clipped *murder* from her thought and finished, "… your father's *passing*."

Katherine again lowered her eyes. "I made this decision before my father died," she said. "And I've discussed it with my mother, and she wants me to do it." Katherine spoke slowly. It was a lie in which she felt safe. Her mother's lethargy was intensifying toward catatonia. Anne Dolan spent her waking hours in a drugged stupor before the television. She slept in the clothes she wore during the day, and it was only at her daughter's insistence that she changed them each morning. Anne Dolan's energetic interference in Katherine's plans was, at present, an impossibility. "She said it would make her happy to see me in the robes."

"Your mother may also be reacting from emotion, Katherine. I imagine that there will be no time in your life when you could be of more use to your mother than right now. She may say to you that she would like to see you in the convent, but it is more likely that she is in great need of the consolation that only a child could provide—and you are her only child."

"Ma—" Katherine faltered. "Ma is upset, of course she's upset, and so am I, of course, at what happened. But Daddy dying, and dying the way he did, hasn't made any difference in my decision. I don't think it's fair to keep me out of the convent just because Daddy was killed, I—"

"Katherine!" exclaimed Mother Superior Felicitas. "This is not a game! There's no *fair* and *unfair* when you're talking about dedicating yourself to God! Believe me, child," she said softly, "it's not that we don't want you here at the convent—nothing would make me happier than to see you one of us, believe me!— but I must tell you that a girl cannot join a religious order because she sees it as an escape from a troubled home life. Things can't be happy for you, or your mother now, but a mere escape could be accomplished by taking an apartment in another part of the city! The convent is full of trouble. Just like the rest of the world, the convent is full of temptation to sin. You will never be entirely free from the tribulations of the world, you will never escape from iniquity. Our sisters are prideful, envious, arrogant, unfaithful, sometimes even blasphemous. We wear these robes not as a sign that we are pure, but only in permanent and continual recognition of our weakness and sinfulness. Remember, Katherine, from the book of Job: *Man is born to trouble as the sparks fly upward*. The convent is no rock for the weary. We must all be indefatigable warriors here."

"I understand that, Reverend Mother," Katherine pleaded. "And I'm not trying to become a nun in order to get away from

Ma or what happened—that's not it at all. It's just that nothing in the world is as important to me as joining the convent. That's what's right for me, I know it is, God's told me so in my heart, that's what he's telling me every minute of the day!"

"And I have no doubt His voice is strong within you, Katherine. None of us here has ever doubted that, but I have to insist that you and your mother take the time to think this matter through. Katherine, we're talking about your whole life that's to be dedicated to God."

Katherine sank back in her chair, her damp hands limp in her lap.

"There are some things I want you to do, Katherine."

Katherine did not answer, but kept her eyes averted: her father, though dead, would still manage to keep her out of the convent.

The nun rose from her chair and came to the other side of the desk. Her habit brushed Katherine's knees. Her arms were folded across her starched scapular. "Katherine, if you start to sulk I intend to terminate this meeting right now. I am not rejecting you, surely you understand that. As I said, we must be warriors here, and I think that you might be one of the strongest and most valiant among us, but with time. That's all I'm asking of you. Time. If you cannot sacrifice now—if you cannot see your duty to your mother for these first difficult months of her bereavement, and *your* bereavement too—what will happen to you once you do get in the convent, when your entire life becomes one long, unceasing, sanctified sacrifice? If you are impatient now, what will your impatience be once you are behind these walls?"

"I'll do anything you think is right, Reverend Mother. You tell me what I should do, and I'll do it."

"I want you to go to school. To college."

Katherine's mouth dropped slightly open.

"Your grades have never been outstanding, I know, but you have been a conscientious, steady student, and in the right school, that will count for much. There's no reason why—"

"What's the right school?" blurted Katherine.

"Why, Boston College, of course!" smiled Mother Felicitas. "So many of our girls go there, and they do quite well. I don't think there would be any trouble in having you enrolled for the summer term, and the courses you take will be applied toward your freshman year credit."

"But it's already May, and I never applied for admission," said Katherine, who remembered that acceptances to college had been received by her classmates in March and April. "It's too late for me to start, I—"

"Katherine," said Mother Felicitas in mild reproof, "you must not think that I am making idle suggestions. I have been thinking about you for some time. I have in fact already made inquiries. My sister works in the admissions office at BC, and I have already mentioned you to her. There will be no difficulty—no difficulty, that is, as long as you are prepared to do your part."

"I'll do anything you want me to," said Katherine meekly.

"I'll call my sister and have her send over the necessary forms. And you needn't concern yourself about finances either—something can always be worked out for deserving students. I'm particularly anxious for you to begin right away, Katherine. You don't need to be in that house all day. I want to see you out of it, and in the summer there simply wouldn't be enough for you to do around the convent. Keep active, keep busy. Your improved spirits will doubtless be beneficial to your mother as well."

Mother Felicitas walked Katherine through the cool convent corridors to one of the side doors. There they stood in the stone shadows of the foyer, and the nun's smile seemed no more than a reflection of Katherine's own happiness at realizing to what extent she had become an object of the convent's interest and solicitude.

"Two of our postulants will be enrolled in the summer schedule as well, and you're welcome to accompany them to and from the school each day. They'll be driving from the convent every morning, and it'll save you the expense and the bother of the subway trip—and give you a little company as well. Believe me, Katherine, this time of waiting will be good for you. It will take you out into the world a little and your decision will be a more realistic one. And I don't want you to worry about grades, either. I want you to *learn*. A good heart is always accounted of more worth than the quickest mind." Mother Felicitas pulled open the

front door, and the hot sunlight of the noon hour spilled over
Katherine's already radiant face.

8

By the end of July, three weeks into classes at Boston College,
with one short paper already behind her, Katherine could scarcely
believe how easily it all came to her. At ImCon, though she had
longed to please the nuns with acceptable work, she had never
seemed to get anything just right. But at the college, although
ostensibly the courses were much more specialized and difficult,
the professors far more rigorous than the indulgent sisters of the
Convent of Saint Agnes, Katherine was working for the glory of
God—and she never passed an uneasy moment in the classroom.
Every scrap of knowledge she garnered was a tiny jewel added to
her trousseau for her marriage to Christ. Every moment, every
movement was dedicated to her future in the church.

Five mornings a week Katherine waited anxiously on the
steps of the Medford Street house for the Volkswagen Beetle
belonging to the convent. She insisted on sitting in the back in
deference to the exalted position of the two postulants who were
also enrolled at Boston College that summer. The ride was nearly
forty-five minutes long through rush hour traffic, but Katherine
only wished it had been more protracted so that she might have
heard more of the gossip of the convent. Jealous of the two postulants, she further modified her own apparel to blend with their
flowing black robes, as if she were a kind of apprentice to the
postulancy. Despite the wretchedly hot weather prevailing that
summer, Katherine wore heavy navy blue skirts, dark hose, and
low-heeled black loafers. To her starched white cotton blouses
she affixed narrow black collars and pinned a tiny gold crucifix
to one flap. When it rained she wore a black scarf over her hair.
Like the postulants, she covered her textbooks in brown paper
cut from grocery bags.

When Katherine had told her mother that she would be
attending Boston College, she did not think it served her purpose
to admit that this was a prerequisite to becoming a Slave of the

Immaculate Conception. Anne Dolan took her daughter's enrollment to mean that Katherine had given over the idea of becoming a nun. She fell into relieved whimpering: "Oh, Kathy, I *knew* you wouldn't leave me! We'll be happy again, and after you graduate you'll be able to get a nice job teaching here in Somerville. You'll meet some nice young man, and even if you get married there's plenty of room here for both of you. And when you start to have children, we can find a bigger place. Oh it'll be so good for both of us! Oh, Kathy, we're going to start a new life!"

Anne Dolan's vision of her daughter's future expanded as her own life contracted. Now the widow slept on the sofa, and the television set was never turned off. Anne Dolan said she couldn't sleep without the late-night static: it made her feel warm, and without it she was so cold! Katherine returned from classes late in the afternoon, shopped at the corner grocery, did housework, and then prepared dinner for her mother and herself. In the evening she studied, coming out of her room only when it was time to say good night. Katherine saw her home life as a continual penance.

One night, as she lay on the couch with her dinner on a TV tray across her lap, Anne Dolan burst into tears without apparent reason. Katherine look up perplexed, and her mother, in a paroxysm, overturned her plate of beans and franks onto the floor.

"Ma! What is it?" cried Katherine angrily, and went to the kitchen for a towel. When she returned, her mother whimpered: "I was thinking about Jim. He's still not buried! Oh lord, Kathy, he was a good man! How he loved you! How he loved both of us! He worked himself to the bone for us, there never was a man to work like he did, and people kept him down! He was a family man and people kept him down! I loved him so much, didn't you, Kathy? You must have loved him like he was your own father!"

"Ma," said Katherine, "you spilled your entire dinner on the rug and now there's not any left. There's nothing else in the house and you're going to have to go without."

Between her schoolwork and her mother's demands, Katherine hadn't an idle moment. At eleven o'clock she'd fall asleep exhausted, but long before morning her sleep would be disturbed by the old dreams. They had come upon her once more, and with more than their former intensity. She'd wake startled, with a fine film of perspiration coating her body, and against the bare wall of her close, darkened room she'd see the lingering image of the girl she might have been. And after that she could not find sleep again.

On the last Saturday in July Katherine took a bus to Cambridge and entered the sprawling Lechmere department store. She slipped into the last in a line of enclosed telephone booths at the end of the appliance department and dialled the number of the Somerville police station. Turning her back to the glass door, she placed three tissues over the mouthpiece. She asked to be connected with a detective, and when it proved that none was available, she told the man on desk duty that she was a neighbor of the Dolans on Medford Street and was certain that James Dolan had been murdered by his wife.

Katherine spoke quickly, fearful that the line would be traced. "You could hear their fights all over the neighborhood, they used to wake up my baby at night. Mrs. Dolan told me she would kill her husband if she thought she could get away with it. Everybody in the neighborhood knew they didn't get along, they were only staying together because of their daughter. People won't talk about it unless you make 'em, though. Go back and ask people, they're mad because she's getting away with it. Go ask the neighbors what they think, ask 'em what they heard. They'll all tell you she killed him."

When the police officer on desk duty asked her name, Katherine wadded the tissue and, in her normal voice, whispered, "I can't tell you . . ."

The next day, as she was returning from mass, Katherine noted a suited man emerging from the house next door to her own. He climbed into a car that was parked beside a fire hydrant and there conferred with a man dressed similarly. Later in the afternoon she saw him ring the bell of the house on the other side.

When Katherine returned from Boston College on Monday afternoon, a policeman was waiting for her at the apartment. He informed her that her mother had been arrested for the murder of James Dolan. The neighbors, prodded with the right questions, had told of loud arguments between Anne and James Dolan. "We learned that a number of these arguments centered on your decision to become a nun," said the detective.

"I don't know . . ." faltered Katherine.

"Didn't you hear them? The neighbors certainly did."

"When Ma and Daddy argued, I left the house. When I couldn't leave the house, I tried not to listen. Why . . . why did it take you so long?"

"To arrest your mother? We weren't sure. Your neighbors didn't talk right away. Then it seems somebody got mad at her and called us up, somebody who was mad at her for 'getting away with it.' That just clinched what we already believed. Listen, I'm sorry that—"

"Who was it?" demanded Katherine. "Who called you up?"

"One of your neighbors."

"Which one?"

"I can't tell you that," said the detective. "It wouldn't do you any good to know."

Katherine, reassured that the detective did not suspect her of making that telephone call, accompanied him to the police station, where she was questioned in much greater detail. She told what little she knew of her parents' history, she tried to excuse her father's drinking and her mother's slovenliness, she attempted to play down the controversy that had surrounded her decision to join the convent. The detectives questioning her came away with a stronger feeling against Anne Dolan than had been generated by all the emphatically negative testimony of the neighbors.

She saw her mother in a temporary cell in the Somerville jail, and only nodded in response to Anne Dolan's plea that she never desert her. "Everything will be fine, Ma," said Katherine. "Nobody thinks you did it."

Katherine returned to Medford Street in the unmarked police car she had seen the day before. Word of the arrest had spread quickly in the neighborhood, and several women were gathered before the house. They parted with little whispered words of consolation as Katherine passed numbly between them and up the steps of the triple-decker.

Reverend Mother Felicitas telephoned that night to tell Katherine that a room had been prepared for her in the convent. "It cannot be good for you to remain in that apartment alone. Shall I send someone for you now?"

"No," Katherine had said in a weary voice, "I'll be all right, at least for tonight."

It was the first night she had ever spent alone in her home, and the first night in a long while she spent without dreaming. Next morning she was wakened by the telephone. She picked up the receiver listlessly, but without either fear or anxiety. It was the realtor to whom the Dolans had paid their rent each month. Katherine realized she did not even know how much the apartment had cost her parents.

"We here at the company just want you to know, Miss Dolan, that we sympathize fully with the . . . um, unhappiness you're experiencing at the present moment. But we also need to know what arrangements have been made for the payment of your rent. We still have not received the check for July's rent, and this month's was due on the tenth. I know it's difficult at a time—"

"I don't know anything about it," said Katherine softly. "But it doesn't matter. No one's going to be living here anymore."

She wandered from room to room through the house, glanced at the worn and scarred furniture and the faded wallpaper, studied the pictures on the wall, and thought, *All this is mine now. This is what I'm giving up to join the convent. This is the material world.*

Her tour ended in her own bedroom, at the door of her own closet. She counted the pairs of shoes she had and touched the sleeves of all the blouses that hung upon the rack. At last, from the shelf above that rack, she brought down a suitcase and opened it upon the bed. In one side she laid out her rosaries and scapulars, a small stack of holy cards wrapped in tissue and secured with a ribbon, and the pendant with the relic of Saint Adelaide. Then she packed her best clothes, and did not sigh to abandon the rest. At the very last, she removed the crucifix from the wall above her bed and laid it atop her diary.

When she had closed and locked the case, she carried it out to the hallway. She walked through the apartment once more to make certain that the lights were out, the windows latched, and the shades drawn. She unplugged the television set and pushed it back against the wall. She locked the door behind her unhesitatingly and dropped the keys in Mrs. Shea's mailbox, without bothering to leave a note. She did not respond to the neighbors who called softly to her from their front porches, but kept her eyes straight ahead as she moved down Medford Street in the direction of the Convent of Saint Agnes.

9

The first part of her life, Katherine had come to see, had been a kind of death—eighteen useless, hideous years filled with meaningless pain, hardly to be endured. It had required a sharp, sudden, *real* death to engineer her rebirth. If James Dolan had not died, pierced to the heart with a carving knife, she would not be in the convent today. Although the hour she would assume the voluminous black habit was still uncertain, Katherine was happier than she had ever been before, and her occasional uneasiness that her necessary and justified crime would be discovered was but a small price to pay for the ecstasy she experienced in the Convent of Saint Agnes even though she walked those quiet, cool halls only as a guest of the order. Her room was segregated from the chambers where the nuns slept, and Katherine chafed nightly at this distance. She was regularly enrolled at Boston College and was taking one course more than the normal load. Her tuition was paid by a scholarship obtained through the agency of Reverend Mother Felicitas's sister in the admissions office, and her incidental expenses were taken care of by a secret fund controlled by the head of the convent. Katherine took a postulant's share of the convent work, and communal confessional was the only activity in which she did not participate. Her happiest moments were those in which one or other of the nuns would slip and address her as "Sister."

The splendor of the evening services at the Church of Saint Agnes drove the remembrance of former distress from her mind, and Katherine knew that she might be happy for the rest of her life, moving from one glorious ceremonial of the church to the next. Her guilt that she had murdered her father she had long ago consecrated to herself as a penance, and she had even begun to take pride in the enormity of that crime and the suffering it engendered in her.

Anne Dolan had been charged with murder in the first degree. She had been so vague and alien during the arraignment, however, that the judge sent her to Bridgewater State Hospital to undergo extensive psychiatric treatment, and there her lawyer, Mr. Giovinco, had thought it advisable to keep her for as long as possible.

As soon as her mother had been locked into Bridgewater, Katherine had broken up the Medford Street apartment. She told Reverend Mother Felicitas that this was the especial wish of Anne Dolan, who had vowed never to return to the place. Most of the furniture was sold to a secondhand dealer from Cambridge, and the rest was got rid of at a yard sale presided over by Katherine and Mrs. Shea. Everyone in the neighborhood wanted a souvenir from the home of the murdered husband and his murderous wife. At the end, Katherine was $1,843 richer and wanted to contribute the money to the convent's coffers, but Reverend Mother Felicitas insisted that it be deposited in the bank to help defray her mother's legal expenses.

It was four months since Katherine had telephoned the police and accused her mother of the crime that she had committed, and still she was not free of the woman. It was a terrifying thought to the girl that her mother might be released on psychiatric grounds; then, Reverend Mother Felicitas would surely insist that Katherine return to Anne Dolan.

So far as Katherine knew, her plight was never discussed openly in the convent. If scandal followed her, Katherine did not feel its breath upon her back. Whenever the subject was mentioned, it was Katherine herself who broached it. As autumn hardened into winter, Katherine began to believe that her mother would never return from Bridgewater at all: she had been found insane or become lost in bureaucratic maneuverings. There were days on which she gave not a single thought to her mother, and those days were blessed.

But when she received a summons to the formal office of Mother Felicitas on the Monday following Thanksgiving, Katherine was certain that it had to do with her mother.

Anne Dolan had been deemed mentally competent to stand trial for the murder of her husband. Court date had been set for the fourth day of January of the new year. "Mr. Giovinco called not half an hour ago, Katherine, dear," said Mother Superior Felicitas, her expression one of pain and concern. "He had tried for another stay, but failed."

Katherine said nothing. Her fingers were wound together before her.

"Your mother will be returned to Middlesex County Jail," said the nun, glancing at a page of notes she had taken during the conversation with the lawyer. "I'm glad that you will be so close. This must be a terrible and a very lonely time for her."

There was a pause, and Katherine imagined that she ought to say something. "I'll be visiting Ma every chance I get," she said in a choked voice. She looked up into the mother superior's eyes, hoping for approval for this promise.

Mother Superior Felicitas had glanced away, troubled. "Katherine," she said, in a tone that suggested she had not even heard Katherine's resolve, "I hesitate to say this to you—"

"What, Reverend Mother?" asked Katherine anxiously, fearful that her mother's transference back to jail would somehow revoke her uneasy position as lay guest within the convent. Waves of hate were tided in her brain against her mother for this anticipated misery.

Katherine's unguarded voice pulled the Reverend Mother up sharply. "Katherine," she said, "my discussion with Mr. Giovinco was more probing than I have indicated. It will be a hard trial for your mother. It is possible that things may turn out . . ."

"Bad?" suggested Katherine.

Reverend Mother Felicitas nodded. "We will all pray, of course, that they *don't*, but . . ."

"Every moment," said Katherine firmly, "I pray God that things turn out for the best!"

"But things may not, dear. Things may not," she repeated sadly. "Though of course I'm not trying to discourage you. This news, too, comes at an awkward time. I'd hoped that this would be a day of unalloyed pleasure for you, dear."

"Reverend Mother?"

"I've set up a series of meetings for you, Katherine, with priests attached to the Mother House in Worcester and with a psychiatrist from Boston College."

Katherine sat bolt upright in her chair. *She thinks I'm crazy . . . like my mother. She thinks I killed my father!* Her fingers wrenched around the arms of the chair.

Puzzled at Katherine's reaction, Mother Superior Felicitas wrinkled her brow and said, "In preparation for your eventual postulancy, Katherine. I think the time has come."

Katherine's breath stopped in her throat.

"It's a requirement made of all young women who wish to become nuns, you know that, so please don't think that you're being singled out. We only want to make sure that you will be emotionally prepared. These interviews will be made for your sake, not ours. We are *not* building any kind of file, as I heard one postulant complain. And of course I wish you to understand that none of this, and particularly not the timing, has anything to do with your mother's unfortunate situation. Do you understand?"

"You're saying that I'm being permitted . . . ?" Katherine's voice was small and disbelieving.

A bell chimed twice beyond the office door and down the halls of the convent. Mother Felicitas checked her digital watch. "You must remind me to tell Sister Jude Thaddeus that her call to matins is a minute and a half early." She sighed. "Sister Jude Thaddeus is *always* early. Come, Katherine, walk to the chapel with me."

Katherine's position, here as elsewhere, was a little apart from the nuns. She did not believe Mother Superior Felicitas's assurance that this decision had nothing to do with her mother's precarious chances in court. Mr. Giovinco had doubtless convinced the nun that Anne Dolan's case was hopeless, that Katherine's mother would be found guilty and imprisoned for the rest of her life. Katherine's eyes were bright as she scanned the bowed black heads of the nuns. Her clasped hands beat violently against her breast as she chanted, "My fault, my fault, my most grievous fault."

When she undressed for bed that night, she discovered a small purplish bruise outlined against her flesh.

*

On the day before the end of the fall term at Boston College, Katherine was once more summoned to the office of Mother Superior Felicitas.

"I have the report of the psychiatrist you saw on Tuesday. As it turns out, he's a Jesuit priest, though I didn't know it at the time. It used to be that you—"

"Did I pass?" asked Katherine eagerly. In the hours after school for the last month, Katherine had been conferring with priests and various members of the order sent out from Worcester. She made daily confession and had talked at length with the psychiatrist, with whom she had been terribly ill at ease.

Mother Superior Felicitas smiled indulgently. "It wasn't a test to pass or fail, Katherine, dear. You're not proving yourself—I had hoped you'd be over that idea by now. We're not sitting in judgment over you. We only want to make sure that this is the life best suited for you. There are other realms in which one may devote herself utterly to Christ."

"I failed," said Katherine miserably.

"No, no, please don't think of it that way! I didn't bring you in here to give you a grade, you know. I only wanted to discuss a few points that were brought out in Father Vane's report."

"What?" said Katherine anxiously. "What points, Reverend Mother?"

"Father Vane said that you were troubled by dreams. Is that correct?"

"Oh, I didn't say that I was *troubled*. No, I didn't say that. I just said I had dreams. But they're not, they're not—"

"Sexual," prompted Mother Superior Felicitas.

"No!" cried Katherine, shamed.

"And it wouldn't matter if they were. A dream of a sexual nature would hardly be sufficient ground to keep you from becoming a nun. You can't imagine that seventy-five women under one roof—even if they are every one of them Slaves of the Immaculate Conception—can't get up an erotic dream among them. No, Katherine, it just doesn't happen that way. The devil has temptations conscious and unconscious, and he never leaves off trying us."

"But I still don't have that kind of dream!"

"They are dreams of a worldly nature—dreams of yourself, but a prettier self, though you seem sufficiently handsome to me. In your dreams, Father Vane says, you are 'pretty, well dressed, surrounded by friends, envied, happy.'"

"They're terrible dreams, Reverend Mother!"

"Why so? None of these things is in itself terrible. Christ's legions are not uniformly ugly, slovenly, diseased, morose, and friendless. I would hope not!"

"These dreams bother me so much," admitted Katherine slowly.

"Why? Father Vane writes that you are 'haunted' by them. I wish that my dreams were half so pleasant as yours seem to be."

"But the girl who's in my dreams—that's not how I want to be, Reverend Mother! I want to be a nun. Maybe I didn't always know it, but now I'm sure that that's the only way that I could be satisfied with my life, if I devoted myself entirely to Christ, and God, and the Church."

"And so says Father Vane. You needn't worry about the dreams. It's natural that when you have determined to forsake the material world, your subconscious rebels. It is human nature to rebel; it is spiritual nature for you to try to overcome that rebellious flesh. Oh, I've seen this countless times, Katherine, the dreams needn't worry you. They pass, and they are forgotten. Ultimately, desire will rot like flesh itself."

On Christmas Eve Katherine was driven to the Middlesex County Jail in East Cambridge. A week previous, Mother Superior Felicitas had spoken to her in the long walk from chapel back to the dormitory: "For the laity, holidays are often more a bane than a blessing, and for those in prison, a holiday is a doubly onerous time. We are committed to delivering packages to the unfortunate on Christmas Day, but there is no reason you cannot spend it with your mother."

"Oh no, Reverend Mother! I'd much rather work here on Christmas. Thanksgiving was so wonderful, I—"

"But your mother! Think of your mother alone on Christmas Day!"

"I'll spend Christmas Eve with her," said Katherine, "but please: I want to dedicate Christmas itself to the poor."

"Your mother is—" began Mother Superior Felicitas, but then thought better. "All right, Katherine. You are so much a part of us already, I confess it wouldn't seem right not to have you around on so joyous a day."

This speech made up for the evil of the promised visit to her mother.

In a corner of the visiting room of the jail was a dreary little lopsided tree, scantily decorated. Katherine regarded it pensively as she waited for Anne Dolan to appear. It had been early autumn when she saw her mother last.

During her confinement Anne Dolan appeared to have aged several years. She looked gray and decrepit; her voice was low and she had developed a cough that interrupted her speech and made her lose her train of thought.

Impulsively, Katherine hurried forward and kissed her mother on the cheek.

"Kathy, Kathy, I'm so glad you've come!" smiled Anne Dolan. "'Cause you know, I won't be here much longer."

"Ma," Katherine demanded, "what do you mean? What—"

Anne Dolan slipped waveringly into a red vinyl chair near a hissing radiator. Katherine pulled another chair close.

"After the trial and all, we'll be back home, we'll—" Anne Dolan coughed and extracted a wadded square of tissue from her uniform. She dabbed it at her mouth and glanced out the window. "Sometimes I get so tired. It's the food here, they put something in the food that makes you tired all the time."

"That's a pretty blouse, Ma."

"Oh, Kathy, I know what I look like." She touched her hand to her hair, readjusting a loose wave. "They won't let me dye it here, and it's starting to look bad. They had a beauty parlor at Bridgewater because they said it made you feel better if you looked nice. Here they don't care what you feel like. I used to have a mirror in my room, but I threw it on the floor and told the matron it fell off the shelf. I got tired of looking at myself getting older every day." She plucked at the puffed sleeves of the white blouse that billowed over her shrunken frame. "I'm losing weight too, that's not the food, the food's okay, I guess, it's the worry. I know it's the worry that's causing me to lose weight."

"Ma..."

Anne gazed vacantly round her, and her eyes alighted on the tree in the corner.

"Oh, Kathy, look at the tree! It *is* Christmas! Somebody said it was, but I didn't believe it—how could it be Christmas in a place like this? I remember last Christmas, don't you? When we were all together. Last Christmas, I don't think I had ever even *been* in a jail before. When Jim and I took our honeymoon in Washington, we had a guided tour of the FBI building, and your father shook hands with J. Edgar Hoover, but that wasn't really a jail, not like this one is..."

"I brought you a present, Ma." From the pocket of her coat Katherine pulled a small gilt-edged book encased in a red leather sleeve. "It's a red-letter testament, with all the prayers in the back. It's on real parchment, Ma, I thought you might like to have it."

"Oh, I do want it!" cried Anne Dolan. "It's the nicest thing I have now, the very nicest thing! I just wish I had something for you..."

"Oh, Ma!"

"... but I didn't have the chance to do much shopping this year." Anne Dolan smiled at her sad, feeble joke.

10

In the hour before the lights of the Hingham convent house were extinguished, Katherine sat in her chamber and opened her diary. She left five blank pages between the last entry of her old life and the first of her new, and to sanctify the separation, she taped to one of the pages a holy card showing the head of the suffering Christ. Blood trickled from the gouging thorns, and His agonized eyes were cast imploringly to Heaven. She wrote the words she had spoken before the bishop that afternoon.

I appeal to the infinite compassion of Almighty God to accept me as his bride and as his humble servant. I ask this with all my heart, with all my humility. I ask almighty God for the benediction of the holy robes. I ask this with all my heart. I ask almighty God to grant me humility, sincerity, and patience as his servant and his slave.

Katherine was a postulant, a new woman, she had nothing whatever to do with Medford Street or her murdered father or her imprisoned mother. The ceremony of Clothing had wiped her clean of her past, and Katherine felt herself free to write of her ecstasy. The Christ of Golgotha had taken Katherine as bride.

She had come to the Hingham convent after Reverend Mother Felicitas decided it would be best for her to perform her postulancy away from the familiar surroundings of the town in which she had grown up. The reverend mother had hoped to delay Katherine's postulancy ceremony until after her mother's trial, but the slight cough that Anne Dolan had when Katherine visited her on Christmas Eve proved to be pneumonia. Her lawyer, Mr. Giovinco, found this the perfect excuse to have the trial delayed until the third week in February. Knowing to what extent Katherine would suffer another postponement of her induction, Reverend Mother Felicitas had decided to initiate the process by which Katherine would become a Slave of the Immaculate Conception. And the first step of that process was Katherine's removal from the Convent of Saint Agnes. "This should be a time of serious meditation," a dismayed Katherine was told. "You must pray for enlightenment. It is unfortunate, but I fear that your emotional attachments to the nuns in this house could hinder your making a right and true decision. And what is right and true, dear, may not be what you want, or what we want either. You love us, Katherine, and we all love you, but there would simply be no challenge if you were to remain here with us. You must decide, for yourself, how much you love *God*."

The thought of leaving the safety and comfort of the Convent of St. Agnes terrified Katherine, and she had wanted to cry out —to beg not to be sent away. But she feared that such an outburst might prejudice the reverend mother against her postulancy.

It was not with an entirely easy mind that Katherine made the trip from Somerville to Hingham, driven by Sister Mary Claire, with Sister Martha, who liked to travel so much that she would go anywhere with anyone, in the back seat. During that ride Katherine resolved that this day would truly be the beginning of her new life: the trepidations and sharp miseries caused by the remnants of her old life would have no place in Hingham.

For three weeks the diary remained at the back of a dresser drawer; it was not so much that she did not wish to record her impressions of the convent—she simply didn't want to be reminded of what lay behind her. But on the evening of her Clothing, she took the diary out again and transcribed the ecstatic ceremony moment for moment, though she could scarcely imagine there would be a time when she would *not* remember it was Sister Martha who had rearranged her veil just before she had reentered the sanctuary, or that the bishop wore black rather than brown wingtips.

The clothing ceremony was the most perfect hour of Katherine's life. The sanctuary was illuminated entirely by candles, the boys' choir sang celestially from the loft, and six nuns from the Convent of St. Agnes attended upon her. She entered the church in a resplendent bridal gown, which in the course of the ritual was exchanged for the black robes that designated her as a postulant in the order. Her head was shorn and covered with a wimple. When her clothing had been completed, she, carrying a lighted taper, led a procession of the bishop, altar boys, and the six nuns down the aisle of the church.

They crossed Mystic Avenue slowly and moved up the wide flagstone walk to the front doors of the Convent of Saint Luke. Katherine blew out the carefully tended flame and knelt on the shallow granite steps. She bowed her head and spread her arms wide.

In the shimmering twilight, her voice was clear and loud: "Admit me, dear Mother, into this house, for it will be my dwelling place until eternity!" She touched her lips to the cold stone. The great mahogany doors of the convent house scraped open, and Katherine raised herself by degrees. The long white hands of Mother Superior Celestine were extended in greeting and welcome.

"We deliver unto your care a daughter," intoned the bishop.

"We accept her in God's eternal love," replied the mother superior.

Katherine rose. Reverend Mother Celestine took her hand and led her through the doorway. When the mahogany doors were scraped closed and the iron bolt shot into place, Katherine had become a nun.

Sitting in the low-backed wooden chair, Katherine wore a white cotton nightdress with tiny wooden buttons at the collar and cuffs. Her habit hung in the narrow closet across from her low metal cot. Her stiff wimple, leather girdle, and large-beaded rosary were laid neatly across the bureau top; she examined them every few minutes in excitement that they were *hers*. The black hose and veil were on a hanger on the closet doorknob. Attached to the cream-colored wall next to the single window was an unadorned crucifix, and it was not the one that had hung in her room on Medford Street. The unpatterned white curtains had not yet been drawn, and the window was opened a few inches to admit the cool evening breeze that blew across the marsh. The tide was swiftly flowing out, but there were still pools in which Katherine, by turning her head a little, could catch the reflection of the rising gibbous moon.

As she wrote, she listened with smiling satisfaction to the soft steps sounding in the long corridor of the third floor as the nuns readied themselves for sleep. Occasionally she heard low voices or an aspirate giggle. The sounds were familiar, for she had lived in the convent for several weeks, but for the first time Katherine felt as if she had the *right* to take comfort and pleasure from such sounds: no longer was she on the outside, an interloper, a suffered participant in the pleasures of the conventual life. Katherine Dolan was dead—and she was *Sister* Katherine, Slave of the Immaculate Conception.

I know that for the rest of my life I'll be just as happy as I am at this very minute. I know that for me, every moment will be a pleasure—just as this moment is a pleasure. The sisters are walking up and down outside in the corridor, and when they pass my door, they think, "That's the room where Sister is, that's Sister Katherine's room." I'm one of them now. Just one year ago, not even that, nine months ago, at the end of my senior year at ImCon, I would look at Sister Mary Claire and at Sister Jude Thaddeus, and I would think, "They call each other *Sister*." They both belonged to God, and they belonged to each other, and they loved each other in God, and it seemed like that was the most wonderful thing in the world, something that I could never experience myself. I didn't think I was good enough to devote myself to God, I didn't think I was smart enough. But Sister Mary Claire said that in God's sight, we're all stupid and we're all sinful, and that it's only here on earth that we have degrees of stupidity and sinfulness. Without the grace of God, we're all insignificant and we're all damned. There's a nun here called Sister Josepha, and I talked to her tonight. She loves the convent too. She said, "When I was a little girl, our priest said that we shouldn't think about heaven as clouds, and people floating around and playing harps all the time, because that's not *anybody's* idea of a good time, but instead we should think of heaven as being the nicest thing we can think of—whatever that is—and then heaven will be twice as nice as that." So from now on I'm going to think of heaven as a convent, just like the one here in Hingham, where I have my own room, and a window that looks out on the marshes. There are trees everywhere you look, and everything is quiet and peaceful.

When she had finished, she turned back the pages, kissed the image of Christ, and closed the book. She snapped the tiny lock shut and slipped the volume into the table drawer.

The overhead light went off automatically, and Katherine moved to sit on the edge of the cot. Beyond the dark window the winter sky was clear and starlit. The moon shone brilliantly on the deep lawn that sloped gently down to the marshes and the rickety pier there. Tall, bulbous-topped cattails swayed gently and with a melancholy swishing at the edge of the marsh.

Stark, dusty Somerville was a world away, and that her mother languished in a prison ten floors above East Cambridge caused Katherine no more discomfort than the remembrance of pain in a wound now healed.

II

"The robes look real good on you, Kathy, I didn't think they would, but they do." Anne Dolan sat in an armless chair, with her back to the sleet-streaked window in the small visiting room of the county jail. A matron, thin and wizened, stood in uniform near the mesh door in the far corner. Katherine sat opposite her mother, in a more commodious chair; the sleeves of her habit draped over the arms.

We've changed places, thought Katherine. *Now I'm the one in power.* It wasn't power, really, it was simply a vast superiority of circumstance: Katherine was honored, satisfied, calm, and—above all—free. Anne Dolan was disgraced, unhappy, nervous, and—above all—incarcerated. Katherine knew that she ought to be patient with her mother, whose situation, after all, was extreme and dire, but patience was hard got for the young nun.

Anne Dolan's eyes were moist and red-rimmed. She glanced shyly up at Katherine and shifted her eyes to her lap.

These robes protect me, thought Katherine, *even from her.*

There was a long silence. Katherine glanced meaningfully at the matron, who nodded deferentially and slipped out of the room. She stood within sight on the other side of the mesh door, but she no longer could hear the conversation of the mother and daughter.

"I'm so glad you came, Kathy, I wasn't sure that they'd let you out of there. I asked another woman here, and she said they never let nuns out, not even for their parents' funerals."

"Reverend Mother Celestine told me that I ought to visit you," said Katherine stiffly, unwilling even that her mother should believe that she had come entirely of her own choice and desire. "Sister Henrica drove me up here, she's waiting outside."

"Are you happy?" said Anne Dolan. "I hope you're happy, the only thing I've ever really wanted in this world is for you to be happy, you know that, don't you, Kathy?"

"I'm as happy as I could possibly be," said Katherine grimly.

"It starts tomorrow," Anne Dolan whispered. "Are you going to be there, Kathy?"

"I'm being called as a witness," said Katherine, "I have to be there."

Anne Dolan looked up: "You're going to tell them how much we loved you, aren't you?" she cried eagerly. "How we did so much for you, Jim and I, we did so much for you, you were adopted, Kathy, and we loved you like you were our own little girl, that's why I can't understand why people could think that I . . . *But I didn't.* You know I didn't. Nobody thinks I did it. You don't think so, the neighbors don't think so. Mrs. Shea came to see me the other day, and *she* doesn't think so, and the nuns at St. Agnes, they know you, and I'm sure that they don't think so. It was just the police, and the people in the court, and the judge, people who didn't know Jim, and people who don't know me, they think I did it, but you're going to tell everybody that I couldn't possibly have done it, you're going to tell everybody that it couldn't possibly have been me that killed Jim, aren't you?"

"I'm going to testify about what happened that day, I'm going to talk about whatever they ask me, Ma."

"Good," said Anne Dolan, relieved in her assumption that Katherine would speak only well of her.

Katherine sat silent.

Anne Dolan looked around her distractedly and repeated, "You look so good in those robes, Kathy, and you've got more color now." She plucked absently at her blouse. "Did that lawyer tell you what to say when you're on the stand?"

"Which lawyer, Ma?"

"My lawyer, Mr. Giovinco. Who else?"

"Ma," said Katherine slowly, "I'm testifying for the prosecution."

Anne Dolan looked up startled. "Against me? You're testifying against your own mother!"

"No," said Katherine, "of course not. I'm just testifying. It was just the prosecution that subpoenaed me first; if they hadn't, Mr. Giovinco would have. I'm surprised he didn't mention it."

"But what will you say, what will you say against me, Kathy?"

"Nothing, Ma, they just want me to talk about—about coming downstairs, that's all."

"I wish you wouldn't say anything about that, Kathy," whispered her mother, "we were both so upset that afternoon, so upset, you know we were—somebody coming in and killing Jim, and we both found his body—oh, Kathy, it was so awful!"

"Yes," agreed Katherine, "it was awful."

Anne Dolan leaned forward earnestly. "What if things don't go right, Kathy?"

"What do you mean?"

"What if they don't believe us? They'll send me to Framingham. I hear stories about Framingham here—it's awful there. I've ridden through Framingham, and I didn't like it . . ."

Katherine did not bother to point out to her mother that were she sent to the women's prison there, she wouldn't be spending much time in the town.

"They have capital punishment here now," whispered Anne Dolan. "I remember when the governor signed the bill, I thought, That's a terrible thing to do, what if somebody's innocent and gets sent to the electric chair? And now it could be me, Kathy, they might end up putting me in the electric chair, have you ever thought about that? I'm scared," she whimpered.

"They don't have the electric chair any more, Ma. It's poison gas."

"I don't know why I'm worried," giggled Anne Dolan, "they'd never convict a woman whose daughter was a nun. I know that's why as soon as all this happened you went in the convent, wasn't it? I was surprised when you told me that was what you were going to do—I thought you had given that idea up. But then I realized that you were doing it all for me. Everything'll be all right when they find out that you're a nun. You knew the jury would never convict a woman whose daughter was a nun."

Katherine didn't reply.

"And then when this is all over, you can come back to me—I'll need somebody to take care of me."

"I'm going to take my final vows, Ma—no matter what happens at the trial."

"Oh of course, Kathy, I know that!" her mother cried, and reached out and grasped her daughter's knee through the black cotton robe: "But you'll put it off for a while, won't you, I know you will, the mother superior will give you some sort of dispensation because I've been through so much, and I'm so sick, they'll let you spend a few years with me, you could get a job, and we'd get along just fine. We'll have to find a new place to live, though, I don't want to go back to Medford Street, you and I won't need much, Kathy, we can get along on very little. When I get out of here, everything will be the same again . . ." She gazed hopefully into her daughter's face.

"I'll pray for you, Ma," said Katherine. "All the sisters at St. Luke's and St. Agnes's are praying for you too. I have to go now."

"All right," said Anne Dolan meekly. "But just stand up and let me look at you once more." Obediently, Katherine stood, her arms stiff at her sides. "Step back, so I can see you better." Katherine did so. "Oh, you're such a pretty girl," exclaimed her mother, "if only Jim could see you!"

When she left her mother at the Middlesex County Jail, Katherine rode with Sister Henrica to the campus of Boston College for their evening class, Special Education for the Mentally Impaired. It was an advanced course, added to her normal undergraduate load, and her favorite. Several long conversations with Reverend Mother Celestine had helped Katherine decide that she would be a teacher of children with special needs.

Following the ideas of a certain Jesuit professor at Boston College, who had taken a particular interest in the elementary school attached to the Convent of St. Luke, Mother Celestine had done away with the "Special Class," in which the certifiably slow and retarded children were kept apart from those with normal abilities. This segregation, even to the children's often dim consciousnesses, was apparent, and their alienation from the other students was thought to hamper their already difficult advancement. In public schools it was often not practical to incorporate these disadvantaged youngsters into the regular classes, where they must inevitably fall behind because their teachers could not provide them with the painstaking instruction they required, but at St. Luke's there was a superfluity of young nuns who were willing to assist in the slow and monotonous care of these children. Katherine was one.

On three days out of the week she assisted Sister Thomasina in her first-grade class, patiently listening to the children—Katherine could hardly believe that she had herself been once so small and tender—inch through their lessons in reading and numbers. She was infinitely patient and formed special affections for those who were slowest and performed with the most difficulty, for in them she glimpsed the Katherine Dolan that was.

She would sit with them for three quarters of an hour and, using crayons and marbles, patiently illustrate over and over the principles of addition and subtraction. She would gently hold their meek little hands and guide their thick pencils in the formation of the letter *A* twenty-five times—and not be disappointed that the children could not then do it alone on the twenty-sixth attempt. She would take a group of six round the school yard and talk to them of everything that could be seen from that limited vantage: clouds, rocks, marsh, and vegetation. And sometimes, in her free time, she would accompany a small group of them for a brief outing to Nantasket, only fifteen minutes away, to walk and gather shells from the winter beach while she talked of waves, currents, and tides to these children who didn't yet understand the difference between fresh water and salt.

For the older classes she sometimes graded papers—just as she had so often imagined helping the nuns at ImCon—or monitored recess periods, occasionally joining in a game of kickball or teaching the smallest children the strange games she had learned in her childhood and forgot all about until now—Spider, Giant, and Crooked Mile. Katherine had never felt so happy or so useful, and her journal was nightly filled with small episodes of the day's work in the grammar school: a child who had suddenly learned to write his own name, a girl who had embraced her in unrestrainable affection, a boy who had said that she reminded him of his dead mother. Katherine looked forward eagerly to the time in which she would have a class of her own; but she knew too that she would miss the opportunity she enjoyed now, of coming into contact with almost every child that was enrolled in St. Luke's.

Katherine's only worry, her only impatience, was for her mother's trial and its outcome. Hingham was years and leagues away from Somerville, from Medford Street, from the Middlesex County Jail, and she had no great fear that she would ever be forced permanently to reenter that world. Her mother could talk for as long as she wanted about Katherine's coming to live with her again when she was acquitted, she could make all the plans she wanted for Katherine's getting a job to support her, she could build the biggest castles that ever existed in an imaginary sky— but Katherine knew that nothing would prevent her from taking her final vows in a year's time.

But the nuisance was that the trial hung over Katherine as well as her mother. Mr. Giovinco, a greasy sort of man, had held several conferences with Katherine, suggesting that she keep her evidence toned down for her mother's sake. "Of course she didn't do it, we know that, she loved your father very much, she tells me so every time I see her, and I know it must be true, but we ought not let the jury know—there'll be a jury, of course—that there was any trouble between them. And are you really sure that you saw her *holding* the knife? You just saw the knife, and it was on the table *near* her, but she wasn't actually *holding* the knife, was she, Sister Katherine?"

12

"Sister Katherine," said the district attorney, "you are certain that you heard no noise from your own apartment prior to the time that your mother returned from her bingo game?"

He stood a discreet distance from her, out of deference to her robes, but also that he might face the jury. He was middle-aged, with dull ginger-colored hair and pale gray eyes that bore into Katherine.

"I heard the television on the back porch. In the summer Daddy sat out there and watched television. There was a baseball game on all afternoon."

The man nodded and bit his lip thoughtfully. "But you testified that you had the television on all afternoon in the Sheas' apartment. How could you also have heard your father's television?"

"I watched television all afternoon with John Shea," said Katherine. "He fell asleep in my lap, and I used the remote control to turn it down very low so that he could sleep. I could hear the ball game from down below."

"And you were also able to hear when your mother came back into the house. You heard her open and close the front door and go up the stairs, and then into your apartment. Is that right?"

Katherine held her hands together in her lap and beneath her scapular. Her palms were sticky with perspiration, and she furtively clawed the material with her nails. Her temples throbbed beneath her wimple, and she fought the desire to thrust her fingers beneath it and massage them. The air in the courtroom was stale and heavy, and the large windows were closed against the frigid winter rain. The radiators rattled and hissed; occasionally they were filled with knocks so loud they covered her halting testimony so that she had to repeat it.

"Yes," she said slowly, "I heard Ma—" She stopped again. It embarrassed Katherine to speak of her parents in such familiar terms before so many strangers. Also, they were so distant from her now—her father dead and, now that the grave diggers' strike was over, at last decently buried; her mother, pale, thin, and subdued, on trial for murder in the first degree. She was a nun, and what were they? "I heard my mother come in," she said.

"How could you be certain that it was your mother?"

"I—I don't understand."

"Perhaps the only reason," said the district attorney, "that you thought it was your mother was that you saw later that she *had* come in. Couldn't it have been someone else—Mrs. Shea, for instance?"

"I lived in that house for eighteen years," said Katherine simply. "I got to know what it sounded like when it was my mother who was coming in the front door."

"Thank you," said the district attorney, "that's exactly what I meant."

"I could even tell if she was in a good mood or a bad—"

"Objection," cried Mr. Giovinco.

"Please, Sister Katherine," said the judge kindly, "just answer the questions that are put to you."

Katherine nodded. "I knew it was my mother by the sound," said Katherine.

"Well," said the district attorney, "was she in a good mood or a bad mood?"

"Objection!"

"Sustained."

Katherine glanced at the clock that was placed between the windows. She had been on the stand for ten minutes, and already felt herself exhausted. She looked down at her lap. Beneath her scapular she felt among the folds of her robe and closed her wet fist over the rosary in her pocket. She was frightened to look out at the spectators, frightened to look at her mother.

"If anyone had come into the house before your mother, you would have heard, is that correct?"

"Yes," said Katherine. "I had left the door into the hallway open for the breeze. I would have heard. Nobody came in."

"And if someone had come in, you would have known who it was, or you would have known it was a stranger, is *that* correct?"

"Yes," said Katherine, wondering how many questions the man would drag out of this single point.

"And if your father had raised his voice for help—"

"Objection!"

The judge was about to speak, but the district attorney rephrased his question: "If your father had called out to you, you would have heard, would you not?"

"Objection! Leading the witness!"

"Sustained."

"*Did* you hear your father call to you, Sister Katherine?"

"No," said Katherine. "The back door was open too, for the cross-ventilation. I think I would have heard him if he had called. I could hear him when he got up to go to the bathroom, or when he went to get something to drink—he always let the screen door slam—but I didn't hear him call out."

"So, Sister Katherine," said the district attorney, "although both front and back doors were opened of the apartment on the third floor, and although the television was set on low volume, you heard *no one* enter the house and move up either the front stairs or the back stairs *all afternoon long*, is that correct?"

"Yes."

"What about the persons who lived on the first floor?"

"There's a separate entrance to their apartment, at least in the front," said Katherine. "We can't hear them going in and out that way. I didn't hear anyone on the back stairs all afternoon," she sighed.

"Did you hear any shouts for help coming from the floor below, any sounds of a struggle?"

"Objection!"

"No," said Katherine, "I didn't."

"Objection overruled," said the judge. "Question and answer may stand."

"All right, then, Sister Katherine. Now would you please tell the court what happened after you heard your mother enter the apartment on the second floor of the house."

Katherine looked up at her mother. Anne Dolan sat back in her chair. Her shoulders were slack and her hands rested limply below the table, in her lap. Her black hair, heavily streaked with silver, was pulled back and fastened by two cheap barrettes at the nape of her neck. She wore a plain white blouse and a dark brown skirt; no makeup other than lipstick. She stared back at Katherine, her eyes sad and vacant, her mouth slightly open.

"I didn't hear anything for about five minutes after the door closed," she began, and described what she had done and seen on the afternoon of her father's murder. Her narrative was straightforward and had been made logical and chronological by repetition, but the images that worked upon her brain were anything but controlled, and did not follow the words she spoke. At the very beginning she remembered being embarrassed by the stain on her father's khaki pants; she thought of her automatic gesture of turning off the television on the back porch; she could recall hushing John Shea upstairs; and, above all, she saw Anne Dolan's face as she held the knife raised above her husband's corpse. Katherine's hand made a fist about the knot of her rosary, while she folded the nails of her other hand info her palm. She broke off speaking for a moment, closed her eyes, and whispered a fervent prayer that she might not break down in tears before so many strangers.

The defense attorney stood. "Your Honor," Mr. Giovinco said, "I think a recess—"

"No!" cried Katherine sharply. "I'll be all right." She breathed deeply; worse than the narration, worse than the visions that narration brought to her mind, was the thought that she would have to return to the stand; it would be better to suffer now than to have respite that would only be followed by another such humiliating public spectacle.

"My mother ran into the bedroom," she concluded. "She dropped the knife in the living room, the police found it there later. I didn't want to touch him, but I went over and closed his eyes—they were still open. I locked the doors and called the police. When the police came, my mother was still in her bedroom."

The district attorney went to the clerk's table and picked up a wooden-handled carving knife. He placed it on the rail of the witness stand. A small tag with the letter *A* scrawled on it had been tied about the wide base of the blade. Katherine drew back, brought her hands from beneath her robe, and grasped the arms of her chair.

"This is the knife that was found, covered with blood, on the floor of the living room of the Dolan apartment. The blood was of your father's type, and the blade would have inflicted just the type of wounds which killed him. Now, is this the knife you saw your mother holding?"

Katherine nodded dumbly.

"We need a verbal reply, Sister Katherine."

"Yes."

"Would you please take the knife, and show us exactly how your mother was holding the knife when you first looked through the screen door, from the back porch, into the kitchen."

Katherine blinked. "Why?" she whispered.

"Please pick up the knife, Sister Katherine."

Katherine reluctantly took the knife in her right hand. Slowly she raised it above the level of her shoulder so that the blade pointed downward at the breast of the district attorney. The sleeve of Katherine's habit slipped and exposed her arm.

A middle-aged woman on the jury gasped audibly at the sight of the nun holding a great carving knife aloft, and it was apparent that the rest of the jury was impressed as well.

Quickly Katherine lowered the knife, blushing with shame and modesty.

"That was how your mother was holding the knife, while she stood over your father's corpse."

"Yes," Katherine replied, her eyes downcast. The district attorney turned to the jury. "I contend," he said, "that this is hardly the position in which one would be holding a knife that had just been pulled from the chest of a man already dead. This position would be one for thrusting forward with the blade—not for withdrawing it."

"Objection!"

"Sustained."

Anne Dolan lifted her hands slowly from her lap, rested her bare elbows on the table, and lowered her forehead into her upturned palms. The jury—seven men and five women: eleven Catholics, Irish and Italian, and one black—turned from Katherine to look at her mother. Katherine dropped the knife onto the railing of the witness box, and it rattled there for a moment; she had to reach out quickly to keep it from falling to the floor. Suddenly she felt weak and faint. Sweat trickled down her cheeks beneath the wimple; the nape of her neck was damp, and the cloth of her habit clung uncomfortably there. She winced when the radiators began a loud knocking.

"Did you love your father, Sister Katherine?"

He wasn't my real father.

"Yes," she said, "I loved my father very much."

"Do you love your mother?"

"I was adopted, and she took care of me as though I were her real child," replied Katherine impassively. *My real mother was burned to death; she was a whore, and she burned to death on the day I was born.*

"And so you love your mother very much," persisted the district attorney.

"Yes," replied Katherine without hesitation.

Mr. Giovinco was whispering into Anne Dolan's ear. She stared at Katherine and nodded dumbly.

"Did your parents argue frequently, Sister Katherine?"

"Objection!" cried Mr. Giovinco, interrupting his whisper to Anne Dolan.

"Rephrase, please," said the judge.

"Did your parents ever argue, Sister Katherine?"

"Sometimes," she replied after a moment.

"How often is 'sometimes'? Once a month, once a week, more often than that?"

As with reluctance, she said: "More often than that."

"And you heard them argue?"

"Sometimes."

"Did they ever become physically violent during these fights?"

"Object to the word *fights*—leading the witness," said Mr. Giovinco, rising a little from his chair.

"These arguments, then? Were they ever violent?"

"I only heard them, I never saw them," replied Katherine.

"Mrs. Shea has said that between the time that you made your decision to join the convent and your father's death, your parents argued a great deal. She said that the quarrels disturbed her upstairs, that sometimes they woke her child. These were, then, I take it, noisy arguments."

"Yes," murmured Katherine.

"Please speak up, Sister," said the judge.

"Yes," replied Katherine, more loudly.

"What were the arguments about?"

"I tried not to listen," replied Katherine.

"But you couldn't help but hear, could you, Sister Katherine?"

"No. They fought about money, and Daddy's . . . his spending so much time at the Paradise Cafe. Other things . . ."

"What other things?"

"They didn't want me to join the convent," said Katherine quietly. "They were opposed to my becoming a nun."

"But if they both opposed it, why did they argue?"

Katherine took a great gulp of air: "Because," she said, "they both blamed each other for it."

"And one of the reasons you wanted to join the convent was to be away from a home in which there was continual bickering, constant friction between your father and mother, is that correct?"

"I joined the convent in order to serve God," said Katherine simply. "That's the only reason. God called me, and I had no choice but to obey Him. I was sorry that my parents were against my decision, I was sorry that they fought about it, but nothing that they could have said or done would have changed my mind. I am very sorry that my father was murdered, because I loved him very much. I was adopted, but he always loved me like I was his own child, and I'll always be grateful for that."

"Thank you, Sister Katherine, no more questions."

When Mr. Giovinco cross-examined Katherine, he went over the same ground as the district attorney. His questions elicited from her the same answers, and those answers produced evidently the same effect upon the jury: though Katherine never said a word against her mother, they all appeared to take the impression that Anne Dolan was a monstrously difficult woman to get along with and that Katherine was an angel of patience, forbearance, and forgiveness.

That day, Katherine had had to sit through the neighbors' testimony—the woman who lived in the apartment below the Dolans' providing the most comprehensive evidence that Anne Dolan was a shrewish, complaining wife who had never tried to hide the bitter discontent of her marriage, her resentment over her husband's chronic insolvency, his alcoholism, and even his impotence. Another neighbor had much to add about Anne Dolan's treatment of Katherine, which she contended was sharp and unjust. Jim Dolan was no prize, she said, but Anne Dolan's conduct toward her daughter—the perfect child—was inexcusable.

After Katherine's testimony, the prosecution rested its case.

Called in Anne Dolan's defense were fellow Daughters of the Sacred Heart, who could say little more than that Anne Dolan had always been civil, that she won fairly frequently at bingo, that she paid her dues on time, and had never said a word that was critical of the church.

The last testimony given was that of the parish priest, who told of Anne Dolan's faithful attendance at mass and, incidentally, Katherine's unselfish service within the Convent of St. Agnes. Anne Dolan did not take the stand. The lawyer and the district attorney harangued the jury, who appeared not to put much credence in either of them, and the judge made his address. At three o'clock on the second day of the trial, Anne Dolan's twelve peers retired to their airless room on the fourth floor of the courthouse to determine the woman's fate.

Sister Henrica, who had spent most of the day at the MIT Library, was surprised when she returned at four o'clock to find Sister Katherine waiting outside in the convent's Volkswagen van. "Oh, Sister Katherine," she exclaimed, "it's freezing out here! Why didn't you stay inside the courthouse where it's warm?" Sleet drove against the windshield.

"The jury came back in," said Katherine. "They were out for only forty-five minutes."

Sister Henrica was too astonished to speak.

Katherine looked at her and said softly, "They said she was guilty."

"Oh!" cried Sister Henrica, "I'm so sorry, I—"

Katherine turned away quickly. "Please don't say anything, Sister. Please, just take me back to Hingham. I—I'll talk to Reverend Mother Celestine later. Just now I—"

"I understand," whispered Sister Henrica, and bit her lip to hold back the expressions of sympathy she could hardly refrain from administering to the convicted woman's unfortunate daughter.

"Sister Katherine," said Sister Henrica after they had left the parking lot. "I'm sorry, but—didn't you want to stay for the sentencing?"

"That won't be until later—sometime next week, I think. Mr. Giovinco will call the convent."

They drove along the Charles River, and Katherine stared silently out at the choppy gray water. It was the beginning of the evening rush hour, when traffic was heavy, and some sort of accident up ahead had slowed things even more. At times they were stopped altogether.

"I should have taken the other bridge," sighed Sister Henrica.

"It doesn't matter," replied Katherine. Their progress toward the next intersection was blocked by a black Lincoln Continental that had broken down in the right-hand lane. A middle-aged man stood before the car, looking perplexed and embarrassed as he waited for assistance from the police or a tow truck. He was wiping the melting sleet from his brow with a white pocket handkerchief.

"Oh, poor man!" cried Sister Henrica. "I'm always so afraid that something just like that is going to happen to me."

Sister Katherine made no reply, but Sister Henrica was surprised when her companion quickly rolled down the window and stared out at the broken-down car.

"Sister Katherine! What is it? What's wrong?"

Katherine made no reply, but thrust her head out the window into the sleet and gazed behind them until the Continental could be seen no more.

"What was it?" demanded Sister Henrica, racing through a yellow light. "What was it you saw back there?"

Sister Katherine made no reply. Sister Henrica's voice was an unintelligible buzz. She placed both hands over the tightening in her breast and tried to still the roaring in her head.

Just as they had passed the black Continental, a young woman of Katherine's age had climbed out of the front seat and stood beside the embarrassed driver. She was precisely Katherine's height. The light blond hair that spilled down over her shoulders from underneath a close-fitting knit hat was exactly the color of Katherine's own. Blinking away the sleet, her eyes were as green and intense as Katherine's. The young woman had caught the nun's gaze, and she cocked her head as if in sudden wonder or puzzlement. In that moment, despite the turbulent wind and driving sleet, Katherine could see the girl full face. The set of her green eyes, the line of her nose, the shape of her mouth and jaw were a mirrored image of Katherine's own visage. The nun was horror-struck. Here was the girl of Katherine's dreams, the Katherine Dolan who might have been. She existed.

PART II

Andrea

13

Andrea Loponti blinked away the snow in her eyes. "Daddy," she said, "did you see the nun in that van? She nearly fell out of the window looking at us!"

Cosmo LoPonti had been watching out for the tow truck and hadn't noticed.

"It was as if she had never seen a car broken down before," said Andrea.

Cosmo sighed and wondered how long it would be before they got home.

It was another two hours. The automobile had to be towed to the garage through rush hour traffic. A car had to be rented, and the drive back to Weston through the early evening darkness and the snow was slow and tedious. Vittoria LoPonti held open the door for her husband and daughter, and exclaimed her worry.

Andrea smiled. "We telephoned, but the line was busy."

"Come on in, come on in, I know you're both cold and wet and hungry. I've laid fires in the living room and the dining room, and the veal is on its second reheating!"

By the time they had finished dinner, Andrea LoPonti had entirely forgotten about the nun who had stared so at her as she stood at the side of the road in the snow.

Weston, Massachusetts, is situated ten miles directly west of Boston, south of the Charles River, and its thirty thousand inhabitants enjoy the highest median income of any municipality in all of New England. Weston's town center is quaintly Victorian, peaceful and well kept, its exclusive shops alternating with the commoner variety of businesses. There are two natural-food stores, a ski shop, two firms that make stained glass, a fruit-juice-and-yogurt bar, a gymnasium and weight-loss clinic, four antique stores, two realtors, three banks, a drugstore, and half a dozen dress shops that wouldn't sell you a blouse for under fifty dollars. Outside this town center, with its broad, clean common and gleaming Civil War monument, the town is New England forest, with fine eighteenth century mansions hidden away at the end of winding drives, massive Victorian houses commanding the best views, and mid-twentieth century homes of redwood and glass set behind tall fences. Much of the land in Weston is given over to parks and recreational areas: several thousand acres of forest, meadows, and ponds are owned by the city, or by Harvard —places that are delightful four seasons out of the year. From merely driving through Weston, one senses its civilized affluence, grace, privacy, quiet, and spaciousness.

Cosmo and Vittoria LoPonti were married in 1957, in St. Anthony's Church in the North End of Boston, on St. Anthony's feast day. When they returned from their honeymoon trip to Marblehead, Cosmo was given a loan of fifteen thousand dollars by his father-in-law. With this capital he started an independent contracting company for electrical work. He and Vittoria lived in a large, cheap, dark apartment above a noisy restaurant on Salem Street, not because they couldn't already afford better, but because Vittoria's father had stipulated, as part of the loan agreement, that Cosmo allow Vittoria to be near her chronically ill mother.

Over the next two years Cosmo's business prospered, and he and Vittoria were a happy couple; their only regret was that she had not yet been able to conceive. Early in 1959 Vittoria's father died, and her mother's health deteriorated seriously. In an effort to prolong the woman's life, she was moved to her sister's house in San Antonio, where the climate was amenable. On the first day of the New Year, 1960, Vittoria LoPonti—carrying the newborn child whom she had surreptitiously rescued from the burning building on Salem and Parmenter streets the night before—flew to Texas and remained there seven months. Her family in San

Antonio much berated her for not having told them that she was pregnant, but for the precious infant she had brought with her, they forgave everything.

During the time that she was absent, Cosmo LoPonti busied himself with his largest job yet: the entire electrical contracting for an exclusive housing project then being built in Weston, the first of its kind—and, because of an amendment to the town charter the next year, also the last. Lonely without Vittoria, Cosmo worked double-time, late into the evenings, on weekends and holidays. The work was completed three weeks ahead of schedule, and the builder was so grateful to Cosmo that he privately offered him one of the smaller houses for a mere $32,000, one third below the asking price. Cosmo obtained the mortgage, purchased the house, and had moved in by the time Vittoria returned to Boston in the same plane that was carrying her mother's corpse.

None of Vittoria's North End friends saw her after the funeral in St. Anthony's Church, and none of them ever learned that when she got off the plane at Logan Airport, Vittoria LoPonti, in a black dress, a black pillbox hat, and a black veil, was carrying a seven-month-old baby in her arms, a child whom she had christened Andrea.

Cosmo and Vittoria LoPonti began a new life for themselves in Weston. Newcomers were not accepted easily by the community, but the couple were quiet and unostentatious and did nothing to offend their neighbors. No one had anything against them, and gradually, by the time Andrea was in grammar school, there were so many more persons in the town of more recent vintage than the LoPontis that people had come to look on Cosmo and Vittoria as established town citizens.

Vittoria was faithful in her attendance at the PTA and eventually came to hold office there; Cosmo granted the city a five percent discount on contracted work. They both attended town meetings, and sometimes Vittoria actually stood up and spoke on such issues as playground safety and public swimming pools. By the time Andrea was enrolled in Miss Britten's Academy, Cosmo was a town alderman, and Vittoria the vice-president of the Society for the Preservation of Weston Antiquities.

Cosmo had prospered. The family had moved to a larger house—not part of the tract—and purchased a summer cottage right on the ocean, at Yarmouthport, on Cape Cod. Here Vittoria and Andrea spent their summers, with Cosmo coming down on the weekends. Andrea's sterling achievements at Miss Britten's had been the crowning of the couple's success in the town. Vittoria thought she had never been so happy in her life as the day on which she announced to the general membership of the Society for the Preservation of Weston Antiquities that Andrea had been accepted at Radcliffe, Vassar, and Wenham, but had decided to go to the last "because it was nearest Cosmo and me."

Cosmo and Vittoria LoPonti had been born and raised in Boston's North End and still bore many traces of that upbringing. Foremost among these was their strict loyalty to the Catholic Church; they believed fervently in the infallibility of the parish priest. They would never be entirely at home in Weston, because of its overwhelmingly Yankee and Protestant flavor, but Andrea was different: she had never known that insular, prying, noisy Italian community, had never been blessed with its raucous happinesses or touched by its pathetic sorrows. She attended church regularly, even went to confession—and confessed truthfully; but religion had never really entered her heart.

Andrea did not look like her parents, both of whom were of obvious Italian extraction. She had green eyes, a fair complexion, and long, thick, blond hair that fell in soft waves over her shoulders. She had occasionally entertained the notion that she was adopted, but had never questioned Cosmo and Vittoria about it. All children have such fantasies, she told her sophisticated self, and she would have died rather than admit to such a puerile insecurity.

She had sometimes wondered about the single earring that pierced the lobe of her right ear. She could not remember a time when she had been without it, and any new acquaintance invariably questioned her, "What happened to the other one?" When Andrea put to her mother the same question, Vittoria had replied, "Oh that—it was the fashion when you were little."

Miss Britten's Academy was housed in a large, Tudor-syle mansion near the town common, across a wide, manicured lawn that had groupings of the tallest and most beautiful blue spruces in the township. The young women who were admitted to this establishment in such small numbers were select, highly motivated, rich, and parent-pressured. High achievements there had been no struggle for Andrea who had excelled from the start. She studied no more and worked no harder than the three forlorn girls who came in at the tag end of the class—girls whose intelligence had been overlooked in the interests of their parents' vast wealth or impeccable social standing. Andrea LoPonti was quick—no fellow student had been quicker. She seemed to retain effortlessly all that she read; she possessed an easy fluency when a pen was thrust into her hands; she had an unfailing instinct for what her instructors wanted of her.

In each of the six reporting periods of each of her six years at Miss Britten's, Andrea LoPonti had maintained a straight-A average. She liked literature and history and could bear up under social studies, so doing well in those courses was no difficulty. She disliked the sciences and mathematics, but had an innate understanding of them and came out better than many of her friends who struggled long and hard with concepts that never really became comprehensible to them. Art appreciation, needlework, "domestic economics," consumer advocacy, astronomy, Italian, French, and Latin posed no difficulties either.

To Vittoria and Cosmo, Andrea was the perfect, dutiful daughter. Any faults she possessed they made themselves blind to; and they had long ago determined that she should never have to struggle, as they and their parents had struggled, in the material world. Her natural intelligence and intellectual attainments, her easy popularity with the other girls at the school they saw as a reward for their years of carefully and lovingly applied discipline; for their years of daily prayers. They had encouraged her in her friendships and, when she was fifteen, allowed her to double-date with one of her best girl friends. Andrea always came home at an early hour appointed by herself, and never with liquor on her breath or cigarette smoke in her clothing.

So far as popularity and ease with studies went, Andrea's freshman year at Wenham was only an extension of Miss Britten's Academy. Although the town of Newton bordered Weston and the college was only twenty minutes from Andrea's home, she had persuaded her parents to allow her to live on campus. Despite the four-thousand-dollars-a-year cost for room and board, Vittoria and Cosmo had acquiesced, and Andrea resided in Wordsworth Hall from September through May.

By the end of October of her freshman year, Andrea was well settled into the rhythm of college life. Many other women of the freshman class were nervous about living up to the standards of the college, hoped desperately they would fulfill their parents' expectations, suffered agonies over which courses to take, and imagined that every move they made would have a direct bearing on their future happiness. It was not so for Andrea. She had tentatively determined to major in history, because history was the sort of thing that would not get in the way of her adult life. Andrea could not imagine that the announcement in the Sunday *Globe* of her engagement to some North Shore scion would read, "Miss LoPonti has a degree in biological chemistry from Wenham." People would expect her to do something with a degree as technical as that—but nobody expected you to do anything with a degree in history.

She took courses that pleased and interested her: Advanced French Literature (concentrating on the late eighteenth century), Regency England (the most romantic era in history, she considered), Mathematics for NonConcentrators (to fulfill distribution requirements), Introduction to Modern Dance (a physical, not an academic course), and Elementary Russian. It was not as heavy a burden of instruction as she might have assumed, but Andrea had the idea that she ought to take things easy for the first few months and grow accustomed to Wenham—it was possible she would be distracted by the novelty of life on campus and away from home, and she wanted a little room to accommodate that distraction.

No accommodation proved necessary, however; Andrea LoPonti adapted readily to the exigencies of college life. She had no fear of her courses, and if she was a little in awe of her professors and instructors, who were ever so much more distant and strange than the young PhDs who had taught at Miss Britten's, Andrea at least did not allow herself to be shy in class. She participated fearlessly in discussion and was not ashamed to ask ques-

tions when she did not understand. Andrea was a quick reader,
even in French, and she was so used to the mechanics of learning
a new language that not even Russian declensions could daunt
her. Andrea had no thought of a career—she saw her mother's life
as the ideal: unburdened and moneyed and free, and she intended
to emulate Vittoria LoPonti in marrying a man who could provide copiously for her comfort. Andrea, however, intended to
differ from her mother in this: Andrea would not marry a man
who was on his way up, she would marry a man who was already
there. Thus, imagining that she would never need to bother with
job applications and resumes and admission forms to graduate
schools, Andrea was not worried about grades—and did all the
better for that insouciance.

Andrea lived on the fourth floor of Wordsworth Hall, a
colonial-style dormitory with ivy-covered walls, close-clipped
yew hedges, and flagstone walkways. For the first few weeks of
the term, she had shared her large corner room with a young
woman from Parkersburg, West Virginia. Andrea had hardly sup-
pressed her unbridled contempt for her roommate—contempt
for her weepy homesickness, her terror of the college, her hour-
long whispered telephone calls to her boyfriend every night. The
third week in October the girl had transferred back to a community college in West Virginia, and Andrea was left the room
to herself. She made the acquaintance of most of the women in
the dorm, a little more than half of whom were freshmen, but
formed no attachment to any but the girl who lived in the corner
room next to Andrea's.

Marsha Liberman—Andrea was sure that she had been called
Marcie in high school—was slender and dark, with thick black
hair that fell in short, permed ringlets about her oval face.

Marsha had a roommate, whom she described as a narcolept
because the girl slept as many as fourteen hours a day, she was
so unhappy at Wenham. In consequence, Marsha spent much
time in the library or in Andrea's room, where the two girls read
their assignments, gossiped and told one another their pasts.
They double-dated, and Marsha spent occasional weekends in
Weston, glad for the chance to be away from the school for a few
days, although her home was only in Waltham, the town neigh-

boring Weston to the north. On campus Andrea and Marsha became a team, and by the end of that first year their friends found themselves unable to refer to one without also mentioning the other.

Occasionally, on weekends that Vittoria and Cosmo spent on Cape Cod, Andrea was allowed to remain alone in Weston, so long as Marsha could stay over. These times, the two girls would invite over their most intimate half-dozen friends, make complicated mixed drinks with exotic names that they found in a bartender's guide, talk about sex, and smoke the marijuana that Marsha had got from her older sister, Joanna. On Sunday morning Andrea and Marsha would run the vacuum cleaner over the shag rugs, open the windows, hide the empty pint bottles in neighbors' garbage cans, and run the waste disposal and trash compactor almost constantly; often the house looked better upon the LoPontis' return than when they had left.

14

On a hot, lazy Saturday morning at the beginning of June, Andrea LoPonti took a sip of coffee and stared listlessly out the bowed window of the breakfast nook. This small alcove, with a dizzyingly busy red-and-white Americana wallpaper, looked out over the side lawn of the split-level house in Weston. Andrea brushed her hair back over her shoulders, leaned her elbows on the table, and watched her father as he stood in the middle of the yard, slowly turning the fine spray of water from the hose in arcs from left to right. Her first year of college was behind her, and Andrea had moved back into the Weston house only one week earlier. She looked forward to a long summer of self-imposed lassitude.

Cosmo LoPonti was a tall, stoutly built man with short, thick, black hair that was combed straight back from his wide, dark face. He was happy during the brief Massachusetts growing season, and he was miserable in the winter. Then, when there was no gardening work to be done, he pored over seed catalogues, visited hardware stores and looked longingly at tools he didn't need, made plans for enlarging flower beds, and nearly killed his indoor plants with excessive care.

Andrea swallowed the last quarter cup of her lukewarm coffee in a single gulp, and turned on her chair. Crossing her legs at the ankles, she rearranged the folds of her new cornflower blue bathrobe and poured another cupful from the electric percolator on the table. A dozen feet away, at the kitchen counter, Vittoria LoPonti prepared dainty egg- and chicken-salad sandwiches for the biweekly meeting of the Society for the Preservation of Weston Antiquities. Vittoria knew much more interesting Italian hors d'oeuvres, but she did not like to emphasize her ethnicity in the club.

"You ought to have something besides coffee," said Vittoria without turning. She wiped her hands on her small tea apron and crossed to the refrigerator. Her hair, clasped at the nape of her neck, fell in a thick ponytail down her back. Andrea was thankful that her mother had resisted the weight that came to so many Italian women in early middle age; Vittoria LoPonti, though not thin, retained a shapely figure.

"What are you going to do today, Andrea?"

"I'm not sure," said Andrea hesitantly.

Vittoria said nothing for a moment. "That means you're not going to do anything, doesn't it?"

Andrea made no reply.

"You know, your father and I have been thinking about you, and what you're going to do this summer."

"You're *not* going to ask me to go to the Cape again, are you? I'll die if I have to spend another summer in Yarmouthport. There's nothing to do there, and there's nowhere to go, and—"

"And no young men," said Vittoria, completing her daughter's thought.

"Well, of course there're boys around there," said Andrea, "but they're always these macho beach bum types, or trying to be, and *all* the really good looking boys turn out to be gay, and where does that leave me?"

"Andrea!"

"Well it's true, and then the ones who are in college always try to maul you to death when they get drunk, and when they're not drunk, they're too shy to speak two words in the same half hour, and you promised me you wouldn't make me go back there, even on the weekends!"

"All right, Andrea, all right. You don't have to get hysterical, but it seems to me that some girls would *relish* the opportunity to go to the shore in the summer. But that wasn't what your father and I were talking about."

"What were you talking about, then?" asked Andrea sullenly.

"Your father and I agreed that you were mature enough to stay here by yourself during the summer, as long as he's going to be here during the week, and as long as Marsha's parents have agreed to let her stay here with you over the weekends. And your father and I were thinking that maybe it would be a good idea if you got a job."

Andrea put her cup down with such a clunk, that the hot coffee spilled out onto the surface of the table. She dropped her forehead into the upturned palms of her hands and shook her head slowly. But Vittoria had not turned round, and the dramatics were lost on her.

"Mother," Andrea moaned, "this is the summer. I need to recuperate—I worked myself to death at Wenham this last year. I wanted to get a tan, I wanted—"

"If you wanted a tan, then you'd go to Yarmouthport. And, Andrea, you have *never* had to work for a grade in your life, and you know it!"

"Mother—"

"It's not that we need the extra money—you know we don't, and we wouldn't try to fool you by telling you we did. But you also know that Cosmo and I weren't always so well off as we are now. There was a time when we had to scrape by, there was a time when Papa had to help us. There was a time when the only heat in the house came out of the oven. Anyway, we think it's important that you get a job, just so that you'll learn what it's like to get a paycheck, and learn about taxes, and making a budget, and sticking to it, and all the things that come together to help make you a better adult. You're nearly nineteen now, and in girls these days, that's certainly adulthood. You had last summer all to yourself, and I just think it's time, sweetheart. I started working when I was twelve. That was the year I got my Social Security card. Andrea, you don't even have a Social Security card."

During her mother's speech, Andrea leaned back in her chair, recrossed her legs, and examined her nails. A noise in the driveway drew her attention, and she was pleased to see Marsha Liberman's apple-green Volkswagen pull up behind her father's black Continental in the garage. A moment later Marsha, wearing a pair of cuffed denim shorts with matching suspenders and a brown gingham blouse, stepped out of the car and went over to speak to Cosmo. As she greeted him, she carefully adjusted the brown gingham bandana that was tied gypsy-style round her head.

Vittoria began to spread egg salad on heart-shaped morsels of Pepperidge Farm white bread. "A job would be good experience at working with people. I love you, Andrea, but I have to say that sometimes you think that the whole world was created just for your own benefit and comfort. Mrs. Marks, you know who I mean, at the Svelte Lady Shoppe, told me just yesterday—"

Marsha knocked briefly at the kitchen door and, without waiting to be called inside, opened the screen door and stepped through.

"Marsha!" cried Andrea enthusiastically.

"Hello, Marsha," said Vittoria, "you just saved Andrea from the end of my lecture. Sit down and have something to eat—do you want to try some egg salad?"

"Sure," said Marsha, eyeing the sandwiches. "Do you have any Diet Cola?"

While Vittoria was at the refrigerator, Marsha looked at her friend. "Aren't you dressed?" she asked.

"No," said Andrea, "as you can see. Why?"

"I thought we were going shopping! If we don't leave soon, we won't get downtown until it's too late to have lunch." She nodded thanks for the drink and three sandwiches that Vittoria set before her.

"So that's what you were going to do today," said Vittoria to her daughter.

"I forgot," said Andrea. "Mother—"

"Yes?" said Vittoria, turning with a knowing smile.

"We're going into Boston, that is, we thought we would go into Boston, and we'll probably go to Filene's—"

"I don't need a song and dance, Andrea. You know where the charge card is."

Andrea rose and hugged her mother, then motioned for Marsha to follow her through the house.

"Take the one for Jordan's too," Vittoria called after them.

While Andrea took a quick shower, Marsha settled herself on the edge of the toilet, smoked a cigarette, and leafed through an old issue of *Vogue*. Andrea quickly dressed in jeans, a blue work shirt the tail of which she tied into a large knot just below her breasts, sandals, and a quantity of gold bangle bracelets. She stood before the mirror, examined herself critically, applied a light coat of pale pink lipstick, and then gave her hair a final quick brushing.

"Jesus Christ!" cried Marsha. "Let's go! You look like you're preparing to elope with the Crown Prince of Denmark!"

"I know, but I feel funny if I'm not dressed right when I leave the house."

"Listen, what are you doing tonight?"

"Nothing special. You want to go to a movie?"

"I've got something better. You want to go to a party?"

There was a suspicious brightness in Marsha's eyes that didn't escape Andrea. "What kind of party?" Andrea asked. "Where is it?"

"It's a party in Boston."

"Oh?"

"Joanna's giving it. Come on, it's a party on Beacon Hill!"

"My parents won't like it."

"They won't be there," shrugged Marsha. "And besides, we'll just tell them that we're just going over there to help Joanna set everything up, and then we're going out to a double feature somewhere, and then afterwards we'll come back to help Joanna clean up, and by then the subways will have stopped running, and we'll just stay over. I mean, my God, you're going to be a sophomore at Wenham next year, they ought to give you a little freedom."

Andrea thought for a few moments and then nodded. "You think I ought to pack an overnight bag?" she asked.

15

"Where did you say you went to school?" he asked. Before she could reply, Andrea was jostled from behind by someone trying to get to the plates of potato chips and pretzels that were set out on Joanna's kitchen counter.

"Wenham," said Andrea hesitantly.

"What year?"

"I'll be a sophomore in the autumn," she answered, with a haughtiness she had not intended.

The young man's thick black eyebrows raised above his beautiful black eyes by degrees. "Ummmm . . ." he mused, unimpressed.

Andrea flushed with embarrassment and took a quick sip from the large tumbler of wine she held tightly in both hands. It was her second glass, and she was already woozy. She felt the carefully practiced facade of sophisticated coed slip away entirely.

The young man was handsome, tall and well built, with the body of a dancer, or perhaps a swimmer. When he'd first come in the door—alone, she had been pleased to note—Andrea was taken by his thickly lashed black eyes. From a distance they appeared deep charcoal smudges on his face.

"I'll be back," he announced suddenly, turned on his heel, and headed for the far side of the room. Joanna's flat wasn't large, but with so many people crowded into it—nearly fifty—he was as effectively separating himself from Andrea as if he had flung himself out the window and bolted away down Mount Vernon Street to the other side of Beacon Hill.

Taking another swallow of wine, Andrea looked about the room for her friend. Marsha wasn't near the stereo in the corner, which was playing a disco album far too loudly, she wasn't by the makeshift bar set up in the kitchenette, and she wasn't waiting in line for the bathroom. And Andrea could not make her out in any of the small groups of loudly talking, loudly laughing guests. Andrea had been disappointed by Joanna's friends—they were neither outrageous, nor sparkling, nor uniformly gorgeous, nor obviously moneyed, nor doing wonderfully crazy things, nor showing their Beacon Hill sophistication in every gesture they made and every word they spoke. Instead they seemed very much like people in Weston or Yarmouthport, only more grubbily dressed. Andrea had very much looked forward to this party, and for a particular reason. She had hoped to extend the range of her social maneuverability to that stratum of persons 25 to 35. It was all very well—and all very easy—to be popular among young women who were one's own age, but Andrea had had no experience whatever dealing with persons who were five to ten years older. She had come to Mount Vernon Street with more than half a suspicion that she would carry the party by storm and that all Joanna's friends would turn to one another and say, "Oh my God! Who is she? And you say she's only *nineteen?* Why, she's like one of us!" It hadn't happened that way: for some reason the guests had been blind to Andrea's true worth, and she had suffered along in anonymity until Derek had turned and offered to refill her glass. And she had succeeded only in putting him off.

Andrea wore one of the outfits she had purchased that afternoon shopping with Marsha at Filene's: three-inch cork wedge sandals, black wide-cuffed cords cinched by a clear plastic belt wrapped twice around her waist, and a plaid, pearl-buttoned western shirt with a solid yoke. None of the other women at the party had dressed with half as much care, and certainly none of them, told herself, could match her for poise and carriage. Yet, as she looked around, she saw another difference between her and the other women at the party—and it was a difference that put *her* deep into the shade. Andrea was certain that if a poll were taken, she would turn out to be the only bona fide virgin present. The other women might not be long on looks or taste or intellectual attainments, but each had had the sense and the energy to get someone into bed—and that, with all her advantages and all her accomplishments, Andrea had not yet achieved. The women all seemed to belong to a sorority from which she had been blackballed.

Joanna Liberman stood near the large plate glass window that looked out over Mount Vernon Street, in serious conversation with the man whom Marsha described as her sister's on-again-off-again-great-love-of-her-life. Joanna was in her mid-twenties, slender, but with none of Marsha's prettiness. Her hair was cut short in an unflattering semipixie that only accentuated the sharpness of her features. Joanna's makeup was always badly done, too heavy and in shades altogether too bright, or too dark, or too colorful.

Andrea made motions to Joanna: *Where's Marsha?* Joanna, not pausing in her conversation, pointed to the open hallway door.

Andrea struggled across the crowded room and squeezed through the doorway into the hall. She found Marsha sitting on the steps that led up to the roof. She was contentedly smoking a Camel and sipping from a can of light beer.

"What's up?" said Marsha.

"Just wanted to get away."

"What happened to your friend—what a gorgeous number!" It was an expression that Marsha had never used before, and Andrea suspected that her friend had just overheard it at the party and was trying it out on her now.

"His name's Derek Something," sighed Andrea desolately. "He's really nice, and—"

"Yes?"

"And he asked me if I wanted to go back to his place."

"Tonight?" Marsha's eyes went wide, and she put her beer can down on the step beside her.

Andrea nodded. "But then I went and fouled everything up."

"How?" demanded Marsha.

Andrea thought to say something to place her actions in an irreproachable light, but instead told the truth: "Oh I was just a little bitchy, being stupid."

"What'd you say?"

Andrea bit her lip. "I got flustered. When he asked me to go home with him, I said: 'Oh, I bet you say that to all the girls.'"

Marsha grimaced. "I would have walked away too."

"Well that's just what he did."

Sadly and thoughtfully, Marsha crushed out the cigarette beneath her sandal. "Did he say he was coming back?"

"Yes, but he was probably just being polite."

"Go find him," said Marsha firmly. "Drop to your knees in front of everybody and beg his forgiveness. Do it loudly. Then maybe he'll be so embarrassed that he'll drag you out of here."

"It might work," said Andrea sarcastically, ". . . but I'm not sure I really want him to. I mean . . . I never went home with a man before."

"Well," said Marsha, "it's just like playing around in a car, except that you're on a bed, and the windows don't roll up and down."

Marsha Liberman was not a virgin, having performed the sex act eleven times. This was a strict accounting, she said, but did by no means include fumblings in her parents' Winnebago with high-school boys. But all her "down-deep" experience had been with her boyfriend, Joshua, a student at Northeastern. In Andrea's eyes Marsha was an experienced woman and the only person at Wenham to whom she had confided the secret of her virginity. Most of the young men Andrea had dated in her freshman year at Wenham were upperclassmen from Harvard and MIT. Although certainly good-looking and pleasant enough, these men had not elicited in her the least desire to establish a sexual liaison. It was their very pleasantness, their willingness to bend to her whims, their fear of irritating her sensibilities as a young independent female that made her discourage their tentative advances.

"The question is," Marsha went on, "do *you* want to? This is your big chance to lose your virginity. It was probably going to happen this summer anyway—it would've happened five years ago if you hadn't been stuck in a goddamn girls' school—and if you do it tonight, you won't have it hanging over you through June, July, and August. And he's so good-looking, Andrea! He's probably unhooked a bra or two before in his life. How old is he, anyway?"

"Twenty-five."

"Probably been out of college for three years," Marsha shrugged. "I'd do it if I were you."

"How can you be so casual?"

"Remember your first cigarette? Your first glass of wine? Your first *period?* My God, Andrea, we've all got to do these things, and it's better to get them over with as soon as possible. Remember: it's your *twentieth* birthday that's coming up. And it's no big deal. It just happens," Marsha concluded with authority.

Andrea leaned heavily against the banister and thought for a long moment. She finished the wine that was left in her tumbler. "All right," she said faintly.

"It's not like you were going home with the Boston College football team, you know. And be sure and do it with the lights on so you can see what everything looks like."

"Marsha!" Andrea pushed herself away from the banister. "Wait, though: I'm not on the pill or anything. I'm not protected at all. What do I do about that?" Andrea did not confess to her friend that this was her principal hesitation in the entire matter. Pregnancy was a chance that she really didn't want to take, as attractive as the prospect was of losing her virginity to so handsome and so much older a man as Derek Whatever-his-name-was.

"Just tell him before you do it," said Marsha. "Men know how to take care of those things, if they've got any sense at all." She took a sip of her beer, wincing as she swallowed the now warm liquid. "You're building this all out of proportion, Andrea. Derek's a man—a *real* man. Not like most of those anemic Harvard types you usually go out with."

"What do you mean?" Andrea asked uneasily.

Marsha hiccuped. "I'm sorry, I probably shouldn't have said that. But I'm glad I did. Listen, Andrea, I don't know why, but you always manage to pick men you can dominate, but then you don't really like it. At first I thought you were going out with those wimps because you were afraid of sex and they didn't pose any threat."

Andrea stared at Marsha. "I am *not* afraid of sex," she said finally.

"So tonight you have the chance to prove it. You've just hooked the most gorgeous guy at this whole party."

"If he ever comes back," sighed Andrea.

16

Derek lived on St. Botolph Street in Back Bay. As they stood in the recessed and unlighted entrance of his building and Derek was searching through his keys for the one that would open the front door, Andrea was sorry that she had come across town with this man. She thought she would have been much happier remaining the night at Joanna's flat. She wished that she had simply declined Marsha's invitation to the party. She decided that she did not really like Derek after all, and that his eyes were probably the only really wonderful thing about him—and those she couldn't even see now, in the darkness and with his back to her. What if her mother telephoned at Joanna's place?

Yet to turn away now would be embarrassing and inconvenient, if not impossible. Once their taxi had sped off, there was none other about. It was past one o'clock, and the subway had stopped running.

Derek's apartment occupied the fourth floor of a very small Victorian townhouse. When they entered, he didn't bother turning on the lights. After latching the door, he took Andrea's hand and led her carefully through a maze of sharp-edged furniture and unrecognizable objects on the floor, down a narrow hallway, and finally into a bedroom at the back. An alley lamp filled the room with harsh sodium light. Derek dropped the bamboo shade, but this only fragmented the light into garish stripes across the unmade bed—and the bed itself was no more than a double mattress, not even neatly stacked, laid flat on the floor.

Soft music and candlelight might have dispelled the uninviting starkness of the room. Andrea waited for Derek to light the fat red candle that stood atop the clock-radio on the floor, but he did not even glance in that direction as he began to remove his clothing.

Andrea looked about her. On the wall opposite the bed was a large unframed poster of Tutankhamen's sarcophagus, the gold coloring shining eerily. There was a painted chest of drawers such as might be found in the room of a very small child, with the bottom drawer missing. In the corner was a five-foot stack of newspapers and, betide it, a scarcely smaller stack of magazines. Andrea realized that she had never before been invited into a room that lacked curtains on the windows or a spread over the bed. Her impulse to flee was stronger than ever, but she said nothing.

How far away I am, she thought. *Far away from everything I've ever known before.*

Andrea wondered if this were the right moment to tell Derek that she "wasn't prepared." But how could she bring herself to admit something so coarse to a man she had only just met? That would spoil what little romance there was between them.

Derek stood before her, his shirt open to the navel, exposing in the pale, striated light a muscular chest covered with downy black hair. He lifted her chin with one hand, leaned slightly forward, and kissed her hard, his tongue rubbing over her teeth, and then drawing her own tongue within his mouth. His other hand rested heavily upon her shoulder, and then slid in one determined motion down to her breast. He caressed it in a manner that Andrea thought rough, but she was startled when her nipples suddenly grew rigid beneath his touch. Strangest of all, she thought, was that he obviously assumed that she wanted him as much as he wanted her. In the way that he held himself against her, he obviously entertained no notion at all that she might be reluctant, or hesitant, or frightened. Simply in fear that he would think her inexperienced, and with the reflection that the sooner she responded the sooner it would all be done with, Andrea mirrored to Derek all the sexual ardor she felt herself confronted with.

I don't even know if I like this, she said to herself. *I don't even . . .*

But that thought was never completed. The sexual passion that she thought only a moment before she would have to feign, suddenly overwhelmed her, and all her thoughts were buried beneath it. She gave herself all the more ardently to this man because she knew she cared nothing at all about him, gave herself up not to Derek, not to this attractive, older, virile man with the beautiful black eyes, but to the passion that lay within her.

*

"I wish you had told me you were untried territory," said Derek sullenly over the edge of the sports section of the Sunday *Globe*.

The rest of the apartment was no better than the bedroom, Andrea discovered the next morning. More outdated newspapers were in dishevelled piles in corners; pamphlets and magazines had been simply tossed against the baseboards. Andrea sat staring out the window; her view consisted entirely of the foliage of a great linden on St. Botolph Street. She lifted the chipped brown mug of instant coffee to her lips. "What?" she said.

"I said I wish I'd known you were a virgin. Those were the only designer sheets I have." He raised the paper again.

Andrea flushed with embarrassment and said falteringly, "I'm sorry, I didn't . . ."

Derek folded the paper and smiled. "Sorry, I didn't mean to sound like such a bastard. It's just that I don't like the sense of responsibility."

Andrea merely stared at him, unable to think how she should react. This business of having her morning coffee with a man whose last name she didn't even know, but who possessed intimate knowledge of her body and had witnessed her in the throes of passion, and was now talking about this and that as if nothing extraordinary had happened between them was an unpleasant mystery to her. It didn't seem right. How could he have been so outrageously carnal just a few hours ago, and so mundane this morning? He had totally occupied himself with her body, until she was certain that nothing on earth mattered to him but the curve of her breasts and the line of her thighs, and now he sat across from her reading tennis scores.

"Come on," Derek laughed, "I was kidding. The blood'll wash out. I was only kidding, Arlene."

"Andrea," she said shortly.

"I'm so bad with names," he replied unapologetically, as if there had been no insult. He shrugged and smiled, but then the smile faded. He slapped the folded paper hard against the edge of the table: "Hey listen, you were on the pill or something, weren't you? I forgot to ask, goddamn . . ." He waited for her answer with widened, fearful eyes.

Andrea tilted her head and fingered the sliver of ruby in her right ear. "Yes, of course I was," she said at last. "I may have been a virgin, but I wasn't stupid. Listen," she said in a hard voice, "I have to get back to the Hill. My friend's waiting for me there."

"All right," he said, and the fact that he did not attempt to persuade her to remain made Andrea feel all the worse. His relief at discovering that she had been on the pill—or something—was evident. *Well, it's done,* she thought, *and it was exciting while it happened, and I don't feel guilty or anything, so I suppose that's something to be thankful for . . .*

Derek leaned and stretched in his chair, and smiled—the host's smile to a departing guest. Andrea was surprised by her own thought then: that she wanted to see this man again, that she wanted to have sex with him again, that she wanted him to ask for her telephone number or a tentative date.

"I think I might have more of that coffee," said Andrea. "I'm still a little groggy this morning."

Derek shrugged. He rose and went into the kitchen, kicking aside the scattered sections of the Sunday paper. Andrea grimaced, and while he was knocking about with the kettle and mugs, she set the paper in order again on the edge of the glass coffee table. She reached over the arm of the couch to pick up the *Times* and *Newsweeks* she found there, and, one by one, stacked them neatly. Under these were newspapers, yellowed at the edges, but still white where the magazines had lain atop them. She draped these over the tattered arm of the sofa.

Derek returned with coffee and set the mugs on the table. "I guess the place is a little messy." He lifted the stack of newspapers from the arm of the sofa. "Where would you like these?" he asked, with a smile of amusement.

Without thinking, Andrea brushed a wave of blond hair back from her forehead and pointed across the room. "On top of that pile in the corner." She caught herself and looked up embarrassed. "I'm sorry, I just . . ."

Derek laughed and did as she had instructed. He idly leafed through the top few papers after dropping them. "I'm a miserable housekeeper," he admitted. Suddenly he yanked a paper out and examined the front page. He glanced back at Andrea, and a smile of wonder crossed his features. "Hey!" he said softly.

"What's wrong?" she asked.

He stepped over, handing her the yellowed paper. Andrea laughed too: "A year ago today—you're *not* a very good housekeeper."

"That's not what I mean," said Derek, and flipped the paper over in her hands. He pointed to a photograph on the lower half of the front page.

"What?" said Andrea. "This article?" She read aloud: "'Somerville Man Knifed to Death in Home.'" She shrugged her shoulders and looked up at Derek quizzically. "So?"

"Look at the picture," said Derek.

Andrea studied the accompanying photograph. In it, two women sat on the edge of a four-poster bed. The woman on the left had dark hair cut in a style that was much too young for her; she was weeping, leaning her head on the shoulder of a sober-faced young woman with blond hair. The caption identified them as the wife and daughter of the murdered man.

With her finger resting on the image of the older woman, Andrea looked up at Derek. "Am I supposed to know her?"

"The other one. The daughter. Look at her close. She looks just like you. The face is the same."

Andrea read the caption again, this time carefully: "Mrs. Anne Dolan is consoled by daughter Katherine, shortly after the brutally slain body of her husband, James Dolan, was discovered in the kitchen of their Somerville home."

Andrea stared several seconds at the image of Katherine Dolan. She looked up at Derek. "She doesn't look anything like me. I'd never wear my hair like that, and I wouldn't be caught dead in a middy blouse. How can you say this girl looks like me?"

17

During the summer months, to please her parents, Andrea took a job as saleswoman at the Svelte Lady Shoppe; and this piece of business turned out to be not so onerous as Andrea had feared, since Mrs. Marks wanted her only for several hours around lunchtime. This gave Andrea ample opportunity to laze in the hot sun.

On the weekends, when Cosmo joined Vittoria in Yarmouthport and Marsha was supposedly staying at the LoPontis' house in Weston, the two young women generally spent their evenings in Boston. Andrea carefully told her parents of at least half these trips, and parroted to them—as if the criticisms had been her own—reviews of the films, concerts, and plays she told them she had seen. She assuaged her conscience over these lies by not accepting the money that Cosmo offered to reimburse her for the tickets.

In Boston, it became Joanna Liberman's habit to let Andrea and Marsha accompany her to whatever bar she intended to visit that evening; and Joanna, because she knew trouble when she saw it, was perhaps a better chaperone than someone oblivious of real danger.

"I can look at a man in a bar," Joanna said to them one evening in a taxi, "and tell if I can handle him or not. If I don't think I can, then I won't have anything to do with him. You could do it too —it's only the really dumb girls who get in over their heads, the ones who just walk around blind. I don't know who first said you can't judge a book by its cover, but I'll bet you anything he never went to a singles bar."

But one weekend Joanna went to Tanglewood, and Andrea and Marsha decided to spend the entire weekend in Joanna's Mount Vernon Street apartment. On Friday night they went to the Brimmer House, where they had been once before—and where, they knew, the bouncer was lax in checking identification of good-looking but underaged girls. The Brimmer House was located only a couple of blocks away from Joanna's apartment, in the parlor and basement of a renovated townhouse on Beacon Street. The basement bar had a dance floor of ample size, where dancers moved beneath soft amber and pink spotlights. Upstairs there were long, angled leather couches and dark-tinted mirrors. Discreet lighting broke the shadows, and handsome men and women, all casually but expensively dressed, leaned close to one another in earnestly flippant conversation.

After looking over the dance bar Andrea and Marsha went upstairs again, out of the range of the disco music. On the parlor level a selection of smooth jazz and blues played at a volume that actually encouraged conversation. The men were mostly in their late twenties, lean and handsome. The two young women found space on one of the leather sofas, and when no waitress appeared after a few minutes, Andrea went to the bar and ordered their drinks.

". . . heavily into mutuals . . ." said a bearded man, who cast Andrea a flattering glance as he spoke to his companion at the bar.

". . . won twice at racquet ball, but I still couldn't get my pulse above . . ." another was saying.

"Best address in the South End," said a young woman standing near Andrea, "and I can't imagine it will be more than thirty thousand for renovation, we'll be able to take care of that in a couple of years . . ."

A man standing at Andrea's left turned to see who was behind him. Andrea smiled, and he smiled in return—but his eye was caught by another woman farther down, and he moved quickly away. Andrea frowned, but then another man, handsomer than the first, stepped in beside her. He brushed back a blond wave from his forehead and smiled with complete self-assurance. His eyes were blue and his teeth perfectly aligned. He introduced himself.

Marsha finally had to go to the bar herself to get the drink that Andrea had bought for her. Andrea introduced her to the advertising executive in a tone of voice that distinctly told Marsha to take her drink back to the sofa alone—and after Marsha had clumsily shaken hands with the man, she did just that.

At half past twelve, Andrea left with the advertising executive and walked the short two blocks to his condominium on Marlborough Street. The man was an affectionate if not an ardent lover. The next morning, after taking her to brunch at Front Street restaurant, he walked her to the corner of Mount Vernon Street. He did not ask for her telephone number, and Andrea, disappointed, wondered if she had proved inadequate in her own lovemaking. Although she looked out for him the next time she visited the Brimmer House, she did not see the man again.

On the next Friday night, Andrea visited the studio of a graphic artist. When she returned next morning to Joanna's apartment building, it was with a feeling of confidence about the way she was able to meet men in the singles bars. She stood in the vestibule and rang the buzzer, and in a moment Joanna Liberman's voice came on: "Who is it?"

"Andrea," she replied into the speaker, and smiled at the young man who had just entered the vestibule with his dalmatian.

Joanna buzzed her in. Andrea pushed open the door and ran upstairs, smiling at her own high spirits. She had conclusively joined the sorority of nonvirgins.

Andrea helped Joanna and Marsha prepare a light breakfast of heated pecan coffee cake, chilled orange juice, and coffee. The three of them chatted idly, but Andrea sensed that something was disturbing Joanna and that Marsha knew what it was. When they finally settled in their chairs at the round dining table between the front windows, Andrea had taken no more than her first sip of coffee when Joanna said, "You're not on the pill or using any sort of device, are you?"

Instead of answering, Andrea looked at Marsha, who appeared absorbed in the task of spreading half a stick of butter onto a small wedge of coffee cake. "No," said Andrea at last.

"I'm not trying to guilt-trip you," sighed Joanna, "*either* of you —but you *might* see your way clear to giving it a little thought," she added sarcastically.

Neither Andrea nor Marsha said anything for a few moments; then Marsha, after taking a bite of the coffee cake, remarked, "Joshua always uses a raincoat."

"A condom is about as safe as wiping up with a Kleenex afterwards," said Joanna severely. "A man who's half decent in bed will break through any rubber that's on the market. The point is that both of you have a decision to make. One alternative is to take the risk of getting pregnant, and go through the hassle of waiting rooms and tests and then telling your parents and then getting up the money for the abortion—*or* you can make a little visit to the health clinic right now, and get a prescription for a little circle of pills."

"What's the number?" said Andrea, wondering at her own stupidity and glad that the matter had been taken in hand.

"The appointment's for eleven o'clock. You've got time for

another cup of coffee," said Joanna. "But, Andrea, tell me something, tell me one thing—"

"What?"

"How could you not have thought of this before? I mean, weren't you afraid?"

Andrea looked up sheepishly from her cup. "I did think about it, but—"

"But she always makes 'em jump ship before the hold blows," said Marsha quickly, and they all laughed.

Andrea smiled stiffly when the female doctor at the women's clinic prescribed birth control pills, but was humiliated when she demanded blood samples and vaginal and throat smears to check for syphilis and gonorrhea. "Is there any reason," the doctor asked blithely, "why I ought to take a rectal smear as well?" Andrea, shocked, shook her head no.

Leaving the place with Marsha, she was silent, for she had realized why she had not gone to a doctor before. She had equated birth control pills with promiscuity: protection against pregnancy meant an insatiable desire for sex. And now, for better or worse, she considered that she had committed herself to a way of life. Promiscuity was perhaps too hard a word, but what would her mother have said if she had known that Andrea had slept with three different men in a single month? Really though, it had been not so much a question of sex as it was one of achievement—she had wanted to master the singles bars the way she had mastered Russian verbs. But how could she explain *that* to her mother? Fearful of Vittoria's discovering the disc of pills in her purse, Andrea had slipped it into her back pocket. And now, back at Joanna's, she begged Marsha to tell her truthfully whether its outline could be seen through the denim.

18

Andrea and Marsha were perched on the top rung of the railing that ringed the enormous roller coaster at Nantasket Beach. Their leather sandals were hooked about the lower rung, and each leaned forward, arms folded, elbows resting on her knees.

A cigarette dangled between Andrea's fingers, and she passed it to Marsha.

The young women's eyes followed the segmented roller coaster cars as they were dragged screechingly up the first and highest arc of the track, paused at the hump, and shot down the other side, the passengers shrieking in gleeful terror. When it came round at the last to where they were, Marsha suddenly sat up straight and waved to two small boys sitting petrified in the last car. The children gazed at her with wide, frightened eyes and clung to the guardrail with white-knuckled hands.

Andrea leaned back and shook her hair; she took the cigarette back from Marsha and inhaled deeply. "Don't you think five times is enough?"

Marsha shrugged. "One more time, and they'll be ready to go home. You know," she said, looking ruefully round the amusement park, "this place is always tackier than I remembered it."

A tall, well-built young man with curly blond hair and set, handsome features passed slowly before them. His wide-set blue eyes scanned Marsha with perfunctory interest, but they lingered on Andrea. He carried a large tan beach towel in one hand and a bottle of Coppertone in the other. Leaning against the railing a few feet down from them, he flung the towel over his shoulder and pretended to watch the roller coaster while he took appraising side glances at Andrea.

Andrea looked him over, but just as he was about to engineer a smile with just the right amount of interest in it, she shifted her green eyes coolly away.

The blond young man sighed in exasperation and sauntered off.

"Well you scared that one away," said Marsha, and waved her cigarette after the retreating figure.

"No loss," shrugged Andrea. "He didn't look as if he could work his way through *Dick and Jane.*"

"Who cares about his reading comprehension?" snapped Marsha. "Honestly, Andrea, ever since you discovered a technique that works in the bars, you act like you invented sex."

"No," said Andrea quietly, "that's not it at all. You're the one who said the men I had been dating were too young and inexperienced, I—"

"I said they were wimps."

"Well," said Andrea, "the men I've met this summer have been older and more . . . experienced."

"I'll bet you managed to show them a thing or two."

"Maybe," said Andrea. "But I've done most of the learning. That boy who wanted to speak to me just now was probably very nice, and he probably *could* have made his way through *Dick and Jane*, but I think he would have barked and rolled over if I'd asked him to. Just like those others—those wimps, as you call 'em. You see what I mean?"

"You want to be dominated?"

"In a way, yes, I guess I do. Not tied to the ceiling or beat over the head with a dead fish or anything like that. And I have *no* interest in finding a man who's going to tell me how to live my life, either." She raised her hands in frustration. "I've been thinking about this, and I can't figure out exactly what it is that I *do* want."

"I'm not sure I want you to find out."

"But I know one thing," nodded Andrea: "I have *no* interest in any man who hangs out at an amusement park."

When Andrea had recounted for Marsha the loss of her virginity to Derek Whatever-his-name-was, she had been truthful; her tale had been unenthusiastic and laden with off-putting detail. But since that night spent on St. Botolph Street, the image of Derek had entered Andrea's dreams. She envisioned his taking her with great force, kissing her with such ardor that her lip was bloodied. No matter with what waking resolution she dismissed him from her thoughts, he returned to her dreams regularly.

Marsha's small cousins walked unsteadily down the wooden ramp from the roller coaster to the asphalt path that went along the railing. Marsha smiled indulgently: "You two want some pizza? Lots of pepperoni and hot peppers? Then some cotton candy and candied apples to take home with you? Snow cones?" she asked.

"Marsha," Andrea protested, "I didn't even take the ride, and you're making me sick."

Pale-faced, the boys shook their heads.

"Why don't we walk around for a little, and then we'll just drive on home. How's that?" said Andrea, smiling.

"Can we play the Superman pinball machine? I won two games on it in Evanston, I bet they have one here," said one of the boys—Andrea couldn't remember which was Andrew and which Michael.

"Sure," said Marsha. "Here's three Susan B's, if you put one of those in, you get five games to the dollar. When that's gone, we go too. Right?"

The boys took the coins and disappeared into the long, low-ceilinged wooden arcade that stank of popcorn and machine oil.

Andrea and Marsha left the boardwalk and crossed the parking lot to the sea wall, seating themselves there on one of the three benches that hadn't recently been vandalized. The wind from the ocean had obliterated all the morning's warmth. They crossed their arms, wishing they had brought jackets, and squinted into the strong sea breeze. As they sat silent, the sky became darker and the cloud cover was perceptibly lowered.

"It's going to start raining any minute," said Andrea. "Maybe we should get Michael and Andrew and go."

"I don't believe in rain until it's soaked my T-shirt," said Marsha. "Let's wait a few minutes."

A line of young children filed before Andrea and Marsha, and the two young women exchanged amused glances, for the students were hardly dressed for an outing at Nantasket Beach. The four boys wore white short-sleeved shirts with butterfly collars and dark blue pressed shorts, while the two girls wore jumpers of the same blue, and white blouses with puffed sleeves. Behind the children was a young nun carrying a shopping bag filled with small sand pails and little metal shovels. She was so preoccupied with the maintenance of order in her group that she did not spare even a glance for the two young women on the bench.

Andrea pulled a comb from her back pocket and ran it through her hair several times with difficulty. "God," she complained, "sea air gives me the kinks. Here we are, sophomores at a Seven Sisters school, and what are we doing with our summer when everyone we know is on an archaeological dig in southern France, or mountain climbing in Yugoslavia? We're on Nantasket Beach! I don't know *why* I let you drag me along."

Marsha didn't reply. She had looked thoughtfully after the nun and her six charges; after a moment, she turned back to her friend with a disturbed expression.

"What's wrong now?" asked Andrea.

"That nun," said Marsha, cocking her head toward the retreating group.

"Yes," said Andrea, glancing toward the black-robed woman, "that's a nun, all right."

Marsha touched Andrea's arm. "Didn't you see?"

"See what? She looked like a penguin? All nuns look like penguins."

"No," said Marsha, her fingers tightening on Andrea's arm, "she didn't look like a penguin, she looked like *you*."

"You got dizzy watching that roller coaster."

"I'm serious, Andrea. I swear to God, she looks just like you."

Annoyed, Andrea stood up and jammed the comb into her back pocket. "Why is everybody always saying I look like somebody else?"

"Who's everybody?"

"That guy I went home with—"

"Which of the multitude?" said Marsha sarcastically.

"The one from Joanna's party," replied Andrea, "that you thought was so gorgeous. My first—*remember*? The next morning he showed me this picture in an old newspaper of a girl he thought I looked like. Somebody killed her father or something and she had horrible hair, and she was wearing this completely tacky middy blouse, for God's sake. Why doesn't anybody tell me I look like Faye Dunaway or Candice Bergen? Instead they point out this cluck who looks like she hasn't had her period yet, or a goddamned *nun* with a shopping bag. Besides, I looked at that nun, I don't look a thing like her."

Marsha ignored Andrea's irritation and stood. "Come on then, and see for yourself."

"No."

"Please, Andrea." Marsha lowered her voice and said seriously.

"I swear to God, that nun *did* look like you. Let's just check her out, and then you can say 'I told you so.'"

With a nod, Andrea reluctantly acquiesced. Marsha hurried her down the boardwalk. The nun and her brood were stopped at a water fountain, the young woman lifting each of the children by turn; the children seemed oddly docile and quiet. Andrea and Marsha stood a discreet distance away and pretended to be in casual conversation as they glanced sidewise at the nun. Andrea kept her hand against the side of her face to disguise her interest. The increasing wind billowed the nun's black skirts and fluttered the veil about her shoulders; at times the child in her arms was altogether lost behind a flap of black cloth.

"I feel stupid," said Andrea, "spying on a nun."

"Her eyes are green, just like yours, and look at that nose. It's the shape of her face too," said Marsha, "it's exactly the same. Remember when I took Life Drawing class and I was using you for a model all the time? Well, I know what you look like, Andrea, I know every line in your face—and that nun has them all, I promise you, she has every line."

"Marsha, she's wearing about fifty yards of black material, she's got a wimple to her eyebrows, no makeup, and her head's probably shaved bald under there—how can you say she looks like me?! She's got green eyes and I've got green eyes and that's it! I look at my face in the mirror for about two hours every day, and I know what I look like—"

"No," exclaimed Marsha, "you don't! In the mirror, you're seeing your face backward. The mirror image is not what other people see. That's why you think she doesn't look like you, because you're thinking of your mirror image, you're not thinking of what you really look like. When I look at you, you know what I see?"

"What?"

"That nun over there. That nun over there is you at a Halloween party. I just wish she'd laugh, so we could see her teeth."

"Oh, Marsha!" Andrea cried loudly.

The nun looked up, but the two young women turned smoothly away and were not seen. The last child in line was set down, and the first one tugged at her skirts. "Can I please have some more, Sister Katherine?" Sister Katherine gathered the child in her arms.

Heavy drops of rain began to fall. Thunder exploded across the sky, drowning even the amplified carnival music of the amusement arcade across the way. The eyes of six children widened, and they stared about nervously, mouths agape. Tentacles of lightning struck through the sky over Hingham. Thunder again blasted overhead. The boy in the nun's arms flinched and cried out.

"Shhh, Patrick," said Sister Katherine, "don't be afraid, it's only the hammers of heaven, that's all it is."

Gnarled fingers of lightning thrust down into the churning ocean as one peal of thunder crowded the growling end of the last before it. The children quaked, hovering at the nun's skirts, and she scurried them up the walk. The boy in her arms burrowed his face into her black shoulder. "Hurry, hurry, let's run," cried Sister Katherine. "God is angry, He's driving in His biggest nails today!"

Andrea and Marsha watched fascinated. The nun, her skirts and veil billowing and flashing black and white, ran past them with her chicks toward a Volkswagen bus in the parking lot. They were joined by another nun, who ran across from the amusement park. The children beat upon the doors of the locked vehicle.

"Hush! Hush!" cried Sister Katherine, "it's only the hammers of heaven! They'll never hurt you! We'll be back in Hingham in ten minutes! Hush, hush!"

Sheets of rain beat against the top of the bus, and the nun herded the children safely inside.

Andrea and Marsha rushed through the pounding rain to the shelter of the arcade.

19

That night Andrea stood before the framed mirror in her room. In her hands she held a large copy of her graduation photograph. Her eyes went back and forth from her reflection to the glossy print. As Marsha had said, the images were not the same. But when she turned the photograph to the mirror, they realigned themselves. What *she* saw in the mirror was not, after all, what other people saw when they looked at her.

Andrea tossed the photograph on the bureau and from a lower drawer took out her makeup mirror. She held it at arm's length and then looked into the wall mirror at the double reflection of herself in the hand mirror. As Andrea studied herself she thought again of what Marsha had said. She observed herself both in profile and full face; she tilted the mirror up and down, she stretched her neck, she lowered her chin; and she concluded that she was looking at a different woman. She shuddered with a sudden sense of alienation—alienation from her own body. What she saw in this doubly reflected image, her *true* image, was not Andrea LoPonti, Wenham sophomore and graduate of Miss Britten's Academy, but rather the young nun on Nantasket Beach, and the girl in the newspaper photograph whose father had been knifed to death in a lower-class suburb.

This realization disturbed Andrea for several days afterward—and in a manner she could not control. Andrea rarely remembered her dreams, and had never thought them important. But through the years, a single figure had sporadically haunted her nights: it was Andrea herself. Not Andrea as she was, bright and popular, applauded and awarded—but Andrea as she feared she really was, Andrea as Andrea would be if she ever dropped her defenses. In Andrea's dreams was a girl who was green-eyed and blond and pretty enough, but who crept into corners and wouldn't speak above a whisper, who abased herself before all others, who hadn't stamina or backbone or anything to say for herself. Andrea told herself that this figure was, of course, the frightened portion of herself, the portion that she had never allowed to gain the upper hand; but now that hapless figure of a girl—no, not a girl anymore, but a young woman—became suddenly more prominent in Andrea's dreams. In the morning, Andrea could never remember in what scenes that retiring creature had played her contemptible part, but was left only with the bitter reflection that this was perhaps her *true* self.

Andrea knew that this girl, who had inhabited her head at night for as long as she could remember, was the goad that had propelled her always toward achievement, popularity, and personal power. But never before had this dream-girl been so prominent, never had she shown up so many nights in a row, never with such clarity. When Andrea woke in the morning, it was with some phrase the girl had spoken beating in her brain.

One day, when Andrea had been several hours alone, she admitted something to herself: that the anger she had displayed toward Derek and Marsha for pointing up the physical resemblances between her and the girl in the picture and the nun on the beach had the same source. She too had seen the resemblances —and worse, she had *felt* them. And in those moments when she had looked at the photograph of the girl consoling her mother, and surreptitiously stared between the fingers of her hand at the nun on the boardwalk, she had had the unmistakable sensation of just having waked from sleep—with the fading, unintelligible words of that other girl echoing in her brain.

On the evening before Andrea was to return to Wenham for the fall semester, the three LoPontis sat together in the den during the evening news. Cosmo was in his recliner with a glass of the imported Japanese beer that Andrea had tried to convince him was so much better than the Budweiser he really preferred. Vittoria was on the couch, clipping newspaper recipes. Andrea sat stiffly apart from them in an overstuffed armchair that she had deliberately pulled out of the range of the television screen.

"Is something wrong, Andrea?" asked Vittoria. "Something's always wrong when you cross your arms that way."

"I don't know."

Cosmo lowered the volume on the television by remote control.

"Are you ill, or—"

"No, I'm not ill."

"Well you don't look yourself, I—"

Vittoria was interrupted by her daughter's harsh laughter.

"Well," said Andrea, "I guess that's it. I don't *feel* like myself, either."

"Cosmo," said Vittoria, "turn off the television." Father and mother looked to their daughter for explanation.

When, after a long pause, she had not spoken, Vittoria gently prodded: "Are you worried about going back to school tomorrow, Andrea? I know it's—"

"No, Mother, I certainly haven't been worried about school. No, *Mother*," she said, laying an ironic emphasis on the word. "I was thinking about my relatives."

"Your relatives!"

"I've been wondering why I've never met any of them. I mean, we must have some relatives. All Italians have relatives. I've never even *seen* my grandparents."

"Yes, you have," said Vittoria uneasily. "You were just too little to remember."

"When was that?"

"When you were in Texas," said Cosmo.

Andrea stared at her father. *"Texas?* When was I in *Texas?"*

Vittoria grimaced at her husband, then turned to Andrea. "You were born in Texas, Andrea. I thought you knew that," she added lamely. "When I . . ." Vittoria cast about for her thoughts. "When I was pregnant with you," she went on at last, "I went to visit your grandmother in Texas. She was very sick. She died, and the next day you were born."

"You flew to Texas when you were nine months pregnant?" asked Andrea. "I didn't think they allowed that."

Vittoria looked confused. "You were premature," she said at last. "I think you came early because of . . . because of everything that happened around then."

Andrea pondered this. "Then my birth certificate says I was born in Texas?"

Cosmo and Vittoria exchanged glances. "You don't have a birth certificate," said Cosmo at last.

Andrea pursed her lips and waited for an explanation.

"There *was* one, of course," said Vittoria weakly, "but we lost it, and when we wrote to get another, we discovered that the city hall in Texas had burned and a lot of the records were lost. We had—"

"Wait a minute," said Andrea, with an unpleasant curling of her lip. "Just cut this out."

"Cut what out?" asked her mother.

"All this bullshit."

"Andrea!"

"All this *bullshit!*" she repeated forcefully. "You're making it up as you go along! The fact is, I'm adopted, right?"

Stunned, Cosmo and Vittoria said nothing.

"Right," said Andrea. "I'm adopted, and you never said a word. I'm such an idiot. I look at you two there, and I look at myself in the mirror, and we don't look anything alike, and it never even occurs to me there might be a reason for it."

"Andrea . . ." her mother pleaded.

"Why did you lie?"

"We didn't lie!" cried Cosmo, but turned his face away.

"Why didn't you just tell me I was adopted?"

"Do you really want to know?" asked Vittoria.

Andrea's smile was merely ironic. "Yes," she replied, "I guess I do. Tell me, Mother, why did you hold it back for twenty years that I was adopted? Why did you and Daddy decide *never* to tell me?"

"Because," said Vittoria, "you *weren't* adopted. We *found* you."

Now Andrea was stunned. "I was *found?* Like on the doorstep or something? In a basket, with a note? And a locket around my neck?"

"No," said Vittoria, "with an earring—"

"Don't!" interrupted Cosmo. Startled, both women turned to him. Andrea nervously pulled at her right earlobe and the ruby chip embedded in it. Cosmo spoke haltingly: "Don't say anything more, Vitti. It won't do her any good to know any more."

"Tell me!"

"Vitti found you," said Andrea's father. "And we kept you because we couldn't have any children of our own. Andrea, you were a gift from God. We couldn't—"

"Who were my real parents?"

Vittoria shook her head. "Andrea, listen, the only reason we never told you all this is not because we didn't think you could handle it emotionally, it was just because it wasn't . . . What we did wasn't legal. Cosmo and I never told anyone, we were so afraid that someone would take you away from us. We couldn't tell you because we were afraid you'd tell somebody else, by accident of course, and the story would get out. We couldn't take the risk, we—"

"Who would I have told?" screamed Andrea. "My God, I—"

"Andrea," cried her mother. "You can't let this make a difference, you can't—"

"It does, though!" shouted Andrea, jerking up out of the chair. "It makes all the difference in the world!"

20

Marsha saw him first. She and Andrea had been sitting for half an hour at the bar of the dance room in the Brimmer House, watching all the arrivals and tentative couplings in the smoked mirror behind the tiers of fancy liquors. When the man stepped through the door, Marsha nudged Andrea with her elbow and discreetly nodded at his reflection.

He was tall and slender, in his late twenties. His features were darkly handsome and just irregular enough to be interesting; his dark eyes were deep-set and heavy-lidded beneath thick black brows. His hair, in short, tight, thick curls, appeared blue-black as he stood on the perimeter of a circle of amber light. The shadow of a beard defined his square jaw. He wore a snugly fitting and evidently new brown leather jacket over a black T-shirt, tight straight-legged, button-fly jeans, and heavy black leather boots. In his large hands he turned a shiny black motorcycle helmet with a mirrored visor. In this place given over to junior executives and administrative assistants, he was a forceful and threatening anomaly.

"Well," whispered Marsha, "I think he's in the wrong end of town."

Andrea watched the man as he moved slowly about the room, evidently in search of someone in particular. He moved near them and leaned against the bar, hoisting a heavy boot onto the brass rail and scraping the gritty sole there until Andrea winced. He set the helmet on the bar and beat an impatient tattoo with his long, thick fingers. He unzipped his jacket with a determined tug, sternly pushed his sleeve to check the time, and continued to beat his fingers against the mahogany. Andrea looked at the matting of coarse black hair that curled across the back of his hands and over the high, tight yoke of his T-shirt.

Andrea turned to Marsha. "I think he's just where he belongs."

"You like him?" hissed Marsha, alarmed by the approval in Andrea's voice.

"Don't you? He's different from the other men we see in this place."

"Yes," said Marsha, "he's not as nice."

"How do you know?"

"His clothes. What he's wearing."

"That jacket cost two hundred if it cost a penny. Those boots are at least a hundred and twenty-five. His clothes cost more than yours and mine put together, and that's counting all the cash we've got in our pockets."

"That may be," admitted Marsha uneasily, "but I still don't like him. I don't trust men who drive motorcycles and wear leather, and besides, I think there's something wrong with him."

"What?" demanded Andrea, glancing at the man again.

Marsha lowered her voice even more. "Look how he's tapping his fingers—he's out of beat with the music. How can you be off the beat when it's disco playing? There's something definitely wrong."

"That's the most asinine thing I've ever heard in my life. I don't understand what you're trying to get at."

"Andrea, the difference between this man and the other men in here is night and day. And this man is definitely night."

"I know," said Andrea quietly, looking at him in the mirror.

"Well I think you ought to forget any ideas you've got about that one."

"Don't lecture me, Marsha."

"What's he doing in here anyway, dressed like that?"

"When are you going to realize that not everybody belongs to a Harvard final club—and not everybody *wants* to either. If I didn't know you better I'd think you were the one afraid of men."

Marsha's eyes narrowed, "I'm not afraid, I'm just cautious, which is something I'm beginning to think you don't know anything about. Andrea," said Marsha carefully, after taking a small sip of her drink, "you've been off lately."

"Off?" Andrea knew what Marsha meant, although she had no intention of admitting it. She had not confided to Marsha the degrading discovery that she was not her parents' natural child, much less that she had no idea who her real parents might be: their names, condition, nationality, or reasons for abandoning her. Though she had pleaded with Cosmo and Vittoria, they had steadfastly refused to tell the circumstances of their taking her in, and Andrea's anger was only increased by their recalcitrance.

She now felt alienated from them, and from her entire life in Weston.

"You've been taking these mood swings," said Marsha. "Subtle, but I can see them."

"What you've been *seeing* is your Remedial Psychology notes."

Marsha lapsed into scowling silence.

The bartender, who had gone upstairs for ice, returned. He greeted the man in the leather jacket with a brief nod and came down to their end of the bar. As he did so, the man in leather withdrew his hand slowly from his jacket and held it out for the bartender to shake. Andrea saw that there was a small manila envelope, bulky and sealed with cellophane tape, cupped in his hand. The bartender, in his, held several folded bills of large denomination. Andrea carefully turned her head away, but kept her eyes locked on the great hairy hand of the man in the leather jacket; the exchange was quickly completed. This done, the bartender pulled a bottle of expensive imported beer from the cooler, snapped off the cap, and slid it across the bar to the man. He took it without thanks or the offer of payment; the bartender moved away without expression. Andrea was flushed with excitement, certain that she had just witnessed a transaction involving drugs, and she would have been willing to bet that it wasn't just grass in the sealed manila envelope.

Andrea glanced at Marsha to see if she had noticed, but Marsha's attention was focused on the dance floor. Andrea continued to watch the reflection of the man in the leather jacket, and now and then she turned to look straight at him. He seemed less tense now, and his foot scraped against the brass rail in time with the heavy disco beat. With one hand kept in the pocket in which he had thrust the bartender's money, the man contentedly sipped his beer; he looked round the room without apparent interest, and did not seem to take any notice of Andrea, or her attention.

Marsha spun slowly round on her bar stool. She had to tap Andrea's shoulder to draw her notice away from the man in leather.

"Do you want to go upstairs for a while?" she asked.

"Not right now. You go ahead."

Marsha looked at her friend for a long moment. "What are you up to?" she asked in a serious voice.

Andrea set her drink down. "I'm not up to anything, Marsha—it's just that I decided to make my presence known to that man over there—to see what happens."

"I honestly don't think—"

"I *know* what you honestly don't think, but there's nothing to worry about." A smile played across Andrea's mouth. "I've got all Joanna's rules for taking care of yourself written down on the inside of my cuffs."

Marsha laughed. "All right, all right." Then she was no longer smiling: "Andrea, it's just that most of the men we meet in places like this are real professional types and—"

"You mean they're 'safe'?"

"Yes. They have their reputations to protect, so they're not going to do anything *completely* outrageous. But this one over here certainly isn't professional, and I don't think he's safe at all. Maybe I'm just overreacting, but if he makes a move or anything happens, make sure the lights are kept on. Oh, and by the way, what about that party on Goodwin Place? We're supposed to go over there with Joanna at midnight."

Andrea shrugged. "Listen, I don't imagine anything is going to happen. This man isn't really my type. But he's a challenge, that's all. He's the most interesting man in this place, because he's so *out* of place, so I'm just trying to see how good my technique is."

Marsha raised one eyebrow. "Well, aren't we the hard woman?"

"Go upstairs, Marsha. Find something hot for yourself."

Andrea stared at her reflection in the mirror. She waited until

Marsha had disappeared up the stairs before turning back to the man.

He was looking at her; he winked slowly, and held her gaze as he tilted back his head in order to swallow the last of his beer. Andrea smiled nervously.

The man shoved his helmet down the bar; it knocked over Andrea's empty glass. He stood and stretched, arching his back. The chiseled muscles of his chest strained the black cotton T-shirt.

"Your friend there ..." he nodded towards the stairs. "She thinks I'm Albert DeSalvo."

"Who?" said Andrea, confused.

"The Boston Strangler," replied the man. His voice was deep and full. "But don't worry, Albert DeSalvo's in prison now." He paused, and tugged at a gold chain around his neck; the pendant was a small gold Coke bottle. "He makes necklaces in the prison shop."

Andrea bit her lip in embarrassment: "You heard what she said?"

"I heard her," he said, and laughed. "I always do it with the lights on anyway."

Andrea smiled and took a sip of her drink.

"My name's Jack."

He got her a fresh drink, and another beer for himself, again not paying. Andrea told him that she had recently begun her sophomore year at Wenham, and that she was supposed to be going to a party in another twenty minutes. He had taken Marsha's place, leaning against the bar on one elbow. One foot was on the floor and the heel of the other boot was caught on the bottom rung of the chair, his legs opened toward her. One of the buttons of his fly was undone.

"Dance?" he said, but it was no question.

Jack moved easily, and as the slow disco built he edged closer to her, dropping his hand onto her waist. He pressed his hips against hers, brushing his crotch against her thighs. Andrea did not pull back, but closed her hands over Jack's, and they moved together in perfect rhythm to the driving beat. His dark eyes grazed over her face every few seconds, down her neck to her breasts and back up, with no apology. Jack's arrogance fascinated her. He flaunted himself and his sexuality—but Andrea did not care.

Sweat gleamed on Jack's forehead and cheeks. The full, heady scent of the leather and perspiration engulfed Andrea, and she breathed it in deeply.

Jack leaned closer to her and brushed his mouth against her ear. "I don't have another helmet," he said. "You afraid to ride without one?"

21

Jack turned the Harley into the driveway of a large two-story, green-shingled house, maneuvering the machine carefully into the narrow space between a battered jeep and the cellar storm doors. He revved the engine once, tensing his body with the sound, and then killed it. He slammed the kickstand with his heel, and in the same motion swung his other leg over and stood aside. Andrea dismounted clumsily; perspiration beaded her forehead and the nape of her neck.

She looked round her at the dark neighborhood. Street lights were obscured by the branches of tall, full-leaved trees. Nearby houses, all with unlighted windows, lay in deep shadow, and although there was no air about them of dilapidation or abandonment, none appeared inhabited. There was a muffled drumbeat from several blocks over, more tom-tom than rock.

"Where are we?" she asked. The ride from the bar had taken no more than fifteen minutes, but Andrea had not recognized their route. This neighborhood was wholly unfamiliar; she supposed that, since they had not crossed the river, they were somewhere south of Boston; possibly they were in one of those places she knew only by its name: West Roxbury, Roslindale, or Dorchester, for instance.

"Jamaica Plain."

"Is that actually within the city limits of Boston?" she asked curiously; then blushed in the dark, remembering that this was not the man to be plied with trivial questions.

Jack did not bother to answer. He walked round to the front of the house, and Andrea, when she realized that she was not going to have an invitation to follow, moved to catch up with him.

The first step to the wide front porch was missing, and two cinder blocks, rough with old mortar, took its place. The warped, unpainted planks of the porch undulated toward either end and creaked softly beneath Andrea's careful tread. Behind the screen door, which bore a gash through it like a sword stroke, burned a pink wall light in a hallway of yellow paper with reflective silver stripes.

She wondered briefly if he would hold the door and allow her to precede him inside, but she contented herself with hurrying through after him when he flung it open.

He tossed his leather jacket onto the hook of a large Victorian hall stand that had recently been spray-painted a light gray. He laid his black, mirror-visored helmet carefully on one of the marble-topped arms.

In the hallway, a wide staircase led to a landing so dark that Andrea could not make out the pattern of the stained glass windows there; double doors opened on either side, and at the end there was a narrow door with a transom. Through the doors on the left, which were partially opened onto a large dining room with corner hutches and a grime-encrusted crystal chandelier, Andrea could see that a motorcycle had been dismantled: the larger pieces were laid neatly in rows on the floor, and all the smaller workings were carefully placed atop the enormous mahogany table that had been pushed up against the marble hearth.

Rock music of the softer variety played at a low volume behind the closed doors on the right. Andrea thought there was probably a roommate, and she told herself she wouldn't even be surprised if it turned out to be a woman. She had heard of strange arrangements in these outlying neighborhoods of the city; of cooperative houses or semicommunes where people sometimes slept together, and sometimes did not, and brought people home, and were casual about sex and strict about vegetarianism. She tried to prepare herself: there would be a man there, or a woman, and they would be introduced, and she and Jack would sit down and talk for a few minutes, and then Jack would say, "Why don't I show you the rest of the house," and the other person would know that they were really going up to have sex, and Andrea would know that the other person knew, and she would smile and not be embarrassed.

But when Jack pulled open the doors, Andrea was dismayed to find not one housemate, but *four*.

A swarthy man with wavy black hair stretched sleeping across the sofa beneath the shaded front window. One dark hand rested on his bare chest and the other was shoved under the waistband of his green army fatigues. The large buttoned pockets on his thighs were lumpy with God-knew-what. A woman whose bright orange-red hair was tangled about her thin shoulders lay beside him, her back to the rest of the room and her face burrowed into the space between the cushions and the back of the couch.

Between the fireplace and the interior wall, on shelving of unpainted planks and dusty bricks, was a fascinatingly large, complex, and expensive stereo system. In the fourth corner were two overstuffed armchairs, upholstered in velour with a green-and-blue bargello pattern that was almost as offensive as the hallway wallpaper.

A tall, slender man with thinning brown hair and a sparse beard sat cradled sidewise in the left-hand chair, his long legs hooked over one arm as he leaned back against the other and leafed disinterestedly through an antique issue of *Time*. In the second chair, like a matching bookend, slouched a woman in an identical position. Her silver-white hair was cut so close that at first Andrea, seeing her in the same blue work shirt and jeans as her companion, took her to be a man. Her face was obscured by a paperback book held so close to her face that Andrea wondered how she could possibly focus the print. The lettering on the cover was too stylized for Andrea to make out at such a distance and in such dim light. She had an almost irrepressible urge to turn on the lamp that stood between the two chairs so that the bookends might not ruin their vision.

"Well well," said the man in the chair, ripping out a page of the magazine, crumpling it, and throwing it in their direction, "Jack Smack returns."

"Hi," said the woman behind the paperback.

"Jack Smack could eat no fat," said the bearded man, and this time threw the whole magazine. "His wife—" He looked more closely at Andrea. "Hey, did she come on the bike—or in a stroller?"

"Say hello to Sid," said Jack. "That's Morgie, improving her mind."

Morgie pushed the book right up against her face to hold the page, and then flashed Jack a stiff middle finger. Her nails were long, pointed, and painted a glossy white.

"That's Dominic and Rita on the couch. They're communing with their astral bodies."

"Hi," grinned Sid, with obviously feigned camaraderie. "Can I call you Flora?"

"My name's Andrea."

The paperback was lowered, and Andrea saw a pair of extraordinarily pale gray eyes, slightly crossed. Morgie's white face was narrow and sharp, and her thin mouth was painted a vibrant red. She looked like a valentine. "I read this book once," she said, "and there was this girl named Andrea in it. She got raped and then put in jail for killing this man who turned out to be her uncle. So it was incest too. It was a good book, did you read it?" Morgie's voice was so thin and rasping that Andrea had to fight the impulse to cringe.

"Want a beer?" asked Jack.

Andrea nodded; Sid and Morgie raised their hands to be included. Jack touched Andrea on the shoulder with a tenderness for which she was grateful in such alien straits.

He was gone before she began to wonder if she shouldn't follow him into the kitchen. She looked around her helplessly. How was she to act toward them? What was she to say? Andrea realized suddenly how genteel her life had been, without her ever thinking it so. She stood vaguely in the center of the faded cotton Oriental rug. No one asked her to take a seat, but Andrea thought perhaps they did not wish to call attention to the fact that there were no other chairs in the room.

At last, feeling herself conspicuous standing in the middle of the room, she seated herself cross-legged before the stereo system and made out as if she were concentrating on the music.

It was the grass they smoked in the alley behind the Brimmer House, Andrea decided, that made her feel so strange. If she had had more, all this wouldn't have bothered her; if she hadn't smoked at all, she would have been able to deal with everything.

The music was on tape, and one incomprehensible song followed another; Andrea, who sat facing that corner of wall where the stereo apparatus was situated, grew almost afraid of turning around, and only now and then glanced at the unstirring sleepers on the sofa. She knew she was still stoned when she realized with what fascination she watched the rhythmical rise and fall of the dark man's hairless chest. Only when he finally moved in his sleep, thrusting his hand all the way down inside his pants, did she look away, in embarrassment. Though it seemed an eternity since he had left for the kitchen, Jack had not yet returned. The tape was nearing its end, and when there was no more music, Andrea knew that she would not be able to continue as she was, staring at the half dozen expensive components.

"You've really got a great system," she said to Sid, when it looked as if there were no more than five minutes of tape left.

"Yeah," he replied, "cheap too."

"It doesn't *look* cheap."

"We bought it hot," shrugged Sid.

Andrea, distressed, turned to Morgie, whose friendliness, if rough, had seemed at least ungrudging and sincere.

"Is Morgie your real name?" Andrea asked, her voice cracking on the first word. "I mean," she said huskily, "what's it short for?"

"Morgan Memorial."

"Your name is *Morgan Memorial?*" asked Andrea, astonished.

"No," she shrugged, "my real name is Betty Page, like in the books—"

"Which books?" asked Andrea, more confused.

"*Betty Page Severely Chastised, Betty Page in Bondage*—you know the ones I mean."

"Oh yes," said Andrea softly.

"Well, before I knew about those books, I hated the name, I mean, what kind of name is *Betty Page*, really? So I changed it to Morgie, because Morgan Memorial's where I buy all my clothes. Their other name is Goodwill, of course, but whoever heard of a woman called Goodwill? They know me real well over there, they all call me Morgie, and they let me in their back room, and there's this big pile of clothes on the floor, like they were building a bonfire or something, and then I buy what I want, and I pay for it by the pound. I like your blouse, where'd you get it?"

Andrea decided she had best not say that she bought it on Newbury Street for sixty dollars. "Filene's Basement," she said at last.

"That place is all right," remarked Morgie hesitantly, "but *so* expensive."

Andrea, not knowing what to say next, said nothing. She wanted to ask what was keeping Jack in the kitchen, but didn't know if, in so strange a household, that would constitute acceptable curiosity. Sid made a great commotion of turning round in his chair, and something about the way he did it left Andrea with the unmistakable impression that he was signifying his complete boredom with her, the evening, and life in general.

"Listen," he said to Andrea, "hand me another magazine, will you?" He tossed into her lap the one he had been reading. She looked round the room, and at last made out a small stack of periodicals in a dark corner.

Glad to be of some use, she went over to it. "Which one would you like?" she asked. "*Life*, another *Time*, *U.S. News and World Report*, *Argosy?*"

"Are you a stewardess?" asked Morgie. "You sound just like a stewardess. Did you ever read *Coffee Tea or Me?*"

"I thought there was a *True Sex Crimes* over there in the pile," said Sid. "Look for it, will you?"

Andrea flipped through the magazines. At last she held up a magazine with the headline "The Montana Rapist Who Barbecued His Victims."

"That's it," said Sid, and Andrea brought it to him.

"What are you reading?" she asked Morgie no longer desirous of entering into conversation with Sid.

Morgie's book, which she had still been holding close to her face, was suddenly thrust at arm's length. On the gaudily illustrated cover, a young blond woman was being stalked down a city street at night by three burly men. The title, in crimson block letters, was *26 Men and a Girl*. In the lower right corner, in small print, was the author's name—Maxim Gorky.

"Oh!" cried Andrea in surprise, "Gorky is *very* good, I think!"

"Gorky?" said Morgie. "You know, I never could stand the taste of vodka. It always makes me throw up, no matter what I've had to eat before."

Andrea's smile faded. "No, Gorky's not a vodka, he was a famous Russian author. He wrote the book you're reading."

Morgie turned the book round, and stared at the cover. "Oh, yeah. Is he really famous? I didn't buy the book because of that, I bought it because of the cover, they've got great books at Morgan Memorial, and I saw this, and I thought, well a book with a cover like this has just *got* to be hot, but I've already read thirty-seven pages, and nobody's doing *anything* to *anybody*. I'm a real sucker for a hot cover. Have you ever read *The Story of O?*"

"I've seen it, I thought it had just a plain cover."

"It does, you're right, it really does, and I never would have bought it, except that somebody at Goodwill had written across the front of it, 'This is a filthy book,' so I bought it. It cost thirty-five cents, and they hardly ever charge more than a quarter, so that's how I knew it was going to be *really* dirty. It's about this girl, they never tell her name, and she—"

Sid flung *True Sex Crimes* at Morgie's head; it hit her. "She said she read it!" he shouted.

"She did *not!* She said she *saw* the book, you fucking smart-ass!"

"You're boring! I hate your goddamn book reports!"

"I may be boring," cried Morgie, "but at least I'm not bald!"

Frightened, Andrea drew back against the shelves. Her shoulder grazed the volume knob of the amplifier, and, at ninety decibels and out of four speakers, Bette Midler shrieked, "Red, red, gimme RED!" On the sofa, Dominic's eyes flew open. He jumped up, and stared around, dazed.

"What the fuck?" he said—or at least his mouth formed those words. No sound could be heard above the music.

Jack appeared between the double doors. Giggling, Morgie got up, throwing her book at Sid, and lowered the volume.

"What the fuck is going on?" said Jack.

Dominic sat on the edge of the sofa and rubbed his eyes; the red-haired woman had not moved at all.

"Sorry!" blurted Andrea. "It was my fault, I knocked against the knob."

Jack looked at her blankly, and then shrugged. She thought he was angry, but then he smiled warmly and handed her a beer. "No big deal," he said. He handed two more beers to Morgie and Sid, and then seated himself beside Andrea on the carpet, just as the tape ran out. Andrea was half glad that she had had the accident, since it had brought Jack in; she felt better with him near, and not so much obliged to take notice of the others in the room. He touched her hand and brushed his lips against her hair. "We'll go upstairs in a little while."

"Is this beer," complained Sid, "or did you piss in an empty can?"

"I stopped to roll some joints," said Jack. "They got warm."

"I like warm beer," said Morgie. "I like it warm and flat."

Dominic looked up at Andrea from the couch. "You broke my ears, goddammit," he whined in a Spanish accent.

Andrea pretended that she didn't hear him; she turned and leaned her head against Jack's shoulder. *What am I doing here?* she thought. *Who are these people?*

She drank her beer quickly, scarcely noticing its taste, but hoping that it would deaden her senses. She pushed the can away from her a little and asked Jack where the phone was.

"It's across the hall, just to the left of the door."

She went out the double doors, crossed the hideously garish hallway, and stepped into the dining room, kicking some piece of chrome out of its careful place.

"Hey, watch it in there!" she heard Dominic scream from the next room. She peered at the telephone, and dialled Joanna Liberman's number, but before it had begun to ring, she remembered that Joanna and Marsha were at the party on Goodwin Place.

She checked her watch; it was half past one. If the party had been bad, as Joanna had predicted, there was a chance they were already back. Andrea let the phone ring twenty-three times. She hung up, and dialled the recorded weather message. She fished in her pocket, and came up with a five-dollar bill. Even if that would

take her all the way back to Beacon Hill, and with the price of
Boston taxis, she knew it would not, she had no way of getting
into Joanna's apartment.

She was almost sick at the thought of spending the night in
this house. She would not consider asking Jack to drive her back
to the Hill. The ride to Jamaica Plain had frightened her; there
were times, when he had taken curves too quickly, that her shoes
had scraped against the pavement. She told herself that she was
only doing right in remaining until the subways started running,
that she might be putting herself into danger by getting on that
motorcycle again—especially without a helmet. But when she
remembered the jeep, she admitted to herself that her excuse
was only a self-deception to cover her real cowardice. She simply
did not have the courage to tell Jack that she was backing out.
Her only comfort was the thought that in six or seven hours it
would all be over. Marsha had called her a hard woman—well, it
was the hard woman who was going to have to make it through
this night.

Andrea, as she still held the telephone receiver to her ear and
listened to the weather report repeated, thought of what her
friend had said. Marsha had been right, of course; she saw that
now. Marsha had known that it would be wrong even to make the
acquaintance of the man in leather.

Andrea turned, not at a noise, but at feeling another presence
near by. Dominic stood between the double doors. His eyes were
half-lidded, and he smiled knowingly; she wondered if he could
hear Virginia with the 1:00 A.M. Boston temperature. His mouth
was wide and his teeth were large, but perfectly aligned. His eyes
swept up and down her body, and his hands pressed deeper into
the pockets of his fatigue pants, inching the waistband so far
down over his flat stomach that she could see the beginning of
his pubic hair.

Andrea jerked her gaze away.

"Rain tomorrow?" he said softly, and walked away down the
hall.

Andrea quickly dialled Joanna's number once more, but hung
up after ten rings—the studio apartment wasn't *that* big. She
returned to the living room. Sid, Morgie, and Jack were pass-

ing a joint between them, and when she seated herself again beside Jack, he handed half the burned joint to her. She inhaled deeply and passed it on to Morgie. The smoke seared her lungs, but she did not cough. If she were to be stuck here for the night, being stoned out of her mind could only make the situation less unpleasant.

Dominic appeared in the hallway, a Sylvester and Tweetie-Bird jelly glass of water in his hand.

"I'm going to bed," he announced loudly, "you coming?"

Andrea looked quickly over to the couch, waiting for the red-haired woman to stir so that she might see her face at last. But it was Morgie that stood and followed Dominic into the hall.

"I thought—" gasped Andrea.

"Ha!" laughed Jack: "You thought Sid and Morgie were together because of the way they were going at each other. We've got a couple of sten guns in the kitchen for when they're *really* going at it. Dominic and Morgie got married about five years ago. This house belongs to them." Jack looked at Sid. "Sid, listen, why don't you take Rita on upstairs, so Andrea and I can have a little time by ourselves here?"

"I haven't finished this story."

"Sid, just do me a favor, huh?"

Sid pulled himself out of his chair, loped slowly over to the sofa, and violently shook Rita into semiwakefulness. She turned over yawning, but did not open her eyes. She held her arms out before her, and Sid, crouching and turning himself almost spastically, maneuvered his long, slender back between them. Rita clasped her hands about his chest and wrapped her legs around his waist. Sid stood carefully, and Rita's head lolled against his shoulder; her long hair fell over her face. Rita would have been a pretty woman, but for the purple birthmark that covered the whole of her right cheek. Sid clapped his hands under Rita's thighs and carried her out of the room and up the stairs.

"Rita's not really much of a night person," remarked Jack.

Bewildered, Andrea shook her head. "Can we smoke that other joint?" she asked.

He reached into his back jeans pocket and extracted not the joint, but a glass vial filled with white powder. From another pocket he took a three-inch silver tube, and then pointed to the record cabinet. Andrea didn't understand.

"Hand me a record album," he said.

"Which one?"

He shook his head in gentle exasperation. "Doesn't matter," he said. "Oh, get one with a solid-colored cover."

Andrea picked one out, handed it to him, and wondered, with growing curiosity and some discomfort, why he placed it on the floor between them.

"What are you doing?" she asked.

Jack emptied a small pile of the white powder onto the record jacket and, with the edge of a razor blade he took from the shelving, quickly divided it into four short parallel lines.

"I want to know what you're doing," she demanded.

Still not bothering to reply, Jack leaned over the record album, held the slender silver tube up one nostril, and snorted up the first line, and then the second. He sat back and breathed deeply. Andrea stared astonished into his watering eyes. He handed the silver tube to Andrea. She turned it between her fingers.

"Just snort it like I did."

"What is it?"

He sighed. "Coke."

"Coke?" she said slowly. "I'm already stoned. How will it make me feel?"

"Like you were queen of the prom."

Andrea snorted the cocaine, and was glad to do it again half an hour later, when Jack made four more lines. They washed the bitterness down with beer, and smoked the second joint to enhance the high. Andrea lay weightless in Jack's arms. The double doors had been drawn together. The candles round the room had been lighted, and the stereo changed over to an all-night soft rock station. From behind the sofa Jack retrieved a thick, soft quilt and spread it in the middle of the room.

He made love to Andrea. In eager submission, she folded herself in his arms. She crossed and locked her legs behind his waist and welcomed his weight upon her. He moved slowly with her, guiding her gently, and his low-pitched groans precipitated her into a febrile excitement she could not have imagined possible. She thought of the other three men she had been to bed with —she remembered the number, but could not recall their faces in sequence. One or the other slipped from her exalted consciousness.

Andrea did all that was asked and demanded of her: Jack was tender, but he took for granted that she wanted what he did. She made no protest when the springs of the armchair cut into her buttocks, or the material of the sofa chafed her breasts and stomach. As she was nearing orgasm, she thought suddenly of her parents, imagining them witnesses to her cocaine-enhanced ecstasies in the arms of a dope dealer—and she cried out all the louder. She pulled Jack harder against her, grated the thick hair on his chest against her breasts as his tongue probed deep into her mouth. His body trembled and shook in rhythmic spasms with her own.

When Jack slid off her, she gritted her teeth; but he caught her up in his arms and held her close against him. He lolled her head back to the quilt. Their bodies were slick with perspiration and glimmered damply in the glow of the candlelight. Andrea propped herself on one elbow and brushed strands of tangled hair out of her eyes. She placed the palm of her hand flat against Jack's chest and measured his breath and heartbeat as they grew slower and more regular. His head had fallen toward her, his filmed eyes closed, and he was asleep. Andrea kissed him gently on the mouth. She carefully withdrew her arm from beneath his head, and stood. She walked about the living room and carefully blew out the candles.

The last was a thick red column of molded paraffin in a blue saucer on the floor by the double doors. She bent down, cupped her hand about the flame—and froze. The doors were parted no more than an inch, and, through the opening, the flickering candlelight fell upon one bare foot. She picked up the saucer and slowly raised herself. Her eyes followed up the body of the naked man. The candle flame reflecting in his full-irised eyes, Dominic smiled at her from the darkness of the hallway.

22

Andrea wrote out for Jack her address at Wenham and the number of the hall phone in the dormitory. Without comment he thrust the scrap of paper into his back pocket. In return he gave her neither his surname nor his telephone number nor his address. While she was waiting for him downstairs, she surreptitiously jotted down the number of the phone, checked his last name on the mailbox beside the front door, and noted the house number. As they were driving away, she got the name of the street from the sign at the corner.

Andrea waited two weeks for his call. When she dialled the number of the Jamaica Plain house one Wednesday afternoon, she prepared herself with the excuse, in case he was hostile, that she only wanted to purchase some grass from him. Morgie, who had forgotten her, took a message and vowed on the soul of Amber St. Clair that she would deliver it to Jack. By the following Saturday Jack had not called, and Andrea was too piqued by her own foolishness to consider telephoning again.

Marsha had made only cursory inquiries about Andrea's evening with Jack, and Andrea, in her replies, had not been candid. "Andrea," said Marsha one evening, as they were crossing from one corner of the campus to the other, "don't you ever worry about getting into a situation you can't handle?"

"You mean Jack?"

"Yes."

Andrea glanced sharply at her friend. The autumn sun had slipped by degrees beneath the horizon and bathed the evening air with luminous gold. "What do you mean: *worry?* I handled that night just fine."

"Yes, you come back with two arms and two legs and everything in between right-side-up—but you haven't handled it all right since then. If he were going to call you again, he would have done it by now. But obviously he's not, so why don't you just forget about it?"

"I know," she said softly. "You're right. I'm being foolish."

Andrea knew full well she ought to have nothing more to do with Jack, should not even allow herself to want to see him again, but she could not drive him from her mind. She was mystified by him and his relationship to his four housemates. She could not ascribe their being together to deep-rooted loyalty when their treatment of one another was so openly caustic. She decided it must be a financial arrangement that kept them under the same roof. Whatever the reality of their coexistence, Andrea felt that a certain danger sparked about them—there was something very wrong in Jamaica Plain. Although she had not dared mention it to Marsha, it was that elusive sensation of danger that represented to Andrea what was exactly *right* about Jack. Through him she had discovered a circle of existence that had always been alien to her, one that fascinated her because it was opposed to all that she had ever known. It took for granted what she considered barbaric and chaotic and—what she had always considered worse —impolite.

As the two women walked along the leaf-scattered paths of the campus in the deepening twilight, Andrea now told Marsha everything that she had previously omitted from the narrative of her night in Jamaica Plain. She even told of Dominic's voyeurism, and Marsha was both disgusted and excited by this detail. Before they went down to dinner that evening, Andrea shared with Marsha the last of an ounce of grass Jack had slipped her as a parting gift.

When Andrea thought of sex, which wasn't infrequently, it was always Jack whose face and form were conjured in her mind. At Marsha's suggestion and by Marsha's management, Andrea went out several times with young men who were either juniors at Harvard or friends of Joshua's from Northeastern—but these had all been mindless, commonplace dates, and if the men had thought of sex as a possibility, Andrea had not. She did not care to be seduced by polite or clever conversation, a fine or at least an expensive dinner, a tentative pressing of thighs in an over-heated theater. All a good-looking man had to do to get Andrea LoPonti into bed was to make it clear that that was exactly where he wanted her; nothing else could work upon her. The men she went out with were not bold enough to approach her in that way, and she had not encouraged them to do so. The sexual experiences she had had the previous summer had been sufficient to form a pattern in her mind: Now only older men would do; she had no use for a man who was within five years her contemporary. Thus Andrea spent most of her evenings on campus, either working in the library or hanging out with Marsha. Occasionally she returned to Weston for the weekend, but these times with her parents were so strained that even Cosmo and Vittoria began to dread them.

She would have liked to visit the singles bars with Marsha, but Joshua now had moved off-campus, to a dreary little apartment on Huntingdon Avenue, and when Marsha went into Boston, it was there she ended up. Andrea was not willing to put up with the inferior company of a female companion who had nothing to offer but transportation.

On a Friday afternoon late in October, Jack appeared at Wordsworth Hall, unannounced, and had the receptionist ring Andrea on the in-house phone to say simply that "Jack's here."

Andrea found him standing by his motorcycle near the front steps of the hall. It was a crisp sunlit afternoon, and Jack's black leather jacket and pants contrasted sharply with the red-gold of the trees and the leaf-blanketed lawns. She moved down the flagstone walkway trying not to betray her anger or her elation. She took each step carefully and stopped several feet from him, her face a mask of cool reserve.

"What are you doing here?" she asked flatly, her voice matching perfectly her expression.

Jack narrowed his dark eyes against the bright sun. "I was thinking of you this morning," he said, "and since I had to be out this way this afternoon, I thought I'd drop by."

Andrea folded her arms beneath her breasts and turned her head so that a blond wave snapped over one shoulder. "Jack," she said, as if with hard-got patience, "I called you at the house last month and left a message. Now you show up like it was only yesterday . . ." Andrea stopped and softened. "Did Morgie forget to give you the message, she—"

"I got it," he said easily. "It's just that I never return calls."

"That's no excuse."

Jack rasped the heel of his boot on the lower step. He pushed away silently, stepped over to his bike, and swung angrily onto the thickly padded seat. "I was thinking about you and I just dropped by."

When his foot was raised to the starter, Andrea stepped over quickly. "I'm sorry," she said softly, and placed a hand on the cool leather of his arm. "I didn't mean to be a harpy."

"Is that like a bitch?" His smile grew until it was dazzling. "Today," he said, "I came prepared."

"What do you mean?"

"I brought an extra helmet. I thought we could go for a ride in the country. There's still a few leaves left."

Andrea did not hesitate. "Let me get my jacket. I'll be right down."

In her room, she could hear him revving his cycle. When she came down again, he tossed her the helmet. She strapped it on, climbed on behind, and pressed herself close against Jack's body. She wrapped her arms about his waist, and with both hands gripped his wide bicycle-chain belt. Jack released the brake and pulled the machine away from the curb.

"Where are we going?" she asked above the noise of the engine.

"Just ride around, out in the country. All right?"

"Yes."

They drove west from the college, to Natick, and then turned north up Route 126, through Cochituate, Wayland, and Concord. The day was bright and clean, and the wind in Andrea's face was exhilarating; the roads were familiar to her until they got past Concord, but it seemed as if she had never really looked at the scenery before—what an immense difference there was between the back seat of a Continental and the passenger seat of a Harley! Beyond Concord, as they neared Carlisle, Jack turned off onto a road that appeared untravelled and forlorn—the kind of road so minor and so little used that it probably was the last to be plowed in the winter snows, if it was plowed at all.

"Do you know this road?" shouted Andrea in his ear.

He shook his head, and slammed the cycle up to seventy so that they fairly flew. Hoary bare trees intertwined their fragile branches above the road, and startled animals hurtled themselves across their path. Andrea was suddenly frightened: they were travelling much too quickly. The narrow road wound, and they might suddenly come upon an automobile and be unable to stop or swerve. "Slow down, please!" she begged, and he did so immediately.

She was surprised that he did not take umbrage at her interference. Instead, he then proceeded playfully at a leisurely pace, running at so low a speed that, for the first time, Andrea could hear something besides the wind in her ears. She heard birds call.

They passed a few houses, but saw no one; there were a few brown pastures and paddocks and a few well-nourished animals —goats and cows mostly; and they passed a flock of noisy geese beside a small gray pool. But mostly they travelled through woodland: dense and gray and silent, almost all hardwood trees, with few evergreens.

Jack suddenly swerved off the road and into the forest, moving carefully but without reduced speed. Andrea clung to him, and shuddered when the toes of her boots scraped the ground. At last he slowed and pointed; Andrea leaned to her right and looked ahead. She saw their goal, a little nineteenth century graveyard probably no more than a hundred feet square, surrounded by a dilapidated cast iron fence, fast falling to ruin. The stones were moldy and awry; some had evidently been vandalized, but not recently. In one corner there was a small square mausoleum of gray stone. Just beyond flowed a rapid brook whose path was constantly interrupted by fallen tree trunks. Its sound rose immediately in the silence that followed the killing of the motorcycle engine.

"Why would they put a cemetery out here in the middle of nowhere?" Andrea wondered.

Jack shrugged. They climbed off the cycle, removed their helmets, and walked slowly through the graveyard. A large break in the fence saved them the trouble of negotiating the rusted gate. Andrea studied the names on the gravestones: "They're all from the same two families: everybody's named either Snow or Bent.

It was a private burying ground for the families. They probably owned the land."

Jack shrugged with disinterest.

They seated themselves on the cold slab of a raised grave. With her finger Andrea traced the almost obliterated letters carved into the stone. Jack lighted a joint and passed it to her. She leaned close against him, and he placed his arm tenderly around her shoulder. She wanted to ask whether they would get back to Wenham before dark, even if they left in the next fifteen minutes; but, thinking that such a question might dispel the romance of the moment, she only remarked, "It's very peaceful here, isn't it?"

She did not care anymore that he had not called her in so many weeks. Her ire had been dissipated in the thrill of the motorcycle journey. Leaning into his strong body, she thought of the times, alone in her bed at night, when her body had hungered for his closeness—and now she had it.

Clouds had gathered over them, and the wind increased and become chill. Dry leaves blew among the gravestones, and Andrea and Jack watched two black squirrels chase one another in and out of the broken door of the mausoleum. No cars passed on the road that was a hundred yards distant and only just visible in a couple of spots; the brook gurgled behind them.

Jack's hand dropped from her shoulder and pushed inside the back of her pants. His nails dug lightly into her buttocks. Andrea turned to face him; she folded her arms about his neck and drew his mouth down to hers. Jack kissed her hard and thrust his other hand underneath her sweater. His fingers and palm were rough and cold against her bare skin. He pulled her against him more tightly still, running his dry lips across her cheek and nuzzling his chin against her neck. His tongue darted wetly and warmly about her ear. Andrea groaned deeply, but when she felt his hardness pressing against her, she pulled back.

"We're in a cemetery!" she cried. "Anybody could—"

He unsnapped the metal fastener of her slacks and, lifting her slightly, turned her round and laid her down the length of the raised tomb of Maria Bent, beloved wife of Charles.

"Not here—" she whispered.

He covered her mouth with his hand, smiled at her, and

slipped his hand down the front of her slacks with one determined motion.

She turned her face away for just a moment, smiled slightly,
and gave in. She no longer felt the cold or the sharp wind or the
mossy stone beneath her. The heat and the selfish preoccupation
of desire flooded her. She touched his face, gently grazing her
thumb against his mouth. He licked the flat of her palm. She
pushed her slacks down herself, as Jack raised her sweater high
on her breast. Her hard nipples chafed against the soft wool. She
pressed her fingers against his ears as his tongue inched lower
down her stomach. She took in her breath sharply as he drew up
into a crouch between her legs.

Her new coral sweater was ruined that afternoon by the damp
moss and lichens that were ground into it on the raised tomb-
stone.

23

That afternoon in the rural cemetery set the pattern for their
relationship over the autumn. Jack would arrive at the dormitory
at odd times and never on the same days or evenings, and Andrea,
no matter what her plans or commitments, would go off with
him. Marsha was blunt in her estimation of the affair and still
tried to set up dates for Andrea, but Andrea would have none of
that. When she was not with Jack, she was perfectly content to sit
in the library or in her room, reading.

For Christmas of that sophomore year, Jack gave her a large
vial of amphetamines and an ounce of grass. She felt a little foolish when she presented him with an expensive navy blue sweater
she'd seen in the window of an exclusive men's shop on Newbury Street. She never saw him in it and was embarrassed when,
visiting his house one evening, she spotted it still in the gift box
on a shelf in his bedroom. Of the drugs Jack gave her, Andrea
kept only a little for herself. She gave half the grass to Marsha
and most of the speed to friends, who were thankful to have it
during the rigorous exam weeks following the Christmas vacation. From then on the girls on Andrea's floor had only to give her

their list of wants in the area of illegal substances, and she made arrangements with Jack to supply them. This was less a favor to her friends than a way to see Jack more often.

On a raw weekend in March Jack brought Andrea to Jamaica Plain. She allowed herself to be flattered that he had telephoned beforehand. It rained heavily both nights she was there, and she and Jack spent the time inside, either in the living room or in his bedroom, listening to music, talking idly, making love. The household was no less strange than on her first visit, but she was able to cope with it now. Sid was indifferent or rude, but Andrea now understood that indifference and rudeness were the entire range of his behavior. Rita turned out to be quiet and friendly, though in a rather distant fashion. Morgie read and chattered, often at the same time, and proudly exhibited to Andrea the great piles of pasteboard boxes in her room, each neatly and fully packed with paperback books. "After about twenty years I figure I'll be able to start through 'em all again," she said. Andrea ignored Dominic as best she could, but was careful never to be alone in a room with him; she always felt his lingering glance on her.

Andrea was no longer afraid of Jack: he was always kind to her, in his brusque way, and he had a certain simplicity that she thought she might as well label innocence as anything else. And the fact was, she had fallen in love with him. Despite what she told herself, or Marsha, about the affair's being no more than a physical indulgence, Andrea could not escape her feelings. But although she often amused herself thinking of what her parents' reaction would be were they ever introduced to Jack, Andrea knew that finally she would agree with their estimation of him: that he was no good, and certainly no good for her. Their affair would not last forever, but this bittersweet conviction only increased Andrea's affection for Jack. When they were in bed together and Jack had drifted into sleep pressed close to her, Andrea, cradled in his arms, felt safe. When bad dreams stirred him, she gently stroked his face and buried his sweating face against her breast.

Andrea tried to educate Jack into a greater emotional sensitivity; she thought that he would be a better person if he had a greater understanding of his own feelings—and of hers. So, frequently, after sex, Andrea would open her heart to him, in whispers revealing to him her fears and secrets, hoping that he would reciprocate. He never did. Once, when she was very stoned, Andrea even went so far as to tell to Jack her dreams of the blond girl who was herself and yet not herself—that nightmare she had found replicated in her waking life when she saw the photograph of the girl in Somerville and the nun at Nantasket Beach. This secondary confession was in lieu of telling him of her unknown parentage, which she had vowed to keep secret.

Jack's imagination was snagged. "Hey," he said, "you mean you've really got these doubles, and they look just like you?"

Andrea nodded.

"Let's find 'em!" said Jack. "I want to see 'em, I want to see somebody who looks just like you!"

Andrea laughed nervously. "No," she said, "I don't want to know where they are, I don't—"

"Don't you want to meet 'em, see if they sound like you and everything? I'll go find 'em and fuck 'em, and then I can tell you if they're *really* just like you."

Andrea laughed: "But that's the whole point: they're like me but they're nothing like me. One's this little frump whose father got murdered, and one's a goddamn nun!"

"Nuns got cunts," said Jack. "I could get it up for a nun!"

Andrea giggled.

"I want to find 'em," laughed Jack. "Maybe you got two sisters your parents never told you about."

"That's stupid!" snapped Andrea. "It's just coincidence. I'm a type and they're a type, and that's all there is to it. You're stoned out of your fucking mind."

"Yeah, but I'm always stoned. So where does this nun live?"

Andrea sighed. "Hingham. I saw her at Nantasket Beach, but I heard her say she was taking these kids back to Hingham. There must be a convent or a parochial school in Hingham, and she's there . . . Jack, let's just drop it—you're bringing me down."

Andrea was certain that this resolve on Jack's part was only the result of too much grass, so she was surprised when, the next morning, he insisted on their driving to Hingham and finding the school and convent where Andrea's double lived. At a gas station, Jack learned of the Convent of Saint Luke and the grammar school that was attached to it. They drove there and parked out front. Andrea tried to persuade Jack not to get out, but he complained, "How the hell will we know if she's here if we don't go see her? I'll just walk over to the playground and look around. I'm not going inside or anything."

"I wish you wouldn't, I—"

Two nuns had crossed the street from the church toward the school, in front of the jeep, but they had stopped on the sidewalk and were staring into the parked vehicle. Wonder was on their faces as they looked at Andrea.

Jack laughed. "Hey, they recognize you, they think you're that nun!"

He grinned at the nuns, then reached over and squeezed Andrea's breast. The two nuns turned quickly and hurried off.

"Jack!" cried Andrea. "You—"

He laughed loudly, turned on the ignition, and sped off down the street, blowing his horn and waving out the window at the two nuns, who had turned once again to watch them go.

Andrea knew that dope dealing on the scale that Jack and his roommates conducted it was far from innocent. It was a simple and safe operation, Jack had told her candidly. Sid drove to Providence twice a week in the jeep and picked up several pounds of marijuana that was sent up from San Antonio. It was brought back to Jamaica Plain and cleaned and packaged by Morgie and Rita; then Jack sold it to petty dealers, mostly in the southern suburbs of Boston. "There're lots of middle men in this business," he said, "and we're just one of 'em." Andrea said little about this, but she nervously eyed the clear vials of cocaine that stood openly on the mantelpieces of the house, or the small manila packets that Jack always shoved into his jeans just before he went out anywhere.

Early one Saturday morning, Andrea found herself in the chilly kitchen with Morgie. The oven had been turned on high and the door left open to help heat the room. Andrea prepared herself a cup of instant coffee, sat at the table, and picked up a packet of white powder that was not the consistency of cocaine.

"What's this?" she inquired idly.

Morgie didn't look up from her copy of *Harlem Hellions*. "Smack," she said.

"Smack? You mean heroin?"

Morgie nodded behind the book. "You know who gets hooked most around here?"

"Who?" said Andrea, not quite ready for such a topic so early in the day.

"Junior college teachers. Wouldn't think it, would you?"

"No," whispered Andrea.

"Somebody ought to write a book about it. Do you write?" she asked Andrea.

"Only term papers and like that," said Andrea uneasily. "Does Jack sell *much* smack?" she asked, hating the word.

"Now and then. The thing about smack is, it's reliable. You get a recession, you know, and people don't smoke as much grass, they can't afford it, but smack—people are addicts, you know, and they have to have it no matter what the economy's like."

Jack drove Andrea to Wenham that morning in the jeep. Just as she was climbing out, he slipped an ounce of grass, bound in a cellophane bag, into her jacket pocket.

"Thanks," she said. She paused with her hand on the door handle. She leaned inside and brushed her lips against his cheek. "Another wonderful time."

He smiled and gave a half-hearted shrug. "Sure."

24

On the first Saturday in April, Andrea and her mother were lunching at the exclusive Cafe Lananas on Newbury Street. Vittoria had telephoned that morning, and her invitation was insistent, although Andrea's assent was less than gracious. Over the top of the handwritten parchment menu, Andrea looked critically at the woman. Vittoria wore a brown tweed suit-dress with an off-white turtleneck sweater. Her black hair was fixed in a bun at the nape of her neck; and, like her daughter, she wore no makeup other than a slight blush to her cheeks, clear lip gloss, and the lightest brushing of pale mascara to emphasize her large eyes. Vittoria had dressed in a manner she knew would be approved by her daughter. She looked up suddenly: "Do you want to share a cold plate for appetizers?"

"Whatever," Andrea replied in a voice that expressed boredom and resignation.

"What were you thinking just then? You had the strangest look in your eyes!"

Andrea didn't immediately reply. Then she said briskly, "I was thinking about the Cape. Marsha and I would like to use the house in Yarmouthport next weekend."

"But it's all closed up. There's no heat and the electricity's been turned off. You'll freeze."

"It's not supposed to be cold this weekend. We'll use the wood-burning stove, or the fireplace maybe. If you don't want us to use the house, please just say so. I don't intend to argue the point."

Vittoria shifted uncomfortably in her chair. "I suppose you could use the house, as long as you promise that if you get uncomfortable, you'll check into a motel. Would you like me to drive you down on Friday, and Cosmo could pick you up on Sunday?"

"No. Marsha's driving her VW, if it doesn't die on her this week."

"Won't you be afraid all alone down there? No close neighbors off-season."

Andrea unfolded her napkin, smoothing it across her lap. "That's the point of it."

A silence fell between them. Andrea glanced at the other tables in the restaurant, she peered through the front windows at the sidewalk, she examined the ceiling—she looked in every direction but her mother's. Vittoria cleared her throat and spoke: "You may be a woman in everyone else's eyes, Andrea, but I still see my pretty little girl." Vittoria paused while the waiter took their order. "You were never a rebellious child," she continued. "Sometimes difficult, of course, but Cosmo and I knew that very smart children are always a little difficult. You never really made us unhappy, Andrea, not for a moment of our lives, not until that day you . . . you got so upset."

"Don't bring it up. I don't intend to go through it again."

"If I could believe you had forgiven us—forgiven us for loving you so much—I'd never mention it again in my life," said Vittoria earnestly. She reached affectionately toward the earlobe that held the ruby chip.

For the first time that day, Andrea looked directly into her mother's eyes. "It's not that I don't want to forgive you," she said grimly. "Of course I do. It's just that I *can't* forgive you . . ."

Vittoria withdrew her hand.

"Your father and I have a surprise for you," she whispered. "I'm not supposed to tell because it's your birthday present, and—"

"I just had a birthday."

"I mean your next one. The Antiquities Society is sponsoring a tour of Europe this summer—July and August, six countries. Well . . ." Vittoria paused.

"What are you trying to say?"

"We thought it would be a good idea if you went to Europe with the group. It's a charter and the price is right and the itinerary is just marvelous. We signed you up, dear. An early birthday gift, or Christmas, or Halloween, or *something*. Some of the members of the Society are a little stuffy, but you and Marsha—"

"Marsha?"

"That's the other part. Marsha's going too. I asked the Libermans if they wanted to send Marsha, and they said of course, so I pulled a few strings and got her included. We thought you might be lonely all by yourself—"

"On a tour, you mean."

"Well, darling, you will probably be the youngest members."

Jack. The name loomed in Andrea's mind, unconnected with any image.

"Maybe we shouldn't have gone ahead with this without asking first, but— Oh, Andrea," cried her mother, "please don't say you don't want to go!"

Andrea thought again, and a vivid but static image of Jack was seared across the back of her eyes. "I didn't expect this," she said.

"Of course not! That's what makes it a surprise. We had already planned to give you a trip when you graduate, but this was too good to pass up. After lunch would you like to go back to that shop on the corner of Clarendon? I think that salmon blouse would look nice on you. And the kelly green sweater for Marsha. Would you like that?"

"Yes," said Andrea absently. "I suppose I'll need a whole new wardrobe for the trip."

"Oh, yes. Keep June free for shopping and shots and everything," Vittoria said giddily. "You should apply for your passport tomorrow, before the rush. You and Marsha will have lots to talk about while you're in Yarmouthport."

"Yes, I know we will."

Mist hung in opalescent veils across Route 6A as they drove toward Yarmouthport early Saturday morning. The air was sharp and cold and smelled of rain. Andrea sighed and scooted farther down in the seat, pressing her knees against the dash. From her bag she took a cigarette and lighted it, flipping the match out the slightly cracked window. The smoke swirled lazily from her mouth and was indistinguishable from the mist beyond the windshield of the jeep.

"Lousy weather," Jack said.

"Ummmm . . ." Andrea replied. "I'm sick of rain. This whole winter's been lousy with rain."

Jack shrugged one shoulder as he shifted gears and swung off the exit ramp for Yarmouthport. The wheels of the jeep hummed evenly. There was little traffic, and he pushed his foot heavily on the accelerator. "It'll be summer soon and you can lay out on a beach the whole fucking day."

Yeah, she thought. *On the Riviera.*

Andrea had not yet told him of her parents' gift, hesitating because she was not certain how he would react. It was not his anger or disappointment she feared—it was his indifference. She had engineered this weekend for them at the Cape simply to be alone with him out of the house in Jamaica Plain. She hoped this time would be so romantic that when she did tell him of the European journey, he would feel regret. She'd like him to ask her not to go. Andrea suspected that, in Jack's case, absence only made the heart grow farther away.

That night, they ate at a small restaurant in Hyannis and

returned late to the beach house. Jack laid a fire in the hearth, and they smoked two joints and snorted four lines of cocaine. They spread several blankets and quilts on the rough-planked floor and made heated love. Andrea had never been so ardent in her love-making and did not restrain her cries. When they finished, she lay on her back, her head resting in the crook of Jack's arm. The firelight played over their sweat-gleaming bodies, and, thinking of the cold that prevailed in the entire house except for the spot where they were just now, Andrea snuggled closer. She told Jack that she would not be seeing him that summer and why. He said nothing, and she was wretched.

She told him she loved him. She wept and turned her face against his chest. Jack remained silent, his body stiffening beneath her weight. Andrea continued to talk, knowing she should stop, but unable to. Finally her voice trailed off. Jack held her until she stopped shaking and the tears subsided. In a thick voice she asked if he loved her.

Jack eased her away and sat up. He stabbed his cigarette out and shoved the ashtray roughly away. The heavy oval of glass slid across the blanket and cracked against the hearth. He stood and moved into the cold shadows where their clothing was heaped by the wicker sofa.

He picked up Andrea's blouse and tossed it to her. "I'll douse the fire while you're getting your things together," he said shortly.

"What?" Andrea sat up, crossing her arms around her knees, feeling the room's chill. "Didn't . . . didn't you hear what I said?"

"Hard to miss."

Her voice was a frightened whisper: "I said I *love* you, Jack. I've never said that—"

"I heard you," he said in a hard voice, roughly yanking up the zipper of his jeans.

Andrea watched as he pulled on his boots and his leather jacket. His heels resounded against the hollow floorboards as he walked away from her. "I'll get the jeep warmed up and then I'll take care of the fire. Just be ready to go."

The door slammed behind him, rattling the glass panes. It wasn't until Andrea heard the engine of the jeep roar to life that she covered her face and began once more to weep.

★

Jack drove her back to Wenham in strained silence. When they pulled up to the dorm, Andrea leaned over to embrace him, but he pushed her back without a word. She did not leave her room in Wordsworth Hall for two days and ate only when Marsha brought her food from the vending machines in the lobby. Andrea had not the emotional strength to relate to her friend what had happened at the Cape house. Marsha stayed in the room with her, reading and saying little and avoiding any reference to Jack. On the third day Marsha insisted that Andrea leave her room, and took her into the village to a double-feature of *Dracula's Dog* and *Nocturna, Granddaughter of Dracula*. The absurdity of the films put Andrea into a better mood, and when they left the theatre, she suggested they drive over the town line to the nearest pub. Sitting in a back booth, they each consumed four large frosted mugs of beer, and talked. After her second cheeseburger, Andrea confessed Jack's coarse treatment of her. Marsha nodded sympathetically through a near-drunken haze, her face screwed into devout understanding.

"I shouldn't have pushed it. I shouldn't have—"

"Bullshit," said Marsha. "You did exactly what you felt like doing and it was right. You didn't do anything wrong. Just what I would have done." She leaned far across the table. "You're better off rid of him now, and by the middle of next week you'll know it too."

"I know it now."

"First time I saw that man I could have told you he's not the kind you fall in love with, Andrea."

"Well then, what do you do with a man like Jack?"

"Just what he did with you: fuck him and have a good time, and that's it."

"Oh, Marsha!"

"It's true. He had no right not to at least talk it out with you, let you down easy." Marsha hiccuped and sat back. "No matter how good-looking he is or how good he is in the sheets, he's just a bum. Personally, I think he's only read one book in his life—the one published by Ma Bell, and he gave *that* up when he heard about four-one-one." Marsha lurched back across the table. "If it'd been me on the Cape with him and he pulled that stunt, he'd be six feet under and I'd be in Framingham. Oh God, Andrea, here we are: two young beautiful women, both jilted and both drunk!"

"Both? You mean Joshua—"

Marsha nodded: "That circumcised asshole—"

"What happened?! When?!"

"Dumped me—like his goddamn laundry that I used to do for him every Sunday. I get an eight hundred on my math on the college boards, and I'm doing laundry every Sunday morning for this creep who can't light a match without reading the instructions! Last weekend, probably just as Jack Jerk was pulling his number, Joshua laid it on. Said he needed to 'expand his horizons' or 'plow new fields' or something. The only new field he wants to plow is this nasty-smelling little blonde who lives in his apartment building. You ought to see her, Andrea—all teeth and no tits. But real Aryan. I got plunged for a shiksa."

"That's awful," giggled Andrea. "That's just awful," she said in a serious voice.

"No no," cried Marsha, holding up her hand in mock solemnity: "I don't want sympathy from you. My little crisis with Joshua is nothing compared to your trauma in breaking up with the leather fiend / dope dealer / nursery school dropout!"

"Well, after this," nodded Andrea, "finals will be a breeze."

"They'd better be. In six weeks, we'll be in Paris—ever get fucked by a Frenchman? It's great. In seven weeks, we'll be in Rome—ever get fucked by an Italian? It's great. In eight weeks, we'll—"

Last call was announced, and Marsha lost her place.

25

Andrea and Marsha had no difficulty in meeting men abroad. Andrea knew French and Italian, and Marsha had French and German. The two young women dutifully spent their bleary-eyed mornings contemplating monuments, museums, and broken statuary. Afternoons were always reserved for specialized sightseeing, which, translated, meant shopping, so the two young women were not put to the trouble of accounting for themselves. In the evening it was usually easy enough to partake of the table d'hote dinner at the hotel, but Andrea and Marsha were rarely persuaded to join a group for the theatre or concert. But after carrying out the obligations they thought necessary for the maintenance of their reputations—the women they travelled with being, after all, quite nice—Andrea and Marsha felt themselves free to explore.

Their lead line to exploration was a European bar guide that Joanna Liberman had recommended. In Italy they found one man better looking than the next, and here they were fabulously courted. In Germany Marsha spent three days with a computer engineer who had a rare collection of Dresden china, telling the leader of the tour that she had to make a spiritual pilgrimage to Dachau. In Munich Andrea one evening had the choice between a thin young man dressed in black leather and a young businessman who was handsome but slightly corpulent; remembering Jack, she chose the businessman. In Amsterdam she went out with a man who taught music theory at the university, and Marsha dated a man who took her to every live sex show in town. In England they found the men pallid or uptight or both, and glutted themselves with the theatre and pub-crawling. During a long weekend in Zurich Andrea received a proposal of marriage from a handsome but overzealous dealer in Oriental art. She tactfully declined the proposal, but remained with the man until it was time to proceed to Paris. By the end of August, when they boarded the plane at Orly, each young woman was struggling with three more pieces of luggage than she had come with.

The previous year at Wenham Andrea had declared History & Literature her joint major, and in her junior year she narrowed her study to that of the period between the world wars in France, Belgium, and Italy. Her upperclassman status provided a single room, directly adjoining Marsha's, on a quiet end of the top floor of Wordsworth Hall. For Christmas that year her parents gave Andrea a bright red Trans-Am and, blushing for the opulence of the gift, said they were only being selfish in the hope that Andrea would visit them more often than previously—but she did not.

Often Andrea and Marsha went into Boston to the bars, and they no longer bothered to wait for the weekend. On these occasions it was normal that one or both did not return that night to the dorm. Whenever Joanna was away for a weekend, the two women took over her Mount Vernon Street flat—and were so blasé about the whole thing that they often found time to get a little schoolwork done there.

In February of that third year at Wenham, at a sleek party in a sleek apartment in Back Bay, Andrea was introduced to a very handsome young man, twenty-six years old with wavy black hair and a thick black moustache, who was an advertising representative for TWA. She became infatuated with him, and he with her, but his frequent absences from the city—although they served to lengthen the term of the affair to the end of the spring—prevented the relationship from taking on the serious character it might otherwise have obtained.

In June she and Marsha returned to Europe, but this time on their own and again at their parents' expense. They visited Germany, Switzerland, and Italy. From their previous year's itinerary they dropped England, France, and Holland, where the men had been dull. They added Greece, of whose male population they had heard much that was interesting. They were not disappointed.

In Zurich the art dealer renewed his proposal, and Andrea again respectfully declined; but she stayed with him two and a half weeks to help him over his frustration. There was a second bedroom for Marsha. In August Marsha met and fell hopelessly in love with a young Greek who had gone to school at Oberlin and was now serving as a tour guide on the Acropolis. He, however, turned out to be more interested in another male guide than in either of the two young women, and Andrea nursed her friend back to mental health during a week on Crete. They did not return to the States until a few days before the opening of school.

Wenham seemed a little draggy as they began their fourth year there, and both were overwhelmed with the sense of *I've been here before*. They even kept their rooms from the previous year, and the contemplation of senior theses was a thrill they might easily have done without. Marsha had tentatively decided to go on to graduate school in mathematics, and Andrea had tentatively decided not to—but they were intent on remaining together after graduation and had already quizzed Joanna on the availability and price of apartments on Beacon Hill.

Andrea was a woman now. She had never been immature, and two summers in Europe—where men had treated her as a fully independent entity—had "finished" her nicely. The short-term, but intense affairs and repeated proposals of marriage had provided her with a certain self-confidence not shared by Wenham women who had spent their summers interning at publishing houses or lying on the beaches of Maine and South Carolina.

Then, on the evening before Andrea was to return to Weston for the Thanksgiving holidays, Marsha appeared at the door of Andrea's room with an incredulous smile on her face.

"There's a call for you—guess who's downstairs?"

Andrea shook her head: "I've no idea. Gloria Vanderbilt? Betty Grable's ghost?"

"That's three guesses. Nope. It's Jack Jerkoff."

It was Andrea's turn to look incredulous. Then both women laughed.

"God," said Andrea, "that's ballsy."

"So," said Marsha, "what's it going to be after all this time? Something between castration and a pardon signed by the governor, I suppose."

Andrea lit a cigarette and moved to the window. It was slightly open to counteract a too zealous radiator. "What in the world would possess him to come back here now? Maybe I owe him for some grass."

"Probably he's horny. He probably thinks you're the same easy lay you were two years ago."

Andrea laughed. "Strike *easy*, read *naive*. God, that was a long time ago, wasn't it! Seems as if I must have had pigtails and freckles."

It had been a year and a half since she had last seen Jack. In the months immediately succeeding their breakup she had thought of him with anger and shame. Now she only wondered that she had ever allowed herself to become involved with such a man. Yet it was odd that he was still important in her imagination—he had become part of her personal mythology—it was his face she often conjured at orgasm. The image of his sweaty, straining face and body taut with desire had never left her, although now it was quite divorced from what she remembered of Jack the man. In her subconscious, Andrea had preserved the physical husk of the man and simply discarded the rotten interior. Whenever she found herself making love with an uninspired and uninspiring partner, she turned her thoughts to Jack and got through it. As soon as he had served his purpose in this way, Jack evaporated, and did not reappear until he was needed again.

"Andrea!"

She turned from the window.

"Well you can't just leave him down there. Are you going to talk to him or not?"

"Why not?" she shrugged. "What harm can it do? Besides, I want to know if he's lost his looks yet or not."

He hadn't. He stood beneath the yellow light of the vestibule, smoking a cigarette. The lines in his face were more pronounced, but Andrea thought that these gave him a bit of character that he'd lacked before—or perhaps it was just that she was even more accustomed now to older men.

Jack smiled, his eyes bright and liquid. Seeing how the girl on reception hung forward over the desk, ogling him, Andrea said, "Let's go outside." She pushed open the door, and Jack stepped out behind her.

He leaned against the brick balustrade and flicked his cigarette across the dark lawn, leaving a little arc of orange sparks in the crisp night air. He jerked his head about and looked at Andrea. In the half-light his expression was soft, and she could read nothing in it.

"You're flying," she said finally, and with evident disapproval.

Jack shrugged. "A little, not much. Want to check my arm for tracks?"

Andrea said nothing. She was trying to determine what she felt, but in fact she felt nothing at all.

"It's been a long time," said Jack, a little uncomfortably.

"I guess it has."

"More'n a year."

"More than 'more than a year.'"

"You been all right? You look great."

"I've been fine. Jack, what do you want?"

"I have to see some friends in Dedham, and I thought that as long as I was in the neighborhood . . ."

"You've played this tape before."

"That was a long time ago."

"'More'n a year,'" she said, but the mockery was spiritless. She leaned against the balustrade beside him and crossed her arms. "You remember my friend Marsha?"

"No."

"It doesn't matter, but Marsha says that a woman doesn't fall in love with a man like you."

"Yeah? Is that what Marsha says?"

"Yeah, that's what she says."

His eyes were playful again as he gazed at her. Andrea realized that the picture she had kept of Jack in her mind had become distorted—she had forgotten how darkly handsome he was.

"So what do you do with a man like me?"

"You ball him and have a good time."

Jack laughed. "Marsha knows what she's talking about."

"I guess so."

Jack slid his arm about her waist. "I think we could work that in—if you want to. No strings, just a good time."

Andrea laughed. "You are arrogant."

He nodded. "You can say no. Your decision. It'd be nice for old times' sake." He pulled her close, and Andrea pulled back; his hand was hot against her hip, and it slid over her buttocks. "I've thought about it lots of times."

"It?"

"You." He smiled easily. "Hey listen, why don't you take a ride down to Dedham with me to my friends' place? It's a sort of pre-Thanksgiving celebration. I won't be there long. Then you can decide if you want to see any more of me tonight. I'll bring you right back here. You'll be back here by ten o'clock, I promise."

Andrea raised her brows skeptically. Jack touched his hand to his breast. "Promise," he whispered.

"You're out of your mind," she whispered.

"Oh sure, I know it," he replied. "But so are you."

"Yeah, I guess I am. I think about it too, every now and again," she added, with sarcasm. She looked across the lawn to the street, "isn't a little cold for the cycle?"

26

Jack's friends lived in a small two-story house in a wooded area between the Route 128 Dedham exit and the Dedham Country and Polo Club. Jack had wanted to drive down Route 128, but Andrea begged him not to: it was too large a highway, and at the speeds he would be travelling, she was certain she would arrive frozen. Jack acquiesced, and they travelled along secondary roads; but Andrea was still frozen.

Andrea hopped off the Harley at the end of the driveway, and Jack spun the cycle farther up and leaned it against a small shed. The Jamaica Plain jeep was parked beneath a great oak. Another vehicle, a rust-damaged Buick, was in the curve of the gravel drive near the front entrance of the house. The tires had been removed, and the car was supported by cinder blocks.

The house itself was little more than a cottage; probably it had been a summer home to some Beacon Hill family at the turn of the century. There was a kind of opulent rusticity in the design. Two sagging wooden steps led up to the front door. The flanking windows were lighted behind drawn manila shades. By this dim illumination, Andrea could see that the porch badly wanted painting and that the house itself was covered in the cheapest kind of aluminum siding. Three green plastic trash bags, their contents spilling out of split seams, were piled to one side. Andrea was certain that Jack had come here only on a drug run, and that at most they would spend an hour here; she hoped most of that hour would be ticked off in one of the upstairs bedrooms. She looked over at him. *My holiday gift to myself*, she thought. It was curiosity that had brought her—curiosity to know what sex would be like with him after so long a time. Emotionally, she felt nothing for the man, she was certain of that—but she wondered how her body would respond to him now.

She stood on the front porch and turned to face the road. No other habitation was visible, and the lone street lamp was masked by an intervening cedar. The forest of gnarled, bare trees with the cold wind singing through the brittle branches made her think that she would never be comfortable or warm again. The moonlight was pale and frigid. Behind her and the house, she could just make out the rumble of traffic on distant Route 128.

They had smoked a joint outside Wordsworth Hall before taking off, and Andrea felt its effects course through her body. She was glad to be bolstered against this evening and this place by some kind of drug.

"Come on," said Jack. He had pushed the door open and was silhouetted by garish white light. Andrea stepped inside behind him.

The interior of the house was worse than she had expected. An exposed ceiling fixture with two hundred-watt bulbs showed a multitude of cracks and chips in the mint green walls of the long narrow entry way. At the far end, a cheap beaded curtain was hung before the enclosed a stairway leading to the second floor. Jack preceded her into the small living room just to the right.

Here Rita and Sid sat cross-legged on the bare linoleum floor before a large space heater, while Morgie and Dominic were sprawled at opposite ends of a daybed shoved into one corner. On a sagging sofa against the opposite wall lay a man and woman whom Andrea didn't know. Their heads were propped against either end, and their feet shoved in one another's faces. The radio played New Wave.

Jack threw himself onto the daybed between Morgie and Dominic. Now there was nowhere for Andrea to sit.

"Marty and Donna-Louise," said Jack, pointing to the sofa.

They were four couples in that room, Andrea suddenly saw, and she was made uneasy by the thought that perhaps she had been selected as Jack's date for an orgy.

"Good evening, all," said Andrea. Marty picked up Donna-Louise's feet and waved them; and this did for greeting for both.

Andrea seated herself next to Rita and tried to warm herself at the heater; but at once she was too hot on one side, and chilled to her spine at her back. She tried to make out the conversation behind her, but it was low and inarticulate. Sid ignored her altogether, but Rita stirred herself to make brief conversation, asking how Andrea had been and what she had been doing. Andrea made her replies as brief as possible. Dominic gave her the once-over, and Morgie grinned and winked.

Out of the corner of her eye she watched Jack rise, go over to the sofa, and drop on Donna-Louise's crotch two handfuls of manila packets secured with thick rubber bands.

"This is more than last time," said Marty.

"I know. You got rid of the last so quick, I thought you could do with more. Might save me a trip."

"You're always welcome here," replied the kind host.

"How long will it take you to get rid of this?"

"You can come again a week from Friday."

"That long?"

"Look," said Donna-Louise, "it's the holiday, everybody goes home to fucking Mommy."

"They won't be back till Monday," said Marty.

"You mean it's college students buying heroin?" asked Andrea with an incredulous laugh.

Rita touched Andrea's thigh, and shook her head. "Shhh!" she said.

"Yeah, shut up, you stupid bitch!" growled Sid.

"Fuck you," shrugged Andrea.

"Who the fuck is that creepola?" cried Donna-Louise, pointing savagely at Andrea.

"I hope at least she's a good fuck," said Marty.

"She is," said Jack casually, and Andrea flushed with anger. "Did you get rid of everything I brought you last week?"

Marty nodded, and Donna-Louise reached down the front of her pants and drew out a thick stack of bills, folded in half and secured with a large paper clip.

She gave it to Jack, who shoved it into the front pocket of his jeans.

"That stuff you brought me Thursday—"

"Forty-eight grams," said Jack.

"Yeah, I got rid of that in forty-eight hours, not bad, and they called me, I didn't have to call them."

Andrea stood. She was suddenly weak, and thought the radiating dry heat of the gas flame was making her ill. "Where's the bathroom?" she asked, of no one in particular.

"Oh God, she's gonna throw up!" cried Donna-Louise. "Point it away from me!" she screamed.

"You okay?" said Jack.

"It's upstairs," said Marty, "on your right."

Andrea hurried through the beaded curtain and took the stairs two at a time to the second floor. She slapped at the walls with the palms of her hands as she climbed. At the top she found the bathroom door and fumbled for the switch on the outside; she couldn't find it, and went on inside.

She eased the door shut, crossed to the window, unlatched it and pulled it creakily up. She stuck her head out and breathed deeply. From here she could see Route 128 in the distance, glowing slightly in the aggregate illumination of so many car headlights. The moon was dimmed by thin clouds. Below her was a slanting roof that shielded a small open porch that ran along the side of the cottage. Pieces of broken beer bottles littered it; she wondered what must have been the condition of the inhabitants of this house to have tossed beer bottles out the windows: then it occurred to her that in summer this would do very well for a sunroof in a yard that was completely shaded. She looked out over the yard, but could see only a slice of the gravelled driveway and the right rear fender of the Buick. Then, hearing a noise, she leaned farther out the window. She glanced up the drive, and froze.

Two cars were parked at the end of the gravel drive. Across the side of one of them she could see "911 Police Dedham" painted in reflective silver. Andrea's body seemed suddenly damp with perspiration. She drew back into the dark bathroom. The radio station downstairs had been changed, and loud rock music blared outside the closed door. The monotonous beat shook the bathroom floor, and Andrea felt so unsteady she was afraid she would collapse.

She went back to the window and peered out again. Two policemen with drawn guns trotted noiselessly in the grass along the side of the driveway. Andrea jerked her head back in, and they passed along toward the back of the house without looking up. She jumped up onto the low sill of the window and slipped out onto the roof, taking care not to step on the shards of colored glass. She crouched in the shadow of the eaves and stared uneasily at the sky: in a few moments the moon would come out from behind the clouds. She waited painfully, and watched three more policemen pass quickly from the parked cars to the front of the house; they stationed themselves well out of her sight.

She waited. The moon came out from behind the clouds, and she watched with horror as the sleeves of her white shirt captured the moonlight and flung it back; fortunately no policeman was near to catch its glimmer.

There was suddenly the sound of splintering wood from the back of the house, and the breaking of glass in the front. The women downstairs screamed, and the men shouted curses.

Andrea ran to the edge of the roof and leapt to the ground; she fell sprawling on her hands and knees. Without glancing back, and half expecting to be shot at, she raised herself and ran blindly into the forest, picking her way from one space of blackness to the next, always avoiding the moonlight.

She ran until her legs ached and she was forced to pause to calm the beating of her heart. She wiped the perspiration from her forehead, then saw that she had badly scraped her left hand; it was bloody. She crouched behind a holly bush and looked toward the house. She could no longer see the lights, but she heard voices, strident and unintelligible. She waited to hear the sound of the car doors slamming, but it did not come.

She realized then that the inhabitants of the house, who had no reason to protect her, would tell the police that she was upstairs; they would see the open window and figure out that she must have escaped into the forest. They would soon be after her. She turned and ran toward the dim noise of traffic on Route 128, desperately praying that she would be able to hitch a ride before the police captured her. With each pounding step she cursed Jack and her own stupidity.

27

When Andrea fled from the house in Dedham and made her way to Route 128, she clambered over the chain-link fence and climbed up the embankment. She ran along the shoulder of the highway, shuddering as each of several passing cars blew its horn at her. At last she took up a station beneath a tungsten light. She stuck out her thumb and attempted a stance of insouciance. She got a ride almost immediately, with a black-bearded man about thirty wearing much-faded jeans and a black leather jacket. "I don't usually pick people up," he said in a surprisingly soft and cultured voice, "because one hears stories . . . But I saw you out there alone, and at this hour I thought it might be best if *I* picked you up, rather than someone else, if you know what I mean."

Andrea nodded dumbly and stared down at her hands. They looked black, and she suddenly realized that they were scratched and bloody. She thrust them into her pockets.

"Thank you," she faltered.

"Where are you going?"

"I don't know," she answered automatically.

The man suddenly lifted his foot from the accelerator. "Wait a minute—" he began, and Andrea saw that she had alarmed him.

"Boston," she said quickly, "I'm going to Boston."

"Where in Boston?"

"Downtown. The Hill."

He nodded, reassured. "All right. I'm going to Copley Square. The bars'll be hot tonight."

Andrea continued to talk to the man. The little pretense of conviviality helped to remove her mind from the terrifying events that had just taken place. Every minute in the car, every word that she spoke and every word she attended to, took her farther from Jack and Sid and Morgie and Dominic and Rita and Marty and Donna-Louise—and the police.

She was let off at the corner of Charles and Beacon Streets and thanked the man profusely for the ride. She was indeed very grateful to him, for she had realized that she might easily have been not so fortunate in hitchhiking, When the man's car was out of sight, Andrea lingered near the Arlington entrance to the deserted and dark Public Garden. The Trailways bus station was no longer located just two blocks away, but, in a recent wave of urban redevelopment, had been relocated to South Station Terminal. Andrea glanced at a clock and saw that even with a fast taxi, she would never catch the last bus of the night that went near the college.

She had several dimes in her pocket, and from a telephone booth outside the Ritz she dialed Joanna Liberman's number. There was no answer. She called Wordsworth Hall, but was told that Marsha had already left for the holidays; calling the Liberman's house, she discovered that Marsha hadn't arrived there yet either. There was no message that she could leave that wouldn't alert Marsha's mother to something's being wrong. Andrea wondered if she shouldn't take the risk of telephoning her parents, making up some story about having come to Boston with Marsha, being separated and lost—but decided that this would require more substantial detailing than she was prepared to give just now. Having narrowly escaped arrest on major drug charges, Andrea didn't yet feel herself up to lying convincingly to her parents.

She went into a garishly lighted coffee shop and nursed a cup of coffee for twenty minutes, trying to decide what to do with herself. The man who had picked her up on Route 128 had said that the bars would be hot tonight; perhaps she ought simply run over to the Brimmer House and hope to get asked home by someone. She had twelve dollars in her pocket; that was certainly not enough for a taxi back to the college, and the first bus wouldn't leave until seven the next morning.

She went to the ladies' room, brushed her hair, straightened her clothing, and hurried out of the coffee shop, headed for the Brimmer House. It was already one o'clock; the bar would close at two, and so she had little time. She felt soiled, going so coldly about the process of offering her body to practically any man who looked presentable. But she had no relish for waking her parents and having them make the half-hour drive into Boston;

and if she did call, where would she wait for them once the bars had closed?

Andrea blamed only herself for her predicament. She'd been a fool to climb onto the back of Jack's motorcycle, she'd been a fool to have spoken to him at all. Of all that had happened that evening, she could be glad of only one thing: that she had not removed her jacket in the house—for she would be very cold right now without it. And, it suddenly occurred to her, the police would have found out her identity by the label in the lining. She wondered anew at the narrowness of her escape. Two summers of adventure in Europe had not prepared her for the excitement of climbing out windows and running through forests to avoid arrest; and, she reflected, she would be just as pleased not to have had the experience at all.

The Brimmer House was quiet on the night before a holiday. Of the dozen men there, most were already partnered, and all were drunk. She ordered a scotch, double on the rocks. She sipped slowly and looked around. The men who noticed her quickly looked away, uninterested.

Andrea went into the ladies' room, and stared dismayed into the mirror at her appearance. She washed her face clean of makeup and trusted to the natural look through her second drink.

Nothing came of the natural look, and last call was announced. Andrea didn't want to waste the little money she had left on a third drink—most would be needed for the bus ticket—and no one offered to buy her one. She was one of the last seven persons in the bar; no one appeared interested in her. She ate the ice in her glass, and at five minutes before two she walked, angrily and a little unsteadily, out onto the street.

Outside the Brimmer House, several men and women lingered sheepishly. Andrea came upon a tall, slender man in a light tan jacket, not drunk at all, leaning against an MG. He glanced at her up and down. She returned the gaze.

"Need a ride?" he said softly, mockingly.

Andrea shrugged, with a smile.

"Going anywhere particular?"

She shook her head no.

"That's good," he said, "because I don't have a car."

*

Andrea got back to college safely and, when she next talked to Marsha, told her friend merely that she had returned very late that night, that she had not slept with Jack, and had no intention of seeing him again ever. She went home on Wednesday, and although her parents commented on her nervousness, she said it was merely the result of overwork. As the days passed, Andrea thought less and less of Jack and his friends. She supposed that they had been arrested, but whether they were out on bail she had no idea. There had been a notice of the raid in the papers, and she read with interest that Rita and Dominic had both given false names to the police. But she had no idea what had become of them: possibly they were all in jail. Suburban police didn't take kindly to heroin, she knew. Evidently they hadn't betrayed her, for the police never appeared, and Andrea allowed herself the luxury of believing that they never would. And even if they did, what could happen? Andrea would simply deny having been there, and there was no proof of her presence.

Over the next few weeks, Andrea studied hard. Her most important project of the semester was due on December twenty-second, a literary and sociological study of Père la Chaise Cemetery in Paris, which she and Marsha had visited two years before. She completed it fully a week in advance of that deadline, and when she handed it in, she returned to her dormitory with an enormous sense of relief and freedom.

That day in her dormitory mailbox she found a short note from her mother explaining that she and Cosmo would be travelling to Quebec City on the day after Christmas and staying until New Year's Eve. Cosmo was to attend a contractors' conference there. There was a terseness about the wording of the note that pained Andrea, but she realized that her mother was only mirroring the coldness that Andrea had displayed toward her parents in the past several months.

In one searing moment Andrea realized her true motive in punishing her parents with distance and cruel words. It was not that they had lied to her—it had nothing to do with them at all. Andrea was merely ashamed at having been the product of unknown parents, parents who had abandoned her: parents who might well have been vulgar, diseased, criminal, or achingly poor.

The revelation that she had not been borne in Vittoria LoPonti's womb had cast Andrea adrift, but instead of falling back on her adoptive parents for their support, she had repudiated them. Now she saw that she was in danger of losing them altogether.

She determined not to let that happen.

Andrea returned to Weston two days before Christmas. There were parties for Vittoria and Cosmo to attend, and Andrea spent the days shopping or in Marsha's company. Andrea was polite, but still reserved; she needed time to observe her parents, and sort out her real feelings. In watching them, Andrea saw to what extent they had always loved her; loved her now. And she saw what pain she had caused them.

On Christmas morning Vittoria and Cosmo were astounded when Andrea appeared at the top of the stairs, straightening the cuffs of her sweater, just when they were about to leave for morning mass. "May I come too?" she asked.

She sat between them and clasped their hands during the prayers. The family sang out of one hymnal. Nothing had to be said.

When they returned to the house, Andrea distributed the gifts, insisting that her parents open first their gifts from her. Vittoria gasped dramatically when she turned aside the paper inside the box, which contained a finely wrought gold bracelet. "Wait, Mother," said Andrea, when her mother started to snap it on her wrist, "look inside, there's an inscription."

"'With a Daughter's Love,'" whispered Vittoria, and leaned far forward to embrace her daughter. "Andrea, I'll never take it off again."

Cosmo opened his gift with agonizing slowness, carefully preserving the ribbon, the paper, and the tissue inside; this was a deliberate tease of both his wife and his daughter. When at last he pulled the chased and enamelled dagger from the box, however, it was with genuine admiration. He took Andrea to task for spending so much money on him, but he blushed with pride over the gift. He was so proud of it, he said, he would never use it once in his life.

"No, Daddy!" laughed Andrea, "I bought it for you to open all your mail with. I *want* you to use it!"

"Well, don't you want to see what Santa Claus brought you this year?" said Vittoria. "Open your presents, Andrea."

There were fifteen of them, in small boxes and large, each beautifully wrapped by Cosmo. As Andrea took apart the first, Cosmo gathered up the ribbon, paper, and decorations as she discarded them. In this, the largest of the boxes, and surprisingly light, she was startled to find nothing but tissue paper—there was no gift inside.

Puzzled, Andrea went more carefully through the tissue paper and found a crisp one-hundred-dollar bill. She laughed in amusement, and Vittoria clapped her hands.

In each of the other fourteen boxes, all exquisitely wrapped and all suspiciously light, Andrea discovered just another such gift.

The next day Andrea drove her parents to the airport and said she would pick them up again on New Year's Eve. "Well," said Andrea softly, as she hugged them good-bye, "I guess we're a real family again."

"Come with us," pleaded Vittoria.

"No," said Andrea. "You two will have a better time without me. Second honeymoon and all that."

Cosmo smiled. "Remember how much we love you," he said.

Vittoria rattled the bracelet on her arm. "I love this," she said, "but your coming back to us is much more precious to me. Thank you, darling!"

On her way back to Weston, Andrea stopped at Marsha Liberman's and asked her friend to keep her company at the house for the evening. The two young women planned to attend a film, but the hours passed so pleasantly in conversation and laughter that they never gave another thought to leaving the LoPontis' house.

It was when she put on her pea jacket and walked Marsha out to the VW parked in the driveway that Andrea first became nervous about being alone in the house. She had asked Marsha to stay over, but the Libermans were all leaving early the next morning to visit relatives on Long Island. Marsha honked twice and backed drunkenly into the street.

Just as Andrea turned toward the house, she heard the roar of a motorcycle engine near by. She stiffened at the sound.

The motorcycle came nearer. Andrea slipped around the edge of the house, staying in the shadows, and hid herself behind the manger her father had set up in front of the living-room windows. A Harley passed beneath the street lamp, but she could not identify the man riding; the light reflected brightly from his mirrored visor.

Andrea did not stop to right the plywood lamb she knocked over in her haste to get back inside.

Over the next two days, she did not leave the house. She slept each morning until noon, drank coffee for the next couple of hours as she caught up on old reading assignments, and spent the rest of the afternoon working on the proposal for her senior honors thesis. This lassitude itself numbed her, and she felt she hadn't even the energy to deposit at the bank the fifteen one-hundred-dollar bills she had received for Christmas. She had placed these in a deposit envelope in the inside pocket of her pea jacket.

She had grown used to being in the house alone and was no longer frightened. After living four years in constant proximity to ninety-four other young women, each of whom possessed a stereo, a hair-dryer, and an electric typewriter and kept one or another going at all times, she relished the silence.

Early on Friday evening, the twenty-ninth of December, Andrea put aside her Russian book and went into the kitchen to prepare her dinner. While she was eating, she decided that she ought to get out of the house. There was the possibility of going to one of the bars in Boston, of course, but Andrea remembered with great distaste what her last exploit, at the Brimmer House, had been, and decided that she'd just as soon make a short evening of it. She would go to a film, get to sleep early and get up early, and go shopping downtown. After changing into jeans, a blue-and-white reindeer sweater and her new lizard-skin boots, she sat at the kitchen table and leafed through the newspaper to see what films were playing near by.

Just as she had determined on *Rebecca* over *Scenes from a Marriage*, the doorbell rang. Andrea sighed with relief: she was certain it was Marsha, who had been due back late that afternoon. She realized in that moment just how eager she was for company; in fact she could not now remember having been alone for so long a time in her life. She hadn't spoken a word aloud in two days.

In the foyer, she flicked on the outside light and pulled open the door.

The glare of the overhead light made deep hollows of Jack's eyes and erased any pleasantry from the crease of his smile. The glass storm door was open and rested against his back.

"Merry Christmas," he said casually, and stepped fully into the light. His half-lidded eyes glittered.

Andrea's fingers were wrapped tightly about the brass knob. "What do you want?" she asked sharply.

He laughed shortly and nodded his head. "It's Christmas," he said. "Old friends get together and they talk about old times."

"My parents are here. You can't come in."

"No, they're not. They left the day after Christmas."

Jack stepped deftly past her, allowing the storm door to slam behind him. After snapping off the outside light, he moved across the marble foyer and ascended the short flight of wide steps to the living room. His movement was unsteady, and Andrea wondered whether it would help or hinder her that he was so stoned. Before she followed him, she peered out the window and saw the jeep parked halfway up the drive.

"Not bad," said Jack, looking around him from the middle of the living room. "Outside looks like a French whore's carnival, though."

He slumped into a chair, slinging one leg over the arm. The heel of his black boot left a streak of grease across the material. Taking a pack of cigarettes from the inside of his leather jacket, he extracted one and lit it. Andrea set a large ceramic ashtray beside the chair, but he deliberately flipped the smoking match into the high pile of the carpet.

Andrea leaned silently into the corner of the sofa. She was cold, and held her hands tightly together to keep from shaking. Her fingers were entwined between her knees.

Jack drew the smoke deep into his lungs and exhaled it with a sigh. "You were always glad to see me before."

"What is it you want, Jack? I've got a friend on her way over. We're going to a movie—"

"I wanted to talk to you for a few minutes, that's all."

He righted himself in the chair and stubbed out his half, smoked cigarette. From his pocket he took a plastic bag of grass and a pack of rolling papers, set them on the end table, and began to roll a joint.

"You want to talk about the bust," said Andrea. "Well," she said, when he did not reply, "I'm glad to see that you're out of it . . ."

"Out of it?" he repeated mockingly.

"Yes," faltered Andrea. "I mean, if you're here now, you weren't arrested, you weren't put in jail, I mean—"

"How do you know I wasn't arrested, how do you know I wasn't put in jail?"

"Were you?"

"Why should you care?" shrugged Jack. "You got away whole-skin."

"Well, I was just lucky that I was in the bathroom when the police came. I could see them from the window, they—"

"*Very lucky,*" repeated Jack.

"Well it wasn't my fault," cried Andrea. "You dragged me to that house—"

"*Dragged?*"

"Well, you *persuaded* me—against my better judgment."

He licked the paper and twisted the ends of the joint. "So you went upstairs to the bathroom, and hopped out the window, and got away."

"Yes," said Andrea. "I did. I hid in the forest. I would have warned you if I had had time, but I didn't. The police had already surrounded the house when I saw them."

The telephone rang in the kitchen. Andrea jumped up and crossed to the steps. She was almost surprised that Jack did not attempt to stop her.

The telephone stopped in the middle of the second ring; Andrea could feel the cold air that blew up from the kitchen below. She was certain that she had not left any of the windows open.

A man appeared in the deep shadows at the foot of the stairs.

"Who is it?" cried Andrea.

Dominic twisted his head into the light. He held up a plastic credit card and touched it to the tip of his nose. "You ought to get better locks," he said, smiling.

Andrea retreated into the living room. Jack's soft laugh filled the space behind her.

Dominic came up the stairs, and as he passed the front door, he jerked it open. Andrea uttered a small cry when she heard the storm door pulled back. In another moment Morgie and Sid were in the foyer.

"Do you want money?" Andrea hissed at Jack. "What do you want?"

"You have any money?" he asked lazily.

"Hi," said Morgie, moving into the living room. "Oh great," she said, staring at the tree. She thumped a glass angel that hung from one of the higher branches, and laughed as it swung. "Can I have this?" she said, and pulled it from its perch.

"Yes," said Andrea weakly.

Sid and Dominic stood beside Jack's chair and puffed on the joint.

"Better get your coat," Jack said to her.

"I can't go anywhere now. I've got this friend coming over."

"Your friend will have to be disappointed," said Sid, and smiled.

"Better dress warm," said Morgie, slipping a porcelain figurine of a balloon-woman into the pocket of her trench coat. "It's real real cold out there."

28

Andrea was seated between Morgie and Sid on the backseat; Jack drove, and Dominic had fallen asleep with his head pressed against the shotgun window, employing someone's sweater as a pillow. They were on the Massachusetts Turnpike, heading west, away from Boston.

They were paying her back, Andrea thought, for having skipped out of the Dedham house just seconds before the police arrived, for not providing a warning, for having escaped when they had been caught. She still didn't know how they were free now—it would have been quite obvious to the police, Andrea was sure, that they had been dealing in large amounts of drugs —but she was determined not to bring up the subject. She hoped that they were merely frightening her: they would drop her off in some godforsaken town at the far end of the Pike, and she would have to hitch back to Weston. They did not know that she had money; to reassure herself, she lightly touched the pocket that held the bank deposit slip and the fifteen one-hundred-dollar bills. She could take a bus, or the train, and be back before her parents returned on New Year's Eve. If ever she even *heard* a motorcycle again, she'd call the police and claim harassment.

"I want a mint," said Morgie. She held her cupped hand before her face, and blew into it. "I've got Hoboken breath."

Sid whistled through his teeth. "Take a down, and get off my ass."

"Fuck you," said Morgie flatly.

Sid leaned across Andrea and grabbed Morgie's thigh. With his other hand he rubbed his crotch vigorously. "Wouldn't you just love it?"

Morgie brushed a hand through her white hair, extracted a barrette, and brought the sharp end of it down hard on Sid's hand. He withdrew with a grunt of pain. "Not from what Rita tells me, I wouldn't," said Morgie.

"Where's Rita?" said Andrea meekly, attempting to make everything more casual than it seemed to her then.

No one answered. Andrea caught Jack's momentary gaze in the rearview mirror.

"Rita gets carsick," said Jack.

"Rita's got a pain in her snatch," said Morgie.

The jeep ground on through the night. Dominic snored in the front seat. Sid rubbed his leg against Andrea's—probably because he knows it annoys me, she thought. Morgie read a John Saul novel by flashlight.

Jack took the exit marked Hartford–New York City. Now they were turning southward, would end up in Connecticut or New York. This business suddenly had grown darkly serious. Andrea had no idea *what* they would do to her. "Where are we going?" she demanded. "Where are you taking me?"

"We're taking you to see the world . . ." whispered Jack.

"This is illegal," Andrea pleaded.

"You bet," said Sid, and rubbed his thigh against hers. "We're taking you across state lines for immoral purposes—"

"Hey," cried Morgie, "do you remember that joke about 'immortal porpoises'? I heard it once, but now—"

"Shut up, Morgie," said Dominic flatly.

"You can't do this!" hissed Andrea.

"Sure we can," said Jack lightly. "Don't you want to know how we got out of that bust? It was close, and it was no thanks to you. Marty and Donna-Louise got it on possession, but we were just present, we didn't know anything about any drugs, we came over for a pre-Thanksgiving dinner—"

"There wasn't any food!" cried Andrea.

"Shut up!" Sid snapped.

Jack smiled at Andrea in the mirror. "I got us all a lawyer, a big lawyer with lots of rep, a big lawyer with lots of strings that he can pull anytime he wants to, a big lawyer who's got a great big craving on for smack, a big lawyer who convinced the judge that we're over at Donna-Louise's being thankful, and the cops jump through the window and interrupt the blessing."

"And it's all your fault," said Morgie, looking up from her book.

"No it's not," protested Andrea. "Even if I had screamed bloody murder up there, you wouldn't have had time to get away. There were cops everywhere."

"You should have warned us," said Jack. "If I had had ten more seconds, I could have hidden that money where the cops would never have found it. We've been strapped for weeks. So it's because of you we're making this trip."

"Where are we going?"

"Seattle," said Sid.

"Truth or Consequences, New Mexico," said Morgie.

"Alcatraz," said Dominic.

"This is kidnapping," protested Andrea weakly.

"Really?" said Morgie, brightly. "I mean, is this really a kidnapping? That's hot, you know, a real kidnapping!"

"No!" cried Jack, "of course it's not a real kidnapping. We're just taking little Wenham girl here for a little ride, we're going to show little Wenham girl a little bit of the world she doesn't know anything about. You don't learn everything there is to know at Wenham, you don't know everything when you've spent your whole life in a split-level in Weston, do you, little Wenham girl?"

Andrea said nothing. In the midst of her anger and terror, she found room to be resentful at being called *girl*.

"Roll a couple of joints," said Jack to Dominic. "Little Wenham girl needs to get mellow in the backseat."

Andrea closed her eyes. Sid pressed against her on the right. The roar of the engine filled her ears as Jack's foot eased down harder on the accelerator and they crossed the Massachusetts border into Connecticut.

Andrea was shaken roughly awake by Morgie. "Hey," she said, "we're here."

"Where's here? "said Andrea, and pulled open her eyes. It was still dark out, but the car had been parked beneath a street lamp in a neighborhood of cramped low row houses with tiny, smudged yards in front of them and twisted television aerials on their pitched roofs.

Her back ached, and she longed to slip her hand round to massage it, but her position between Morgie and Sid made this impossible. She ran her fingers through her hair and felt it tatty. "Where are we?" she said.

"Can't you tell?" said Sid. "This is the World Trade Center."

"We're in *New York City*," said Morgie, with pride. "We're in the *Big Apple!* This is the *City of Dreams!*"

Andrea looked around her with more interest: the neighborhood appeared distinctly lower middle-class. At this hour of the night it was grubby and deserted. The only lighted house was the one before which they were parked. It didn't *look* much like New York, but then, she hadn't visited the city since 1978.

On the front seat, Dominic was slouched against the window, snoring. "Where's Jack?" Andrea asked.

"Inside," said Morgie, and then giggled: "He's selling soap."

"Soap? What kind of drug is that?"

"No," said Morgie, with exasperation, "the stuff you take a bath with."

"Why is he selling soap?" said Andrea, the sleep still not cleared from her mind.

"They think it's *meth!*" cried Morgie, laughing at the wonderful joke of it.

"Shut up!" said Sid. "It's because of you we're doing this," he grumbled to Andrea.

"Me?"

"Yeah you, bitch. We never sold bad stuff in our lives, not once. But all our supply went to the lawyer, and all our cash got confiscated at the raid, so we're just about starting over again. There's no credit in this game, and now we're having to *sell soap* in fucking *Queens!*"

"I thought this was New York."

"You ought to take geography at Wenham," said Morgie. "Queens is part of New York, if you read more you'd know that. There's five boroughs that make up New York City, there's Queens, and Manhattan, and the Bronx—"

"Can it, Morgie!" growled Sid.

Jack emerged from the house and moved swiftly down the walk. "God, let's get the fuck out of here before they find out the stuff isn't meth." In another moment they had taken off again.

"Why'd they trust you to begin with?" said Morgie.

"Because they're friends of Donna-Louise, and they hadn't heard of the bust yet. I didn't tell 'em, either, they'll find out soon enough."

"How much did you get?" said Sid.

"Two thousand. It was one of Donna-Louise's regular runs."

"Good," said Dominic, rousing himself slightly, "we can start over now . . ."

Andrea was pleased that when they left Queens, Jack headed for Manhattan. She could escape in Manhattan: when they stopped she would jump out of the jeep into a taxi—there were always taxis in Manhattan, at any time of the night. She would ask to be taken to the train station. The first train for Boston would be leaving probably in a few hours, and she could get on that: her only worry was that the taxi driver would balk at a one-hundred-dollar bill.

Manhattan was larger than she had remembered. She had a glimpse of the tall buildings, but when Jack turned north, these were quickly lost to sight. She saw signs directing them to the George Washington Bridge, and it was this route that Jack took. Andrea grew more frightened in the backseat.

With some complex maneuvering that Andrea tried to memorize, they arrived at a little terrace overlooking the Hudson River. Five or six small apartment buildings shared a splendid view of the New Jersey shore, and Jack pointed out the one they were interested in. "Everybody out!" he said.

Despite the fact that he was selling hard drugs, despite the fact that he had kidnapped her, Andrea in her well-bred propriety could not understand how Jack could bring himself to visit someone, previously unannounced, at four o'clock in the morning. Jack rang the bell, and they were immediately buzzed in.

A pale, thin man with a sparse beard and shaggy black hair sold Jack a small quantity of Demerol and fifteen grams of heroin. Andrea was rather attracted to this man, Paul, because of his benign smile. He wore a short-sleeved madras shirt, and Andrea noticed that the insides of both forearms were covered with clusters of reddish puncture marks.

From the drawer of a magazine rack he brought out a glass syringe and a plastic tie-off cord; he produced a packet of heroin from his own supply. While Morgie, Sid, and Dominic talked with Paul, who was evidently an old acquaintance and once had lived in Jamaica Plain, Andrea sat in a dark corner and watched, fascinated, as the heroin was prepared for injection.

He mixed the white powder with a small amount of water inside a small tin measuring cup, and held it over a candle flame until it was heated through. This cooled for a few moments while he listened with half a mind to Morgie's ramblings; then he poured the liquid into the syringe, depressing the plunger just enough to expel the air trapped within. Conversation stopped as Paul tied off his arm and then inserted the tip of the needle into a vein just deep enough to produce a drop of blood. Jack nodded: "Good," he said, "you've got it." Paul plunged the needle in deep, and depressed the plunger by degrees until the syringe was empty.

Andrea cringed, sucking in her breath. Jack turned to her and laughed: "Want to be our guest?"

Andrea stared back coldly.

A smile of even greater benignity crossed Paul's face, and froze there. He withdrew the needle and yanked the cord free. As he continued to talk, he became more effusive and less coherent. His moods and his speech changed, it seemed to Andrea, moment by moment.

What was left in the tin measuring cup was offered to his guests, and Sid and Morgie readily partook. Because he was driving back to Boston in a while, Jack refused the hospitality; and he refused Dominic permission as well, saying that he might be required to take his turn at the wheel.

"Stay here," whispered Paul, "everybody stay here. It's getting light out, you can't drive to Boston when it's light out, ruin your eyes driving when it's light out . . ."

Jack, admitting he was tired, accepted this invitation.

Andrea watched as Morgie, Sid, and Dominic—permitted by Jack—repeated the ritual with the heroin. Jack contented himself with rolling joints.

Andrea decided that she would escape when they had all passed out. She wished she had change for the subway—did the subway reach this far up in Manhattan? Probably—and perhaps she could find some quarters in Paul's apartment. New York subways were dangerous, but no more dangerous than this place.

She didn't want to take the joint that Jack offered her, but he quietly insisted. She puffed twice, then tried to pass it back. "I have my own," he said, "you play with that for a while."

She tried to stay awake. She stood at the window and watched the dawn breaking against the Palisades. When she turned round, she saw that Sid lay unconscious on the couch. Paul was not to be seen. Jack, who lay on the floor at a right angle to the couch, opened his eyes slowly. "Come here," he said.

Andrea went to him, and he made her lie down beside him on the threadbare carpet. He turned her over and wrapped his arms tightly about her. His regular breathing in her ear told her he slept.

For a while Andrea looked through the door into the kitchen. There, at a Formica table beneath a garish fluorescent light, sat Morgie and Dominic, holding an incoherent conversation. She began to sweat in Jack's tight and unrelenting embrace. Morgie's and Dominic's endless babbling droned in her ears. Her eyes grew heavy, and she fell into an exhausted sleep.

29

Andrea groggily opened her eyes and immediately closed them again when a dull pain welled up at the base of her neck. She turned her face into the pillow. Her body ached and she was cold, but she didn't have the strength to reach down for the covers. A draft blew across her naked back. She took a deep breath and tried to draw herself up into full consciousness, but she was without strength or coordination.

The draft was suddenly warm. Andrea snapped her eyes open and turned her head. Inches away from her was the clean-shaven face of a man she did not recognize. She stiffened, and a fine shower of cold pinpricks covered her naked body. The man, also naked, was sprawled on his stomach close to her, one hand clutching the dirty case of the pillow beneath his head.

She stared at him for a long moment, certain that she had never seen him before. She ran her eyes about the darkened room, realizing in that moment that she had no idea where she was. The door into a hallway was ajar, and pink light fell in a strip across the bare wood floor. Blinds were lowered, and curtains had been pulled hastily across the two windows. Andrea could not tell it if was day or night.

Perhaps she was in one of the back bedrooms of the drug dealer's apartment in Manhattan. Falling asleep in Jack's arms was the last thing she remembered. She listened for the voices of the others, but could hear nothing. If they were still asleep, maybe she could escape.

But who was this man? Quickly she recalled the hour she had

spent awake in Paul's apartment—there had been no one else there, she was certain. She tried to remember if someone had mentioned Paul's roommate. But even if this *were* Paul's apartment, and this Paul's roommate, why was Andrea in bed with him, naked?

She eased up into a sitting position, taking care not to disturb the man beside her. She could not shake the feeling of weightlessness that almost overwhelmed her. She ran her fingers through her hair and pressed the backs of her cold hands to her eyes. As her consciousness returned slowly, she looked round the room again and saw that her clothes were scattered about the floor. Her jacket was balled in one corner.

She bit her lower lip in concentration, trying desperately to jar her memory. Pain shot through her jaw, and she touched her fingers to her mouth. It was quite tender, and she felt an encrustation of blood there.

There was something familiar about the room, but she could not immediately determine what it was: something about the molding, or the papering, or the height of the ceiling . . .

It was all three. She was not in Manhattan at all, but back in Jamaica Plain; this was one of the rooms she had seen only in passing down the second-floor hallway of Jack's house. But how had she got here without any of the journey impressing itself upon her memory? She hadn't had more than a single joint after they had arrived in New York, but that was hardly sufficient to affect her in this fashion—unless Jack had treated it with something. She remembered now that he had prepared a joint especially for her, and not allowed her to share his. She had been drugged and brought back to Jamaica Plain; there had been no chance to escape at all.

Andrea looked at the man beside her and wondered if she had had sex with him. Probably several times, considering the pain between her legs and the uncomfortable stickiness there. Yet she could remember nothing.

Andrea wondered if she had responded to his love-making. Or had she been under such heavy sedation that she had known nothing at all? It was rape, wasn't it, when a man took you when you were unconscious?

She touched her feet to the cold floor and padded quietly to the window. Parting the blinds, she discovered that it was dark out—but what day? Had the sun just set, or was it just about to rise? When was it her parents were due back from Canada? Was that today or tomorrow? Or were they already at home, frantic because of her absence and the missing porcelain figurine?

A wave of nausea swept over Andrea. She leaned against the wall to steady herself. When she had recovered a little, she looked round at her clothing on the floor and decided that she hadn't really the presence of mind or the energy to dress. She went to the door and eased it open just enough to slip through.

She moved along the wall toward the staircase. Now she could hear soft music floating up from the first floor; several voices melded in simultaneous conversation, but she could not distinguish or identify any of them. On her way past an open door she halted and stared inside. On the platform bed within the room a man and woman were having sex. The woman moaned softly and flung her head from one side to the other on the mattress as the man moved rhythmically on top of her. The man caught sight of Andrea, smiled at her, and with a flick of his head motioned her to join them.

Andrea shook her head quickly, moved on to the top of the stairs, and grasped the banister convulsively. Leaning over, she could see the open doorway of the living room and several shadows that fell across the floor of the first-floor hallway. The music, New Wave rock, was suddenly turned louder, and she heard Jack's voice demanding it be lowered again. Footsteps sounded in the hall below. Andrea saw Morgie, with a can of beer and a box of crackers, walking unsteadily from the direction of the kitchen. She wore her work shirt and a pair of fluffy white mules—nothing else. Morgie hiccuped, fell back a step, giggled, and then, concentrating hard, stepped through the doorway into the living room.

Andrea's head throbbed. She had become aware of a prickly pain on the inside of her left elbow. She rubbed it and looked back down the hall. Groans came louder from the couple in the bedroom. Andrea shivered violently with the cold, and wiped away the perspiration on her forehead. Unwatched, she could make her escape. There was a back staircase in the house, and she would have to hope no one was in the kitchen when she descended.

She closed her eyes and wondered at the chain of circumstance that had brought her here: to an unheated house in Jamaica Plain, where people had sex without bothering to close the door, where people shot up heroin and screamed at each other, where people were kept against their will. How could she have explained to her parents that she hadn't meant any of this to happen when she tried to catch Jack's eye in the Brimmer House?

Unsteadily—for she felt sore in a dozen different places—she stepped across the landing and into the bathroom. Easing the door shut, she pulled on the chain light and stood before the mirror. The tiles were gritty and sharply cold; she took a towel from the rack and placed it beneath her feet. Her hair was dishevelled and greasy. Her lip, surprisingly, was neither bruised nor swollen, though still tender to the touch. As she lowered her hand, she caught sight of a mark on the side of her elbow. In the middle of a blotched circle of purple was a puncture mark. She had been kidnapped and then shot up with heroin. She had been put in bed with a strange man—and it might be that he wasn't the only one. Andrea watched her expression harden in the mirror. It was the first time in her life she had ever really been victimized.

She ignored the pain she felt, she ignored the lassitude that pervaded her body. She pulled a comb through her hair, washed her face, and sponged her body clean. As she leaned forward, the heady scent of perspiration that was not her own filled her nostrils. She towelled dry and swallowed three aspirin.

Creeping back to the bedroom in which she had wakened, Andrea found the other side of the bed vacant now. She left the door ajar for light and bent stiffly to retrieve her scattered clothing. A rasping on the floor behind her caused her to whip around startled. A man leapt from the darkness behind the door. One hand was cupped over her mouth, and the other locked her arms to her sides. She was shoved roughly onto the bed on her back. The clothes she still held were flung away from her. In the slash of light from the doorway, she saw Jack's face above her; his eyes were bright, hard, and angry. His jeans chafed against her belly as he straddled her. His stale breath came hot against her face. Without a word he took a syringe from the upended crate that served as a nightstand. Andrea screamed beneath his muffling hand; he poked two fingers down her throat until she gagged and choked.

The syringe was full; a minuscule arc of liquid sparkled as he emptied it of air. Jack lowered the syringe and slipped the needle into the hollow of her elbow. His thumb jammed down the plunger, and he whispered, "Relax, little Wenham girl, relax yourself, or this is going to hurt you. Janis died because she didn't relax, you ever hear that, she didn't know when to relax herself . . ."

She went limp; her eyelids were heavy, heavier than she had ever known them to be, but she could not lose consciousness. All the movement she was capable of was spiraling her eyes in their sockets; she saw the room as through gauze.

Jack took off his clothes, and suddenly he was on top of her, grunting, pressing her sluggish, damp body into the mattress. She had no strength to fight him, none to respond. Jack had not finished when she saw, over his heaving shoulder, another man in the doorway, naked and unconcernedly pulling himself into an erection.

One face blended into another. She tried to distinguish them by their shoulders, by their sweat. Sid smiled leeringly, and never even removed his jeans. Dominic grabbed her arms roughly and turned her onto her stomach before he climbed onto her.

Thumbs were pressed against her throat in ecstasy; other hands held her arms to the mattress. She was smeared with tongues and hot breath until she felt she could never be clean again. Either her memory faulted or the humiliation became a circle: faces and shoulders and smells began to repeat.

At last, at some point, she realized that she was alone. There was no weight on top of her. She lay on her side; her groin ached, and her breasts were sparked with pain. Her cheek was slimy against the pillow. Painfully, Andrea opened her eyes. She was staring at the doorway. Morgie stood there, silhouetted in pink light.

"Oh please—" whispered Andrea, and choked on speech.

As she approached the bed, Morgie slipped the work shirt from her shoulders and kicked her slippers into the corner.

*

When Andrea found consciousness again, she was alone in the bed. She heard excited hushed voices in the hallway, but could see no one through the open door. Jack's voice, nearby, harshly commanded, "I said get it now!" Footsteps came down the hall, and Andrea clawed at a button on the mattress—the sheets had long before been worked free. Sid passed the doorway without even looking in; she felt the vibrations of his heavily shod feet as he mounted the stairs that led to Jack's room on the third floor. Dominic, wearing a heavy corduroy jacket, paused before the door and shouted, "Hurry the hell up! God, what does it take to get you people moving?!"

Morgie appeared in the doorway, zipping up a green army fatigue coat. Andrea closed her eyes. "She's asleep," said Morgie, and Dominic replied: "The whore's exhausted."

Andrea heard the heavy footsteps descending from the third floor. Through the chink in her heavy-lidded eyes, she saw Sid hand Dominic a small, shiny revolver.

Dominic spun it round his fingers. "Were there enough bullets to fill it?" he asked.

"No," said Sid, "I put in five, though."

"How do you feel, Morgie?" asked Dominic.

"I feel great," said Morgie.

"You drive, then," he said.

"Oh great!"

Their voices trailed off as they descended the stairs, and Andrea could hear no more. She held her breath and listened for the front door scraping open. She felt the vibrations of their feet on the front porch; she heard the doors of the jeep slam. The house was deathly silent. The jeep started up, and she followed it as it backed out of the driveway.

She struggled to raise herself, but before she could sit up, the breath deserted her. She fell back heavily, panting, and in a few moments drifted again into oblivion.

30

When she waked again, the house was still silent. There was a change in the density of light; it was probably day now—but what day, following what night, Andrea had no idea. She stirred and turned on the sheets—those sheets felt cooler and crisper. And she was clothed—that was different too.

She was in her own bedroom, in her parents' house, in Weston. The last thing she remembered was Morgie's form back-lighted from the hallway. How had she come back? Had she escaped, and had that escape been so harrowing she retained no memory of it? Or had she been brought? She didn't like the stillness and silence of the house. She could hear the blood beating in her ears. When she began to tremble, she clawed the bed covers to quell the shaking.

When her hand slid underneath the pillow, it slid over hard, cold metal. When Andrea pulled out the revolver, the acrid scent of gunpowder stung her nostrils.

She pulled herself up onto the edge of the bed. Weak light from the window fell across shapes familiar to her. She pressed the palms of her hands against her eyes and rubbed, hoping to clear her mind of sleep and confusion.

What if Jack and the others were in the house, rifling the bedrooms or waiting to jump out at her from behind half-opened doors?

Rising unsteadily, she moved quietly to the window and drew back the curtains and sheers. Beyond the glass the light was weak; a thick winter fog shrouded everything, and she could not even make out the greenhouse she knew to be no more than fifty feet away. A sense of unreality began to overwhelm her; she pressed her hand flat against the cold glass pane and was steadied. She was aware of a wavering nausea and jabs of aching in her joints.

She cocked her head slowly: still she heard nothing. She let the curtains fall back into place.

The digital clock-radio by her bedside had been unplugged.

She had no idea what time it was, but supposed it must be soon after dawn. She looked all round the room in hope that something she saw might tell her how she had come to be there. She adjusted her pants and blouse, and realized that she was wearing no underwear; she knew then that she had not dressed herself. Very probably then she had been brought here.

Andrea was dizzy. When she feared she was going to faint, she sat on the edge of the bed and lowered her head to her knees. She took many deep breaths and then sat up again. She wondered if the amount of heroin she'd been shot up with was sufficient to create an addiction in her system. The sickness she felt now might be a result only of her incarceration, the lack of food, the repeated rapes—but it might also be withdrawal.

The continued silence in the house allowed Andrea to believe herself alone. She didn't yet know what to do, but at least she was safely home and her parents had learned nothing of her ordeal. If she were allowed a little good fortune, they never would. She flicked on the outside switch of the bathroom light and opened the door. Her bare foot had no more than touched the threshold when she stopped and sucked in her breath. Her hand clamped over her mouth to hold in her cry.

Squeezed awkwardly between the blue porcelain toilet and the blue tiled wall, her back to Andrea, was Vittoria LoPonti. Her long black hair was loose and matted with congealing blood from a gaping wound at the back of her neck. Lines of blood mapped the floor tiles around the corpse. Vittoria's shoulders were hunched, and one arm was extended above her head. It rested flat against the wall. The skin had been broken where her diamond wedding ring had been wrenched off.

Andrea slapped her hand against the light switch, dissolving the image. She yanked herself away from the door and pulled it shut. Her breath seared her lungs as she expelled it. No longer convinced that she was alone in the house, she forced back the screams that welled in her throat.

She went to the door into the hallway, unlocked it, and flung it back, more than half expecting to be confronted by Jack or one of the others.

The hall was dark. When she moved nearer the staircase, she

could just make out the slight glow of colored lights that blinked on the Christmas tree downstairs. It wasn't until she flicked on the hallway light that she saw the dark blotches on the gray carpet. The bloody prints of four fingers were streaked on the door frame of her parents' room. Andrea moved down and looked within.

Cosmo LoPonti lay beside the bed. He wore a winter jacket, the thick quilted material ripped with tiny red explosions of batting across his unmoving chest. His head lolled to one side and his glassy eyes stared blankly at Andrea. She stared back, but her own eyes remained dry. The house was cold, and she returned to her room for a sweater.

She was no longer quiet in her movements. She felt neither weariness nor fear nor grief. In her bedroom she took the gun and stood at the window fiddling with it until she had succeeded in opening the chamber: of the five bullets that had been loaded, three had been fired and two remained intact. She went downstairs and unplugged the Christmas tree. Her boots and jacket had been tossed at the foot of the couch; she sat down to put them on. She thought for a few moments where she had last left her car keys and, after a moment, went directly to them on the dining room buffet.

A few minutes later Andrea started her car and backed out of the drive. She had left the house unlocked. Now she was glad of the fog and the sense of timelessness it lent to the world.

She drove to Jamaica Plain and, following a street map of Boston in the glove compartment, located the street on which Jack lived. She drove past the house, then parked on a side street three blocks away.

As she expected, the back door of Jack's house was unlocked. She peered through the grimy glass, but nothing stirred in the kitchen or in the hallway beyond. She went quietly inside. She moved down the hall slowly and carefully, staying close to the wall to avoid the creaking boards in the middle.

Sid lay on his back on the sofa. Andrea watched the rhythmic rise and fall of his chest until she had assured herself that he was in deep slumber. Rita was curled up in one of the armchairs. She dreamt, not pleasantly; moaning and twisting, she pushed herself into the back of the chair. Her arm twitched and dropped to her side.

From Rita's wrist dangled a gold bracelet. Andrea moved to the side of the sleeping woman, leaned down and examined the bracelet. With the nail of her index finger, she pulled the bracelet back just enough to see the words *Daughter's Love* engraved on the inside.

Andrea fell back on the carpet. She rocked herself on her haunches, covering her mouth to keep from crying out in her anguish.

She stopped of a sudden, lowering her hands by force of will and fisting them in her lap. She regulated her breathing and stared blankly at Rita's birth-scarred face. She turned slowly on the carpet and studied Sid's immobile form on the sofa. Her eyes skitted about the room, catching at items randomly. On one of the low shelves beneath the stereo amplifier were several packets of heroin bound with a rubber band, and next to these an empty syringe—and an enamelled dagger in a heavy chased sheath.

Andrea stood, her face a mask of cold determination.

She no longer considered her own safety. They were all asleep, they wouldn't wake so long as she was quiet in doing the things she had to do. She was in the kitchen, heating three packets of heroin in a little cup above a candle flame. Remembering carefully what Paul had done in New York—and how long ago had *that* been?—she filled a syringe and returned to the living room. Without hesitation she jammed the needle into Sid's neck. He flinched but did not wake, and she slowly pressed the plunger.

She returned to the kitchen, filled the syringe, and again pressed it into a vein in Sid's neck. She reached into his pocket and pulled out all the drugs that were there: three more packets of heroin and a plastic bag labeled by marking pen: Demerol. This she ground into a powder in a mortar, mixed with the last of the heroin that she had prepared, and filled the syringe a third time.

Andrea came up behind Rita, holding the syringe in her fist, thumb on the plunger. Rita shifted in her sleep and twisted her head. Andrea retreated to the kitchen: she could not risk Rita's waking with a scream that would alert the rest of the house.

She entered the hallway through the kitchen and went up the

stairs quietly. In their room at the end of the second-floor hallway she found Morgie and Dominic in bed. On the table beside the bed was a silver clip of cash she recognized as her father's, and a tangle of gold chains. A pendant that was set against the base of the lamp she recognized as Cosmo's gift to Vittoria on their fifteenth wedding anniversary; Andrea had helped him to pick it out. Her mother's wedding ring was on Morgie's right forefinger.

Dominic was on the far side of the bed. His snores filled the room; Andrea hadn't to be so careful about the noise she made. She plunged the needle into Morgie's arm, and held her hand tightly over the women's mouth, digging her nails sharply into her cheeks almost in hope that she would wake. The needle nearly broke as it struck bone, but Andrea persisted until the glass chamber was empty. Morgie never roused out of her drugged sleep.

Sweat gleamed on Andrea's face as she stood. There was more heroin, and she would inject them all. Pocketing the bills on the bedside table, she went down the hall quietly, and froze as she heard someone—it must be Rita—climbing the stairs. She slipped into the empty bedroom where she had been raped, and held her breath in the darkness there. Rita went into the bedroom where Andrea had seen the couple making love; she heard Rita mumble something to Jack, who replied thickly.

When they were quiet again, Andrea slipped out into the hall-way. She hurried past the half-opened door, not daring even to breathe, and descended the stairs again. If she could wait until they all fell asleep again, she could kill Dominic with the last of the heroin, and then there was a bullet each for Rita and Jack. She wished now that she had gone into Jack's room first; it was he who had instigated the entire business, she was sure of it, and he ought to have died first.

At the foot of the stairs, Andrea checked her reflection in the mirror of the hall stand, and then, seeing Jack's black knit watch-man's cap dangling on a peg, she snatched it up and pulled it over her hair, completely concealing her blond strands beneath it.

Why am I doing this? she wondered, and smiled at the incongruity of the action.

A board creaked heavily, and Andrea snapped her head up, her hands still on the rolled edge of the watchman's cap. Rita stared down at her from the top of the stairs, alarm flaring in her eyes.

"Jack! Jack!" Rita called in a thick voice.

Louder footfalls came behind Rita. Andrea did not wait to see him, but ran back down the hall into the kitchen. She yanked open the back door and fled the house.

"Fucking bitch!" Jack's voice boomed behind her, but Andrea was already running down the fog-shrouded alley. In a few moments more she was back in her car, without having heard footsteps behind her. She turned on the ignition, pulled on the headlights, and headed slowly through the fog toward Boston. At a stoplight she counted the bills she had taken from Morgie's bedside table—nearly four hundred dollars—and pushed them back into her pocket. She was very much surprised to discover that the package of cash she had received from her parents was still inside the jacket as well. When the light changed, she threw the car into gear and drove on. She slapped hard at the rearview mirror, twisting it so that she could no longer see her own image in it.

Though she had no idea now where she would go or what she would do, she knew one thing for certain: Andrea LoPonti no longer existed.

PART III

The Hammers of Heaven

31

Sister Katherine sat at her small table at the back of the empty classroom. Spread out before her were twenty papers with simple addition problems painstakingly scrawled in the children's handwriting. Across the top of the desk were three pillboxes containing red, blue, and green stars, corresponding to *excellent*, *good*, and *needs improvement*. It was Katherine's own idea that the green star should be used instead of the great glaring red check mark that Sister Mercedes had employed for years. "I remember when I was that young—check marks used to make me feel so bad," Katherine had said to the sister, "let's just give everybody a star. The ones who 'need improvement' will feel bad enough as it is."

The last paper deserved a green star, but Katherine was hesitant to end her grading in that fashion, and so awarded a blue star instead. She shuffled the papers into a neat pile, lidded the boxes of stars, and turned her gaze to the playground just beyond the tall windows.

It was mid-morning, and Sister Mercedes had taken the twenty students out for free-activity recess. On the swing set three little boys were deliberately swinging in a rhythm that pulled the posts out of the ground; a little boy and little girl were performing a nice set of acrobatics on the jungle gym; two girls on the monkey bars were kicking one another with giggling viciousness, and on the slide a boy and a girl were attempting to come down the shiny tin ramp on their backs, heads toward the ground, with a handful of pine straw thrust under them to cut friction. Sister Mercedes, her head bowed, sat alone on the green bench in the midst of them all; Katherine would have thought that she prayed, or said her rosary, had she not seen the glint of sunlight on Sister Mercedes's watch carefully thrust out of her sleeve. Sister Mercedes had never hesitated to confide to Sister Katherine her dislike of recess and its concomitant noise; and this was the first day of school after the Thanksgiving vacation. The children had been particularly rambunctious today and kept Sister Mercedes in constant motion through the morning.

Katherine envied Sister Mercedes her full teaching schedule; and it was no comfort to know that Sister Mercedes would gladly have traded places and duties. However, it would not be long before Katherine had classes of her own: after three and a half intensive years of classes at Boston College, she had her bachelor's degree, and one more semester of advanced courses would secure for her a teacher's certificate. Conducting her own classroom, Katherine knew, she would be of that much greater use, and—although it was sinful to think it—of much greater effectiveness in her first year than Sister Mercedes had ever been.

Katherine was special in the Hingham convent: set apart first by the drama of her admittance, tangled as it was with her parents' disapproval, her father's murder, her mother's trial and conviction; and with her dedication to the children, her high scores on examinations at Boston College, her willingness to assume the most rigorous tasks of the convent. She seemed never to weary of poring over her studies or volunteering to visit ill parishioners, take gifts of clothing and food to the destitute, or assume house chores that made her hands raw and her body sore. Silent chants of prayer sustained Sister Katherine through these self-imposed ordeals, and in the years of her postulancy at Saint Luke's she was never once reprimanded. A month after Epiphany, at the beginning of February, she would take her final vows. In a ceremony far less elaborate than the one for her Clothing, Katherine would become officially a Slave of the Immaculate Conception. She was eager for the event, which would take place on her twenty-first birthday. In the convent no notice was taken of these personal holidays, but Katherine suspected that Mother Celestine knew and did not disapprove of the coincidence.

Katherine placed the graded papers on Sister Mercedes's desk. She retrieved her cape from the cloakroom, dropped her pencils and her stars into her canvas book bag, and opened the door to the playground.

She waved at Sister Mercedes and pointed at her wrist, although Katherine wore no watch. Sister Mercedes stood in relief, crossed herself, turned around in a little circle of pleasure, and clapped her hands loudly.

The children all seemed to go limp. Sighing, they dropped from their perches and lined themselves up at the door, some of them timidly waving to Sister Katherine, who crossed the playground heading toward the convent house.

In the entrance hall Katherine draped her cape on a hook and, still carrying her book bag, ascended the wide front staircase. She planned to read for an hour or so in *Problems of Early Childhood Development*.

"Sister Katherine?" a soft voice called from behind her.

Halfway up the stairs, Katherine turned, resting one hand on the glossy banister that she had polished and oiled the evening before. "Yes, Sister Prudentia?"

"There's a call for you."

Sister Katherine smiled and nodded, although she had longed for the hour alone and uninterrupted. It was not unusual for parents of Sister Mercedes's students to phone at odd hours to consult Katherine on their children's progress: Sister Mercedes gave the parents short shrift, and Sister Katherine was always patient and encouraging. "I'll take it on the library extension," she said.

Sister Prudentia disappeared, and Katherine hoisted her book bag over her shoulder and hurried back down the steps, hoping that the worried mother could be consoled with only a very few well-chosen and softly spoken words.

Sister Katherine found the library empty. She eased the doors shut and dropped her bag onto a table. Bright early December light poured through the double layer of sheers. Sister Katherine settled into the wingback chair next to the telephone and pressed the only extension button that was flashing.

"Yes? This is Sister Katherine."

She pulled back her veil and loosened the wimple over her ear. The receiver clacked against her earring. Although it was against order policy for any nun to wear adornment of any sort, there were days when Sister Katherine surreptitiously pressed the ruby chip into her lobe again. It wasn't that she was vain, it was only that she never felt entirely like *herself* without it.

Sister Katherine hadn't heard the first response. "Yes?" she repeated pleasantly. "Who is this, please?"

"Kathy?"

Sister Katherine sat up slowly in the chair. "Who is this?" she demanded. The sunlight seemed to hurt her eyes, and she turned away from the window.

"It's me, Kathy."

"What?"

"It's me," said her mother again.

Katherine said nothing for several moments. "Ma, why are you calling me here? I told you never to call the convent. So why are you calling? Are you sick? Because you can't expect me to come all the way out to Framingham to see you if you are. I was just there last month, and it's hard for me to get permission—"

"Oh, Kathy, no, I'm fine! I'm just fine!'

Katherine now heard the giddiness in her mother's voice. "Why are you calling, Ma?"

"Oh Kathy, I can't wait to see you!"

"Ma, I said I couldn't get out to Framingham—"

"I'm not in Framingham any more."

Sister Katherine was shocked. "Where are you? Where—"

"I'm in Boston," said her mother. "They've let me out."

Katherine slumped back in the chair. Her mother's voice became a scatter of incomprehensible speech.

Katherine had visited her mother four times a year at the prison in Framingham. Reverend Mother Celestine would gladly have given the postulant permission and funds for more frequent journeys, but although the visits cheered Anne Dolan, Katherine told her superior that they left her mother depressed for days afterward, and that the prison psychologist had advised against any greater frequency of meetings. Katherine wrote her mother weekly and carefully saved the postcards that she received in vague reply; these she would have thrown away, but that they bore religious images on the recto. Every visit and every letter closed with the command that Anne Dolan was not to telephone the convent upon any pretext whatever. Sister Katherine said that the receiving of personal calls was a severe infraction of convent discipline.

When Sister Katherine informed her that Anne Dolan had been paroled from prison on good behavior, Mother Superior Celestine, astonished, wondered aloud why Sister Katherine had not before mentioned the possibility of release. Sister Katherine explained uneasily that her mother had kept the parole board meetings a secret even from her, and that she too had been greatly surprised.

"But where is she now? Will she return to her home—to Somerville?"

"No," said Sister Katherine, "she says she'll never go back there. Right now she's in a halfway house in Boston, in the South End."

"On Tremont Street?"

"Yes, that was the address."

"I know the place," replied Mother Superior Celestine. "You must go there tomorrow morning."

"I—"

"Oh, Sister Katherine, your mother will need so much help in this time of readjustment to society. I suppose she'll stay in the halfway house until she finds work and a place to live. It's as nice a place as can be expected, but I don't think your mother will be able to recover fully until she's well out of there. The place is crowded just now—overcrowded, actually, so we must put on extra effort to take care of your poor mother. When you see her, tell her that all the prayers of the convent go with her."

"Oh, yes," murmured Sister Katherine, "of course I will."

"I worked in the laundry, and I hated it. I sorted everything, then I washed it and ironed it. I sewed on labels, and I had to make sure it got back to the right person. Every time I raise my hands to my face I can smell ammonia and starch—I think I'll smell ammonia and starch until the day I die, Kathy! They give you fifteen cents an hour and you have to work nine hours a day. That's one dollar and thirty-five cents a day, I used to figure it up every day, how much I was getting—and it was always one dollar and thirty-five cents. And you work six days a week—that's eight dollars and ten cents a week. There's not much you can buy with that. All I can say is, it's a good thing that I don't smoke. All my money would have gone to buy cigarettes. I always did what they told me. I never gave 'em any trouble. Some of the women there wanted to drag me in at first, but when they found out my little girl was a nun, they left me alone. So you protected me in there, honey, though you didn't know it, it was all because of you being a nun that I got out of there so soon!"

Anne Dolan looked shyly up from her hands, which were folded neatly in her lap. "There's a coffee machine downstairs. You want to me go down and get us some? I've got money—when I left, they gave me all the money I had earned in the laundry." She started to rise, but Sister Katherine waved her back.

"No, Ma, I don't want anything."

Anne Dolan nodded distractedly and fell back. They were sitting in a narrow room, in mismatched straight-backed chairs on either side of a small wooden table that had been painted bright red—as if on purpose to clash with the green walls. Katherine's skirts brushed against the narrow iron cot, and she turned her face away from the meager winter light that found entrance through the dust-streaked window. The radiator beneath hissed and clanked noisily. Anne Dolan wore a too vivid floral print housedress and flat black shoes. Her hair was entirely gray, cut short and unstyled. She wore no makeup and, despite her release from prison, looked as old and as thin as when Katherine had last visited her.

"Did you keep up Jim's grave, Kathy? I thought about it a lot—every time it rained or snowed, I thought of him out there under the ground."

Katherine did not even know in what part of the cemetery her father's grave was located. But she said, "He's been well taken care of, Ma. What are you going to do, Ma? Now that you're out."

"I have to get a job, and keep it. That's part of the parole."

"Maybe you could get a job in a laundry," suggested Katherine.

"No!" cried her mother, hurt. "I could never do that again. It'd be like I never left Framingham."

"There's not much else you know how to do, Ma," shrugged Katherine.

"Well I had an idea," said Anne Dolan, brightening. She leaned forward, resting her bony elbows on the scarred table. "It came to me yesterday right after I talked to you."

Katherine adjusted her robes impatiently. "Please, Ma, get to the point. I have to get back to the convent."

"That's just what I was thinking about—the convent."

"What about it?" Katherine asked warily. "I told you all about it in my letters."

"That's what gave me the idea, honey." Anne Dolan's voice rose. "You said it's a big place and told me about how hard you and the sisters have to work. You must get awful tired sometimes, and it might make a lot of sense if you had somebody there to help, you know, like a priest has a housekeeper. It's a big place, and there's probably an extra room up at the top of the house, I bet, and I wouldn't want any money—or maybe just a little— they'd have to pay me minimum wage so it would be legal, but that's not much, they—"

The coldness in her daughter's green eyes stopped her excited speech.

"No, Ma," said Katherine.

"I'd be right there in the house with you, Kathy!" whispered her mother.

"The nuns do all the work in the house. It's required. It's done for penance. Outside help isn't allowed."

Anne Dolan shifted uneasily in her chair. "Are you sure you've got that right, Kathy? 'Cause you remember Mrs. Lomax at Saint Agnes every week, in the kitchen, when the nuns were too busy at the school."

Sister Katherine stood and moved to the window. She undid the latch and slid it up a few inches, allowing cool air into the room. She pressed her hands against the top of the radiator until she could stand the burning no longer. She turned back to her mother. "I talked to the director downstairs, and she said that there shouldn't be any trouble finding you a job. Most businesses would rather employ a murderer than a thief. We'll find you a place to live—"

"It's got to be nicer than this!"

"Apartments in Boston are expensive, Ma," said Katherine evenly. "Maybe you should try to find something out from the city a little—in Lowell or Springfield, maybe. Why don't—"

"But that would be so far away from you! Maybe if I called the Mother Superior down there and explained things to her, she'd—"

"No!" cried Sister Katherine. "Don't you ever call the convent again! I told you not to, but you went on and did it! There's no work there, and I don't want you annoying Mother Celestine! I'll help you all I can, I'll do everything I can, but don't you dare pick up that phone!"

Anne Dolan began to weep. "No," she said, "I wouldn't hurt you for the world, Kathy."

Katherine picked up her cape from the bed and tied it round her shoulders. "Good-bye, Ma, I'll—" She stopped, fished inside the pocket of the cape and extracted a rosary of red beads with a heavy silver-plated crucifix. She moved back to the table and took her mother's thin hand. The fingers fell open, and Sister Katherine laid the chain of beads across the calloused palm.

"It's been blessed. I had it blessed this morning."

Anne nodded dumbly and closed her hand over the rosary.

"I'll call you later this week."

Anne Dolan couldn't speak for her tears.

"Mother Superior Celestine told me to say that the whole convent was praying for you." Katherine stepped into the dimly lighted hallway and closed the door softly behind her.

32

Within a month of her release from Framingham, Anne Dolan secured employment as a part-time sales clerk in a large variety store in Central Square, Cambridge. She had wept to think she would be so near Somerville, in a place where she knew former friends to shop, but nothing else had presented itself, and she did not venture to object. She received $75 a week, and her weekly rent was $31.50.

She occupied a single room in an East Cambridge house popu-
lated mostly by unmarried male factory workers. It had a high
ceiling and three windows that looked out over a playground
noisy with children in the day and teenagers at night. A sink had
been thrust into one corner, and she had a hot plate that had been
given her by her employer because only one burner worked. She
shared a bathroom down the hall with the three men who also
lived on the third floor of the house.

The first time that Katherine visited her mother in this place,
Anne Dolan had been ashamed of her circumstances. She felt
old and wasted and helpless. In the course of the hour-long visit,
she begged her daughter to pray for her, she demanded that she
quit the convent, she asked that she pay for a television set. Anne
Dolan wanted consolation, she wanted a dye-job and permanent,
she wanted to die. Katherine had left with the vow that she would
never return. But Anne Dolan yelled out the window after the
retreating nun: "Kathy, if you're not back here next Saturday
afternoon, I'll call the Mother Superior and tell her you hit me!"

Katherine's dreams and expectations of life were soured by her
mother's reappearance. Daily Katherine vowed to strike Anne
Dolan's image from her mind, and daily it loomed larger before
her. Sister Katherine couldn't hear the telephone ring in the convent house without dreading it to be a call from her mother. Each
day, although she fought desperately against the sin, hate for her
mother's very existence grew within her. Most nights, despite
the inclement weather, Katherine would steal down from her
chamber, cross silent Mystic Avenue, and in the church pray for
God to forgive her evil and destructive emotions. She returned to
her room with trembling hands, lips still moving automatically
in supplication and a sheen of perspiration glowing on her pale
brow. In the morning, however, she felt no better for her effort
and could do nothing but vow to pray still harder.

It was just at this difficult time that another issue began to tug
at Katherine's already burdened mind. One winter afternoon,
after she had taken her last examination in the morning, Katherine sat at the back of the chapel and prayed her gratitude for
the test's having gone easily. She was alone except for the organ-

ist practicing Bach fugues. After a while Sister Henrica entered, genuflected before the altar, and slipped into the pew with Sister Katherine. Sister Henrica wet her lips as if hesitant to speak, and then slipped closer to Sister Katherine.

"I was in Boston yesterday," she whispered, and then looked at Sister Katherine with significance.

"Yes?" asked Sister Katherine, also with significance—for she could not approve of the chapel being used for casual conversation.

"I was *downtown*. At *Park Street*. At *one o'clock*."

Sister Katherine's eyes grew wide. "Yes?" she asked again.

"I *saw* you," hissed Sister Henrica, and sat back suddenly, as if with relief at a great confession.

Sister Katherine was confused. "I wasn't—"

"Shhh! Please don't try to deny it, Sister. I'm not jumping on you, I'm just warning you! What if it had been Mother Celestine or Sister Winifred instead of me?"

"What are you talking about?"

Sister Henrica made a face at what she considered Sister Katherine's wilful misunderstanding. "I saw you in street clothes. I saw you walking right by the subway, and you had on a short jacket and blue jeans. You came very near us—I can't understand why you didn't see us—and I got Sister Winifred to look the other way just in time, I—"

Sister Katherine blinked. "No," she said. "That wasn't me. That was somebody else. I wasn't in Boston yesterday."

"Yesterday. At one o'clock. I know it was you!"

"I had an exam yesterday at one o'clock. And in the morning too. I ate lunch at the cafeteria at BC with Father Dickerson, who teaches that course on problem adolescents. I was at Chestnut Hill the entire day, Sister."

Sister Henrica looked bewildered.

"Then it was your twin! It must have been! You must have a twin sister!"

"No," said Katherine. "I'm an only child."

On the following Saturday morning, Katherine was given money to cover the expense of a round-trip bus ticket to Boston, subway fare to and from East Cambridge, and lunch for herself and her mother. But when it happened that Mother Superior Celestine had to drive to Worcester that morning, she offered Sister Katherine a ride into the city, which Katherine gratefully accepted. She was let off at an Orange Line subway station in the South End, near the halfway house that had sheltered her mother, but with nearly two hours to kill before Anne Dolan got off from her morning shift.

The South End was an area of accelerating change: a population of the ethnic poor—Spanish, black, Puerto Rican—being displaced by the relentless gentrification of young professional childless couples and gays. Strings of four or more four-story town houses were run-down, one more derelict than the next, with drunks and bag-ladies encamped on the steep carved stoops, while the next several had been recently sandblasted, fitted with new carved doors, leaded glass, painted shutters, and winter window boxes of clipped evergreens. It was all a strange mixture of sagging decay and explosive restoration; but despite the signs of rejuvenation, everywhere visible, Katherine felt ill-at-ease. All the streets themselves were dirty and, she was sure, dangerous.

The idea came to her suddenly; she would not visit her mother at all. Nothing but misery waited for her in East Cambridge— nothing but pleas and recriminations and complaint. It would be unpleasant to wander the streets of Boston for the entire day, but that unpleasantness was nothing in comparison to what she would suffer in spending the afternoon with Anne Dolan. In fact, if she only went to the public library—which in the past three years had become a place well known and comfortable to her— she might pass the day in relative contentment.

It occurred to her, as she was walking past the great police station on Berkeley Street, that in her habit she might be recognized by one of the nuns also in town for the day, by a parishioner, by the parent of one of her students. This possibility made her distinctly uncomfortable, and she almost resolved to go to her mother after all. The thought of her deception becoming known to Reverend Mother Celestine was terrible.

Just before the bridge that crossed the railroad tracks, she stopped and stared at her reflection in the windows of the

Morgan Memorial, determined to remain still until she had made some decision. Looking at herself, she began to wonder if the young woman that Sister Henrica had mistaken for her was actually identical in appearance. She glanced around as if in timid expectation of finding her duplicate standing near. Katherine thought for a few minutes more, not realizing that she was drawing some attention to herself by the intensity of her gaze and her motionlessness. Then, quite resolutely, Katherine entered Morgan Memorial. She moved past the shelves of housewares and the cases of paperback books, toward the racks of women's clothing at the very back. She laid her book bag on a table, settled her cape far back on her shoulders, and one by one went through a long rack of dresses. At the last, she selected a burgundy flannel with high collar and long sleeves. She folded it and set it atop her book bag. From a table of scarves she pulled out one that was long, soft, and gray. A stiff blue vinyl coat with a rip hidden beneath the sleeve brought the total up to only a little more than eight dollars—and she had more than fifteen with her.

"It's for a woman whose apartment building burned down last night," whispered Katherine needlessly to the checkout girl.

"Great," she replied.

Katherine looked up and saw that the girl had an eye heavily ringed with purple bruises.

At a sewing notions shop on Boylston Street, Katherine purchased a ring of safety pins and slipped these into her book bag.

She mounted the steps of the Boston Public Library, stared for a moment up at the names of the world's philosophers, artists, writers, scientists, and enlightened rulers, and then entered through the swinging doors. Climbing unhesitatingly the vaulted marble stairway, she ignored the dark, dim murals that had so intrigued her in the past. She walked through an exhibition room, where she was happy to find no more than two men whispering before a large mounted poster. At the far end, beside the closed door that led to the library's rare print section, was a ladies' room. Katherine turned the handle with a perspiring hand.

As she knew, the rest room was intended for the use of only one person at the time. She locked the door behind her.

Avoiding her reflection in the mirror, Katherine made the sign of the Cross and then prayed for forgiveness as she untied her cape.

Five minutes later Katherine stood before the mirror and stared at herself in it. Her short blond hair was almost hidden beneath the gray scarf that she'd tied at the back. The burgundy flannel dress was a size too large, but the safety pins fixed to the inside of the waist gave the illusion of a comfortable fit. Beneath the skirt she had pinned up her long slip well above the hemline, and the black hose and simple black shoes had been left—they did not clash.

Someone tried the door of the room. Katherine saw a woman's shadow through the frosted glass.

"Just a minute," she called softly, in a voice that she could scarcely recognize as her own.

The shadow retreated.

Katherine folded the items of her habit and placed them neatly inside the wrinkled paper bag; she was especially careful of the wimple, rolling it about the scapular. She pulled on her jacket, adjusted a wisp of hair that had fallen across her forehead, and left the rest room. She nodded shyly to the librarian, who leaned against the wall tapping her foot impatiently.

Katherine went to the elevator and pressed the button. She threw the book bag over her shoulder and pressed the bag of clothing far up under one arm. She tried not to walk like a nun. The elevator door opened, and Katherine stepped into it alone.

For the next hour she wandered through the newer section of the library, picking books off the shelves and leafing through them. She sat at tables where serious students bent over their volumes and their notes, and avoided tables where the drunks slept and old women muttered to themselves as they worked cross-word puzzles. In the theatre in the basement she sat among a couple of hundred children and watched a film called *The Whales of the North Atlantic*. She followed some of the children into the juvenile reading room and looked through the books there with a view to recommending them to her own students.

Without her habit she was almost at her ease. The guilt that had attended her deception had been folded up and put away with the wimple, scapular, and rosary. Even if someone from the convent saw her and word got back to Hingham that she had been seen in street clothes in the Boston Public Library, Sister Katherine would have Sister Henrica's testimony that there was an exact physical duplicate to Katherine in the city. She was safe.

In the section on sociology, Katherine examined a large picture book on famous female criminals. There was a photograph of Winnie Ruth Judd, the trunk murderess, smiling as she entered the courtroom on the day of her sentencing. Reminded of Anne Dolan, she slammed the book shut and walked on. *Why should I visit her at all?* Sister Katherine thought. *She's not my real mother.*

Passing from the new portion of the building back to the old, Katherine stumbled across the microfilm viewing room. She stopped suddenly, went in, and filled out a slip for a particular month of the Boston *Globe*. She took the spool of film to a machine in the far corner of the room and, after carefully reading the instructions on its operation, threaded the film and flicked on the light.

She didn't have to go further than the first frame. The microfilm was for the month of January 1960, and on the front page of the January 1 edition was the story of the burning of the tenement building at the corner of Salem and Parmenter Streets in the North End.

Trembling as though cold, she read of her own rescue, thrown from a fourth-story window into the firemen's net. In an interview with the midwife who had visited the building only an hour before it caught fire, she learned of her twin sister, whose tiny corpse had never been found. And she found out her mother's real name: Mary Lodesco.

I'm Katherine Lodesco.

She twice advanced the frame. At the top of page three was a frightful photograph of a woman whose limp body was thrust through a broken window; flames were frozen into a flat pattern of shredded ribbon behind her. "Moments after hurling one of her hours-old twins to safety, Mary Lodesco died when her stomach was punctured with a large shard of broken glass remaining in the window frame."

Katherine pressed the switch that killed the light on the machine.

*

Katherine sat alone at the back of the overheated bus to Hingham. There were not more than twenty other riders this Saturday afternoon, mostly women who had gone into town shopping and now napped fitfully or talked in low, gossiping voices to one another. Several had nodded friendlily to Katherine when she boarded at the last minute. Katherine had so much relished the anonymity of wearing her street clothes as she wandered the rooms and corridors of the library that she had lost all notion of passing time; when at last her consciousness had registered a clock above the information desk, she had returned to the single ladies' room, changed back into her habit, and hurried out of the library. The guard on duty had not, of course, bothered to check the packages of a habited nun.

Staring out the tinted window, she thought of her mother, Mary Lodesco, who had sacrificed her life so that Katherine might live. She had died in hot flames.

Once back in Hingham, Katherine hid her purchased clothing in her locker at the school. She had thought originally to secrete it beneath her mattress at the convent, but she could not be certain that the women assigned to clean the rooms would not find it there.

After dinner in the refectory, Katherine returned to her room, drew her diary from the desk drawer, and penned the following entry:

> I rode into Boston with Reverend Mother Celestine. We talked about my classes and courses. She thinks I ought to attend the ceremony in February when I get my diploma. I never imagined that I would be a college graduate. When she let me off, I took the subway to Cambridge. I visited my mother for about four hours, from 11:30 until 3:30. We had lunch together at a small restaurant across from Lechmere. The food was very good. While we ate lunch, she told me all about my real mother, Mary Lodesco, who died trying to save me from a fire in her apartment building in the North End. That happened the same night I was born. My twin sister died, my mother couldn't save her too. My twin sister will be waiting for me in heaven when I die, but will

she still be a baby, and I'll be an old woman? God will take care of things like that, I know. Of course I always knew I was adopted, but I never knew my real mother's name and I never knew that she died trying to save my life, and I didn't know I was one of twins, and I was the lucky one. I will ask Mother Celestine if there can be a mass said for my mother, Mary Lodesco, and my sister, who never even got to be named, who both died by fire on January 1, 1960. That is my real birthday.

33

Three days later Mother Superior Celestine came up to Sister Katherine on the playground of the school. "Your mother's parole officer called a little while ago, and I took the liberty of speaking with him. You know how much interest I've felt in your mother's case—even though I've never met her."

Sister Katherine did her best to smile. "Thank you, Reverend Mother. What did he say?"

"Your mother is in a severe depression. She has missed three days at work, and also her scheduled meeting with him. That is a very bad course for your mother to take, dear. She evidently wants to see you, she evidently *needs* to see you very badly. I think that you ought to go to see her this afternoon, Sister Katherine."

"I have—"

"Your duties will be reassigned. There's a bus at eleven-thirty, and I'll have Sister Prudentia drive you to the station."

In the bottom of the book bag that Sister Katherine took with her on the bus were the clothes that she had purchased at Morgan Memorial; but today she felt that she must visit her mother in truth. In her present state, Anne Dolan might not even hesitate to get on the bus to Hingham.

Anne Dolan was happy indeed to see her daughter, and Sister Katherine was as affectionate as she could be—until she discovered that her mother's story to the parole officer had been a lie.

"Oh, Kathy, I didn't know what to do! I knew you weren't coming back for two weeks, and that seemed like such a long time! So this morning, when it was time for my meeting with Mr. Jameson, I called him up and told him how bad I felt and how much I needed to see you. I told him I had missed three days at work, but really I hadn't. I can't afford to miss work, no matter what happens. I'm sorry, Kathy, but I just had to see you! You don't know how much your visits mean to me."

"Ma," said Sister Katherine calmly, "if you ever do anything like this again, I will apply for a transfer. I'll get transferred to Oregon or Taiwan or somewhere like that—and you will never see me again. Do you understand that?"

"No! I just wanted to see you. It didn't matter—"

"Your parole officer called the convent. Mother Superior Celestine had to drop everything to talk to him, then she had to come find me on the playground. Sister Prudentia had to skip a class so that she could drive me to the bus station. Sister Birgitta had to take over my classes this afternoon, and that kept her from going to see *her* mother in the nursing home. You see the trouble you caused?"

"I didn't know, Kathy, I just thought—"

"You didn't think, Ma. You never think of anybody but yourself. Now listen, I don't intend to be your nursemaid. I'm always willing to come and see you, and come and visit you whenever I can get away from the convent. But I have my own life now—and my life is in the convent. I've devoted myself to God. I'm the bride of Christ. You seem to think I'm still a little girl and we all live happily ever after on Medford Street. Well Daddy's dead, and you're an ex-offender, and I'm a nun: things just aren't the same any more. You're different and I'm different, and you're trying to treat me like things were just the same as they always were!"

"No I'm not, I—"

"Ma!" cried Sister Katherine. "You're not listening to me. Listen to me! You've got to leave me alone!"

Yet Katherine knew that remonstration was useless. Anne Dolan, so long as she had breath in her body, would be her curse and bane.

On Christmas Eve Katherine again found herself in her mother's small rented room in East Cambridge. The window blinds were up, and beyond the glass a light snow was falling. In each window Anne Dolan had suspended wreaths of long-needle pine encrusted with red-sprayed cones. A large paper pop-up crèche rested on the table. Arranged round the nativity scene were a number of small packages done up in brown paper and bright ribbons—gifts of homemade jams and jellies, fruitcake, nuts, and sweet bread, prepared for Anne Dolan by Sisters Henrica and Prudentia. A larger package contained a shawl of white virgin wool knitted by Reverend Mother Celestine herself. She had even embellished one corner with three ornate crosses representing the Crucifixion.

In her canvas book bag Katherine had two gifts for her mother. One was wrapped in shiny blue foil with a white bow; it had been purchased at the last minute at the small Christmas shop run by the sisters in the recreational hall of the Church of St. Luke. The second was a bottle of sweet berry wine made in the kitchen of St. Luke's—Sister Prudentia's special recipe. It was wrapped in bright red foil with a green bow round the neck. Into the bottle Katherine had poured enough rat poison to kill every inhabitant of her mother's rooming house.

Katherine apologized to her mother for her sharpness the previous week, and Anne Dolan waved away that apology in embarrassment. "Oh, Kathy, of course you were right, I guess. I'm just an old woman now, and I can't expect you to take care of me. I guess I just keep thinking about things, and how I'd *like* them to be, that's all. And you know, I've never been alone before, never in my life, like I'm alone now. I lived at home, and then I married Jim, then you came along. Even at Framingham, I was never alone. But now I am, and it's hard . . ."

She was sitting in an armchair she'd raked close to the table. Katherine sat stiffly in a high-backed wooden chair only inches from her. Anne Dolan kept one bony hand dangling against her daughter's robes. For the occasion she had tied a red velvet ribbon in her hair and attached a sprig of vibrant green plastic holly to the breast of her brown sweater. There was a chill in the room, and Anne Dolan held the collar of the sweater closed with her other hand. When once it fell open, Katherine saw to her astonishment that her mother was wearing the red-beaded rosary as if it were a necklace, with the heavy silver crucifix resting against her breast.

Katherine had advised her mother to wait until Christmas to open the gifts, but Anne Dolan protested, "I'll be all alone tomorrow, what would be the fun in that?!" As her mother slowly unwrapped each present, Katherine told who it was from and promised that she would relay her mother's gratitude. Katherine prepared instant coffee and brought plates for the cake, and slowly ate as her mother arranged the gifts in a little arc on the table. She had already wrapped the shawl round her shoulders.

"I've saved yours for last," she said.

"Well, Ma, the shawl is the nicest. Mine's not nearly so nice."

"Yes, but it's from *you*, and that's what matters." She pulled over Katherine's gift and slowly unwrapped it. Inside the box, wrapped in tissue, was a hand carved crèche of wood and ivory. Anne Dolan moved her chair so that the meager light from the window fell full upon it. "Oh, it's so beautiful, Kathy! Did the sisters make it?"

"It's from Germany, Ma. It's all done by hand . . . But when I got it I didn't know you already had one," she said, indicating the paper scene on the table before them.

Anne Dolan frowned. "Oh that!" she said disdainfully. "That's just nothing. I got that from the store. I just took it home with me one day."

"You stole it!" cried Sister Katherine, amazed.

"No," said Anne Dolan wonderingly. "I just brought it home. Like all the other ladies there do."

"Ma—"

Anne Dolan took up the paper crèche and tore it in half. She dropped the pieces on the floor with the discarded paper and ribbon. The carved manger took its place on the table.

"You remember that big manger scene your grandma used to have on top of the TV set every year? That was nice, but it wasn't as nice as this one. I miss Mama sometimes. You know, the only time I got to leave Framingham was to go to her funeral. She wrote to me once. She said she heard I was in prison, and she wanted to know what I had done. I never wrote back. I miss her sometimes. I miss Jim, too. You know, when I'm at the register,

I can see the Necco building out the front window. So when I'm at the register, I think of Jim all day long. He was so good to us! Kathy, didn't you say you had *two* presents for me?"

"No, Ma," replied Katherine after a moment, "there was just the manger."

Anne Dolan begged another Christmas gift that her daughter was reluctant to bestow: she wanted to visit her husband's grave. Katherine pointed to the increasing snow; she thought the cemetery might not be open on Christmas Eve; they had no way of getting there easily—but Anne Dolan pressed, and Katherine gave in. She would be able to tell Reverend Mother Celestine that she had at last persuaded her mother to visit James Dolan's grave.

They travelled to the cemetery by taxi and, once there, had to ask a caretaker to locate the plot for them. There was no marker —the burial policy money had run out just at that point—and only a slight sinking in the blanket of snow indicated that it was in fact a grave. Anne Dolan began to sob. She took the rosary from around her neck and ran the beads through her fingers. After three decats she dropped to her knees in the snow.

"Ma, get up!" hissed Katherine, heartily embarrassed despite the fact that they were alone. "You'll catch pneumonia down there!" Katherine gripped her mother's thin forearm and pulled her to her feet.

"Poor Jim!" she cried. "Kathy, you should say your beads too!"

"We'll find a church, Ma. Where it's warm and dry."

Katherine tugged her mother away. Anne's low heels slipped in the snow and she flung out her arm to maintain balance. The rosary flew from her fingers and dropped in the snow near her husband's grave. She jerked away from her daughter and stumbled toward the rosary. She fell onto her side, and, trying to raise herself, she only rolled over onto James Dolan's little sinking plot.

She didn't even try to get up, but only turned her weeping face into the snow.

Sister Katherine stooped, grasped her mother's arms, and lifted her up. "Ma," she said quietly, "this is why I didn't want us to come. Look what you've done: you've got snow all over Mother Celestine's shawl."

"My rosary!" she sobbed. "That's the rosary you gave me!"

Sister Katherine retrieved the rosary and placed it in her mother's hands. She readjusted the shawl about Anne Dolan's shoulders. Unmindful of the wet ground, she knelt and brushed the snow from her mother's legs and shoes. Then, holding her arm tightly, she led her from the cemetery.

When they returned to Anne's room, Katherine took out the bottle of wine and placed it on the mantelpiece. "Sister Prudentia made it, Ma. She said you shouldn't worry about how much you drink, because it's not really alcoholic at all. I like it a lot."

That evening, an hour after dinner, Reverend Mother Celestine called Katherine to her office. There was a little fire of birch in the hearth, and the only other illumination in the room was the antique lamp on Mother Celestine's desk. Dim firelight played shadows about Katherine when she entered the room. When Mother Celestine requested that she take the chair nearest the desk, Katherine declined and stepped just to the edge of the pool of light cast by the green-shaded lamp. Her face was mostly obscured by the changing shadows. Her wimple, and that of the superior across from her, were made a pale, crackling orange by the fitful light of the fire.

Mother Celestine rose from her armchair and moved to stand in the bay of the window. Her expression was deeply troubled. She laid one hand lightly against a pane of cold glass and stared distractedly into the chill night as she spoke.

"Sister Katherine," she began, "your life, since you came to us, and even before, has been full of unhappiness . . ."

"But I've never been as happy as I am now, Reverend Mother, now that my final vows are so near. And," Katherine added, "now that my mother has been able to begin her new life."

Mother Celestine turned from the window to face the young nun, said nothing for a long moment, and then stepped into the perimeter of green light. Katherine became increasingly uneasy. Mother Celestine rested the tips of her fingers on the desk; Katherine could see the sorrow in her eyes.

"Oh, Sister Katherine . . . my poor child." Mother Celestine's voice was no more than a whisper. "I would give anything on earth not to have to—" She drew in her breath: "Your mother is dead, and she died by her own hand."

The fire crackled and hissed in the steely silence that fell between them. Katherine drew her hands up slowly and closed them, fist into palm, before her. She said nothing, but waited for Mother Celestine to continue.

"It happened this evening, probably no more than an hour after you left her."

Katherine drew further back into the shadow. She turned toward the low fire, away from Mother Celestine. It was necessary to hide the relief that flooded her: at last she was entirely free.

Mother Celestine came round the desk and stood behind Katherine. She placed her hands firmly on the young woman's shoulders. Katherine lowered her chin and said in a low voice, "How? How did she do it?"

"Not now, child."

"Please, Mother, I ought to know. Ma—"

"She hanged herself—with the shawl that you gave her this afternoon."

"What!" cried Katherine. "She *hanged* herself?"

Mother Celestine nodded, and when she spoke, her voice broke. "I'm so sorry, Sister Katherine." Her hands closed tighter over Katherine's shoulders.

Katherine went to the fire; she bent forward and stared into it. With her cupped hand, she covered the smile that would have betrayed her.

The next day Katherine returned to her mother's room. She bundled all Anne Dolan's clothing and meager effects into the bed cover, placed them on the doorstep of the building, and called for the Salvation Army to pick them up. The poisoned wine was poured down the sink, and the bottle deposited in the trash can on the neighboring playground.

34

Sitting at the small table in her room, Katherine unlatched her diary and turned to a blank page. She'd removed her veil and wimple and run her fingers through her short blond hair, massaging the nape of her neck and bowing her back slightly as she stretched. Tension seemed always to be with her lately, and now a headache throbbed dully behind her eyes. She wrote:

> When I think about the Ultimate Sacrifice that Christ made upon the Cross of Calvary, I am filled with a sadness so great it can't be measured. This sadness doesn't leave room enough for grief over Ma's death. We are told that this is the way it should be, but the sisters look at me strangely, and think it is strange that I'm not crying because Ma is dead. I can't cry, I try to think of Ma and pray for her, but I end up thinking about Christ on the Calvary Cross—and that's the way it should be. When I came in this order I left the world behind. That's what I'd like to tell the sisters: *I've left the world behind.*

No announcement had been made of the death by suicide of Katherine's mother, but all the convent knew of it. Katherine felt herself constantly observed; and the attention was disconcerting and wholly unwelcome. The eyes that fell upon her were sympathetic and genuinely sorrowful, but Katherine wanted only to be ignored. She dreaded to find herself alone with a sister, for then the other nun would invariably take the opportunity to speak a word of consolation; Katherine was ever at a loss for a response to this kindness. She looked away, she thanked the sister, and she moved quickly on. It was thought that Sister Katherine was grief-stricken over her mother's grisly and unholy death. Her plight had provided hushed conversation over the preparation of meals, in minutes before bedtime, while a hundred different duties were carried out in the convent and the church.

Katherine felt no sorrow. Her apparent unhappiness was the result of the attention that was paid to her because of her bereavement. For Katherine, the death of Anne Dolan had but a single meaning: it was liberation. That her mother had died truly by her own hand and not Katherine's was an unmistakable sign of God's favor. Katherine saw a parallel with the story of Abraham and Isaac: she had been willing to sacrifice her mother in order to obey God more perfectly, but at the very last, the sacrifice had not been required of her. Katherine had not yet found opportunity to dispose of her street clothes, but the certainty that she would never again have to employ them in deceit was a distinct relief. Her past lay where pasts should lie: far behind her—it no longer encroached on her present contentments. Now that Anne Dolan was dead, there was no one to preserve the memory of Katherine Dolan. Now there was only Sister Katherine of the Order of the Slaves of the Immaculate Conception.

After the autopsy had been performed on Anne Dolan's body, it was released for burial. James Dolan's burial policy through Necco would have covered the expenses of Katherine's mother's funeral, but because of her suicide, Anne Dolan could not be buried in a Roman Catholic cemetery. Katherine refused to claim the body. Reverend Mother Celestine had gently suggested that Katherine find a Protestant or municipal cemetery, which had no directives against those who took their own lives, but Katherine said that she would accept humbly the teaching of the church in this matter. Katherine signed a certificate donating her mother's body for medical research. There would be no funeral to attend, no grave to visit.

And why *should* she attend the funeral or visit the grave of a woman who had not loved her, and who was, after all, not her real mother? Anne Dolan hadn't loved Katherine, she had only *needed* her. Her real mother had died on the night she was born; her real mother had died just hours after giving birth to twins.

The following day Katherine volunteered to help scrub the tiled floors on the convent's kitchen. She was granted permission by Sister Lazarus, whose duty was to organize work details, and so Katherine spent the hours after luncheon on her knees, alongside Sisters Philomena and Alfred. The floors of the convent were scrubbed twice a week, the work devolving either by rotation or penance. Grime was painstakingly scraped from between the small squares of quarry tile until the mortar shone; the baseboards met the floor in a clean, straight line. The sisters used buckets, small wire brushes, and putty knives. It was neither easy work nor happy, but to Katherine it was preferable to remaining silent and alone in her chamber. With her sleeves pinned up to the elbows and a large denim apron protecting her habit, Katherine crawled along the outside wall and chanted prayers in time with Sisters Philomena and Alfred. Singing and conversation were forbidden when performing work that was deliberately menial.

Katherine had been on her knees somewhat more than an hour when Sister Henrica appeared in the doorway and quietly told her that she was required directly in Mother Celestine's office.

She wiped the perspiration from her cheeks with the corner of her apron, undid her sleeves, and removed the apron. She shot a look of apology to Sister Alfred because she must walk across the space just waxed by the nun.

On her way to Mother Celestine's study, Katherine inwardly prepared herself for more bad news. She suspected that, in some unforeseeable manner, her mother was going to reach from beyond the grave to trouble her. Mother Celestine nodded silently to Katherine and motioned her to take a chair.

Katherine sat and did not return Mother Celestine's comforting, forced smile. Mother Celestine, correctly interpreting the postulant's despairing dread, then said quickly, in a level voice, "Sister Katherine, I will come directly to the point."

Katherine nodded her thanks for this kindness.

"I have conferred with my superiors at the Mother House in Worcester, and after some difficult debate we have decided that it will not be . . . *expedient* for you to finish your trial of postulancy at Saint Luke's."

Katherine drew in her breath sharply and stiffened.

Seeing Katherine recoil, Mother Celestine rose, stood behind Katherine's chair, and placed an arm gently about the young woman's shoulder. Katherine did not move, and would not look at Mother Celestine.

"In a week or so, you will be transferred from Hingham to the Mother House in Worcester, and there—"

"You're not going to let me take my final vows!" cried Katherine grimly.

Mother Celestine's grip tightened on Katherine's shoulder. Then she let go and came around to face her. "How could you think such a thing! No, child, you will certainly remain a blessed Slave. That is your chosen life, and you have consistently demonstrated your love of it. There are few young women more suited to the conventual life than you, Sister Katherine, we would—"

Katherine, flushed with relief, pressed her burning cheek against the back of the leather chair, crushing her starched wimple. In a few moments she turned back to Mother Celestine. "I'm sorry," she whispered, "I thought—"

"No," smiled Mother Celestine, "we were thinking only of you. No young woman in our memory has undergone so difficult a postulancy as you, Sister Katherine. I needn't remind you why. We had thought that removal from Somerville would be sufficient, but we fear that you are still too close to the scenes of your unhappiness—"

"Yes," said Katherine quickly, "I am. I'm too close . . ."

"And for that reason, you are being transferred to Worcester—"

"But what about my work at BC? I've only got one semester to go, and then—"

"Sister Katherine," said Mother Celestine, "please don't interrupt, or I shall never be able to finish."

Katherine bowed her head.

"Both Holy Cross and Clark are very good schools, and with your grades, I think you will have no difficulty in signing up—even at this late date. The order does not intend to deprive you of your teacher's certificate."

"Thank you, Reverend Mother. I apologize. It's just that—"

"I know, dear: it's sudden. Now, Sister Katherine, you have spoken to me several times with real interest, I think, of our missions—"

Katherine looked up sharply.

"Yes," smiled Mother Celestine. "You *were* interested, weren't you?"

"Yes, very," she whispered.

"We have decided that as soon as you have taken your vows, we will give you the opportunity to assume a post at one of the mission schools. In most cases, the teacher's certificate will not be necessary. The BA that you already possess will be sufficient for the purpose. Now these are almost always difficult positions, and our charges there are often *most* unfortunate, but our missions' work in these places is doubly blest of God for its very difficulty. It is, moreover, far removed from anything you've ever known; you have never travelled, have you, Sister Katherine?"

"I've been to Worcester, Reverend Mother, when I visited the Mother House with Sister Mary Claire. And once I went to Springfield, to a play."

Mother Celestine smiled. "Our missions are farther removed than that, I fear. In any case, the matter will be left up to you. You can always return to school after a few years and pick up your certificate. This, after all, should be a spiritual and not a secular decision. And you need not—"

"I've already made up my mind," said Katherine hurriedly.

"Yes?"

"I want to teach at one of the missions."

Mother Celestine cocked her head as she smiled. "All right, Sister Katherine. You must know that I'm pleased with your answer, but for now, we'll have to consider this a conditional decision. You should not hesitate to change your mind."

"There is nothing that I want more, Reverend Mother, nothing!"

After the lights were extinguished that night, Katherine stood a long while at her window and gazed fixedly at the fresh blanket of snow on the back lawn and the frozen grass at the edge of the marsh. At last she slipped beneath the blankets of her cot, and her slumber was not disturbed in the least by unwelcome dreams.

35

Several nuns stood cleaning and chopping vegetables at the enormous butcher's table in the center of the basement kitchen. Sister Prudentia stood at the counter, brutally kneading one of several large bowls of bread dough. Eighteen greased bread pans were lined up ready to bake the two-day supply for the house. As had been the custom at the Convent of St. Agnes, there was a radio playing here, but Sister Prudentia, complaining of the depressing news, had turned to easy-listening music. This was technically an infraction of rules, but no one made any objection.

Nodding cordially to Sister Katherine when she came down the stairs, Sister Prudentia flicked a drop of perspiration from her cheek and left a streak of dough behind to mark the place. Sister Katherine smiled, but said nothing. Often she came to the kitchen in the late mornings, although she was rarely assigned to duty there. She enjoyed the warmth—the convent was kept very cool, for reasons of economy and self-denial alike—as well as the smell of fresh fruit and vegetables and rich chicory coffee. Katherine poured herself a mug of that coffee and sat on a stool at the far end of the counter, near the window that overlooked the withered herb garden and the salt marsh. It was the second day of the new year, and although St. Luke's school was back in session, Sister Katherine was no longer required to attend to her former duties there. This might have been a lazy time for her, but that her mind, at least, was always busy with the future—the future as she had always imagined it, free from the restraints of her family, free to accept entirely the strong bonds of the church. Soon she would be in Worcester; in another month she would have joined the Order; and a month after that might well see her heading up a classroom at one of the far-flung missions maintained by the Slaves of the Immaculate Conception. The steam of the coffee began to fog the windowpanes, and Katherine felt wisps of cold air over the backs of her hands. She blinked and turned from the glass.

The morning's edition of the *Herald-American* lay nearby. Idly, Katherine drew it over. The front page recorded rumors of a new Middle East War, the vandalism of a Rembrandt portrait, and a graft scandal in the Boston police department. At the bottom, however, was the headline "Weston Couple Slain New Year's Eve."

Katherine closed her eyes and breathed a quick "Hail Mary" for their souls. Below the headline was a photograph of the murdered pair: Vittoria Marie and Cosmo Antonio LoPonti—the copy of a photograph taken in a hotel bar in Quebec City, Canada.

Katherine sipped her coffee and read the story.

An electrical contractor and city alderman for the town of Weston, Cosmo LoPonti and his wife Vittoria spent the days between Christmas and New Year's attending a convention in Quebec City, Canada. They left at home their only child, Andrea, a senior honor-student at Wenham College. Returning on New Year's Eve, about 4 p.m., they were surprised not to find their daughter to meet them at the airport, as she had promised. They took a taxi home, and from there telephoned several of their daughter's friends, who however could give no indication of Miss LoPonti's whereabouts, or any reason for her failure to appear at the airport.

What occurred over the next twelve hours is unknown. The following morning, about nine o'clock, a friend of Andrea LoPonti's, Marsha Liberman, also a senior at Wenham, telephoned the LoPontis in order to ascertain whether her friend had returned. There was no answer, and after an hour or so, Miss Liberman drove over to the LoPontis' house. Finding the front door unlocked and ajar, she went inside and discovered the body of Mr. LoPonti. He had been shot twice in the chest. Miss Liberman found the body on the floor beside the bed in the master bedroom. She telephoned the police immediately, and waited for them in the kitchen. The body of Vittoria LoPonti, with a single bullet fired at close range through the back of her neck, was later found by the police, wedged between the wall and the toilet in the small bathroom off the daughter's room.

Neighbors questioned said they heard nothing unusual that night.

Drawers in the bedrooms had been gone through, and jewelry and some cash had evidently been taken. Police speculate that the couple were murdered by burglars. Preliminary medical reports place the time of death at around midnight, New Year's Eve.

The whereabouts of Andrea LoPonti are unknown. It is also not known whether she returned to her home before the robbery took place. If she did, the police fear that she may have been abducted by the killers.

The story had been continued on the third page. When she finished reading it, Katherine realized that there was a second picture accompanying it—a photograph of the dead couple's only child—with the caption "Daughter sought."

Katherine stared at the photograph of Andrea LoPonti. "Dear God . . ." she whispered. A nun shredding carrots looked over at her. Katherine fumbled for her canvas book bag and drew out a black marking pen. She uncapped it and gripped it violently over the photograph. Then, holding her breath, Katherine ran the pen over the photograph in a definite pattern of lines and blackened spaces.

Around the shoulders and head of Andrea LoPonti, Katherine drew a crude version of the habit of the Slaves of the Immaculate Conception—the same habit she wore now. The photograph had become a portrait of herself.

Katherine crossed herself feverishly as she thought of the fire in the North End on New Year's Eve, 1960. The newspaper account swam before her, and for the first time it possessed immediacy and importance. When she had read it off the microfilm, she had not felt that she was actually part of that terrible story. Katherine was the twin who was saved, the twin who was thrown from the window.

But had her sister really died? Their mother, Mary Lodesco, was unquestionably dead; Katherine had seen her picture, flames behind, her belly pierced with a shard of glass. But the corpse of the other child had never been found. And if Andrea LoPonti were that missing sister, then all of their adoptive parents were dead. And all of them, Katherine's and Andrea's, had died violently.

Katherine looked about the kitchen. Sister Prudentia was dividing the dough into the pans. The nuns at the butcher block were putting together a carrot salad for luncheon. Andrea folded the newspaper and slipped it into her canvas bag; she murmured an excuse that she must write some letters, and left the kitchen.

In the sanctuary of the Church of St. Luke, Sister Lazarus and the sixth-grade choir were in rehearsal for Sunday's mass. Katherine had hoped to find a place alone, but resigned herself to the music. She dropped her bag onto a pew near the front and knelt on the velvet cushion. She rubbed her eyes, feeling suddenly weary and drained. In the loft a dozen unsteady soprano voices sang "Ave Maria." Late morning sunlight streamed through the stained glass behind the altar, showering Katherine in gold and scarlet.

Katherine thought about Andrea LoPonti. She had become convinced that Andrea was her twin sister, although there was, and could be, no final proof of this. And what did it matter? She could never see the young woman again, never have the opportunity to reveal their strange, unexpected kinship. Katherine would be in the Hingham convent for no more than another two weeks. Then she would leave Boston, very possibly forever. Her life would be devoted wholly to God and to the Church. And now, to God and to the Church she commended her spirit, her life—and her past. She would have no roots now but those that struck deep into the soil of the conventual life; she would have no parent but the Mother Superior; she would have no loved ones but the children and the unfortunates who were placed under her care.

Katherine knelt in thankfulness. The sunlight burned brightly into her forehead, like a benediction from God's searing hand. Behind her in the loft, Sister Lazarus led her choristers in one of the youthful anthems that would be sung on Sunday:

O blessed souls are they,
    Whose sins are covered o'er!
Divinely blest, to whom the Lord
    Imputes their guilt no more!

They mourn their follies past.
    And keep their hearts with care;
Their lips and lives, without deceit.
    Shall prove their faith sincere.

While I concealed my guilt,
    I felt the festering wound;
Till I confessed my sins to thee.
    And ready pardon found.

Katherine's elation remained with her through the day; she did not write in her diary for fear of betraying too much even to that silent conspirator. That night, her sleep was fitful. Stylized images of the day she would celebrate her final vows shimmered in her taxed brain, and she experienced the ceremony in its modest splendor. She sensed a double line of nuns behind her as she knelt before the altar of an imagined church. Katherine raised her eyes, but not to the attending mother superior. It was Andrea LoPonti who stood there, smiling, uttering words Katherine could hear but could not understand. Katherine lifted her hands to her twin sister and discovered they glistened brightly with fresh blood. She would have wiped the blood away on her new black garments, but Andrea LoPonti, still smiling, descended the steps of the altar and took Katherine's hands in her own.

The blood spilled into a thick crimson pool in Katherine's black lap. And although she pleaded, Andrea LoPonti would not let go her hands.

Sister Katherine received permission from Mother Celestine to go into Boston that next afternoon in order to return several volumes to the Boston Public Library. This was a request not much out of the ordinary, and it excited no comment either from the mother superior or from the other sisters whom Katherine informed of her destination and purpose.

In the ladies' room of South Station terminal, Katherine stood at a sink, splashed water on her face, and dabbed her cheeks dry with a paper towel until the two women already there had left. She took the vinyl jacket, the dress, and the scarf from her book bag and stuffed them into the trash receptacle farthest from the door. Retrieving from the bottom of the bag the newspaper containing the story of the LoPontis' murder and the altered photograph of Andrea LoPonti, she placed it in another can at the opposite end of the room. She had not dared dispose of these items in Hingham, and now that she had destroyed the last link with her former life, Katherine was dizzy with relief. She crossed herself, following in the mirror the movement of her fingers against her scapular. She adjusted her wool cape and walked resolutely out of the room.

In the main waiting room, Katherine could see a tall, slender man with dark, tanned skin and shining black eyes. He had turned at the sound of her heels on the granite steps. Katherine was used to being closely observed: all nuns were objects of interest when they appeared in their robes in public. Katherine put on her face of inconsequentiality and passed him by without looking again.

He grabbed her arm.

"Hey, little Wenham girl," he said in an insinuating, Spanish-accented voice that made Katherine tremble, "you in mourning for somebody?"

She was too startled to withdraw her arm immediately, but then she resolutely yanked herself free.

"Little Wenham girl got all dressed up to go out of town, didn't she? Stay awhile, little Wenham girl," he whispered, and his smile was a leer.

Katherine kept walking toward the front doors. The man followed closely, his hand tight about her elbow. Katherine looked out for a policeman from whom she might claim protection.

"Little Wenham girl—" the man whispered in her ear.

"No!" cried Katherine. She again jerked away from him, hurried through the front doors of the station, and fled into the back of a taxi.

The man who had so evidently mistaken her, or who was perhaps just crazy, stood on the sidewalk and made a halting attempt to reach for the handle of the taxi door.

Katherine slammed down the lock. "Washington Street," she demanded of the driver, and looked with terror at the grinning face that peered at her through the streaked window.

Katherine was let out on the corner of Washington and Stuart streets. She was glad that she had had the sense not to tell the driver to take her to the public library, for the man—if he followed—would easily have found her there. Heavy wet snow had begun to fall from the slate-gray sky, and Katherine knew that she must get quickly away. It was still possible that the man in the bus station would find her—he might have heard the little she did tell the driver.

She pulled up the hood of her cape and looked about, not certain in which direction to go. Suddenly she realized the full implication of his words: "Little Wenham girl, little Wenham girl . . ." He had thought her Andrea LoPonti in disguise. Katherine shivered and felt weak. She took a deep breath of the cold air and moved down Stuart Street in the direction of Chinatown. At the corner of Harrison Avenue, as she was waiting for the traffic light to change, she remembered the church that was just around the corner. She turned and hurried toward it. There she would be safe.

36

Andrea drove from Jamaica Plain into downtown Boston. On that ride through the fog-shrouded streets the realization had come to her in all its terrible force that she had just murdered two human beings—murdered them in an almost casual fashion. Yet her only regret was that she had left Jack alive. She thought of her house in Weston, and of her parents who lay dead inside it. Brutally to herself, Andrea remembered how she had last seen them: cold, stiff, spattered with blood. The gun that had killed them now tugged in the pocket of her jacket. She parked the Trans-Am on a quiet street in the South End that was labeled Resident Parking

Only and walked up Tremont Street until she came to a coffee shop. Here she sat with a cup of coffee that grew cold as she tried to gather her wits and control the shaking of her limbs.

She could not return to Weston, knowing that her parents lay dead in the house. She could not go to Wenham, either: the dormitory would not open for another two days. It was impossible to go to the police before her parents were found, because she would be forced to account for her absence. And it would be improvident to tell of the house in Jamaica Plain before the murders were discovered there. She had come to a hopeless pass.

Andrea, badly confused, wandered Boston all that day. It was with trepidation that she turned every corner, and with terror that she saw any jeep parked or moving in traffic. Although the morning had dissipated the fog, it had brought with it cold air. Nevertheless, Andrea sat on a bench in the Public Gardens and hurriedly devoured the hamburgers she had bought in a McDonald's near the Common. The afternoon she spent in a sordid cinema on Washington Street: it played a double bill of two fifties horror films, a serial from the forties, and half an hour of trailers. Through it all, Andrea was distracted by the snoring of tramps sleeping in the seats around her and the wail of a trombone from the strip joint that adjoined the theatre.

Although she wasn't hungry, she returned to the McDonald's for dinner, and that night she sat through *The Empire Strikes Back* two and a half times. She had been four days now without a bath, and in that time she had been kidnapped, gang raped, and shot up with heroin—it was no wonder she was stared at in the street.

That night she took a room in a small hotel on lower Washington Street: she was too dishevelled to be admitted to any of the better places; she had no identification for the YWCA, and her plight there would doubtless excite curiosity. She paid in advance with some of the money that had been stolen from her father. The clerk asked for how many hours she wanted the room.

"All night," she stammered.

He shrugged and handed her the key. "Do you want to leave your name, honey?" he asked. "In case there are any messages, I mean?"

"There won't be any messages," said Andrea, entering the rickety elevator. All night long, as she lay fully clothed on the soiled sheets, she listened to doors opened and slammed all along the corridor. On her way to the bathroom she had seen two frowsy women assisting two very drunken men into one bedroom, and a still more drunken man exiting from another.

Finding no cloth or towel in the bathroom, she returned to her room, ripped off a strip of material from the curtains hanging across the single grimy window, returned, and washed herself clean with that. Toward morning she slept a little, but a man with a gimlet eye and a bucket opened her door at nine o'clock and told her she had to get out.

"Who are you?" Andrea whispered.

"Oh," he leered, "I'm just the chambermaid."

That morning Andrea purchased a *Globe* from a machine and, while she drank coffee at a booth in Burger King, read the account of her parents' deaths.

On the obituary page she found another notice of both her father and her mother, detailing their civic accomplishments. In the column *Other Deaths*, subdivision "Jamaica Plain," she hunted in vain for notice of Morgie and Sid. The fact that they had not yet been reported dead made Andrea apprehensive. By all rights their deaths should have been listed—how had Dominic and Rita and Jack kept them secret? Andrea shoved the paper aside with a trembling hand.

At a clothing store on Washington Street, she purchased two new outfits, and next door, at a discount drugstore, she picked up a large selection of toiletries and a cheap suitcase. In a restroom at City Hall she changed into one of the outfits, leaving her much-soiled other clothing on the hook in a stall, retaining only her pea jacket. She applied makeup carefully but sparingly and, in the early afternoon, checked into a Holiday Inn on Huntingdon Avenue.

She wanted time to think. She was almost certain now that she would turn herself in to the police; even if worse came to worst, she could admit to the killings of Morgie and Sid, pleading insanity by reason of drugs and multiple rape. Not even the jury that had convicted Patty Hearst would declare her guilty after she had told her tale. She needed only a little time to get her story straight. She did not yet know whether or not she had best wait until the deaths of Morgie and Sid were made public before she went to the police.

But as she sat alone in the motel room and stared out at the traffic along Huntingdon Avenue three floors below, she could think of nothing but that her parents were dead, and that she was alone in the world. How was she to deal with that? Even if she were to come through all these crowding troubles, there would be nothing of value to her on the other side. There would be no more shopping trips with her mother; her father would never trim another tree. The Society for the Preservation of Weston Antiquities would have to elect a new recording secretary, and the hydrangeas would die of neglect.

Eventually she slept, a heavy, unrestful slumber. When she waked, it was to find that she had merely fallen across the bed. Her feet still rested squarely on the carpet. It was ten o'clock. Andrea walked dazed out of the motel, ate at Brigham's in Prudential Center, and returned. Having thought of nothing at all, she undressed, turned down the covers of the bed, and fell immediately asleep again.

She rose at noon, roused by the knock of a more respectable chambermaid. She secured the room for another day and decided that she would walk around for a few hours, allow the air to refresh her and clear her mind —and then, if she had convinced herself that nothing was to be irretrievably lost by it, she would turn herself in to the police. She would appear on their steps as Andrea LoPonti, the unfortunate daughter of the upright couple who had been brutally slain in their house in Weston.

"I was kidnapped," she'd say. "I was taken to this house in Jamaica Plain, and I was raped. I was given drugs, and I've been wandering Boston in a daze."

Andrea had had a lunch of boiled duck on rice in an out-of-the-way Chinese restaurant that seemed to be frequented principally by pimps and nurses. As she walked through the beginning snow toward the center of town, her attention was attracted by a nun, in full black habit, who was let out of a cab on Stuart Street.

There was something familiar about her, and while the traffic light continued against them, Andrea studied her.

It was the nun that Marsha had pointed out on the boardwalk at Nantasket Beach. It was Andrea's double.

The lights changed, and the nun crossed the street. Backing out of the way into the recessed door of a bank, Andrea watched as she passed.

The nun crossed Harrison Avenue between double-parked cars and mounted the steps of a church. She stopped for a moment at the schedule of services and then went inside. Impulsively, Andrea followed her.

Inside the church, Andrea took a place in the last pew. She watched the nun perform the Stations of the Cross. When the nun had finished, genuflected before the main altar, and started back up the aisle again, Andrea stood in the pew to face her. Andrea knew that she would speak to her. But what she would say, she had no idea.

The nun stopped a few feet away, and the ashen expression on her face convinced Andrea that she too was strongly affected by their resemblance. When Andrea took a single step toward the aisle, the nun all but ran toward the doors. Still acting purely on instinct, and not knowing why it seemed suddenly vital that she speak to this young woman in black robes, Andrea quickly followed her.

Within the dark vestibule, lighted only by a buzzing low-watted bulb in the ceiling, the nun struggled to pull open one of the heavy brassbound front doors. A thin slash of gray light and a dissipating line of snow spilled inside.

Andrea grabbed the nun's arm, jerked her back into the vestibule, and slammed the door shut.

The nun twisted her arm free and cowered against the door. Her bag slipped over her arm and dropped to the tile floor. She fumbled with the great doorknob behind her.

"The police are looking for you!" the nun hissed.

"How do you know that?" said Andrea. Her voice, to her surprise, sounded normal. It was as if she were responding to a remark made in a classroom.

The nun managed to pull the door open. She jumped forward

with the knob in her hand. A blast of snow-laden wind gushed inside and billowed the nun's cape about her head. Andrea retreated a step.

"How do you know that?" repeated Andrea, more forcefully. The nun's face shone in the pale daylight. A middle-aged couple slipped through the open door and smiled at the nun. "Thank you," they said, and hurried through the cold vestibule into the sanctuary.

"Close that door!" cried Andrea.

The nun allowed the door to slam shut.

"Don't you know who I am?" she said.

"Who *you* are?" demanded Andrea. "How should I know who *you* are?"

"I'm your sister."

Andrea's mouth dropped open. Her breath was stopped.

"I am your *sister*," the nun repeated, her voice almost defiant.

Andrea blinked, and did not conceal the grim smile that began to crease her mouth.

37

Katherine laid her hand next to Andrea's. "Look at our hands, they're exactly alike. If our hands are exactly alike, and everything else is the same, then we've got to be twin sisters."

Andrea saw only that her nail polish was chipped, and that the nails of the nun had been bitten almost to the quick.

They sat in the last booth of a narrow restaurant two doors away from the church. Andrea had her back to the entrance; she had removed neither her hat nor her coat. Katherine sat with her right arm pressed firmly against the inside wall, as if for support.

The waitress placed two white porcelain mugs between them. The steaming coffee sloshed over the rims of both cups and splashed the table. Katherine pulled several paper napkins from the holder and began wiping up the liquid. Andrea held the mug in her hands, but did not drink from it.

"Why do you think I'm your sister?"

"We look just alike," replied Katherine.

"I know that. I've seen you before. I saw you on the boardwalk at Nantasket Beach, with some children," Andrea said, and then added carefully, "but I've got other doubles too, you know."

"Other doubles?" asked Katherine. "Did your other doubles wear earrings just like yours?" asked Sister Katherine softly. She pushed back her wimple and turned her head so that Andrea saw the ruby chip embedded in her left ear.

Andrea began to stammer.

Katherine said: "I'm not supposed to wear this, of course. It's an infraction of rules. But I've had it all my life, and it's hard to give it up. Now it's the only thing that's left of my former life. My father is dead—he was murdered in Somerville."

"That was you too!" whispered Andrea. "I've had this earring all *my* life too. I've always worn it. How—"

"Because we're sisters, that's *how*. We're twin sisters."

Katherine told Andrea about the tenement fire in the North End: their mother's death and the second baby whose body was never found. "These earrings must have belonged to our mother —so she gave one to each of us. And then she died."

"I don't know . . ." said Andrea doubtfully.

"You're my sister," said Sister Katherine adamantly, "I know you're my sister. I dreamed about you my whole life. I used to think I was dreaming about myself, but all the time I was just dreaming about you. And in the past few days I've been having nightmares . . ."

"What about?" asked Andrea guardedly.

"I don't know. I can't remember. But I wake up scared. Why haven't you gone to the police?"

Andrea looked up startled.

"I read the paper this morning," said Sister Katherine. "I'm sorry—"

"Thank you," said Andrea stiffly. "How do you know I *haven't* gone to the police?"

"Because if you had, you'd be in Weston now. Your parents are dead, and you'd be in Weston now, seeing about their funerals."

"I have my reasons," said Andrea. "I have reasons for not going to the police yet. And listen," she cried in a menacing whisper, at the same time crushing Sister Katherine's patent leather shoe with her scuffed boot, "don't say a word—don't say a word about seeing me, you hear, nobody knows where I am, and for right now, I don't *want* anybody to know."

"You didn't have anything to do with . . ." began Sister Katherine tremulously; she was afraid to complete her question.

"Of course I didn't!" cried Andrea. "I loved Mother and Daddy, I loved them—" She wiped away her angry tears.

"I'm not going to tell anybody," said Katherine, "but I really think you—"

"I don't care what you think," said Andrea. "If you're really my sister—"

"Don't you believe me?!"

"Yes!" cried Andrea, "I believe you, whatever you want to tell me, I'll believe it! But if you're my sister, then you're going to help me."

"How?" stammered Sister Katherine. "I can't—"

"You said you were in a missionary order, didn't you, and your mission is to help people, isn't it, you've made vows to help people for the rest of your life, haven't you?"

"Yes . . ."

"Then you'll help me, you'll help your long-lost twin sister."

"Do you need money? I have a little, I don't think I have more than—"

"I don't need any money, but I may need your help with something else, I've got to think all this through first, though, I've got to think what's the best thing for me to do."

"The best thing to do is to go to the police."

"No it's not! Not yet anyway. You're right, and I'm in trouble, and it's because I think the people that killed Mother and Daddy are going to try to kill me too."

"Why don't you just go to the police then? They'll protect you."

"No! I can't do that yet!"

"Why not?"

Andrea turned her head away for a moment, and did not answer.

"Listen," said Katherine.

"What?"

"After I got off the bus this morning, I was in the station, and this man stopped me, and he thought I was you, he called me 'little Wenham girl,' and I didn't realize he was talking about you, I was scared, I—"

Katherine could see the fear in Andrea's eyes.

"He called you 'little Wenham girl'?"

"Yes," said Katherine.

"What'd he look like?"

Katherine gave a description of the man.

"Did he have an accent?"

"Yes."

"It was Dominic," said Andrea with despair. "How did you manage to get away from him?"

"I jumped in a taxi, and he didn't have time to follow me. I thought he was just crazy. I wasn't thinking about you, he scared me so much."

"He scares me too," said Andrea grimly. Then she looked closely into Sister Katherine's eyes. "I've got to see you again."

"No!" cried Sister Katherine. "I can't come into Boston any more. I'm being transferred—"

"You're lying," said Andrea mildly. "Listen, if you're really my sister, then you'll talk with me again, I just want to talk. See me tomorrow, just for a little while, just to talk. Tonight I'm going to think about what to do, I'm going to make my plans, and tomorrow I may need to talk to you, that's all, just *talk*."

"I really can't come back to Boston again, I got special permission today to—"

"I don't care about that," snapped Andrea. "I'll be in Hingham tomorrow."

Katherine was startled. "How did you know the convent was in Hingham?"

Andrea smiled. "We're sisters, remember. Twin sisters. We've got a special kind of telepathy, I guess. You've heard of that. What time is convenient, I'll visit you there, you can tell everybody I'm your sister. I *am* your sister," Andrea laughed, softly.

"No! They know I don't have any sister. Listen, I'll be out on the playground from ten-thirty to eleven, I'll be sitting so that you can see me from the street—that's Mystic Avenue. Don't come any earlier. Come up to the hedges there, and I'll talk to you, but if you don't come then, don't come at all."

Andrea nodded. She touched the back of Katherine's hand lightly with her broken nails and slipped out of the booth.

The man behind the cash register cursed the snow and cold wind that blew inside when Andrea opened the door.

Katherine paid the check, carefully computing the tip at exactly ten percent, and slowly left the restaurant. Outside, as she adjusted her cape against the snow, she looked for Andrea, but the young woman had disappeared.

Katherine glanced back through the plate glass window of the restaurant. Just on the other side of it, a man dropped a dime into a pay phone and punched out a memorized number. He turned and smiled at Katherine: it was the man from the bus station, whom Andrea had called Dominic.

38

With entirely feigned interest Katherine attended as Sister Mercedes led her twenty third-graders through their spelling lesson. From her table at the back of the room, she took repeated glances out the window, watching the deserted playground for the approach of Andrea LoPonti. Early that morning Katherine had requested that Sister Mercedes allow her to help with the students once more before she left Hingham for the Mother House in Worcester. The day was bright and cold, the ground blanketed with the snow that had fallen the day before. It was nearing recess, and the children had grown restless in anticipation of being the first to trample that newly fallen cover. Katherine watched the traffic along Mystic Avenue and wondered uneasily whether it was her sister in the jeep that had already passed three times that morning. As she glanced that way again, the jeep appeared once more, slowed before the school, then disappeared around the corner of a side street.

Katherine had been a fool, she told herself, an irresponsible fool to have stopped even to look at the girl who had stood in the row at the back of the church. She had been even more of a fool to have revealed to Andrea what it served no purpose for Andrea to know—that they were sisters. Katherine had only just managed to rid herself of all her earthly ties, and now she had been stupid enough to resurrect another! Neither of them would be helped by this information. Andrea, if she had believed it at all, had not seemed overly pleased by the new connection; and Katherine herself was now obligated to deal with this long-lost sister, who was on the run from the police and a man called Dominic. Three years ago, finding her twin sister might have been a marvelous and exciting thing to have happen to her, but this meeting today was likely only to cause still more difficulties in Katherine's troubled life. She could not shrug off an ominous feeling that Andrea was plotting *something* that could have dire consequences for her, something that she must be on guard against when she met her sister. Katherine was comforted by the knowledge that she would be leaving for the Mother House in only another week —Andrea LoPonti couldn't touch her there. But *today* . . . what to do with Andrea today? Katherine decided that she would talk to her sister, urge her to go to the police, and then send her away.

Sister Mercedes clapped her hands once. The students stood at their desks and filed toward the cloakroom with carefully repressed excitement. Katherine glanced once more toward the playground, breathed a prayer of gratitude that it was still empty, and rose to help bundle the children into their coats and boots. She continued to hope that Andrea would stay away altogether.

"Let me go out with them today," said Sister Katherine, knowing that Sister Mercedes, who disliked the cold intensely, would gratefully accept the offer.

"Thank you, Sister," said Sister Mercedes, "I think that I'll be very sorry to see you leave."

Once outside, most of the children fled to the corner of the playground with most snow in it, fell into leaderless teams, and launched into the snowball battle that had been anticipated in whispers throughout the morning. They were only playful, and astonishingly quiet about it, so Katherine, although the battle was stretching rules, allowed it to continue. She pulled the hood of her cape loosely up about her head and turned toward the bench that was set near the front hedges.

Andrea LoPonti, wrapped in a black pea jacket and wearing a black knit cap covering her hair, sat at one end of it, absolutely still, staring at Katherine.

Katherine approached her. "Morning recess is just twenty minutes," she said to her sister.

Andrea, weary and tense, only nodded.

"Did you have trouble finding this place?"

"No," Andrea answered. She shoved her hands deep into her coat pockets. "That's the convent over there, isn't it?" She cocked her head toward the house on the other side of the school.

"Yes," said Katherine cautiously. "I'm sorry you had to come all the way down here—for nothing. I should have made it clearer yesterday, there's nothing that I can do for you."

"Yes there is. One thing."

Katherine looked up over the hedge. The jeep she had seen pass several times had pulled up to the curb: now she could see that there were three persons inside, two men and a woman. The driver got out. From the other side a taller, clean-shaven man and a woman with long red hair and a large purple birthmark on the side of her face emerged. They huddled before the jeep in conversation that appeared somehow not casual. Katherine, about to speak, looked down at Andrea, but it was Andrea who spoke first:

"I want you to let me stay in the convent for a while."

"No!"

"I want you to go to the mother superior and tell her that your sister—"

"That's impossible! I couldn't do that, Mother Celestine knows I don't—"

The young woman with red hair had climbed into the driver's seat of the jeep; the two men were approaching the playground. Katherine's objection was broken off by the menace in their appearance.

Andrea noted Sister Katherine's absorption in something behind her. She twisted round and saw Dominic and Jack's heads appear over the horizon of the hedge.

"Oh dear Jesus," she breathed.

Katherine was as shocked by the terror in her sister's voice as by the blasphemy of her words. "That's the man who grabbed me in the bus station yesterday," she whispered. "And I meant to tell you, he was in the—"

The snowball battle grew suddenly shrill behind them as one side mercilessly pursued its temporary advantage. Andrea's hand closed over the revolver in her pocket, and she slowly withdrew it.

Katherine saw this, and, fearful that Andrea was planning to shoot the two men, uttered a small stifled cry. Andrea held the gun close at her side and swung about again to face Katherine. She aimed the gun at Katherine's breast.

"Get me inside—*now!*" Her voice was cold and hard.

Jack and Dominic had stepped up their pace and were coming rapidly nearer the hedge that separated the playground from the front lawn. Katherine turned around immediately and headed for the school building, Andrea following only a foot or so behind her.

Andrea glanced over her shoulder: Jack and Dominic were looking for the easiest way over the four-foot hedge. "Hurry!" she insisted.

Katherine glanced at the children at the other corner of the playground; their game continued, but a few had paused, and their bewildered expressions made Katherine realize that they saw the gun in Andrea's hand.

"Not the classroom!" said Andrea. Katherine looked about her bewildered, then turned sharply and went to the gray metal door that opened onto a long corridor behind the gymnasium. She swept inside, and behind them Andrea yanked the door closed and snapped the security bar into place.

A couple of moments later, the door was rattled and kicked, and they distinctly heard two voices, sharp and metallic: "Goddammit to hell!" growled Dominic, and Jack echoed him.

"Your fucking plans," complained Jack harshly, "you had her yesterday in the fucking diner—"

"We'll get her—"

"Yeah, and how the fuck are we supposed to get through this door, fucking nuns are gonna call the cops—"

"Look for—"

Katherine heard no more, for Andrea had pushed her through

a swinging door into the boys' locker room. It was deserted at this hour.

Andrea ripped off the nun's veil. Katherine began to shake, and her breath came in convulsive gasps. Andrea slapped her hard across the face.

"Take off your clothes!" Andrea hissed through clenched teeth. She sat on a bench, placing the gun beside her, and pulled off her jacket. She looked up at the nun and repeated the command, *"Take off your clothes!"* Then she added, in a lower, sneering voice, *"Sister!"*

Katherine stood numbed. She made a move as if to undo her cape and then lunged at Andrea. Andrea jerked out of the way, and the revolver fell from the bench onto the cement floor.

Both women leapt for it.

Outside, Jack and Dominic suddenly left off their mutual denunciations when they realized that the playground had become quiet. The children stood mute, watching them. Jack glanced up, and when he saw several nuns appear at the upper windows looking for the cause of the unexpected silence, he pulled Dominic around the corner of the gymnasium. They leaned back against the bricks and tried to revise their strategy.

Not five minutes had passed before the gray metal door through which Katherine and Andrea had disappeared flew open and the woman in the pea jacket and watch cap stumbled out and fell into the snow. Jack and Dominic left their hiding place in time to see a black-sleeved arm yank the door shut again. The two men advanced toward the fallen woman as she struggled to her feet. Dominic thrust his leg against her backside, and she sprawled in the snow once more, softly moaning. When she twisted her head around, the two men were standing in menace above her.

"Oh, little Wenham girl came out to play," whispered Dominic.

Sister Philomena stared down from her second-story classroom with an expression of curiosity and alarm. She unlatched the window and leaned out for a better look.

Another window scraped up and the black-veiled forms of Sisters Henrica and Alfred appeared only twenty feet down from where Sister Prudentia observed the trio. The children, sensing danger, were herding together in the most distant corner of the snow-blanketed playground.

Sister Alfred gasped and covered her mouth when each of the men grabbed one of the fallen woman's arms, lifting her out of the snow. Sister Prudentia leaned precariously far over the sill and shouted for them to stop. The two men had pulled the young woman off in the direction of the jeep, which was idling at the curb. Tiny faces began to fill the lowest panes of glass along both stories of the grade school as more black forms of women came to view the disturbance.

"No!" the woman shrieked as she struggled between her captors. She brought up the heel of her boot and scraped it down hard against Jack's shin. He let go her arm, cursing. She swung loose against Dominic and tried, ineffectually, to jab her elbow into his stomach. His grip on her arm tightened, and he twisted it until she cried out inarticulately.

"Stop it! Stop!" Sister Prudentia shouted.

The children fled toward the school building, sending up wails of terror.

Sister Henrica reeled to face Sister Prudentia. "Mother Celestine!" she yelled. "Run and get Mother Celestine!"

Sister Prudentia disappeared from her post just as Sister Philomena appeared through one of the classroom doors on the ground level. She tried to gather the horrified children about her.

Jack pushed his victim to the ground and stepped on her back with such force the breath was knocked out of her. Dominic lifted her by the collar of her coat and dragged her toward the hedge.

She struggled again to free herself, gasping all the while for breath. She dug her fingers into Dominic's crotch and pulled and twisted as hard as she could. He dropped her and jumped away. "You fucking bitch!" he shouted, and kicked her in the stomach. The woman's scream of pain matched those of the nuns in its intensity. Jerking with anger, Dominic took from the pocket of his jacket a band of cold steel studded with gleaming spikes, feverishly pulled it over the back of his hand, and lifted the woman once more. She whimpered and pleaded pathetically with him.

"This is for Morgie, you fucking bitch. That's what this is for—"

A chaos of shouts cascaded about the trio from the windows and across the playground.

"No, Dominic!" shouted Jack, and grabbed the young woman's arms. The spikes stabbed once into her nose and right cheek. Blood flecked the snow. Jack jerked her away before Dominic could bring the spikes down again. "The fucking nuns are watching, the fucking nuns—"

Jack dragged the unconscious woman out of Dominic's reach. When he reached the fence of bare-branched shrubs, he lifted the woman under the arms, hoisted her up onto the hedge, and then shoved her over on the other side. Then he and Dominic scrambled over.

Sister Mercedes exploded from the school building, brandishing a mop.

"Fuck you! Fuck you!" screamed Dominic as he and Jack dragged the unconscious, bleeding woman across the front lawn to the jeep. They shoved the woman into the back of the vehicle, and before the doors were shut, Rita had taken off in the direction of Boston.

Sister Mercedes let fall the mop and stared stuporously after the jeep. Behind her, Sister Katherine's charges huddled together and wept in terror.

39

Andrea Loponti remained confined three days in Sister Katherine's room at the convent. Shortly after Katherine's abduction, she had been found cowering in a corner of the girls' locker room. When Mother Celestine delicately questioned her whether she had seen any part of the violence on the playground, she had nodded dumbly.

She was led to Sister Katherine's chamber and laid upon the cot. The blinds were drawn against the late morning light. Sister Henrica wanted to remove Andrea's habit, but Andrea signalled her away.

An hour or so later, she was questioned briefly by the police —the young woman who was attacked had been seen talking to

Sister Katherine just before the violence occurred. Andrea identified the abducted woman as Andrea LoPonti, whose parents
had that same week been killed in Weston. Andrea, in a scarcely
articulate manner, managed to suggest to the police that she was
but a poor witness just now, but that she would be happy to speak
again in a day or so, and in greater detail. The police would have
persevered if not for the kind interference of Mother Celestine.

Dinner was brought to the chamber, and Sister Philomena sat
perched on the windowsill, clucking encouragement to Andrea,
who only picked at the dishes. It was only after Sister Philomena
left, with soft words of consolation, that Andrea, searching Sister
Katherine's desk, came across the leather-bound diary.

She leafed through it and judged the diary to be the work of
a timid, immature mind. The handwriting itself was enough to
put her off: a girlish, undisciplined scrawl. But then she realized,
just when she was about to throw it aside, that the scrupulously
detailed lists and explanations of conventual procedure and
duties might be of use to her. Even prayers and the times they
were to be recited in chapel were written out, although Andrea
supposed that this would be basic and mundane knowledge to a
young nun—a postulant, to be exact.

When she came to a list that contained the names of each of
the Slaves of the Immaculate Conception resident at the Convent
of St. Luke, and beside each name an identifying physical charac-
teristic or behavioral peculiarity, Andrea thought, *My God, it's as
if she knew I was coming to take her place . . .*

Andrea had no doubt that her sister was dead. Jack and
Dominic—having committed themselves to a daylight attack
and kidnapping—could not allow Katherine to live. Andrea
only hoped—she actually prayed—that they did not discover
that the twins had switched clothing. She imagined to herself
Katherine's bloody death beneath Dominic's spikes, and heard
his voice damning *Andrea*. If they thought they had killed Andrea
LoPonti, they would not return to the convent. Just as Katherine
had, Andrea began to look on St. Luke's as the only refuge in her
troubled life. She did not dare step beyond its walls. For the time
being she refused even to look out its windows.

Sister Philomena brought her meals; Sister Henrica visited her twice daily and read to her from *The Imitation of Christ*; Mother Superior Celestine sat on the edge of her cot, held her hand, and wanted to know how she was feeling. But it was to Sister Prudentia, young and voluble, that Andrea ended up most grateful. Late on the first morning that Andrea spent in the convent in the guise of Sister Katherine, Sister Prudentia crept into her chamber, perched on the edge of the desk chair, and breathed, "Oh, Sister Katherine, we're all so sorry for what happened! We're all so sorry that it had to happen to you! And after everything else, after what happened just last week, with your poor mother, God rest her soul—I've prayed for your mother, Sister Katherine, I've prayed for her every day since we heard the news. Everyone in the convent says it's just terrible what happened on the playground, but that it was worst for you, because you were so much nearer—and you had just talked to the young woman. That poor young woman! The way those two men hit her! And the way they dragged her away—they were taking her away for more of the same! If she's not dead now, she's probably wishing she was ... Sister Katherine, we're all hoping that you'll just stay here for a while, and pray, and try to get everything out of your mind. Some sisters say it would be better if you got out and went about your work, but Sister Philomena said when she found you, you didn't look yourself, you looked like your own ghost. When something like this happens, it's best to rest for a few days. I don't blame you for not talking, you must be thinking about it all the time ..."

This monologue, which would only have distressed the real Sister Katherine, was very welcome to Andrea. It told her what her conduct should be in the coming days. She remained quietly in her room, reading and rereading the diary, catching the names and memorizing the duties—and, after the first time, skipping over the ruminations of Sister Katherine's heart. She spoke as little as possible and tried to give the appearance of being constantly distressed and preoccupied. Since this was Andrea's true state, it was not a difficult demeanor to feign.

She knew from Katherine herself, and from the diary, that she was soon to be transferred to the Mother House, and from there to a mission school. If this moving about had not been immediately in store, Andrea thought she might well have given the

entire deception over—she could not imagine maintaining it
beyond the week's grace that would be allowed her for trauma.
But if she was being sent to places where the true Sister Katherine
was not known, then there would be only the difficulty of keeping up the pretense that she was a postulant in the missionary
order. The possibility that the real Sister Katherine would return
and unmask her was one that Andrea dismissed out of hand. She
had come to know Jack's cruelty.

In the last entries of the journal Andrea found that Sister
Katherine was to take her final vows once she reached the
Mother House, but she had not included the instructions for that
ceremony. This omission sent Andrea into a panic. She searched
through the few books Katherine had on the shelf of her closet
and went twice through the papers stacked neatly within the desk
drawers, but found nothing. And it was, of course, impossible for
her to question any of the nuns about it: her ignorance would
betray her. In desperation one night, hours after the house was
slumbering, Andrea went to the library and searched every shelf
until she found a slim volume outlining the ceremony of the final
vows. She took the volume back to her chamber and pored over
it until she was almost as familiar with it as her sister had been.

Andrea knew she would not remain a nun forever, of course.
She hoped it would not even be necessary to take the final vows
—perhaps she could get away before that. Her twin sister had
had a rough time of it, Andrea learned: her father murdered, her
mother tried and convicted. Her mother had committed suicide
one week, and—the other nuns thought—next week she had
seen a young woman beaten nearly to death before her eyes. All
these things could easily cause a mental imbalance that would
prevent her from becoming a nun. She might ask for a leave of
absence, without the intention of ever returning. Once out of
the convent, she would have a new identity. It was a shame, of
course, that she would not be able to have any of her parents'
wealth or their insurance money—Andrea LoPonti was dead; but
with some boldness, Andrea resolutely looked on the prospect of
beginning a life from scratch.

She began to wonder if she should apply to graduate schools
when she got out of all this business with the convent and the

Slaves, but then brought herself up short: She wasn't out of the woods yet. The police were coming back to have her testimony on what she saw; there was at least one more week to be spent among nuns who had been Sister Katherine's daily companions; there were a thousand mysterious details of convent life that she would have to pick up immediately by close observation.

When she was alone, the diary was Andrea's study. And when she was elsewhere in the convent, or in the Church of St. Luke, she participated in the life with a certain hesitancy, it was true, but also with a courage born of her determination to bring off the deception.

Late one night, when the lights of the convent had been extinguished, Andrea sat at the window of her room and, by the light of a candle and her reflection in the panes of glass, cut off her hair, imitating the shorn style of the Slaves. The two ruby earrings, together for the first time since Mary Lodesco had removed them from her own ears and divided them between her twin girls, were placed on the windowsill. They sparkled in the candlelight.

40

A few days after Katherine's abduction, Andrea waited in the convent library for the police detective who would take her testimony. Mother Superior Celestine had said it would be well to put this off at least another day, but Andrea gave her to understand that the sooner the interrogation was over, the better. Andrea sat stiffly in a high-backed chair with her long black sleeves draped neatly over the arms. The heavy maroon curtains had been drawn back, and bright afternoon sunlight poured in behind her. She kept her eyes on the double mahogany doors of the library, and when Mother Celestine opened them to admit the police detective, Andrea made no movement to greet him.

The detective was a man in his late forties, wearing a tan overcoat atop a closely fitted but inexpensive suit. He crossed toward Andrea, pulling a notebook from his suit jacket; he flipped it expertly open as he stood in the sunlight that spilled over her head and onto the Oriental carpet at her feet. Andrea watched with weary, calm green eyes. The police detective pulled over a straight, narrow chair and seated himself on a little corner of it.

"Good morning, Sister Katherine," he said, and nodded as he scanned the page of notes he had taken on his last visit with her.

Andrea said nothing, but waited for him to begin. She had insisted to Mother Celestine that it would be best for her to give evidence alone. With the policeman she would be all right, but it was vital that none of the nuns overhear Andrea speaking at length; she had not spent long enough with Katherine to know or to recreate her speech. She could not have reproduced Sister Katherine's gestures.

"This isn't easy for me," said Andrea with a weak smile. "But I've gone over everything in my mind, and I'll tell you everything I know about the young woman who was . . . the young woman who came to see me."

The detective was startled by the calmness of Sister Katherine's voice, but he nodded his agreement. From his overcoat pocket he took a cassette recorder and placed it on the edge of the desk. When he asked if she minded his recording her evidence, she hesitantly shook her head no. Andrea was uneasy to have her voice recorded: if anyone who had known Sister Katherine heard it, he would know that it was not the nun who had made the tape. But to refuse would have excited suspicion immediately. She must take her chances.

"On Wednesday I went into Boston. I was returning some books to the library." This Andrea knew from Sister Henrica. "I had an hour to kill before the next bus, and so I walked around a little. It began to snow, and I decided to go into the church on Harrison Avenue to pray for a few minutes, and just outside on the street, this young woman stopped me. Of course I didn't recognize her at first, but it was obvious she was in some kind of trouble—she acted very nervously, and thought someone was after her. It was then I remembered about the poor woman whose parents had been killed in Weston on New Year's Eve. I asked her if that were she, and she said yes. She said there were people out to get her and kill her because she knew who did it. I told her she ought to go to the police because the police would protect her, but she wouldn't—and she wouldn't say why, either. She wanted to talk to me, so we had a cup of coffee—"

"Excuse me, Sister," said the detective politely, "but why did Miss LoPonti approach *you* on the street?"

"I was wearing my robes. Andrea LoPonti was a Catholic. She knew that she could turn to a nun for help. She would have stopped a priest too, probably, it's just that she came across me first, that's all. She said we looked a lot alike—"

"You do, you look very much like her."

"That could be," said Andrea with a small smile, "but we don't think much of appearances here. But it could be that's why she came up to *me*. She felt safe with me, I suppose."

"And she told you she was in trouble."

"But she wouldn't say what kind. She said she wanted to talk to me again, and I told her where my convent was. I had hoped she would come, because I thought then I'd be able to talk her into giving herself up. And if she got out of Boston, where those people were hunting her, she'd feel safer. I told her I'd be around in the school in the morning, and she could look for me there. I'd introduce her to Mother Celestine, and I was hoping that Mother Celestine could talk her into going to the police."

"But you didn't tell any of this to Mother Celestine when you got back here that evening?"

"No, I didn't. I didn't think she'd show up, she was so jittery when she talked to me. We were having coffee, and at one point, she just got up and walked out."

"Why didn't you go the police, Sister Katherine? You knew that Miss LoPonti was wanted by the police. Why didn't you tell them that you had seen her?"

Andrea paused, perplexed. "I don't know," she stammered. "I suppose it was because I was taking everything she told me in confidence, as if it were confessional or something. It never occurred to me to go to the police. I should have, of course, I see that, I should have gone right to the police, and if I had, she wouldn't be dead now. She *is* dead, isn't she?" she asked softly, her eyes averted.

"We don't know," said the detective soberly. "We think the people who came after her may be the same ones who murdered her parents. In that case . . ."

Andrea nodded sadly.

"Go on," urged the detective. "Please, Sister Katherine ..."

"She showed up the next day. I was surprised. She was even more nervous than the day before. I tried to get her to come inside, but she wouldn't at first, and when she saw those two men getting out of their jeep she got hysterical. Then she pushed me inside the gym—she had a gun that she took out of her pocket—"

"Yes," said the detective, "some of the children saw that."

"I tried to get her to go through into the main building, but she was afraid they would cut her off. She wasn't thinking straight. She made me go in the gym. If she had let me, I could have gotten her out of there."

"How long were you inside?"

"About five minutes. It may have been longer, I'm not sure." Andrea closed her eyes and touched her temples. She had carefully rehearsed her story, but for a few moments the real memory of that time took the place of her fabricated tale.

Katherine's robes hampered her movement, and Andrea easily retrieved the gun from the floor. Shifting it from one hand to the other, Andrea clumsily removed all her own clothing until she stood before her sister wearing only her underpants. Katherine trembled in her coarse cotton pants and brassiere; the nun's habit was a mound of black on the concrete.

Andrea pushed her bundled clothes toward Katherine: "Put them on!"

While Katherine fumbled, Andrea quickly dropped the nun's underslip over her head, yanked on the flowing black skirts, and secured the leather girdle and white scapular. She pulled on the hose and slipped into the heavy-heeled black shoes. Everything fit her perfectly.

After she had buttoned the blouse and fastened the unbelted jeans, Katherine, without being told, pulled on the knit hat and carefully concealed her hair beneath it. She had to sit down to pull on the tight-fitting boots, and when that was accomplished, she slipped into the pea jacket. Shaken, slack-mouthed, and with glazed eyes, she stood as if for Andrea's approval.

"You *do* look just like me," Andrea whispered. "I think you really *are* my sister." She tied the wool cape about her shoulders and concealed the gun beneath the black material. She thrust out her hand, palm up. "Give me your earring."

Katherine hesitated a moment, but Andrea waved the gun menacingly. Katherine pulled the earring sharply from her ear, leaving behind a spot of blood.

"It won't work," she said as she handed the ring to Andrea. She spoke as if struggling out of a deep and troubled sleep. "Whatever it is you're planning, it won't work."

Andrea dropped the earring into the pocket of her skirt. By the clock in the boys' dressing room, six minutes had passed while the two sisters exchanged clothes and identities. The unfamiliarity of the habit was emphasized with every step that Andrea took. She pulled open the door and waved Katherine into the hall. When Katherine did not move, Andrea took the gun from beneath her scapular. "You may be my sister," she said, "but I'd kill you just the same."

"*You* killed your parents," Katherine whispered.

"No," said Andrea calmly. "I loved them very much. Those two men out there—they're the ones who killed them. *They're* the murderers, not me."

"But you'd kill me."

"Yes, I think I would," said Andrea. She released the safety catch on the revolver.

Katherine, on whom Andrea's clothes fit strangely well but who felt uncomfortable in them all the same, passed out into the hallway: Andrea poked the gun into Katherine's back and propelled her toward the metal door at the end of the corridor.

Katherine turned her head slightly and asked, "Are we going outside? Those men are still out there—"

"*I'm* not going out," said Andrea, as she reached round her sister and lifted the bar across the door. She turned the knob. "But you are," she whispered. She pushed the door open and then, in a single, sure motion, shoved Katherine out into the snow.

She instantly pulled the door shut again and locked it. The revolver she tossed onto the top of a large ceiling fan that was set into the wall directly above the outside door. Then she ran breathlessly back down the corridor.

★

"Sister Katherine?" The detective's voice was softly prodding.

Andrea opened her eyes and dropped her hands back onto the arms of the chair. "Where was I? Oh, yes—she was talking crazy. I don't even remember what she said. She pointed the gun at me, and then she pointed it away, and I was so frightened, I didn't pay any attention to what she was talking about. I still can't remember that part, and I probably won't ever remember it."

"But what made her run back outside where she knew the men were waiting for her?"

"I don't know," said Andrea. "She was acting very strange. I thought maybe she was on some kind of drugs or something, but maybe she was just very upset. Anyway, she ran back outside, even though I tried to tell her not to."

"What happened to her gun? When she went back out on the playground she didn't try to defend herself with it."

"I don't know," replied Andrea, shaking her head. "Those two men must have taken it away from her. We were in the boys' locker room—she made me go in there—and I know when she left there, she had it in her hand."

"You saw what happened outside, didn't you, Sister Katherine?"

"Yes," whispered Andrea. "After a couple of minutes, I followed her out into the corridor. The door onto the playground was open a little, and I went up to that. From there I could see what they did to her. I tried to look away, but I couldn't. I had to watch it all, even though I didn't want to. After that, I went in the girls' locker room, and I got sick. I haven't begun to recover from it yet," she said apologetically.

"Did you get a clear look at the two men?"

"Yes," said Andrea. "I was looking right at them. But nothing registered. I can't remember anything about them, except that one of them had a dark complexion and the other one was light. That's all I can remember."

"Well," said the detective, "you've been a lot of help to me. I'm sorry to have to put you through all this. You'll have to make an official statement, but what I'll do is have someone type out what's on this tape, and you can read it over and sign it, that's all we'll need."

Andrea nodded.

"Sister Katherine," said the detective, "I thank you for talking to me like this today, I know it's been hard for you. You—"

"It had to be done," said Andrea. "I'm just so sorry it all had to happen. That poor girl, I can't help feeling partially responsible—"

"You shouldn't say that, Sister Katherine. Andrea LoPonti was in a great deal of trouble, we're not exactly sure what yet, but there was probably nothing you could do."

"You haven't caught them, have you?"

"No, not yet. But one of the children gave us a good description of the jeep, and we're looking for that. We'll find them soon enough."

Mother Celestine, though she was fond of Sister Katherine, could not be sorry to see her leave the Convent of St. Luke. The girl seemed to have been born under a black cloud. Trouble followed her. In the past year she had suffered more misfortune than most persons know in a lifetime. For a nun, she was of altogether too dramatic a nature. And it was this last piece of terror that seemed to have done her the most damage: she was as withdrawn as she had been when she first came to St. Luke's; her silences were morose and unbroken. Three days after the interview with the police detective, from which meeting she had gone directly back to her bed in exhaustion, Sister Katherine was driven to the Mother House in Worcester by Sister Henrica. When she returned, Sister Henrica sadly told Mother Celestine of the terrible change in Sister Katherine: "We were close, Reverend Mother, we were very close because of our classes at BC, but on the drive up to Worcester, she hardly spoke a word to me. She's like another person."

Epilogue

The nun stood just inside the doorway of the single-storied concrete block building in the waste desert ten miles outside Taos, New Mexico. The sole of one heavy-heeled white shoe inclined against the raised threshold. A sun-browned hand was drawn up to shade her eyes against the sun. She waved to the last of the seventeen children climbing aboard the ramshackle school bus at the end of the dusty school yard. The arid wind that raised clouds of dust between her and the bus also lifted her gauzy white veil and played about the white folds of her habit. In a year she had grown used to it.

Only when the dented yellow doors had clanged unevenly shut and the vehicle sputtered off toward the Indian reservation to the north did the nun draw back into the scarcely cooler shadows of the mission schoolroom. Sister Maria, short and rotund, bobbed up and down in the farthest aisle, retrieving pencils and scraps of paper from the tiled floor.

"Oh, Sister Katherine," cried the nun, standing erect and reaching round to massage the small of her expansive back, "I can never thank God enough for weekends! I declare, they are a taste of heaven!"

Andrea smiled, and turned her head slowly. The bones of her spine cracked a little. "I'll finish the cleanup, Sister Maria," she said. "You've worked very hard this week. Go back to the house if you like."

"No no!" cried Sister Maria, wiping beads of perspiration from her sun-darkened face, "I'm the assistant and it's my job. Besides, my work is nothing to what you do. If I had those children all day long, I don't know *what* I'd do with myself. But they love you so. Poor things! I wonder what it's like to grow up at the end of the world?"

"This is hardly the end of the world," said Andrea, seating herself in the high-backed wooden chair behind the teacher's desk. "You forget that we have missions in Taiwan, and Manaus, and Mozambique. I grew up in Boston—that's supposed to be the hub of the universe—but I was never happy there. And here —well, here, I haven't been unhappy."

"Why were you unhappy in Boston, Sister?" asked Sister Maria curiously. "Did it—"

Andrea smiled. "Please, Sister Maria, the fact is, the children *did* tire me out today, and I'd just as soon sit here quietly for a while."

"All right," said Sister Maria. "Just let me get the windows." Sister Maria secured all the latches and then softly left the room without speaking again to Sister Katherine, whose head was bowed over her folded hands.

Up until the very day that she was to be taken from Hingham to the Mother House in Worcester, Andrea had thought she might reveal her true identity, claim temporary insanity as an excuse for her incredible behavior and assumption of her twin sister's identity, and return to Weston to claim her inheritance as her dead parents' surviving daughter. But what she read in the paper on that last morning made it impossible for her to turn back.

In disgust over the brutal kidnapping of Andrea LoPonti from the convent-school playground and Jack and Dominic's vowed intent to murder the young woman, Rita had taken the first opportunity to flee the house in Jamaica Plain. Having had nothing to do with either the robbery or the murders, she told the police all that she knew. But by the time the police presented themselves at the house. Jack and Dominic—and Andrea LoPonti —were no longer there. The corpses of Sid and Morgie were exhumed from their shallow graves in the Middlesex Fells, and it became known that Andrea LoPonti, the kidnapped girl, had murdered the two in revenge for her parents' death.

Andrea, in the guise of Sister Katherine, had been at the Mother House for only two weeks, hiding herself easily among the two hundred women resident there. If she was occasionally clumsy or appeared not to know some simple rule of procedure, the lapse was ascribed to the traumas she had recently under-gone. It was with three other postulants that she took her final vows, and Andrea was more amazed at the tears she shed at the ceremony than at the strangeness of her taking part in it at all.

At the beginning of March she was transferred to the mission at Taos and given fourteen children in the third and fourth grades. That she knew nothing of children or the mechanics of classrooms beyond what she remembered from the time that she was herself in elementary school was a considerable worry to Andrea. But as it happened, she need not have been bothered. The poor Indian and Hispanic children were so far behind that a modicum of love and patience and attention were of more value than all the courses in childhood psychology that the real Sister Katherine had taken in four years at Boston College would have been.

But Andrea was weary of being constantly on her guard against betraying herself. It had been only her sister's detailed diary that had allowed her to succeed at all. Andrea kept the book hidden in her room, and actually brought it with her when she came to class every morning—feeling safer to have it near, in her desk drawer. As soon as she could duplicate Katherine's childish script, Andrea had continued the diary with an assiduity that matched her sister's own.

She had filled the last page that afternoon.

The next morning, Sister Katherine borrowed one of the three vehicles belonging to the convent. She said she was driving into Taos in order to buy materials for her students' art lessons the following week. She declined Mother Superior's offer of money from petty cash, saying she might be reimbursed upon her return.

Andrea drove not to Taos, but to Sante Fe, seventy-five miles distant. She made two stops. The first was at a bank in Fairview, where she changed into more convenient denominations the fifteen carefully preserved one-hundred-dollar bills. The teller eyed her curiously, wondering why a nun had so much money, but thought it impertinent to ask questions. Shortly after she left this town, Andrea turned the car off on a side road and changed into jeans, a red polka-dot blouse, and much-scuffed boots that she had some time before taken from the church's charity box.

The discarded habit she folded neatly and placed in the trunk of the car. To the scapular she pinned a note that read simply, "I am perfectly safe, but I do not intend to return. Sister Katherine."

In Sante Fe she abandoned the car in the lot of a shopping mall, unlocked and with the keys in the ignition. Inside the mall she went into a jewelry store and had her left ear pierced and her sister's ruby chip inserted.

At a department store she purchased cosmetics and a leather flight bag. She took a taxi to the bus station and purchased a ticket to Los Angeles. While waiting for the bus, she borrowed a pen from the man sitting next to her and filled out the identification card on the leather flight bag.

Her new name was to be Katherine-Andrea Lodesco—her sister's name, her own name, her mother's name. That felt right, as did the new ruby in the lobe of her left ear.

The bus arrived, and Katherine-Andrea Lodesco climbed on, smiling. She relished the light-headed exuberance that had swept over her—a sense of achieving, at last, real freedom. She swung her bag onto the overhead luggage rack and scooted past a grumbling old woman to settle into the window seat. "Katherine-Andrea Lodesco," she whispered, under the noise of the slamming door and the engine grinding to life. In a moment the bus pulled out of the Santa Fe terminal and moved slowly for several blocks before angling onto the highway and picking up speed as it headed west.

She had purchased the previous day's Los Angeles Times, and, after reading and circling promising advertisements for employment and housing, she turned idly to the news sections. On page three her eyes drifted down and stopped abruptly at a block of three photographs, her attention riveted by only the first. At first she giggled to see there her own high-school graduation photograph—and the caption Andrea LoPonti. It seemed so long since she had thought of herself in that identity that the significance of the photograph did not strike her until she had examined its two companions. Though as much out of date as her own, they were unmistakably portraits of Dominic and Jack.

Her hands began to tremble so badly that she was forced to press the newspaper flat against her thighs. The old woman in the next seat grunted and shifted her weight closer toward the aisle.

Diesel fumes seemed suddenly to overwhelm Andrea when she had not even noticed them before. Nausea swept over her as she feverishly read the article.

She learned that Dominic Batista, already wanted in Massachusetts for armed robbery and murder, had been shot and killed in a police raid on a large-scale cocaine ring in southern New Jersey. His accomplices, tentatively identified as Jack Schifler and Andrea LoPonti, also wanted in Massachusetts, had fled the scene and were being sought in four states along the eastern seaboard.